THE CIRCUS

OF THE

EARTH AND

THE AIR

H.A. Atwell/*Circus World Museum, Baraboo, Wisconsin.*

BROOKE STEVENS

THE CIRCUS OF THE EARTH AND THE AIR

Harcourt Brace & Company

NEW YORK   SAN DIEGO   LONDON

Requests for permission to make copies
of any part of the work should be mailed to:
Permissions Department, Harcourt Brace & Company, 8th Floor,
Orlando, Florida 32887.

Illustration on page 247 courtesy of Milner Library Special Collections, Illinois
State University. All other illustrations courtesy of Circus World Museum,
Baraboo, Wisconsin, including the photographs by H. A. Atwell on the
frontispiece and page 35.

Definition of "stage" on page 185 copyright © 1992 by Houghton Mifflin
Company. Adapted and reprinted by permission from *The American Heritage
Dictionary of the English Language,* third edition.

Library of Congress Cataloging-in-Publication Data
Stevens, Brooke.
The circus of the earth and the air/Brooke Stevens.—1st ed.
p.   cm.
ISBN 0-15-117987-5
I. Title.
PS3569.T447C57   1994
813'.54—dc20   93-19163

Designed by Trina Stahl
Printed in the United States of America
First edition
A B C D E

For all of my great family with deepest love and affection:
Mac, the Old Maria, Carla, Eddy, Steve, Nancy, Merle,
Melvin, Tim, Sara, Chris, Luke, April, Sandy, Pat, Anthony,
Mark, Little Carla, Alessandro, Isabelle, Sebastian, Sabra,
Raphael, Lily, Hal, Marian, Robin, and Weasel.

And for Giulietta Masina and Federico Fellini.

ACKNOWLEDGMENTS

Heartfelt thanks to Craig and Meera Bombardiere, Fenner Brownell, Betsy Causey, Rachel Cline, Martin Duff, Craig and Lu Marcus, Douglas McMullen, Donald Nitchie, Chris Pratt, Nelly Riefler, Don Rogers, Oren Rudavsky, Alison Salzinger and family, Robert Schroeders, Joseph Sharkey, and Celia Wren.

Special thanks to the staff of Circus World Museum, Baraboo, Wisconsin.

And to my agent, Jane Gelfman, and my editor, Alane Salierno Mason.

And warmest appreciation to Pamela Dewey for her insight and patient support of this book from its earliest stages.

THE CIRCUS

OF THE

EARTH AND

THE AIR

CHAPTER 1

IRIS came up on the other side of a high wave, swimming hard and fast and climbing the crest of the next wave without going under. Beyond the breakers in the calm blue-green sea, three gulls opened their wings to fly. She swam toward them steadily, lifting her hands high over her head, kicking up white foam behind her. Soon all Alex Barton could see through the late afternoon light was a glimmer of movement from an arm or a leg and flashes of white.

A few pink and white clouds gathered on the horizon; gulls flew by from land toward sea. Alex scooped sand into his hands and let it sift through his fingers. Then, looking out at the water, staring at the reflection of blue that his wife had become, he thought of how much he loved her and how strange and lucky it was that they were together.

Iris came into sight again, a dark speck of movement becoming clearer, an arm coming out of the water, arching out over her head, and once again the foam from her kick. Alex turned and threw his towel onto the sand, dove through white foam and under waves until he could see her clearly, stroking so steadily and seriously that she didn't look up. When she was near, he dove deep into cool water, rolled onto his back, and watched her white, naked body kick rapidly as she went overhead. Coming up again, he blew air out quietly and followed her, reaching out for her kicking feet, then touching one.

She turned and screamed.

He put his arms around her muscular body, which felt cool and light underwater, and kissed her lips; she was laughing.

Together they swam in, feeling the slow lift of the big waves, finally riding a small one all the way up onto the sand of the beach. Facing the ocean, they sat down and let the surf's foam drain from their backs. High-flying seagulls caught the yellowing rays of the sun.

She tapped his knee and pointed to a large white shape moving far down the beach through a light blue mist that had risen from the breaking waves. Soon they saw a horse, a white horse with a frisky white mane, kicking up water as it ran through the foam of a wave, nearing them quickly, rocking back and forth, galloping. They climbed up to their belongings and picked up their towels, aware of being naked in front of it.

It was coming up on them now, its ears erect, its neck arched. Iris stepped toward it, but Alex held her back. It slowed to a trot as it crossed in front of them, its neck and shoulders lathered with frothy yellow sweat. Vapor jetted from its nostrils. Turning away from the water, it climbed inland, through the deep white sand, finally disappearing over a steep dune. A tern flew straight up into the sky above it.

Iris and Alex followed the horse's tracks, sand flowing beneath their feet, up the steep knoll. They let go of each other's hands and used all fours to make the climb. Alex looked across a wide field; sharp blades of saw grass gave way to curly tufts of salt gray crabgrass. In the middle of the field stood a tall circular tent, a circus tent with red, yellow, and blue stripes on its roof converging on a center pole from which a forked flag hung limply. There were trucks parked to one side, some with their doors open, and far off to their right the windshields of parked cars reflected the diminishing red light of the sky. The horse, far away and small, headed toward an opening in the tent. A person with yellow hair, perhaps a woman, came out and put a bridle on it, leading it through the door.

Alex turned to Iris. Her eyes were fixed on the tent and the cars. Taking her hand, he led her back to the beach, where they dressed, picked up their belongings, and climbed back to the field and started across the grass.

Spotlights had come on around the circular border of the tent. They could hear several engines, generators perhaps. To one side of the field they saw a tree with a perfectly flat top like a tree on an African plain. A black bird roosted high in its branches. Behind the bird, fiery yellow and orange clouds streaked the sky.

A long line of people waited in front of the barred windows of a ticket booth. There were young couples, older couples, families with children, and tourists with cameras. Alex and Iris joined the line behind two young boys who stood behind their parents, punching each other in the arm. The older boy was hurting the younger boy, who looked as if he would break into tears soon, but the parents paid no attention to either one.

The long line moved slowly. Darkness settled across the field, the moon came out, stars appeared one by one in the purple sky.

Iris and Alex had been the last ones to get in line. When they finally reached the ticket window, they could hear the ringmaster inside the tent already starting the show. "Children of all ages . . ."

Behind the ticket booth's thin black bars, they saw an old woman in dark sunglasses, her gray fingers on the counter waiting for money.

"How much?" Alex said.

"Thirty dollars."

He slipped his hand into his wallet and laughed. "I've only

got a twenty." He rubbed the single twenty-dollar bill between his thumb and forefinger hoping it would turn into two. "Do you take credit cards?"

"No," the woman said.

"Any chance you'd let a showperson in for free?" Alex asked. "My wife is an actress."

"No." She was already reaching up for the wooden curtain.

Alex turned to Iris. "Are you sure you don't have any money on you?"

She shook her head. Her hands rested in the back pockets of her jeans.

Alex turned back to the window. The wooden curtain had been pulled down. On it was a painted mural of a circus ring in the open air before a placid blue sea. In the ring, seagulls roosted on an elephant that lay on its side with its eye closed.

The back door to the ticket booth opened and closed. The old woman, who was surprisingly short, walked with a limp toward the big top.

A tiger or lion growled so deeply that Alex and Iris could feel it in their chests. They looked into a menagerie tent and saw five elephants separating hay from broken bales with their trunks, curling it up to their mouths. Farther down they saw large steel cages stacked on top of each other.

They could smell dung and hay and feel the heat from animal bodies. They heard different sounds: hay swishing in the trunks of elephants; the rattling of a steel cage; a hiss of air, perhaps from a big cat; then a whinny answered by another whinny.

They turned and went back toward the clear, mournful notes of a trumpet coming from the big tent. A trapeze artist must be working. Stepping back, they looked at the roof of the tent as if they'd be able to see through it. The forked flag on its crown had yellow and black tigerlike stripes.

Somewhere outside the tent they heard hooves; a white horse appeared, galloping, perhaps the same white horse, but now ridden by a man dressed as a Cossack, a sword at his side and spurs on tall black boots. He narrowly missed Iris and Alex, then yanked the reins to one side and turned the horse around rapidly, coming up alongside them.

He was no older than Alex. His face had a European look, Italian or French. He had beautiful dark eyebrows; his narrow, muscular features made him look feminine for an instant, then masculine, powerful and sleek. High cheekbones and large, alert eyes. His expression changed as he looked from Alex to Iris; the horse beneath him pranced back and forth excitedly, but the man's eyes were trained on Iris.

"You'd like to see the show?" he said. "Sure, you can see it, but you"—he lifted a rein and pointed at Iris—"I've seen you, you are an actress aren't you?"

Iris nodded her head.

"Then you must volunteer for an act. It'll be your admission fee."

The man's legs squeezed the excited horse and it bolted toward the opening of the tent where somebody lifted the flap and the man and the horse disappeared. The trumpet still played as Alex and Iris followed him in.

The space inside was bigger than they had imagined; high above, a woman in a silvery blue suit was flipping and twisting in the air, catching the hands of men on opposite swings. Standing in center ring a dwarf in clown attire played the trumpet, pointing the instrument toward the ceiling.

A woman with a plume on her snowy white hat smiled at Iris and Alex and led them to the bleachers, pointed with a riding crop toward their seats, then took Iris's arm. "You must stand up," she said, "when Father Fish looks your way." She handed her two tickets. Iris gave the tickets to Alex. One was torn, the other whole. He put them in his pants pocket.

A heavy man and a small white monkey with pale fur and bright yellow eyes worked together selling concessions, the monkey delivering food and collecting money from hard-to-reach people on the bleachers. To Alex and Iris he made several trips, bringing a snow cone, a beer, and two hot dogs, then chattered impatiently as he waited for payment.

During one of the animal acts, Alex took out the tickets she'd given him and looked at them. Their peculiar shade of red matched the shade of the tent and the shade of Iris's shirt. *The child will follow,* the untorn ticket said. A wire mesh fence with barbed wire on the top and ripples of water before it had been drawn behind the thin black letters.

The show was more than two hours long. Among the acts was a contortionist, a Chinese woman who moved from one posture to the next on a little pedestal in center ring so gracefully and fluidly that she looked like she was underwater. Folding herself backward she rested her buttocks on her back and wrapped her legs over her shoulders and down her chest. A man came out into the ring, lifted her with one hand, and carried her away under his arm like a package.

Finally, the lights were extinguished and the ringmaster, a stout, ruddy-faced man in red coattails, called out, "Ladies and gentlemen, our final act of the night is our most spectacular: the great, one and only *Father Fish's disappearing act!*"

When the lights came on again, they saw that a circular wooden platform, a stage of some sort, had been wheeled into the ring. A black box, like a coffin, rested on end at its center. The door opened. A man in a dark blue tuxedo decorated with silver scales stepped out. The tuxedo's tails were shredded to look like a fish's tail. He wore an enormous top hat and white gloves. There were thick layers of white makeup on his cheeks, caked and layered like fish scales. Stepping away from the coffin, he took short bows, turning to all members of the audience, then, with enormous bulging eyes, he looked straight up to Alex and Iris. Like a blowfish he puffed out his cheeks, then burst out laughing.

"Ladies of the audience," the ringmaster called. "From among you, the amazing Father Fish needs a volunteer. A volunteer of great faith, a volunteer of great courage. Those with great faith, please rise!" he shouted.

Iris stood up smiling and made her way down to the ring. The lights in the arena suddenly became a watery blue and green, caressing the skin of every face and hand in the audience. Taking Iris by the elbow, Father Fish put his wand under his arm, then turned and looked up into the stands. He stared at Alex for an instant, tipping his hat with his white glove and blowing him a kiss. Stepping to the side of Iris, he put his arms behind her back. As if fainting, she fell back into his arms, and he held her horizontal body effortlessly.

Swiftly he lifted his hands high over his head and stepped around her. She floated before him. Demonstrating her independence, he waved his stick over and under her floating body, then placed his arms beneath her again and she descended into them. He lowered her feet gently to the stage. She bowed slightly as if in a trance, then stepped back into the cushioned coffin. The man closed the door and draped a blue cloth over the box. To one corner he set fire with a lighter. The fire climbed the fabric until the whole box was engulfed, yellow flames rising high up into the trapeze rigging. Once the cloth burned away, Alex saw crumbling, charred strips of the box itself collapse onto the platform around it. Smoke filled the upper regions of the tent, then the stands. People coughed, raising handkerchiefs to their noses. Finally, there was nothing left onstage but charcoal and embers; the smoke began to clear. Father Fish bowed several times, then turned and walked away.

The ringmaster stepped out. "Ladies and gentlemen, tonight Father Fish is having difficulty bringing his subject back from the dead. Rest assured that this is only a temporary failure of communication," his voice echoed. "Another night . . . another night . . . Thank you, and have a good evening."

The band played, the lights came on, and the crowd stood up, talking loudly amongst themselves, lining up in the aisles of the bleachers to leave, walking slowly. Alex stared down at the

black circle where he'd last seen Iris. He waited for the crowd
to move down the steps, then climbed over the bleachers and
down into the arena toward the exit that the ringmaster and the
magician had taken. Workmen in jumpsuits pushed past him.
Outside he met with the crowd and pushed across the river of
people to the back of a trailer.

Lights shone through drawn curtains. The same yellow-and-
black forked flag hung from a pole on the roof. Alex knocked
on the flimsy aluminum door. The door opened and he saw
the burly ringmaster. The monkey stood on the ringmaster's
shoulder, its long tail curling around his neck like a scarf, its
yellow eyes glaring at Alex.

"Well?" Alex said.

The ringmaster, his face beet red, had unbuttoned his jacket,
vest, and shirt. A pale white undershirt stuck out from beneath
his layers of clothing; his belt was unbuckled, but his pants were
still buttoned. The monkey chattered loudly.

"Yes?" the ringmaster said above the din.

Alex smiled. "Where is she?"

"Where is who?" the man said.

"I'm her husband," he said.

The man looked at Alex gravely. The monkey kept chattering.

"Whose husband?" the man said.

Alex saw other performers behind the ringmaster and monkey: the face of an old dwarf, who had already wiped off most
of his makeup, and the face of a woman, a heavy, defiant, European face: healthy, muscular, and unhappy. She wore one long
black false eyelash. Another woman stood behind her.

"My wife—the woman who just volunteered."

The ringmaster stared at Alex; the faces behind him pressed
closer, those of the women over his shoulder and that of the
dwarf at his legs.

"Are you some kind of prankster?" the man said.

"What? The woman in the show—with Father Fish, the performer. I'm her husband."

"Father who?" the man said.

"The man with the black hat, the woman in the box, the disappearing act."

The man put his arms up across the door as if to hold the others back from Alex.

Alex smiled, turned, and followed the last of the crowd over to where the man on the white horse had met them. He looked up at the clear sky, at all the stars. The moon, well above the water, looked much smaller, more distinct. He could barely see the ridge of dunes that divided the field from the sea. He turned and looked at the cars leaving the field—a line of taillights slowly rising and falling over bumps and ditches, making their way to the main road. He went back toward the mouth of the tent. Inside, a haze of wood smoke drifted. The workmen were breaking down the rigging. The trapeze and tightwires were coming down, the ring curb was dismantled and loaded on a truck inside the tent. Men had folded a section of bleacher.

He stepped outside. The salty and grassy night air was cool. He was tired, anxious to get back to the guesthouse. Workmen were leading the horses out of the tent. One was pulling the white horse by a painter up a trailer's ramp. The horse swung his head back, snorting and whinnying, fighting the workman's rope. Finally, it bolted up through the dark door.

Four elephants with two men next to each one worked outside the big top. The elephants wrapped their trunks around the tops of tent stakes and pulled. The long stakes came out slowly with clods of dirt clinging to the ends. The sound of the generator filled the air. The lights of the last few cars shone against the brush at the far end of the field.

Every component of the show was being torn down. Alex stopped a workman carrying a huge coil of cable toward the back of a truck and asked him where the woman who had volunteered for the last act had gone. The man, who evidently didn't speak English, shrugged his shoulders and went on.

He went to another trailer he thought might be for performers and knocked on the aluminum door, shaking the curtains inside. The door opened and the man who had been on the white horse—his face kind, sleek, and effeminate—looked out at him.

"Where's my wife? We have to go," Alex said.

"What do you say?" he said.

The man wore a white sleeveless undershirt. Veins bulged from his arm and shoulder muscles.

Alex smiled a little. "You asked us to come to the show," he said. "Me and my wife."

"Who are you?" the man said. "Go away." He started to close the door.

"The husband of the volunteer."

"I don't know who you are." The man slammed the door.

Alex grabbed the handle. It was locked. He banged on the door. "I'll call the police!" he yelled.

He saw the silhouette of an elephant pulling back on a guy rope. Workmen carrying props, boards, and wires moved quickly back and forth. A man lifted two bales of hay, one in each hand, toting them to the animal truck. Performers came out of the trailers, helping to set up spotlights on the roofs of several trucks, as the other lights were pulled down off the tents.

Alex went to every trailer and knocked. Nobody answered; the doors were bolted.

He stepped out into the field in the direction the cars had gone and watched for Iris's silhouette, waiting for her to come up to him. It was quite a show, he thought, but what he couldn't figure out was how they had gotten her to go along with them. It wasn't like her. She must have known that during the last hour he had been feeling a little anxious and had wanted to get back to their room. She knew his feelings, that it was quite a novelty finding this circus in the field behind the beach, but that the novelty had worn off, and he just wanted to take a shower and lie down in bed. It was more like him than like her. She played tricks on him, but they were mild tricks; the few times she'd hid from him she'd whistled when he couldn't find her.

At least an hour had gone by and she still hadn't appeared. He walked to the edge of the light from the spotlight so she'd see him, squatted, and watched the elephants lined up in pairs, two on one side of the big top and two on the other, holding guy ropes taut with their trunks. A workman yelled a command and the elephants moved forward, slowly collapsing the canvas.

The other tent, the animal tent, was down now too and an elephant, guided by workmen, rolled up a section of canvas with the front of its trunk.

Alex spotted the stout ringmaster with the chattering white monkey on his shoulder walking away in the dark. Alex called to him from behind.

"Excuse me, excuse me."

The ringmaster kept walking.

"Hold on, would you. I still haven't found her. I'm getting tired of waiting!"

"Get lost," the man said, still walking away.

"Don't tell me to get lost! I'm freezing. Now just hold on here." He reached for the man's shoulder to turn him around, but as he did the monkey spun around screeching and bit Alex's hand. A needlelike pain shot through it.

"Goddamn it!" Alex yelled. The man kept walking away.

Small drops of blood dripped down the back of his hand. He held his thumb against the bite to stop the bleeding.

He turned and started across the dewy field toward the empty parking lot.

He wasn't positive where he was. The narrow dirt road must lead back to the main road. He'd have to hitchhike back to the guesthouse, or call a taxi from a public phone. He'd seen a telephone in the small town near the dirt road they had walked on to get to the beach.

He kept his thumb pressed against the shallow cut. He thought of Iris. She must have gotten a ride out of the area, but he wasn't sure why she had done this. He thought of what they would say to each other when he got back and saw her. Maybe she hadn't known that they weren't going to tell him what was going on. He could hear her apologizing to him back at the guest room.

"But I got bitten, bitten by a monkey!" he'd say. "You think that's funny? Well I'm pissed off . . . Why did you go along with those cruel bastards? . . ."

The dirt road at the edge of the field cut through short, scraggly trees and waist-high bushes. He could hear crickets in the grass and the crunch of the gravel under his feet.

He imagined how fast and easy this would have been in a car. Usually he liked walking, but he was tired and anxious to get back to the guesthouse.

"Where did you go when he was burning that box?" he kept saying aloud.

The terrain along the dirt road changed from low brush and small trees to bigger trees. The air smelled less like the ocean and more like the dark earth. There were no crickets. The taller trees made the road darker and quieter and he felt small.

He released his thumb from the shallow cut and realized it had long ago stopped bleeding. He tried to laugh at himself for thinking his problems so momentous when, in fact, he was so small compared to everything else.

He made it out to the main road. Cars drove by quickly. Because there was no shoulder, he had to keep climbing the bank through the tall wet weeds to avoid being hit. This added to his anger. "I almost got killed on the road. A drunk swerved . . ." He hated the sound of cars at night. They didn't know he was there; people were probably drinking, laughing in their comfortable little enclosures. In their headlights they'd catch a glimpse of him walking through the grass along the embankment. They'd think he was crazy.

He came to Towson, a town with only one small country store, which was closed, and one public telephone. He fingered his pockets for change, then crossed a parking lot next to the store where he saw two cars with their lights on parked next to each other, facing different directions. Two teenage boys with their arms around girls were talking through the car windows. Alex walked into the headlights and held out a dollar, asking for change as he approached. The two teenagers came up with four quarters. Alex thanked them.

There was no dial tone; the pay phone was out of order. He thought of Iris. "You wouldn't believe what this cost me," he said to her. He didn't know how he'd get back, so he couldn't finish off the scenario in his head. He went back to the teenagers. Both cars started moving; he stopped one of them and went to the window.

"Is there another pay phone around here? That one's broken."

"Nope," the boy said.

"Any idea how I might get a cab? I missed my ride back to Verrehaven."

"Nope."

"I couldn't offer to pay you to drive me there?"

The boy looked at the girl next to him.

"I'll pay you ten dollars," Alex said.

"That's two six-packs," the girl said to the boy.

Alex got into the back of the car.

He crossed the porch of the guesthouse near the center of Verrehaven where he and Iris had rented a room. He walked through the living room, then started up the stairs. First he tried the handle, then he put the key in and opened the door. The light was off. He turned it on. Mrs. Burns, the owner, had made the bed.

The room was untouched.

Iris must have gone back to look for him. He was a little relieved that she hadn't been comfortably waiting for him all this time. He went into the bathroom, cleaned off the back of his hand, and examined the bite, which looked like just a scratch now that it had scabbed. Though tired, he took a quick shower, expecting to see Iris's hand pull back the shower curtain at any moment, then in the bedroom he expected to hear the key in the door. He dried his hair and got into bed, turning on the reading light behind him. He stared at the door for a moment, then picked up a book and tried to read. He laughed to himself; somehow this whole trick with the circus was something that he could have engineered himself. He was always playing tricks on people; when he was little, he played dead in front of his foster parents. Maybe this was such an elaborate stunt that it would cure him once and for all of tricking others.

He was still angry and a little upset just from having to spend the last two and a half hours alone, but he was also slightly amused at the whole thing. It was certainly something to tell their friends when they got back. He closed his eyes, and, in a flash, he felt deeply exhausted; something was yanking him down into the darkness of sleep.

CHAPTER 2

WHEN he woke up, he found he'd kicked the covers off and a bright blue ray of sunshine was focused on his stomach. He'd been sleeping deeply all night and now he was groggy. He reached over quickly for Iris and found she still wasn't there. He jumped out of bed calling her, expecting her to be in the bathroom. But he could tell that she hadn't come in the night before; she definitely hadn't come in.

He pulled on his clothes and ran downstairs. He suddenly thought of the circus people. It was their trick; it wasn't Iris's; she wouldn't do this. Maybe it was the man on the white horse. The sidewalks were already filling with tourists in their yellow and blue summer clothes. He ran down the center of the street to a car rental agency near the ferry landing and filled out the papers for a car. He drove up-island through the town of Towson to the entrance of the dirt road he'd followed the night before. As he turned in, a dump truck was coming out. Farther along the dirt road he met with another dump truck and pulled the car over to let it pass.

He came to the edge of the field. The tents and trailers were gone. In the distance across the grass he saw more dump trucks, two yellow backhoes, and a bulldozer. They'd already plowed a great deal of the field. Alex gripped the steering wheel of the small car tightly as adrenaline surged through his muscles. He recognized the flat-topped tree that looked like a tree on an African plain. He was sure he was in the right place. He parked the car next to a number of pickup trucks and station wagons and closed the door. He felt tiny and helpless, he felt like crying.

He could see workmen in sweatshirts and blue jeans, some smoking cigarettes, several with cups of coffee in their hands, standing back and watching the bulldozer and backhoes working.

They didn't notice Alex until he shouted to one of them over the noise of the machines. "What happened to the circus that was here last night?" he asked one man.

The man held a cigarette between his lips, smiled without taking it out, and jerked his head back as if Alex had made a joke.

"There was a circus here last night," Alex said, pointing to the ground. "Do you know where it went?"

"What kind of circus?" the man shouted, then looked at the others to see if they were listening. Another man came over.

"A real circus, with animals," Alex said. "My wife and I came here last night."

"Here? Not here. You sure you're on the right island?"

"What do you mean?"

"Are you sure this is the right island?"

"Right island?" Alex said. He stared at the oddly shaped tree he'd seen the night before. "Of course it's the right island. They must have packed up and gone."

"Maybe," the man said.

"No circus out here," the second man said. "Not yesterday."

"I'm sure of it." He knew the workmen were islanders; he'd seen them driving their equipment through town.

He walked out toward the beach, finally climbing the dunes.

The water was calm; the waves, hardly bigger than lake waves, were gently slapping the shore. A few white gulls floated serenely on the still water. He saw the mysterious black head of a cormorant rise up, then dive down again.

Iris's yellow towel. He hadn't remembered that she'd left it behind, but there it lay, wet and crumpled in the white sand. He ran down to it and picked it up, turned around and came back. From the top of the dune he could see the bulldozer pushing a huge mound of dirt to one side. It was her fault, it could only be her fault, he thought. What did people do in magic tricks? There was always a trapdoor through which they escaped. She had to have been somewhere; she had to have made the decision to play the trick on him.

"My wife and I were on the beach right down there. We saw a circus here and went to it," he told the workmen, holding up the yellow towel as if to prove it. They looked at him silently. "I don't know what happened to it," he said.

He returned to the guesthouse, certain once again that when he opened their door, he'd see Iris. As he climbed the stairs he heard a vacuum cleaner and saw his room door open. Mrs. Burns had already made the bed and was now cleaning the rug.

She didn't hear him come in. "Miss?" he said, "Have you seen my wife?"

She wore rimless glasses with wire shanks; her hair was a light yellow, a strange color, though Alex was sure she didn't dye it.

"No, no one's been in here. I'll be right out of your way."

Alex wrote a note and left it on the dresser. "Iris, I'm in the café." He left it against the mirror, stepped over the vacuum cleaner cord, and went downstairs.

He sat in the little open-air café where he and Iris had had breakfast most mornings, flipping through the *Gazette*'s weekly calendar, looking for the announcement of a circus. Before he ordered from his waitress, he asked her, "Did you know there was a circus in Towson last night?"

"A circus here?" she said. Her blond hair was pulled to the back of her head in a bun. She smiled.

"You didn't hear about it?"

"I love circuses," she said. "I can't believe I missed it."

"Any of the other waitresses go to it?"

"Nobody mentioned it."

"Would you ask them when you get my order?"

When she returned with his breakfast, she told him that nobody had heard about it, not even the two people who lived in Towson.

He poured cream in his coffee, buttered his croissant, folded the paper and placed it to the side of his food, then got up and ran from the café to the guesthouse.

The room door was closed; the vacuum cleaner cord ran around the corner. He bolted up the stairs as if he was sure she was back now that the door was closed. But the room had merely been freshened up. The bed was tightly made and bare, and the books on the shelf above had been straightened. His pants from the night before had been folded and placed on the end of his bed. He went through the pockets and found the two tickets, one torn and one whole, then he went back downstairs to the café.

Steam was still rising from his coffee. He examined the ticket again. *"The child will follow,"* he read. Looking at the letters now he saw that they must have been hand drawn because the *The child* of the torn ticket was definitely different than the one on the other ticket; the fence, too, was different.

His waitress came by and topped off his coffee.

After breakfast he stopped into the office of the *Gazette* and asked a roomful of people sitting before computer screens if anybody had heard of a circus the night before. Everyone turned in their chairs and looked at him, some shaking their heads.

In the police station Alex asked a woman dispatcher the same question.

"A circus?" she said.

Two officers in navy blue uniforms were coming out of a back room. One was quite a bit older than the other. He had jet black hair slicked to his head, large ears, and a wide face. His crooked nose looked like it had been broken and never set.

"You mean a fair," he said.

"No, I mean a circus with elephants, tigers, a high-wire act."

The older officer glanced at the younger one. He was smiling when he looked back at Alex.

"Where?" he said.

"By the water," Alex said. "Near King's Beach, that's where we saw it."

The men shook their heads. "Nobody told us about it."

"Well, I don't know how to do this," he said. "But I have to report somebody missing."

A voice broke from the static on the radio, and the woman dispatcher picked up a microphone and began talking through it.

"I don't know how to say it, exactly . . ." Alex started telling his story. The younger officer left and the older officer sat down behind a desk and told Alex to have a seat. After Alex finished talking, the older officer called the Towson police and asked them if they'd heard of a circus. Nobody there had. He looked at Alex a moment, then opened a pack of chewing gum, dropping the plastic strip on the desk, and offered Alex a piece.

"No, thanks," Alex said. The officer put a piece in his mouth and chewed for a moment, then stopped.

"Are you all right?" he asked.

Alex showed him the two tickets. The man examined them, then handed them back. Then Alex held out the back of his hand. "A monkey bit me."

"A what? A monkey?" The man glanced from the cut to Alex's eyes.

"Look, I'm not crazy."

"I didn't say you were," the man said.

"I'm telling you, this happened—"

"But I can tell you right now, there wasn't a circus in Towson last night if the Towson police didn't know about it. This is a small island," the man said. "We have a ferry system." He picked up the phone and called the steamship authority and asked to speak to someone. Alex listened half to the man and half to his own thoughts. *Iris must be back at the guesthouse now.*

"Bob, yeah, how you doing. Listen, I have a guy down here who saw a circus last night in Towson . . . Yeah, of course . . . He says it's not there now . . . No, this island. King's Beach or something"—the officer looked at Alex for a second then back at his desk—"We just wanted to check a circus didn't go through on the ferries, he says they had big semis . . . Look, I'll talk to you later."

Hanging up, the officer took a deep breath and looked at Alex. He smiled gently. "This sort of thing ever happen to you before?"

"No. I don't think this is funny. I'd like to report my wife as missing."

"All right with me," the officer said. He opened a desk drawer and pulled out a form and began filling out the top of it. "Name?" he said. He looked up. "By the way, my name is Marlin." He got up and shook Alex's hand.

Alex introduced himself, then said, "Listen, I'll be back. I just want to see if she's back yet. It'll save you the trouble."

In the guesthouse hallway he dialed a friend of Iris's, Claire, who was also a good friend of his, and asked her if she had heard from Iris in the last twenty-four hours.

Claire hadn't, but she wondered why he was calling. Alex told her not to worry; they were supposed to meet somewhere but had gotten mixed-up. "I thought she was going to call you this morning," Alex lied. "I thought you might know. We've just gotten a little mixed-up. We lost each other."

"She's going to call?"

"I think so; I thought that's what she said."

He drove back up to the construction site in the field. The equipment was parked next to the piles of dirt and some men were leaning against a pickup truck; others sat in their trucks eating lunch. Alex thought, *Christ, they must think I'm weird.* He avoided looking over at them and walked toward where the horse had crossed the dunes. The soil became sandier. Carefully he looked for hoof prints. After a long time he found one, a clear one in the dry, sandy soil, pointed in the right direction, right toward the place where the tent had been.

"Who was the first to get here this morning?" he asked. The workers looked up from their sandwiches and stared at him curiously, registering the question. Their faces were red and tanned.

"What for?" one said, biting an apple.

"I was wondering if there were any tracks out here. Did anybody notice any tracks?"

"There wasn't any circus out here," said an older man from inside a pickup truck. He could have been the foreman.

"Were you the first one out here?" Alex asked.

"Yup, and you got the wrong place; there was nothing out here but that grass."

"Was the grass flattened? Did you notice any animal droppings, any litter?"

"Nothing," the man said. "It was just like it was when the surveyors were here. You got the wrong field. There may have been a circus somewhere, I don't doubt your word, but you got the wrong field."

"Is there another field around here?"

At first the man looked irritated, as if his men shouldn't be exposed to this nonsense, but then he seemed to be thinking about the question sincerely.

"As big as this? Not without a house on it."

That night Alex opened up Iris's bags, pulling everything out
of her pockets, turning her underwear inside out, looking in her
shirt sleeves. She had brought a program to a play that she had
been in the year before in New York, and three books, two
thrillers and a more serious novel by a writer whom they both
knew personally. After flipping through the pages, he put it
back.

The next morning, from the telephone downstairs, he called
Claire and explained to her from the beginning what had really
happened.

Claire was silent. Then she spoke in her usual cool and rational
manner, apparently unaffected by the hysterical tone in his
voice. "It's simple, Alex. She has to be somewhere."

There was a pause during which Alex could hear her breathing.
He crumbled a dried flower in a vase on the table next to the
telephone. Realizing what he was doing, he scraped off the pieces
and put them into his pocket. He could see out the front door.

"Alex?"

"What?"

"Are you guys playing a joke on me?"

"Claire, listen, so help me God, it happened exactly as I just
told you. We weren't having a fight. It isn't funny anymore. If
Iris is playing a trick on me, it isn't funny, and it isn't like her."

He went on trying to convince her of the gravity of the situation. "I'll pay for your flight out here, please, Claire, this is an
emergency!"

Claire agreed to come. They hung up and she called back to
tell him the flight she had booked. Alex pulled the two flowerless
stems from the pot, broke them in pieces and put them in his
pocket, then started up the stairs.

Later that morning an issue of the *Gazette* came out and Alex
found a short article on his police report in the back pages.

Circus Sighted on King's Beach. Evidently his story was too fantastic for the conservative little paper to take seriously. Returning to the police station that afternoon, he spoke to Marlin, who was busy filling out court forms and seemed annoyed by Alex's persistence. Finally, Marlin put the forms away, took out a notepad, and began asking Alex questions.

"What were you doing on that part of the beach?"

"Walking."

"It's a private beach. It's a hell of a long way from where you started."

"We like to walk, both of us like to walk."

"You went swimming. How many times did you go swimming?"

"Three times," Alex said.

"And her?"

"Three times."

"Did you see her get out the third time?"

"I got out with her."

"You're sure she got out with you?"

"Positive." He tried to see what Marlin was writing down on the yellow pad.

"How long after that before you saw this circus?"

The questions went on, concentrating on details about the circus. Finally Marlin told Alex to get into his car with him, and they drove up-island and turned onto the long dirt road.

Marlin waved to the construction workers as he and Alex got out of his car. Alex crossed the field, looking for the hoof print. Instinctively remembering where it was, he squatted and pointed it out to the officer who bent back blades of grass and found another print. Marlin looked up at Alex, then stood up and walked to the dune. Alex followed him. From the top of the dune, Alex pointed to the place where he and Iris had been.

"I found our towel down there yesterday morning."

Marlin was writing something down on a clipboard. "You know, this is quite a story," he said.

Alex pointed to where backhoes were digging a foundation. "Right there," he said. "That's where the tent was."

They walked toward the site. Marlin stopped to write something else down.

"What makes you think this was the spot?"

"That tree right there," Alex said. Marlin looked at the tree, then at Alex. "I'm sure this was the field. I walked home on the dirt road."

"But that was at night."

"I remember that line of trees over there. I remember that tree; how could there be another like it? Look at it."

"Your wife like circuses?" Marlin asked, as they walked toward the construction workers.

"Not particularly, no more than anyone else. We kind of laughed to ourselves at this one."

"Why'd you laugh?"

"I don't really mean laugh. It was just so surprising."

The officer went over to the men and talked to them. Alex stood a few feet away, squatted, and pulled up grass. He could smell the freshly turned earth. The backhoe shut off and Alex suddenly heard their voices clearly. "He's crazy," a worker said. Evidently he hadn't meant for Alex to hear this. Marlin gestured as if to quiet him down. Alex couldn't see their faces.

The front seat of the police car was deeply cushioned. Except for a trace of cigarettes the interior smelled new. The radio kept crackling as they drove away from the field and along the dirt road. Before reaching the main road Marlin turned up a driveway leading to a small brown house hiding among the trees. Alex followed Marlin to the front door.

An old man in white coveralls came to the door. "Mr. Kinney?" Marlin said. "This is Mr. Barton. Could we come in?"

The old man wore a coffee-brown hearing aid. He nodded and held the door for Alex and Marlin.

Alex sat down on one end of an old sofa and Marlin at the other. Kinney sat in a chair in front of his blank television screen.

"Any trucks going by two days ago?"

Kinney stared at Marlin.

"This fellow here thinks there was some kind of circus."

"Circus!?" Kinney said, as if that were the only word to get through to him.

"There was a circus down there three nights ago," Alex said, "I saw it."

"On this island?" the old man yelled. He squinted at Alex.

"Yes, did you hear anything?"

Kinney appeared to be figuring out what Alex had said. Then he said, "As a matter of fact, I thought I did hear something out there. But I'm not sure."

"What did you hear?" Marlin asked.

"Eh?"

"What did you hear?"

"Activity!" the man yelled. "Car, maybe a truck or two."

"How long ago?" Marlin said.

"What?"

"How long ago?"

"Hell, about a month ago," Kinney yelled back.

"Anything more recent?"

"No," Kinney said. "It's been quiet. Nobody bothers us down here."

That evening Alex drove to the airport to pick up Claire. It started raining so hard that the heavy drops danced on the pavement and the cars in front of him slowed almost to a stop.

Claire got out of the small plane first, holding a crumpled black canvas rain hat to her head and leaning into the wind. In the lobby of the small airport they embraced and Alex told her that he was no closer to understanding what had happened than when he'd talked to her last. He became very upset.

That night Alex and Claire walked through the small town until it had nearly emptied of people. Alex kept slapping his hands together, pounding his fist into his leg, and stamping his feet. "It's crazy," he kept saying. "But really it's impossible. It just couldn't have happened."

He told her the story three times, each time remembering new details but none of them helped; he'd gone through every motion. It was all absurd. The circus people must have brought a boat to shore somewhere, that was the only thing Alex could imagine. "But the coast guard said there was no way a big enough boat could have come and gone undetected, and besides how could they possibly have gotten everything from shore onto the boat without a dock or a pier?"

After breakfast the next morning, he brought her to the police station. Marlin spoke to them first together, then alone. At lunchtime they made a list of things to do. They'd get both local newspapers more involved, contact the bureau of missing persons, go to the radio station again, interview people around Towson.

Two days later, they had accomplished everything on the list. Except for the tickets and the barely visible mark left from the cut on the back of Alex's right hand, not a shred of hard evidence pointed toward the existence of a circus. Not once did Alex bring up the possibility that what he had seen was not real. After a week, Claire contacted an organization that kept track of American cults. No one had ever heard of a kidnapping plot this elaborate. That evening at a small restaurant in town, Claire put her hand over Alex's hand and told him what the cult organization suggested. "They said tragedy can produce hallucinations. Alex, if you saw something that you couldn't face, your mind could well have produced this circus, like a strange dream to avoid facing reality."

"But the tickets," Alex said. "How about the tickets?" He

reached into his wallet and laid them on the table. Claire looked from their smudged surface into Alex's eyes.

"You could have drawn them, Alex; it's not inconceivable."

"Then what the hell happened to her?"

"What do you think happened to her?" Claire said.

The next morning Claire ended her part in the investigation by hiring a private detective, one of the best within reach of the island. He commanded a high fee. Claire felt that if he couldn't find out anything about a circus, then the case for the existence of a circus would have to be put to rest; other theories about what had happened to Iris would have to be adopted. Claire left the island two days later.

CHAPTER 3

ALEX and Iris had come to
the Island of Verre with the intention of staying a week. Four
weeks after they'd first arrived he was still renting his room.
His story, his problem, spread among the islanders quickly. The
waitresses in the café knew about it, the store owners, the
woman who ran the guesthouse. Reporters had taken pictures
of him. The local paper ran a humorous editorial including
quotes from islanders about circuses and elephants. Columnists
told jokes about people hiding elephants in their basements.
Some people were kind to him, others treated him like an insane
man who may not have had a wife to begin with. No one explic-
itly told him he was crazy, but he knew how they really felt.

He became irritable. He wanted to argue with somebody
about his case, but he knew that this would only make matters
worse. He had a falling out with the detective, who finally told
him that there was definitely no circus on the island, and that
his story would only continue to embarrass and humiliate him.
The detective told him to go home and seek psychological help.

"You're hiding something from yourself," he said. "I'm sure you don't want to find out what it is unless you're safe at home."

He dismissed the tickets. "You may have bought those somewhere in New York. Maybe if you remember where they're from, you'll remember what happened on the beach."

Of everyone Alex met, Marlin offered the most sympathy, taking everything at face value and never so much as intimating that Alex had hallucinated. Once he even invited Alex to dinner at his house, introducing him to islanders. Several times he drove Alex to houses in the area near the field to question people about the circus.

Finally, one morning, Alex packed his bags, bade farewell to Mrs. Burns, and walked down to a bench along the pier to wait for the next boat to shore. He watched tourists, most of them gray- and white-haired retirees wearing light-colored, jovial summer clothing, walking along the docks, snapping pictures, speaking to each other in mild voices, laughing and smiling. "We were going to be older someday," Alex said to himself.

He saw a shadow at his feet and looked up. It was Marlin dressed in uniform with dark glasses.

"You didn't tell me you were leaving," Marlin said.

"I know. I was going to write you and thank you."

"Can you take a later ferry?"

"What for?"

"I'd like to show you something."

Alex put his bags in the back of the police cruiser and got in. They drove along a beautiful country lane through the center of the island, along stone walls and cow fields. The road rollercoastered; sharp bends pushed Alex against the door. In some places tree branches swept low overhead and spots of green light flashed across the hood.

"I've meant to ask you something," Marlin said. "Have you got any Indian blood in you?"

"Why do you ask?" Alex said.

"No reason," Marlin said. "You look a little Indian."

"And you, are you an Indian?"

"Half-blooded," Marlin said. Marlin slowed the car to a stop. Before them, a small goat herd crossed the road with two young girls in blue jeans clapping their hands behind them. A baby goat was the last to cross.

Marlin asked Alex again about his heritage.

"I don't know," Alex said quietly as they started up. "I don't know who my real parents are."

They went by a farm built of gray stones. Even the barns were made of stones. Through a gap in a wall that paralleled the road, Alex saw sheep lying down in a pasture of long grass.

His throat began to tighten. He tried to swallow but couldn't. He thought the feeling would pass quickly, but instead his arms and legs trembled. He could barely force words from his throat to ask Marlin to stop.

Opening the door, he rushed up the grass bank, fell to his knees, and began choking up tears. He could smell the long late summer grass and hear cicadas calling in the sun and in the trees. When he finally got up again, he saw Marlin in his dark sunglasses, standing with his hand on the hood of the idling car. Marlin looked aloof and indifferent, but as Alex came back down the hill, Marlin took off his glasses and his eyes looked suddenly small and sweaty, innocent and tender.

"Look, I know how all this sounds—" Alex said in the car.

"You don't have to explain," Marlin said.

"I mean, you know, you come up with something like this and people think you're crazy."

"I've seen some things that other people have laughed at."

"Have you ever heard of anything so—?"

"Maybe not quite like you described it."

"You're saying you believe it though, don't you?" Alex had

taken out the ticket. He held it up for Marlin while they were driving along the winding road through pastures and under trees.

"I do believe it," Marlin said. "But I don't believe it too, you see."

He looked at Alex out of the corner of his eye. "Some things happen only to certain people."

"But not to me," Alex said. "Things like this don't happen to me."

"Maybe they're starting to happen—"

"No, I'm sure they're not starting to happen. I mean, I had a hot dog that night . . . I could taste the hot dog the next morning—I burped it up—believe me, you just don't—"

One of Marlin's hands rested on the wheel, the other on the seat between them. He looked at Alex.

"It's one of those things," Alex said. "Most of the world will think you're crazy or something—because, I know it doesn't make any sense. For Christ's sake, I saw something real."

"You love her a lot, don't you?"

"A lot?" Alex said. He turned toward Marlin and began to speak, but his throat constricted again.

"You don't have to say," Marlin said. He parked the car in a field that sloped down to the ocean, one of the most beautiful fields Alex had ever seen. At the bottom of it, before the beach, he could see a pond with three wild swans drifting on the pale blue water. Cattle were grazing at the bottom of the field before the dunes. The grass was long; the cattle were very red. The sun shone in a wide path through the middle of the ocean. The ocean looked big enough to show the roundness of the earth. A dark blue surrounded the white path.

"Sit down," Marlin said. A warm breeze brushed their backs. "I want you to listen to me. I want you to answer a few questions for me, just answer them truthfully, and don't try to second-guess my intentions because I'm trying to help you. I don't think you're crazy, and I happen to like you quite a lot. I've dealt with a lot of people on this island, rich and poor; I don't like many of them; I like you, and I think something did happen to you, but I think something else happened to you that you don't know about."

Alex pulled up a long blade of grass. He sat quietly.

"When you saw that white horse," Marlin said. "Did you feel different?"

"Different?"

"Think about it. Were things in any way different than they were before, when you were, let's say, walking down the beach?"

Alex broke the blade of grass in two pieces, then in four, put one piece to his mouth, and looked out over the great wide path of sun on the ocean.

"What would be different?" he asked.

"Were the colors brighter?"

"The colors?"

"Did the horse seem brighter than other horses? The water bluer?"

Alex nodded. "The horse was unusually bright—of course. I told you that. But if you're suggesting it wasn't—"

"When you saw the tent, was there anything peculiar about it? Did it seem entirely foreign, or very familiar?"

"It just seemed weird that it was there. We were swimming . . ."

"Did it make you feel lonely?"

Alex laughed for a minute, then he looked at the veins on Marlin's crooked nose.

"Why would it make me feel lonely?"

"I'm just asking you. Just answer the questions, Alex, don't think about why I'm asking them."

"The tent looked a little lonely. It looked strange," Alex said.

"All right then. Now, think of how that tent and then that horse made you feel. Don't think why I'm asking, just tell me what comes to mind."

Alex looked at Marlin's wide face.

"It made me feel like I was in a place I'd never been in before."

"What kind of a place would that be?"

The light breeze stopped. There was silence.

"Look," Alex said, "anything like that would make you feel like you were in a strange place."

"Sure, but what kind of a strange place?"

"An old place," Alex said. "Something out of the past."

Marlin didn't speak. Alex looked down at the red cattle grazing slowly in the long grass next to the pond. He saw Marlin taking something out his pocket. A piece of cloth, a bathing suit. Alex fingered it, and slowly began to remember it was the suit that Iris had brought with her.

"This was found on the beach two days ago. It matches the description that you gave us of her bathing suit."

"But we weren't swimming with bathing suits."

Marlin was shaking his head.

"You know, there are many different worlds. You may have seen that circus . . . I mean, it may be as real as I am sitting right here. And I believe you. I don't think you're crazy. I've seen some things too, believe me, I've seen some things that I would never tell people, not the way you've gone around telling people about the circus, but right now, I don't think your wife is with a circus."

Alex turned toward Marlin. "Did you find her? Her body?"

"No," Marlin said.

"Tell me, tell me if you did find her."

"No," Marlin said. "We didn't, just the suit."

"But she wasn't wearing a suit; she wouldn't have worn one."

"Do you know where her suit is, if this isn't hers?"

Alex shook his head. "You didn't find her, did you, you're sure?"

"I'm sorry," Marlin said. "There's just nothing that points toward a kidnapping or even a disappearance any longer. Your wife, as your friend Claire said, was extremely stable."

Marlin got up and started down the hill toward the pond and

the cattle. There were many yellow and blue flowers with tiny petals in the field. There were dried cowpatties in the grass and many cow tracks. The sun fell brightly on Alex's face.

"Come on," Marlin said, looking back.

He went on into the herd of red cows. Alex got up and started down the hill to him.

"You really think she drowned, don't you?" he called.

Marlin turned. He'd put his hand on the neck of one of the cattle.

"I'm not going to say what happened to her."

"She didn't drown, I can tell you that."

"You love her, fellow. I can feel how much you love her, I've felt it since I met you . . ."

H. A. Atwell/*Circus World Museum, Baraboo, Wisconsin.*

CHAPTER 4

ALEX decided to return to New York City. There was nothing more he could do to find out what had happened to Iris. It was also time for him to start the semester at the school where he had been teaching for several years.

On his way into his apartment building, he stopped at old Mr. and Mrs. Lovlor's apartment on the first floor. They were the superintendents of the co-op building. Neither of them had seen Iris. Mr. Lovlor handed Alex a pile of mail, and Alex took the elevator up to his floor.

Opening their apartment door was like accidentally opening the door to a morgue. The haphazard condition they'd left the place in was unchanged. A mop Iris had left in a yellow bucket of water near the kitchen door hadn't been moved. The water was gone, the mop threads dried and hardened. In their bedroom, he saw their mattress was covered only by sheets and he remembered that they'd brought the bedspread to a dry cleaner. There were messages on the answering machine, some for Alex, some for Iris, but none from Iris. Alex sat down on the couch, sorting through their mail. But as soon as he realized that there was nothing addressed to him from Iris, he lay down on the couch and started to cry.

A week later he was standing before his class of eighth graders at a small, private elementary school in Greenwich Village. From the first moments of class, looking out at the audience of young faces, an almost irresistible urge to tell them the whole truth about what had happened came over him. After each boy and girl in the class told of what they'd done that summer, they turned to Alex and asked him what he'd done for the summer. He told them he'd gone to the beach with his wife. When they said "Where?" he hesitated and said, "Coney Island, we spent only a day in Coney Island, the rest of the time we were looking for something."

"For what?" they asked.

"Nothing," he said. He asked a young boy to watch over the class, stepped out to the bathroom, sat down in one of the stalls, and cried.

As the semester got under way he found himself dreaming during classes. He could no more pay attention to his students than he could walk on his hands. He tried to assign special reports to each student to take up time. He counted on the smart students—they would be listening when he wasn't—to ask the appropriate questions. As he'd done when he was in eighth grade himself, he counted the minutes of each class until it was over. Fifty minutes seemed—as it had back then—like three hours, a day seemed like a week, a month an entire year. The thirty-minute subway ride to and from school was more like a commute from Pennsylvania.

Sometimes he'd hear a child calling "Mr. Barton" several times before he'd realize who was being addressed. Other times, a student would ask about getting a drink of water and he'd snap, "Don't you drink at home? Don't you have water at home? Why don't you drink when you're at home?!"

On his way to and from school, he was so anxious to get to his destination that he couldn't read. But looking at the faces of commuters was dangerous. Once on his way to school he thought he saw Iris from behind. When he walked up to her and saw a stranger's face, he stepped off the train, phoned the principal's office, and told the secretary he was sick.

But he kept faith that she hadn't drowned; he still had the tickets and the vivid impressions of her disappearance. Besides, he remembered swimming out to meet her, remembered diving under and touching her foot, remembered her tapping his knee and pointing out the white horse, remembered waiting in line for tickets and then wandering over to the animal tent, and remembered the screech of the monkey before it had bitten him.

His memory of the incident became more real every day. He wrote it down, every second he'd spent with her on the final day. He'd paid two dollars for the hot dogs, a dollar for the snow cone, two dollars for the beer. All he'd had that morning when they'd left for the beach was a twenty; he'd paid the driver ten dollars and that left him with five dollars and that was exactly how much money he'd had on him the next morning. Nobody was going to convince him that all that had happened that night wasn't real.

But that fall an emptiness came into his life, an emptiness such as he'd never felt before. It was a dryness, a barrenness. He held strong to his belief in the reality of what he'd seen, but the force of this emptiness kept crowding in on him. Sometimes it became so strong that it made him nauseous and he'd spend part of the day in bed.

On the rare occasion that he talked to friends about Iris, he could tell what they were thinking. At least once every few weeks Claire and her friends asked him for dinner. One evening, Claire took him aside and told him that she was worried about him. "You've got to see a counselor, Alex. You need to talk to a professional."

"Nobody can help me," Alex said. "Not without getting her back for me."

"How do you hide an elephant?" Wasn't there a joke that children told about that? But for Alex there had been at least five elephants, many horses, cages, tents, trucks, people. Cars, somebody should have at least seen the cars emptying out of the dirt road after the show was over. It was a small island, thirty miles long. Even if somebody had masterminded a plot to get them off the island, the detective surely would have traced it.

The magic trick itself was the easiest to explain: mirrors, trapdoors. But you can't hide an entire circus.

There were the tickets; how could anyone deny the tickets? How on earth could he have gotten such tickets, tickets that fit perfectly with this dream? The tickets were real; the drawings on them were real. Sometimes after telling people his story he showed them the worn red admission tickets. "I'm not a calligrapher," he said. "That was drawn by a calligrapher."

But other times his stubbornness and defiance of what others considered the facts turned into a feeling of self-disgust. He was a man deceiving himself, living a lie. Like a cartoon character, he had walked off a cliff and had kept on walking—in thin air.

Before Christmas of that year, the school administration asked Alex to take an extended leave of absence starting the following semester. He felt no regrets. A year before he had worried about keeping his job, now this notice of dismissal—couched in polite terms—seemed like a Christmas present. After the holidays he crossed town to the unemployment office and got in line.

He spent most of his hours in his living room, pacing, sometimes talking to himself; often he'd go entire days without eating. Every time the phone rang he picked it up expecting to hear her voice. There was a certain irony in any voice other than hers. Something inside him would scream, "Where is she? Where the hell is she?"

Claire kept in touch with him still. Alex tried to sound cheerful to her so she'd leave him alone, but it felt like something black lived inside him, so black that he'd rather die than face it. He rarely slept more than four or five hours. When he woke up everything came back to him in a split second. He counted the days, sometimes the hours, since he had held her hand, since he had kissed her.

CHAPTER 5

DURING this time he'd kept a secret from everybody, even, in a way, from himself. The secret was a memory he'd had of an event that had been in his thoughts up until the time of the circus.

It had happened less than a year after he'd met her, a time when he was falling deeper and deeper in love with her. A time when he was thrilled with his new relationship on the one hand, but afraid of losing control of his feelings on the other. He was falling and the fall had to end somewhere, some boundary between them had to be drawn, some invisible line had to appear. This feeling of oneness was heightened every time they made love. Making love hastened the descent, and the faster he fell the more noticeable became a subtle tension within him, a tension which stemmed from not knowing where he was going, a tension which would only be relieved when he knew he was at the bottom, when the boundary was drawn, when there was no further descent into this dangerous position of having your life placed wholly in somebody else's arms.

It had happened during a January snowstorm, during winter

break of the school year. For the previous month and a half, Alex, at Iris's encouragement, had been acting in an amateur play. It was the first time he'd attempted something like this since a bad experience of stage fright at boarding school when he was fourteen. This experience had made Alex so terrified of audiences that he always bowed out of speaking in front of even a few adults. But this fear—of which he had many nightmares—was in both his and Iris's opinion symbolic of bigger fears. Acting in this small play had seemed like a good idea, a way of tackling a crippling frustration that he'd felt for over twenty years.

But during the play's dress rehearsal Alex became overwhelmed with stage fright and began doing what he'd done onstage at fourteen. He put his hand up to his mouth and began mumbling a phrase. He was so embarrassed and humiliated that before the play was over, he dashed out the theater's back door and ran all the way home through the streets of New York in a heavy snowfall without his jacket. When Iris caught up with him, she told him that she had borrowed a car and that she had the keys to a friend's house in Connecticut.

The two-hour drive that evening took them four. By the time they reached the house, the snow had stopped falling, the clouds had cleared, and the moon was out, shining on the unsettled top layer of snow crystals.

Upstairs in a bedroom, they climbed into the cold, clean-smelling sheets. Leaving the curtains open, they turned out the light and looked out through the window next to the bed at the pasture behind the house. A deep, beautiful layer of snow covered the hill.

Though he had wanted to make love, when he felt her lips against his, he could barely keep his eyes open to say good night. He fell into a deep sleep, into a dream in which he and Iris were living in a dark blue château, a beautiful, ancient château that he gradually discovered was also a prison. When he came out of the dream an hour or so later, Iris was on top of him, kissing his neck. She'd taken off his nightclothes, pulling him tight against her. He was already erect, but he was not sure where he was, for part of him was still back in the château. Gradually, as they made love, he came out of it.

He had seen it then—the blue light—perhaps from the moonlight on the snowy hill behind the house, the deep blue light. It was so strong that he had been sure somebody was shining an artificial light on the area outside, playing a trick on both of them. He'd pulled back the curtains to see more of it. The tree on the hill behind the house cast a blue shadow; the fresh snow was as blue as water. He started to tell her about it.

"I've been watching it," she said.

"What is it?"

"It began while you were inside me. I was watching your face turn blue."

"But what is it?"

"Maybe it's the cold."

He turned and looked at her. She was as blue as the snow, as blue as the Indian Ocean. The shadows around her eyes and under her nose were dark blue. She smiled. She looked morbid, then uncannily real, like some kind of fish or mermaid come out of the sea. He lay back and looked her body over. She was sitting up. He brought his hand up to the blue shadow under her arms then under her chin. He ran his hands under her eyebrows, then dragged his fingers in the ripples of light across her face and down to her breast. He watched the blue shadow under her breast as he touched it, the silver-blue nipple between his fingers.

Then it started to come to him. He was looking up at her, speaking to her before he was aware of what he was saying, telling her something that sounded disembodied at first, but soon took on the air of truth. If she died, he'd kill himself. It was as simple as that, words, nothing but words, but by the morning he knew that these words had already embedded themselves deep in his mind, so deeply, so strongly that their meaning was as true, as concrete, as reliable as any other physical object. It was something to think about, yes, but fortunately it was merely a dictum that would not come into effect unless she died before him; perhaps he'd die first. The words were the native words of that light, engendered by it.

In the morning, the snow reflected harsh white daylight. Alex waited for Iris to awaken, then started to tell her.

"No," she said. "I know what happened."

Lying awake early one morning, Alex remembered this incident and felt an enormous sense of relief. This memory of blue light, which had been so prevalent in his mind for the past few years, had been locked away, forgotten at the crucial moment when Iris had actually disappeared. *This is what it's all about,* he thought. *It's not that I couldn't face her death, it's that I couldn't face my own.*

He went into his kitchen, put on water for coffee, and sat down. A steep angle of yellow sunlight cut the room in half. The light, usually so fresh at this hour, looked perverse. He started giggling, short little laughs at first, like hiccups almost. There may have been tears, but he wasn't sure. He laughed harder and harder, coughing to catch his breath.

He didn't stop until he heard somebody knocking on the door. It was the people who lived upstairs. Their bedroom was over his kitchen. He apologized through the closed door, then flopped down on the living-room couch and kept laughing. "That's what it is," he said. "So that's what it is. This whole thing . . ." He thought of Father Fish. "That was my doing . . . That was my mind, my creation . . ." He thought of the smell of the horses, the dung on the wooden ramps, the tiny hairs around the eyes of the elephants, the strange look in eyes so small compared to their heads, the sound of hooves, and the man with the tall black boots . . . the white horse. *That's all mine,* he thought. *Every bit of it is mine. I made it up!*

He repeated these words. "I made it up! I made it up!" He began laughing again, louder and louder. "I made it up! I made it up! I'm a genius! A genius at keeping myself alive! I can make up a whole circus when I have to! I can make a tiger's beautiful orange-and-black fur and his long tail. I can even make up my wife—my wife, Iris—the most complicated, beautiful person in the world; the intricacy of her beauty is mine, all mine. I'm a genius, nobody in the world is a genius like me." He held out his hands and imagined a tiny white horse in his palm. "Look," he said. "Look at the galloping white horse." The little horse was galloping across his palm, slowly making its way over the wrinkles. "I can make you as big as I want. I can make a beach, an ocean, a bird flying up from the dunes. I'm brilliant, nobody can do what I can do, not even Iris . . ."

The rest of the day he went over it in his mind. Now he knew exactly what to do.

"Nine months is not so bad, Iris, nine months is nothing compared to the rest of time . . . I've slipped up only momentarily, darling."

CHAPTER 6

I DIDN'T think you'd ever come back," Mrs. Burns said.

"It's where I was with her last," Alex said. "I'd like to pay you in advance for my room."

Mrs. Burns laughed a little. "You needn't do that," she said. "I trust you."

"Thank you, Mrs. Burns. You were very kind to me last year. I'm sorry if I caused you trouble. You see, I was a little out of my mind."

"They should have been kinder, Mr. Barton. People should have understood."

"But I *was* out of my mind then. I was absolutely out of my mind." He stared at her, held his eyes on her until she laughed nervously. His voice became slow, quiet, and dreamy. "You see," he whispered. "I loved her, Mrs. Burns. I loved her more than anyone in the world will ever imagine. No one has ever been so in love with another as I was with her. But I'm so sorry for all the trouble I caused you, and I thank you for your kindness . . ."

That night he didn't sleep at all. He saw no reason to sleep. *Why should I preserve my body? Insomnia?* He laughed at the word *insomnia.* At three in the morning he parted the silky white curtains of his room and saw the whiteness of the rising moon over the roofs and through the trees. In the morning, he dressed and put on a red baseball cap that had belonged to Iris. It was a little too small for him, but it would stay on if there was no wind.

He had to wait until eight-thirty for the car rental agency to open.

From the agency he drove up-island, his stomach empty, his body tired, but his mind more awake than he ever remembered it. On the dirt road to King's Beach, he drove slowly, then suddenly slammed on the brakes, jumped out of the car, and began walking down the road, looking up through the tall pale green oaks at the light blue sky and imagining what these trees had looked like in the darkness when he had been walking back from the show.

He came to the field and crossed the dunes to the water.

It was perfect. The waves were still breaking. "Still breaking," he said to the waves. "You haven't given up, have you?"

He threw down the baseball hat, stripped off his shirt and pants, then walked naked to the water, dove forward, and began to swim. His promise to Iris would be kept. The water was cool, but he swam hard to keep warm. He wanted to get far enough out so that there would be no chance of making it back.

It was amusing to think of the intricacy of the trick he'd played on himself: all of the people he had met in his dream, all of the strange acts, which were admittedly like nothing he'd ever seen before. His mind, a cunning being within him, had not only tricked him into believing that she had returned to shore after her swim, but it had created an entire circus, including box-office personnel, elephants, a light show, trapeze artists, clowns, bales of hay, the smell of canvas, the strange noises of cats, cars moving out of a parking lot, an entire crowd. And it had done it so realistically that it still didn't seem possible that it was a dream.

The really strange thing about it, he thought, *was the fact that there was no suggestion of the tragedy it was meant to hide.*

After a long while his muscles began to cramp and he felt satisfied. Soon the choice of whether to live or to die would no longer be a choice. He swam close to half a mile out. A current picked him up and carried him; the water became warmer, the sky bluer. He was glad to be out here; he was closer to her. "Iris," he said. It felt good to say her name out loud. Ever since she'd left him his words had been strained and false. Now she would hear him.

"Iris," he said, and started to cry.

Treading water, he turned toward shore. It looked so incredibly tiny, just a white strip, and he could see the light green hill crowned by a fire tower at the most distant part of the island. A gull crossed in front of him. "I love you. I was glad to have you for the time that I did have you. That's what I must remember, the time together . . ."

He swam on, doing the sidestroke, his ear against the water. Staring up at the sun, he wondered how much longer he could last before he'd never see the sun again. The sun beat down on his face, and now there was salt in his eyes; his eyes stung. He looked back at shore. Perhaps the current was carrying him farther away, or perhaps the sun had weakened his vision, but it appeared even smaller. He turned and began swimming again. He was out of breath but he kept going, lifting his stiff arms over his head and pulling down.

He heard a noise, a knocking noise coming from behind him. It came steadily; he wasn't sure whether it was coming from inside his head or outside somewhere on the water. After a few more strokes he stopped and put his face down in the water and opened his eyes. His eyes stung, but he kept them open, kicked off and went down underwater. He had a vision of her as he went down, a vision of her body under the water, her white

skin in all the blue. *If this is where you are, then this is where
you are.*

His lungs were bursting. He turned and swam for the surface,
blowing air out on the way up just in time to lift his mouth
above the water and suck air in.

His vision was blurry. Above him a dark figure loomed.

"What the hell are you doing?" a voice said. Alex's eyes stung
too much to really see the person. "Hang onto the boat." The
voice was familiar; it was Marlin's voice.

Alex was breathing hard. He reached out for the gunwale,
then drew his hand back. "Leave me alone," he said.

"Grab onto the side, I'm not asking you; I'm telling you.
Grab onto the side!"

"No," Alex said. He turned and swam away. But soon he
heard the knocking noise, the sound of oars.

A hand grabbed Alex's hair and he jerked his head free. "Leave
me the hell alone."

"Get back here," Marlin said.

Alex had little energy left. He swam as hard as he could, but
his arms were stiffening so that he could hardly extend them.
Marlin grabbed his hair again, and Alex thrashed and pulled his
head away from him. He was out of breath. "Get back here!"
Marlin screamed.

Alex swam a little farther, then took a deep breath and went
under, kicking down into the deep water. He was tired and knew
he couldn't hold his breath for long. He felt patches of colder
water. His eyes were open but everything was a dark blur. Soon
his lungs became tighter and tighter; the air was forcing itself
out, but he wanted to get as deep as he could so that getting up
would be impossible. He went deeper. The water was darker
and his ears were bursting. Then he did it: he blew the air out.

A hand grabbed his ankle.

He was lying on the seat of the rowboat choking and coughing,
Marlin right above him. He got up to dive overboard, but Marlin

slapped him so hard across the face that he fell back against the seats and gunwale. When he tried to get up again, he felt another slap. Marlin picked up the oars and started to row.

Alex kept coughing, choking; it felt more like he was throwing up; his throat hurt as if he had been screaming; he was so dizzy that he just heard snatches of Marlin's speech.

A wave hit them as they came in and toppled the boat upside down and Marlin put his arm across Alex's chest and began dragging him into shallow water. Then Marlin was pushing him from behind, onto the beach. He turned him around. "Look at me," he said.

Alex looked at him. He saw Marlin's hand coming around the side of his vision, then felt another extremely powerful slap across his cheek. Alex fell down, coughing. Marlin picked him up again, this time by both shoulders, swung, and slapped him just as hard.

"Now lie down in the sand," Marlin yelled. "I'm going after my boat. You move from this spot, and I'll hit you like you've never been hit before."

Welts had risen so high on the side of Alex's face that his eye was closing. He put his hand over the pain and lay down on his side.

After a while he saw Marlin's boots in front of him and felt a towel and clothes drop on his back, then he felt Marlin's hands grab under his arms and he was standing up pulling on his pants and shirt.

Marlin pushed him up and over the dunes.

"Look up," Marlin said. Alex looked across the field toward where he'd seen the horse and the circus tent.

"What do you see?" Marlin said. Alex could see a wide circular platform about five feet off the ground with a diameter of about fifty feet. Its smaller circular base made it look a little like a mushroom.

Marlin pushed Alex down the back side of the dune, then across the field. The field appeared untouched except for the structure. There was no road leading to it, just long grass and flowers. Marlin brought Alex up to it and then told him to climb up. Alex put his arms up on its surface and Marlin gave him a boost. Alex rolled onto the smooth surface, his wet clothes sticking to his body. He turned to see Marlin get a running start then push himself up over the edge with surprising agility.

"Ever seen a house before it's finished?" Marlin said.

Fine floorboards had been laid across the surface. Instead of nails, tiny wooden pegs held them down. The deep red wood had been varnished.

"Let me explain something to you, Mr. Barton. This house is finished. There's no place for walls, no place for a roof. Don't ask me what it's for because I haven't got the slightest idea what it's for. And I asked the men who built it what it's for, and they said they don't have the slightest idea, either. But do you know what I think?" Marlin said. Alex held his hand on the welts across his face. "Whoever built this thing is insane . . . that's all I know."

"Has anybody been out here?"

"Nobody," Marlin said. "I've been watching this thing every goddamn day since it was built. I haven't got the slightest idea what this thing is. A corporation owns it, but all that is is a mailbox. But if somebody built it, somebody wants to come out here eventually. The land itself cost almost a million dollars. You don't build something like this and just leave it, understand?"

Alex nodded his head.

"So somebody's going to come out here one of these days and when they do I'm going to arrest them for something, believe me, and I'll find out what the hell it's all about."

They drove back down the dirt road to the main road and then followed another dirt road up a steep hill until they came to a small salt gray house with rocks and patches of red dirt in the yard. Marlin got out and helped Alex out of the car and up through the long grass of the yard to the front door. He pushed the door open with his foot and brought Alex up a short flight of stairs to a living room with a couch and television and a thick rug. He laid him down on the couch.

"I want to tell you something when I get back from work tonight. It's about your wife. Don't go anywhere. Just stay in here today."

CHAPTER 7

THAT evening when Marlin got back from work he took Alex behind the house, down a path that came out at the bottom of a hill. Alex could see the entire western end of the island all the way to the sea. The waves looked like tiny strips of freshly fallen snow; the hills leading to the water were a pale green. The sun drew a long line across the moving water.

Marlin climbed up a path through the tall grass and Alex followed. In the thinner grass at the very top of the hill, Marlin knelt. Alex stood before him, then turned and looked out over the land to the ocean. Sailboats were scattered across the darkening water. In the bushes bordering the field, Alex saw the flickering wings of small brown birds.

Marlin did not appear to be staring at anything in particular, just out at the green hills and dark blue sea. Alex sat down and then knelt next to him.

"Last year, when you were here, I wanted to tell you about something that happened, but I didn't know what it meant," Marlin said. "You see, every year, on the first full moon in July the tribe I come from gathers and sets up tepees near the crown of this hill, then a man is chosen to sit up here and sing while groups go inside each tepee to pray. As the man on top here sings, he takes in the prayers of the group and his song changes according to what he hears. Sometimes he finds himself singing about an animal, sometimes a person, sometimes a tree, and sometimes a flower. If he happens to sing about a flower, it's a good sign for everyone. It means the people will flower, maybe not this year, maybe not for a hundred years, but someday. The gathering must be when the moon is full, when the moon is bursting with light, and it must be when the grass is long and the shadows have grown long and are turning into the shadows of evening.

"Last summer the night before you came into the police station you might remember there was a full moon. It was a beautiful night. One of the most beautiful nights we've ever experienced because the sky was a stranger and deeper blue than I've ever seen before. I was the man chosen to sing on top of the hill," Marlin said. He let the words die, and he was silent.

Alex heard the wind in the grass. He could smell the air, not from the sea, but from the earth. He did not ever remember smelling the earth like this.

Then Marlin went on. "Last summer after sundown the birds took forever to disappear. They flew back and forth in the night. They were not owls or nighthawks, but birds of the daylight that had forgotten to go to sleep. We saw them, moving through the sky over our heads against the stars and the moon. Eventually they landed on all the tepees and finally one landed on my shoulder next to my ear so that I could hear its flickering wings as it was preening itself. That night I know that nothing that was part of the true world slept anywhere; that night as my people prayed, the tepees began to glow as if there were lights inside each one. All became different colors. Meanwhile a song came from my throat, a sad song that was speaking to the whole world. Nothing will ever explain it, but I knew there was a deep sadness inside someone somewhere and that my song was coming from the person. I gave my heart to it that night, gave everything I had to it. The song became stronger and stronger until I felt almost as if I were about to give birth to something. Stretching out my arm and opening my hand, I saw something that I realized I had been holding all along. Something sad and very beautiful."

Marlin held out his closed hand and opened it, and Alex saw the head of a blue flower in his palm. It was very small, but Alex recognized that it was an iris.

CHAPTER 8

THE next day Marlin told Alex to climb the hill and rest and keep watch out over the sea. He told him that he would come up later and meet him.

Alex didn't question Marlin; he merely climbed through the long grass to the top and sat, crossing his legs, watching the changing light over the water.

He could hear cicadas in the afternoon in the hot sun when the grass and the trees were dry. Beyond the rising pale green light of the fields, shades of wind moved on the water making more fields, fields of dark blue, then lighter blue, the reflection of light changing with the clouds. Grazing cows sauntered in the grass below, feeding under the bands of moving light like fat red fish in shallow water.

Toward the late afternoon he became more and more aware of the smells of the earth and the lichen-covered rocks, the dry grass and the salty air that blew across it. He felt the skin along his arms and on the back of his hands with his fingers; he felt his leather shoes and the blanket on which he rested. He listened to the wind in the trees and against the stones. And all around him he watched the changing light.

Crows flew up over the crest of the hill of grass. He counted for a while then lost count. They flew lazily in pairs, some distance apart but vaguely together. They could have been dropping behind a line of trees and coming around behind him in a big circle; he didn't know, but there were many of them and they all seemed to be going somewhere.

CHAPTER 9

IN the early evening Marlin came back up the hill, and brought him to his house for dinner. Afterward they got in his police car and drove down-island onto the dirt road and parked at the edge of the field where Iris had disappeared almost a year before. The sun was low and red on the horizon of low land and flat silvery blue water. The platform in the field cast a wide shadow in the sparse grass. The sea birds, the gulls, the terns, the herons, the pairs of wild swans that had come up off the brackish ponds that lay behind the dunes crossed into the diminishing light, the soft red rays covering them like a thin coating of oil. Alex followed Marlin across the field into the shadow of the platform, then into the light again. Marlin threw the blankets and sleeping bag up, cupped his hands, and boosted Alex, then climbed up himself.

Alex walked along the edge of the circular platform then stopped and looked out toward the sea. The sun dropped behind the hill. The water where he had tried to drown himself grew darker and bluer, then almost black.

He continued pacing the perimeter of the strange structure of wood and cement before squatting and looking down.

"It sounds hollow if you tap on it," Marlin said.

Soon the stars were out. The dark shadows of herons moving from one pond to the next flew by, and he heard the wings of swans, the short, graceful whipping sound of their wings in the moist night air. Marlin sat with his legs hanging over one side.

"I didn't know if seeing this platform just once would keep you from doing what you set out to do yesterday morning. You must believe in it. Its insanity, its bizarreness, whatever you want to call it, is all you have left right now."

Alex looked at his face in the half-light.

"Do you want me to sleep here? I don't think I can," Alex said.

Marlin laughed a little. "You'll sleep." he said. "First, keep your eyes open and watch the birds. There is nothing so beautiful as birds of the night. They do not sing; they move as fish move, silently; they are stalkers, stalkers of the silver light of the fish, stalkers of the moving surface of secret waters."

Alex lay looking up at the stars. He felt he was shrinking, everything was getting farther away. He fell asleep, but woke up and looked at the luminous dial of his watch and saw that he had only slept an hour. He rolled over and looked out toward the dunes. He saw Marlin's dark silhouette standing high on the dunes against the blue-and-white light of the night sea.

He fell asleep and woke again, looking at the stars. Now Marlin lay next to him, his blankets and bag casting a short blue shadow onto the platform. Sleep was coming on again. He felt someone holding his hand and looked to the side: Iris was seated next to him. They were on a bleacher inside a circus tent. Alex could hear a man selling popcorn, and a child clicking the trigger of a plastic gun. A cannon had gone off somewhere in the arena and the smoke was just clearing. This circus tent was not quite like the one where he had lost Iris. Instead of looking down at center ring, they were looking up at it. A giant stage like the platform on which he slept had been raised high by a hydraulic lift. On it was a silvery blue man, the same man who had appeared on the white horse. His eyes were darkened by makeup and his muscles under his shirt rippled. The spotlight changed from blue to yellow to green, and each time the muscles of his arms and neck were accentuated. He wore some kind of lipstick, a dark lipstick, and his mouth, slightly open, looked black. He stepped to the edge of the ring and took a deep breath. His chest rose. Suddenly he leaped out toward the audience. The people in front ducked and leaned to the side to avoid him, but his fingers hooked onto a trapeze and he moved fluidly from bar to bar, diving forward, catching the one in front of him, then doing a flip onto the next one, forward and backward, ending up on a high wire directly over Alex's head. He ran across it, his feet turned to the side, his knees bent. In a flash, just as he was over Alex, one leg slipped and he fell forward. The crowd moaned, but he grabbed onto the wire and swung from it, then swung himself back up and continued high across the tent, eventually descending to the stage above the ring.

He stood there catching his breath. Alex could see his intricate, bulging muscles. Sweat streamed down his forehead and neck, dripping from his fingers. When his breathing returned to normal, he cleared his throat and began to whisper. It was the loudest whisper that Alex had ever heard; it carried all the way to the back of the tent. "Forgive me for my error," he said. He took another deep breath, his beautiful chest rising before him. "Normally one would use nets for such a feat. Normally, though, a flying man would not slip.

"But among you is a couple whose relationship I must characterize as strange. Among you is a woman who has already reached a stage far beyond what any of you or even myself could ever hope to achieve. And among you is a man, the husband of that woman, who has fallen desperately far behind her. He is no doubt quite alone.

"Forgive me for my presumption. I do not know who this couple is, only that they are here this evening with us. They have joined us without knowledge of what they're joining; they have come to see a show, to leave their lives behind.

"Their love for each other is so strong that it almost caused me to fall when I was over them. I felt devotion from the man, such devotion as I've never experienced before, but have only read about in the ancient texts."

The beautiful, limber man in the blue suit stood at the edge of the ring facing the audience. He put two fingers on each temple, closed his eyes and climbed down. Bumping into seats and steps, he made his way up the aisle toward Iris and Alex.

"They're nearby," the man said. He stopped next to Iris and put his hand out.

"Touch me," he said.

Iris reached up and touched the man's outstretched hand.

"It's you," he said. "You're the one, and your husband?"

He reached his hand out for Alex. Alex touched the man's sweaty hand.

"Am I right?" The man opened his eyes and smiled.

"Come with me, both of you. I need a volunteer. Have you ever been hypnotized?"

Iris looked at Alex.

"No," Alex said.

"It will help you to see yourselves; please come with me."

They got up and followed the man down the aisle. Every step that the man took, Alex could see his muscles shifting. He appeared even bigger than before, more grotesque, more extraordinary close up than when he'd been on the platform in the ring. He lifted Iris onto the platform, then Alex.

The platform sounded hollow. Lights shone brightly into Alex's eyes. Everyone was staring at him, and he was terrified.

The man held something in his hand, a pendulum on three strings. On it Alex saw a tiny ring and stage that held a tiny black horse. Red paint, signifying pools of blood, covered the tiny stage at the horse's hooves. Some of the little ring was metallic.

"What does your ticket say?" the man said.

He was not speaking loud enough for the audience to hear. He spoke at a normal volume.

Iris touched Alex's hand and told him to take out the tickets. As if waking from a dream, a dream of fear, Alex reached into his pocket for the two red tickets and read them. *"The child will follow,"* then looked up at the man. The man appeared calmer; sweat still ran down his body; his muscles glimmered in the light. It seemed the sweat could no longer be from the physical exertion of the trapeze act; it must be from something else. But the man's chest moved gracefully up and down, like a kudu's or an elk's chest, Alex thought. He couldn't tell whether this man was evil or benevolent. His makeup, his lipstick, the color of his skin, and his abnormal musculature was too bizarre.

"First, I must have your consent to be hypnotized. But I must say," the man said, "it can only help you in the end. There is nothing dangerous about it. It will open up worlds, new worlds to both of you. You see," he said and waved his arm upward. "Someday you'll be able to fly like me. That is just one of the many things I will teach you to do."

Alex found himself gazing toward the top of the tent. It seemed much bigger in here than it had been from outside; the tightwire was much higher.

"Yes, or no?" the man said.

"This is our chance," Iris said quietly.

Alex said yes, then Iris said yes. The pendulum and stage with the tiny horse began to swing.

"You must think only of the horse," the man said. "Not just

any horse, but the horse that stands before you. You are wondering what he's made of—of flesh? you ask. Not of flesh, I say."

Alex turned from the swinging pendulum and looked at Iris.
She was different now; the look in her eye was older, more
mature; her arms for some reason appeared stronger, her hands
stronger.

The man pointed in slow motion to the audience. Instead of
people Alex saw blackness gathering around a point, railroad
tracks receding into a tunnel. He was astonished that this tunnel
was in the tent, astonished that there were black sod and large
green plants on the stage, astonished that the man, though standing far away from him, reached out and touched him.

"Go on," the man said. "You've got work to do."

He followed the railroad tracks toward the darkness. He
stopped on the ties and turned and looked back at the man. A
jungle had grown up around him. Alex suddenly recognized him
as Marlin. Marlin was pointing toward the hole where Alex had
to go.

"I thought you were a policeman," Alex said.

"Go on, go on." Marlin waved, his hand flapping up and
down loosely.

Alex turned and kept going. Soon he was in utter darkness;
he stumbled on the ties of the track, then got up. A light came
on up the track, a light which was the same shade of blue as
Marlin's shirt.

He headed toward it, slowing his pace, stepping more carefully.

When he got to the source of the blue light he saw that it was
coming through a long rectangular window, like the window in
an aquarium. He stopped at the window and saw, behind the
glass, the tiny stage, and the horse. The horse, now half the size
of a normal horse, had fallen forward onto its knees. Blood
flowed from its back onto the stage. The stage slanted toward
Alex and right near the glass he could see a stream of blood

dripping over the edge. The blood looked viscous, but too light colored to be real blood.

He turned around; now there was darkness behind him. Only forward could he see a light; this one was a soft twinkling green and it too came from a wall in the tunnel. He moved toward this green beacon.

A doorway led into a light green room with a huge swimming pool with a silver ladder. Diamond patterns of light reflected off the water onto the ceiling. Stepping inside, Alex saw mosaics of tiny blue, green, and white tiles covering the floor. The designs were of Egyptian sphinxes, goddesses, and servants.

"*The child will follow,*" he heard. He could not tell from what part of the room the voice was coming.

"Iris, is that you?" he asked.

"Yes, darling, I'm in here, but I can't get out."

"Where?"

"Alex, use the ticket."

"The ticket, what for? How?"

"Read it, please, darling. Please."

He noticed a man standing in the shallow end of the blue-and-green pool. The man's flesh was emaciated; his ribs and most of his skeleton showed; his belly button stuck out; his head was shaved. His thin legs did not look like they could hold him. In one hand he held a tiny violin, no bigger than a soda bottle. With the other hand he began to swim. He appeared so thin and weak that Alex could hardly believe that he'd remain afloat. The man did not look like a person swimming, but something else altogether, a water insect or an animal.

A hand passed over his face, brushing his nose; he opened his eyes and saw Marlin standing against the backdrop of the night sea, his face lit with the faint wash of starlight. Alex felt horrified, as if he had never seen this man before him, as if he were dreaming the dark shape of man on stage before sea; perhaps he was sleepwalking. "Who are you?" Alex said.

"It's me; it's Marlin," the man said.

Alex remained silent, watching the shadows under Marlin's eyes and his slick black hair reflecting the light of the stars.

"I'm tired," Alex said. He lay back down and pulled the blankets over him.

CHAPTER 10

HE woke up. He could see the
brightening sky where the sun was coming up and the dew-
covered gulls moving toward it as if it were calling them. The
surf had risen, but the water beyond the breakers was still
smooth and blue. Alex stood up, covering his shoulders with
his blankets.

Marlin's blankets were in a pile at the edge of the platform.
A corner of his green sleeping bag stuck out, but Marlin was
not in it. Alex climbed down from the platform, crossed the
dewy grass to the dunes, and looked out over the water. The
pounding surf misted the air at the edge of the beach. It was
nearing high tide; a large wave sent foam over a crest of sand
into a pool of water at the base of the dunes. At the edge of the
pool, half in the water, Alex saw a pile of clothing.

He climbed down to it; there were shoes, socks, a shirt, and
even a wallet in the pants. He pulled the credit cards out and
saw a police identification card with Marlin's picture and name
on it. He dragged the clothes up to where they would be safe
from waves and looked for movement beyond the breakers, but

he saw nothing except the gulls. He waited for what he thought was a long time, too long for somebody to be in the water, then he turned and ran with the clothes to the top of the dunes and started across the field toward Marlin's car. He stopped before he got there, dropped Marlin's clothes and then ran back to the top of the dunes. *He must be swimming,* he thought. A gull lifted off the smooth blue surface. Three tiny black-and-white ducks floated facing the same direction. The foremost one lifted off the surface, its rapidly beating wings stirring water before it was up. The other two followed.

He ran down into the water up to his knees. "Marlin," he called. "Hey, Marlin. Hey, Marlin! Hey! Hey!" he called. He was yelling loudly, but the waves swallowed his voice. "Where the hell? Come on . . . I mean where the hell? You didn't, I mean, you couldn't, how could you?"

CHAPTER **11**

HE walked down the main street of Verrehaven, passing the small bookshop. Mrs. Burns stood up from her rocking chair on her guesthouse porch as soon as she saw him, her mouth open in astonishment.

"Where have you been? I had to move your belongings out of your room. I thought you had left."

"I was staying with somebody," Alex said, calmly.

"Why didn't you call?"

"I thought you'd know I'd be back," Alex said.

"But there were other people who wanted the room," she said. "I'm sorry. I just couldn't risk it. They're staying for a week, and you might have been—"

"That's all right," Alex said. "I'm not feeling well. I just want to leave the island anyway."

She took him to the triangular storage room under the stairs where he lifted his bags out and carried them to the porch.

"A young girl was looking for you this morning," Mrs. Burns said.

"Do I owe you any money?" Alex said.

"No," she said. "Just for the one night."

Alex handed extra money to her, but she took what he owed and refused the rest. He thanked her, picked up his bags, and started along the main street, passing the café where he and Iris had eaten breakfast. Suddenly the young waitress who had served him came running out.

"Mr. Barton," she said, as he walked. Alex stopped and watched her carefully.

"You didn't stop in to say hello. I thought about you all winter," she said.

He stared at her even more carefully. She was wearing the same uniform she'd worn the year before when he was with Iris. "How long have you been here?"

"I've been busy," he said, quickly. "I came on business."

One of the waitresses from the café began calling her. "Evelyn!"

She turned quickly and said she would be there in a minute, then she looked up into Alex's eyes. "Please, wait. Put your bags down and wait, please."

She ran quickly back to the other waitress, disappeared into the café, then came running back to where she'd left Alex.

"Can I call you Alex? I'm so glad I caught you, my name is Evelyn. You do remember me, don't you? I'm so glad I caught you. Do you have to go right now? Could you spend some time with me? Just briefly. I've thought about everything that happened last year. It's silly, but I've had so much to say to you, Alex. God, I've been dreaming about you. Dreaming about you!" She laughed, then suddenly took his arm and pulled him away from his bags and up toward a side street, then turned and ran to the bags and carried them back to him.

"You know, everybody thought you were crazy last year. Everybody but me."

They walked up a very steep hill with houses, lawns, gardens, and white picket fences on either side of the narrow road. An old cemetery lay off to the left of the road between houses. Two aging fir trees grew in the center of it between mounds of grass and slanting gravestones.

They entered through an iron gate. Evelyn climbed ahead of Alex and rested the bags at the top of a knoll.

"You're the only one," she said as he reached her. "I mean—I knew you weren't like the others in this town and on this island. I knew you weren't trying to get attention. You know, about that circus—I learned some things this winter, and I believe you. I believe you. I believe what you saw."

Alex sat down in some shade. The young woman had pulled her thick, wavy, sandy blond hair back with a headband. Her shoulders were bare and her skin smooth.

"After you were gone last year, everybody laughed at you. I mean they laughed at you while you were here, too. But it was during all the laughter after you were gone, all that making fun of you that something happened to me: I fell in love with a young man, a young man who looked just like you. I'm serious," she said. "Here." She pulled her wallet out of her dress pocket. "Look." Alex saw a dark and narrow face and black hair like his own. The picture looked similar to the way Alex himself had looked ten or twelve years before. "His name is Peter Michelman. He's a painter," she said. She spoke quickly, almost out of breath. "His paintings are so beautiful; I cannot tell you what they do to me." She slapped her belly. "They hit me right here. They bring me right down into myself. I don't know why. I have no idea why they do that except when I look at them all the words, all the words that are in my head, stop and I suddenly feel whole in front of the picture. I feel like every goal I've ever wanted I've suddenly reached instantly, and I'm there. There is no going forward in my mind nor going backward. I am living in the present."

Alex could hear crickets in the cool shade of the stone wall. A thrush with a white tail swooped down in front of him and landed on one of the long upturned branches of the fir.

"Anyway, that's neither here nor there, Alex." She suddenly

turned to him, kneeling and facing him. "I must ask you something. Please don't leave the island, please, please, not for at least one more night. You can sleep in my den on my couch. Please don't leave the island."

Alex shook his head. "I can't stay long."

"Then wait and at least listen to what I learned last year." Alex nodded his head and watched her. "I'd hear fishermen and construction workers call you 'that nut, that crazy maniac.' I didn't realize what it was doing to me to hear them call you names like that. But then, you see, I've always wanted to fall in love, always . . . and I thought it was you when he sat down in your chair and I had to serve him. I thought it was you, only he was younger. But he was alone like you, just like you, like you were last year, and he looked like you and I kept thinking it was you only he was younger and I started to say something to him. I didn't even know where it came from. I said that I loved him and I meant it, I meant it truly and then he brought me back to his studio. He lived up-island, and he showed me his paintings and when I saw them I understood not only him but you."

An old car drove up the hill past the cemetery, a pickup truck with a rounded front end and plank rail back. An old woman was driving it. Alex saw that she wore light green gloves.

He looked back to the lively young waitress.

"You aren't after what everybody else is after," she said. "You're after something else.

"You see, Peter's paintings were inspired by something that had happened to him, something that was strange and really quite beautiful. Several years ago he and his best friend, a young priest, took a one-week trip to Rome. Nothing spectacular happened on the trip or so they thought. But after they'd been back from their trip a few weeks, both of them began having vague memories of something that had happened to them."

"Memories? What do you mean?"

"Something had happened to both of them that they must

have forgotten right away. Later they remembered it like a dream. They'd met a clergyman who'd told them all kinds of wild stories, and this clergyman, they came to believe, wasn't just some ordinary guy, he was the pope."

"That's impossible," Alex said.

"Well, it is impossible because after a little research they found out that the pope hadn't even been in Rome at the time of their visit. Not only that, but before and during the time they met the pope they remembered that it had been pouring rain. But when they called a weather bureau in Rome they found out that during the seven days they'd been in Rome, not a drop of rain had fallen."

"What does that prove?"

"They didn't know what to think of it. But the more they talked about it, the more they remembered. A beautiful acrobat had led them into the Vatican to the pope's chambers. Eventually, Peter and his friend decided that they must have had a hallucination together."

"Couldn't they both have had the same dream? That happens with best friends."

"It wasn't a dream they remembered. It was too real and its influence on their lives was too powerful. It was as if the hallucination was inside them and living and growing the way madness must grow inside a person.

"As time went on it became more and more meaningful to both of them. Peter's friend went back to where he was from, somewhere in Mississippi, and became the priest of a small Catholic church there in a town called . . . I can only think of my own name when I think of it, Evelyn, Mississippi, but I know that's not the name. But even there the madness of this vision began intervening in parts of his life. Eventually, he joined a circus to keep his sanity."

"Why a circus?"

"During their meeting with the pope, he had talked to them about circuses."

"Did Peter join one too?"

"No. He became an artist. He said it wasn't a choice. Like joining a circus, being a painter was also an attempt to keep from going mad. To resist madness, he felt, would only make things worse. The paintings were exploding out of him. Please let me show you one of them. It's behind the house we lived in."

She got up and told him to wait for her, that she was going to get her car. Five minutes later she parked a rusted green car in front of the cemetery gate. Alex brought his bags down the hill, the soft earth sinking under his feet.

She drove him away from town and onto a small road shaded by the overhanging branches of trees.

They parked the car at the bottom of a yard of long grass below a stained wood house with a dark porch. Inside, the house smelled of creosote and pine and the floorboards creaked as they walked over them. A dog in the backyard scratched on the screen door. Evelyn and Alex let him in as they went out and climbed the hill behind the house. Alex stopped in the sun to catch his breath. Evelyn walked ahead, then realized he had stopped and came back down and asked him if he was tired. He was very tired, he said.

They went on, walking along a path under tall pines to a round hut made of thin split logs. Skylights had been built into the roof. Evelyn opened the split log door and Alex stepped in. A painting was set up on an easel.

In it he saw a field, like the one where the circus had appeared, and in the long yellow grass he saw a yellow-and-red circus ring. A milky blue strip of sea lay behind it and light green grass lay under it. Zebras, a lion, two elephants, a llama, and a camel had fallen in the grass on the slope upward to the sea. The elephant was farthest away. Its body was badly maimed. Patches of red flesh were exposed to the elements. A zebra's head had been cut off; its body eviscerated. The camel's mouth was open, and blood flowed into the grass. As Alex looked closer he saw inside the ring a chimpanzee with a patch over his left eye and an arrow in his heart, and a white dove, its wing torn from its shoulder. Also within the circle were the wire and poles of a circus tent, and off to the side red-and-yellow canvas was blown into a heap.

The light in the small studio fluctuated from shadow to light as the wind blew the clouds overhead.

"That's the only one left," she said. "He had an exhibition on the island two months ago and he sold them all, every one but this one, which he was working on."

Evelyn turned and left the studio and began walking down the path toward the house. Alex followed but he saw something in the woods, a red-and-yellow cloth, eaten by the weather. The branch of a bush with tiny green leaves grew through it. The cloth crumbled in his hand. He turned and looked at the outside of the round studio. Spots of red-and-yellow paint were flaking from its long, thin planks. Farther into the woods he saw the hull of a gray boat rotting into the pine needles and earth. Evelyn took his arm and brought him along the path to the top of the field above the house.

She stopped. Her tone of voice changed suddenly. She told him that Michelman had disappeared at the beginning of the summer. "He said he was just getting some milk at the store and nobody has seen him since."

She laughed. "This was the first man I ever loved," she said. Alex could see the dog looking out of the screen door of the house. Evelyn sat down. "I've wanted to fall in love with somebody for so long, but I was too critical. How old do I look?"

"Nineteen," Alex said.

"My birthday's tomorrow. I'll be twenty-seven," she said. "Twenty-seven, and last year was the first time." She laughed a little, lying back against her elbows in the grass and looking up at the sky. Alex knelt next to her. He saw big, round salty tears on her cheeks. "I'm told I'm a bitch, everybody tells me that. Why can't you go out with somebody? I can't go out with just anybody; I'd rather be a bitch than go out with just anybody. And then it happened last year, Michelman walked into the restaurant, and I knew. His gestures were so similar to yours, Alex, you're reminding me of him right now."

She pointed to the tar-paper roof of the house. "I spent all winter with him, and then he left me two months ago without saying a word. He left his house; he left everything."

She brought Alex down to the house and they went through it to the front porch.

"I don't understand it," she said. "One minute he's here and the next he's gone. It was right after his exhibition—all of his paintings were bought up. It seemed too good to be true. I knew something would happen. I'm not superstitious, but sometimes you can tell."

Alex looked down the hill of long grass to the road. Evelyn stood next to him, looking up at the side of his face.

"Did you go to the police?" he asked.

"Yes, of course. They didn't think it was abnormal, you know, for a man to leave a woman. They kept asking me for proof that he was kidnapped. But I had none. I just know that he isn't the type to ditch someone like that. I trusted him. I'll be honest with you, it was the first time I've ever really trusted anyone. I gave him everything in my heart."

Tears came to Evelyn's eyes again. She looked away. "I can't stand it," she said. "You look so much like him. I can't stand it."

"Have you any idea what might have happened to him?"

She walked to the end of the porch and crouched down away from him. The dog scratched on the screen door. Alex let him out. The dog wagged his tail against his legs as he went over to Evelyn.

"You must be related to him," she said.

"No. I don't have any relatives," he said.

He went inside the house and gathered a handful of tissues for her. They sat together on the end of the sagging porch boards. Evelyn blew her nose. "I miss him so much. You have no idea how much I miss him." She held onto his shirtsleeve and stared up into his eyes. "You have no idea what it feels like. I thought talking to you would make it better, but it's only made it worse."

"What happened?" Alex said. "Tell me exactly what happened."

"Well," Evelyn said. "Last winter Michelman was so desperate for money, so broke, that when he sold his paintings he wasn't thinking of the consequences it might have on him emotionally. In the back of his mind he believed he could always buy them back or at least visit them. But he could never have guessed what would happen: whoever bought them bought *all* of them and took them without leaving so much as a name to contact."

"But he had slides of his work, didn't he?"

"Nothing could replace the originals for him."

"What were these people like, the ones who bought them?"

"I wasn't there when the purchases were made. But the gallery sitter said there were several people, all in the same group."

"They took them away right then and there?"

"Cleaned the little gallery out. The gallery sitter thought Michelman would be overwhelmed with joy. They paid with a certified check drawn off the bank in Verrehaven."

"What did the gallery owner say?"

"He was happy. Of course, he was happy. But Michelman went nuts. A day before he had been complaining bitterly about being broke. He had been so damned obsessed about being broke that he once told me his greatest fear was starving to death. But then, suddenly ten thousand dollars richer, and he was telling me somebody had stolen his soul, that he was a dead man without his paintings. He said he could have endured selling some of his paintings but not all of them. He didn't think anyone would buy all of them."

"That makes sense."

"To a point, yes, to a point. But he became obsessed. Believe me, I had to live with his obsession all winter. It got worse and worse. Then one day he told me he had it all figured out, that there was a man named Volenti who owned an island called Cea. Volenti was the one who bought them, he said."

"Where is Cea?" Alex asked.

"About forty miles from here. It's bigger than this island, almost twice as big."

"One man owns the whole thing? Was there any evidence that this man bought them?"

"No. That's the way Michelman is. He didn't know. He had nothing to go on but his own paranoia. And nobody is allowed on the island so he could make up whatever he wanted about it. He stopped being rational right after the sale. I got him to paint what you saw in his studio, but as soon as his inspiration dried up again, he turned back into an obsessed man."

Alex followed Evelyn into her living room. Leaning against the dark pine wall was a backpack fully loaded with a sleeping bag, pots, and pans. Evelyn opened the top of the pack and began pulling out bags of dried camping food, dinners, lunches. "He told me he was going to do something courageous. He was going to go over there and steal a few of his paintings back. He found somebody on this island who had lived and worked over there, a man who was terminally ill, and got him to help him. I want to take you to see this man's brother, his name is Astley . . . As Michelman planned it, he would sneak onto the island and steal back at least three of his paintings—but before he left on his mission he disappeared, vanished . . ."

CHAPTER 12

LATER in the afternoon, Evelyn drove Alex to a shack covered with tar paper at the end of a dirt road. A short man wearing black pants and tall work boots opened the door and smiled. Some of his teeth were missing, some were black and rotted. His skin was sun-wrinkled and gray, and he looked to be in his early seventies. Evelyn introduced Alex. The man's name was Chester Astley.

"Come to see my turtles?" he asked.

"Turtles?" Evelyn said.

"People come over all the time to see my turtles."

"Could we see them later? We've got some questions about your brother."

"Velman?" he said, raising his voice.

"Yes, Velman."

"He's dead."

"Yes, I know, but we want to ask you some questions."

Limping, he led Alex and Evelyn into the kitchen in the back of the house where he poured three cups of coffee and set them on a blue-and-white checkered tablecloth. Two bird feeders

hung from a tree in the backyard near the window. Chester lifted
a newspaper on which he had been rolling cigarettes and dumped
the tobacco remains into an orange tin.

His eyebrows were thick and white.

"Velman worked for a man named Mr. Volenti, didn't he?"
Evelyn said loudly and clearly.

"Yup."

"Did he tell you about him?"

"Some stories." Chester lit a hand-rolled cigarette. The smoke
was thicker and bluer than from other cigarettes.

Sparrows and chickadees pecked from the bird feeders. On
the grass, squirrels were eating the fallen seed.

"What kind of stories?" Evelyn asked.

"Velman worked for him as a soldier," Chester said.

"A soldier?"

"That's what he did as a profession."

"Mr. Volenti?"

"No, Velman, he was a soldier, a veteran. Soldiering was his
profession."

"Where did he meet Volenti?"

"Joined the army in New York. That's where he was living.
He wasn't in touch with me, you know. Turned out he'd joined
a private army. Turned out this man Volenti owned it. So where
does he end up? Not too far from Verre even though he hated
it here.

"Didn't write, didn't even let us know where he was. He
hated Dad, you see. But two months ago he knocked on the
door here and set down right there in that chair.

"Told me how come they let him out of the army. He had a
tumor that was making him crazy. Besides it looked like he was
going to die soon and he wanted to say good-bye to me and
settle accounts with the old man. But the old man's been dead
pretty near fifteen years. He didn't know that."

"What's this army for?"

"That I couldn't tell you."

"Did they pay him?"

"He didn't come here with much money. But he said he stayed because he'd become addicted to the army, the way of life in it, like Dad was addicted to booze, and like I'm addicted to these." Chester raised his cigarette a little. "He said had he and I not been twins he'd never have come back to Verre. He said even those who are dying never leave the old man's island, as they call it, but his was a special case."

Chester took another drag from his cigarette. "It's different for twins," he went on, looking into Alex's and Evelyn's eyes. "Twins feel things that others hardly know about. I know because during most of my life something was missing, you know, and sometimes I wondered what the hell I was doing alive at all. But he came back to me and I understood right then what I'd been feeling all my life. It was because of him not being around that I was feeling it."

Outside the window Alex could see a squirrel standing on its back legs breaking apart a sunflower seed.

"But the last days of his life I really began to question him and question his stories about his life. I stopped believing him, but I never stopped listening. I just tried to translate what he was saying into something else."

Chester put his cigarette down, got up slowly, and left the room. When he came back he held a pair of khaki pants in one hand and a dark purple cardboard box in the other. Unfolded, the pants looked like army fatigues. "Let me show you something else." He dug through a pile of black-and-white photographs in the cardboard box, pulling out a picture of a group of soldiers standing on a platform in front of a line of tall trees. The picture was taken from above the platform and Alex could barely make out its circular shape.

"Velman told me there's a mountain on the island and that there are people living inside it."

Alex lifted the pile of photographs and looked through them slowly. He saw another one of a circular platform.

"Who is this guy Volenti?" Alex asked.

"His name is Edward Volenti. He's the guy who ran the army," Chester said.

"But why does he have this army?"

"He's rich, that's all I know."

Alex turned to Evelyn. "Did you know about him before?"

"I've heard his name. You can't live here without hearing his name."

"But what's he have an army for?"

"Paranoid, I guess," Evelyn said.

"Of what?" Alex asked.

"Of people coming to his island."

"What does he have on it?"

"A mountain," Chester said. "He's got his very own mountain."

"But nobody's going to take his mountain."

"The richer you are, the more worried you get about losing everything," Evelyn said. "I've heard people say that."

"I'll tell you something about Velman," Chester said, slowly. "His last few days, he got worse fast. He started thinking that he was back on the island and that he was an animal—I mean it. He thought he was a bear. He growled like a bear. I had to feed him a special diet, the doctors told me to feed him a special diet. But he didn't want it. He wanted berries. Berries, berries, berries he kept saying. He got mad at me. He took swipes at my face like he had claws. Sometimes he pretended to hold the bars of a cage and shake them."

"What did he say about Edward Volenti?" Alex said.

"He said he's a rich man," Chester said.

"That's all?"

"He may have said something else. I don't really remember. He got mixed-up at the end with so many mixed-up stories that I really don't want to go over it."

Evelyn asked Chester a few more questions but he didn't seem to want to talk. "Don't you want to see my turtles?" he said.

They crossed his back lawn to three cages of dark, heavy mesh, with sheets of fluted roofing across the top and heavy rocks to hold the roofing down on each one.

The old man slowly picked up one rock after the next, dropping them down into the grass, then he reached in and lifted by the tail a large, green-backed turtle that opened its mouth wide, exposing its pink-and-red gums. Chester laid it in the grass and walked behind it with his hands in his pockets as it made its way toward the shade of a small tree. After carrying it by the tail back to its cage, he brought out another one with orange and black stripes on its shell. Its sharp beak clapped down on itself. In the grass, it moved in the same direction the first one had gone.

CHAPTER 13

THAT evening they went out
to dinner and later Alex came back with Evelyn to her house.
She made up a bed for him in the den and said good night.

Later that night, on his way back from the bathroom, Alex
heard her crying and saw that her light was on. He knocked and
opened the door. She looked up from her pillow; her eyes were
red.

"I'm sorry," she said. "You remind me of him so much."

"I know how you must feel," Alex said. He sat at the edge
of her bed and patted her back under her long hair. After a long
while she fell asleep, and Alex turned the light out and went
back to his bed.

The next day they read the paper after it was delivered on the
front porch.

POLICE OFFICER DROWNS

Officers found Marlin Fisher's clothes on King's Beach late yesterday afternoon after he did not report to work earlier that morn-

ing . . . Though no note was found all evidence points toward suicide, the second such case on the island since early this spring.

Brian Thrum said Officer Fisher had attended a wedding reception for Thrum's daughter the day before. "He was the same, the same as he always was. We talked about going fishing in two days. He'd just paid all that money to have his boat overhauled and he said he was really looking forward to getting back on the water . . ."

"I hardly think it was suicide," Evelyn said.

"What the hell is going on?" Alex said. "I mean why would this Edward Volenti guy be kidnapping people?"

Before Evelyn's shift began at the restaurant, she brought Alex into town to pick up his rented car and Alex drove back to the house. In a closet in Evelyn's room he found a box of slides stored next to a slide projector. Holding one of the slides up to the light, he saw a painting. After setting up the projector, he turned off the lights.

The first slide was a painting of a circus tent on green grass under blue sky and a few drifting white clouds. A tranquil sea lay in the background in which the only discernible figure was the tail of a huge fish descending behind the horizon far in the distance. As Alex examined the slide he saw at the top of the tent a small forked flag that matched perfectly the flag of the circus he had seen with Iris.

In the next slide a strong wind had apparently destroyed a circus tent. Strips of torn canvas lay across a field exposing circular bleachers and a wooden circus ring. Lying in the center on his back was a huge curly haired man wearing a gold hoop earring. He was a circus strong man and he was still clinging to a barbell that said 10,000 Pounds on each bell. But his eyes were closed, his mouth was half open, and blood dripped from the corners of his lips down to his ear. A red gash slanted across one of his biceps.

There were more slides of demolished circuses, then a

photograph of a woman under a tree. Focusing the slide, he saw that it was not Iris, as he had first thought, but Evelyn dwarfed by the huge branches of the tree. Her baseball hat cast a shadow across her face. She looked sad, he thought.

Then he saw another photograph. He almost said it out loud. *That's me.* He could not say exactly why it looked like him. It was the way he was standing and the shadows to the side of his face and the unhappiness, the deep unhappiness that made him think of himself.

Alex left this slide on for a long time thinking, *This is what it's like to look at yourself. More so than seeing yourself in a photograph, more so than seeing yourself on film. The only way to see yourself is in a reality in which you've never been, of which you have no memories whatsoever.*

Another slide was of a pencil sketch of an island. At the top he saw the word *Cea.* A mountain had been drawn on one end of the island and an arrow pointed to it with writing that said, The Melancholy Resides Inside Here.

Alex turned off the projector and sat in the dark for a while. Then he got up and climbed the path in the backyard that led to Michelman's studio. Before reaching the top, he sat down in the grass. Looking down toward the dark house, he felt something come over him. It was the old feeling, the feeling that he had experienced all winter in New York, the feeling that Iris was gone for good. For three days since his swim it had left him—and now it was back.

It's all madness, he thought. *Marlin committed suicide. And what was I standing on in the field but the foundation to a circular house that lost its funding before it was finished! And now I've resurrected myself, as if my pact with Iris didn't matter!*

As he lay back looking at white clouds moving across the sky, the feeling came on stronger, and he thought he would feel better if he could cry, but something prevented him from crying. *There's only one thing to do now,* he thought, *and that's go back and do what I tried to do before Marlin interrupted me.*

The back door to the house opened and Evelyn came up the hill barefoot, wearing her black-and-white waitress uniform, an apron in her hand and on her head a cone-shaped cardboard hat that said Happy Birthday. "I'm glad you're here. I had this feeling . . . I've got to watch over you."

"Do you really believe all that stuff?" Alex said angrily.

"What's happened to you?"

"You don't think just because there's a private army that I'm going to believe there really was a circus?"

"What have you been thinking about?"

"I don't know why people bother me."

"Who's bothering you? You didn't even wish me happy birthday."

"Sorry, but I hope you know you wasted the last two days of my life."

"Are you all right?" Evelyn knelt next to him.

"Let's not pretend we don't know the truth when we both know it. Your boyfriend left you. I don't know where he went, but he left you and Marlin committed suicide and my wife is dead—dead! Do you hear?"

Evelyn spread the material of her black dress against her legs, then got up. On the way down the hill, she reached to her head, pulled off her cone-shaped hat and dropped it in the grass.

Alex ran past her to his car. He backed up, turned around, and drove quickly along the back roads that led up-island to King's Beach. When he reached the dirt road, he sped up, small stones battering the underside of the floorboards, dust rising high behind him.

He parked at the edge of the field, opened the door, and ran for the beach. He heard another car come into the field as he ran. The car drove quickly across the field behind him, then in front of him and stopped, and Evelyn got out.

She stepped in front of him and grabbed onto his belt as he passed. He dragged her a little ways, then tried to unhook her fingers from his belt.

"I've got something to show you. Stop!"

Evelyn held her arms around his waist. He pulled her through the grass up the side of the dune. At the top he fell to his knees. Evelyn handed him a white envelope, already torn open.

"I wanted to show this to you before you did anything stupid," she said.

"What is it?"

Dear Michelman,

Not long ago you requested that I draw you a map and tell you the best way to get onto the island to recover some of your paintings. I didn't believe that you should really do it, not until after you told me what you'd do to yourself if you didn't get them back. Now I know how badly their loss must hurt you. You told me that you would be back to see me but something is delaying you, and knowing that I might not make it even one more day, I thought I should write down the instructions I wanted to give you verbally.

It is only as I'm beginning to die that I see that what Mr. Volenti has been doing there is not altogether right. I see the people who once meant so much to me in a different light. Their practices are immoral and must cause an extraordinary amount of anxiety. Chester's story of missing me, which was like mine of missing him, convinced me that I should have come back earlier, that I shouldn't have left without at least letting him know that I was alive.

But read these words carefully. All has changed. Everything has evolved toward violence. Earlier this year a man tried to break in to find a lost friend. Not only was the invader severely punished, but so was his friend—inexplicably. What justification does Mr. Volenti have for that? Of course, they say that it's impossible for somebody to get on the island. But what do they know?

I've marked a way in, if someone can get past the beach guards—at night such a thing might not be that hard. They patrol, but there is over two hundred miles of shoreline to watch. It's getting into the mountain, that's what's impossible. Volenti has the mountain blocked off and guarded—I know because I worked there for eleven years, and as far as I know there was never a moment when two guards weren't standing there with guns. I haven't the plans for the mountain; besides they're always changing.

But I do know one thing. New soldiers are sent down to the barracks to join the troupe with only the password: Volenti—and if one is dressed right, this is the way inside—simply show up at the barracks prepared to be a soldier and when asked who sent you say, "Volenti." They don't expect new soldiers to understand the island, just a few basic rules, so everything else will be explained. Follow my route through the woods. There's a river to walk along most of the way. And bring enough camping equipment and food to last at least four days—the hike might take you that long.

What's needed is an adventurous spirit, an adventurous spirit, an adventurous spirit!

A hand-drawn map marked a route across the large island. The route started from the beach facing Verre, crossed through a long valley, and ended up near a mountain at a building marked Barracks.

"I'll get you Velman's uniform," Evelyn said.

CHAPTER **14**

THAT night in Evelyn's den
Alex dreamed that he was high over the ocean traveling in a hot-
air balloon. He was licking cherry-flavored shaved ice in a
cup. Below he saw the white foam of a person swimming at
great speed with powerful and beautiful strokes. Dropping
his shaved ice, he reached for the controls of the balloon but
realized they didn't work. Gusts of wind brought him farther
away from the swimmer, then closer until he could see the person's face.

"Iris! Iris!" Alex called.

But Iris kept swimming, kicking up a frothy wake.

"Iris, Iris!" He kept yelling until finally she stopped swimming, treaded water, and looked back at him.

She was not the least bit surprised that it was he.

"Darling, swim under me. I'll lift you up," Alex said.

She didn't swim toward his balloon. She merely lifted her
hand with one finger pointing out of the water.

At first he thought she was sending him a signal, a special

signal that would unlock the mystery of where she had been. "What is it? What are you trying to say?" he yelled.

But then he realized that she was merely pointing above his head.

Turning, he saw that the balloon that held him up was a thin rubber child's balloon that said Happy Twelfth Birthday on its side. The balloon had been blown up so much bigger than its real size that surely it was about to burst. When he turned back to Iris, she had already swum so far away that she was tiny and had nearly reached the horizon.

His own cries for help woke him up, and he kept calling once he was awake. "Evelyn! My God, Evelyn help me!"

She opened his door and came in tying the belt of her white bathrobe.

"I'm sorry," he said, catching his breath. "I didn't mean to yell like that. I woke you up, I know."

"Did you have a nightmare?"

"Who is this Volenti guy? Who the hell is he?"

"I don't know any more about him than you do, now."

"But how do I get there? You've got to help me get a boat. Do you know anybody who has a boat?"

"But I don't know if you should go."

"Do you think it will work, camping out the way Chester's brother said in his letter?"

After she went back to bed, he lay awake the rest of the night. At daybreak he got up, dressed, passed the sleeping dog by the back door, and climbed the hill to the painting studio. He opened the split log door and went in.

Something about the painting on the easel was different; perhaps it was the early morning light coming through the skylight, but the colors were bluer. And something else seemed changed—the chimpanzee with the arrow in his chest had a different face, a more human one than he remembered, like that of a man in extreme pain; more than just the arrow in his chest was hurting him, there was anguish in his face.

He noticed that the paint glistened as if it were fresh. Touching a corner of the face, he found it dry. The rest of the canvas was dry too.

As he walked through the shadow of the pines out into the field, he felt drowsy, as if his body would pass out despite the efforts of his mind to stay awake. Quietly he opened the door to the house, stepped back over the still-sleeping dog, and went into the den to his bed. Within a few minutes he was asleep.

When he woke up late in the morning, he found a note on the kitchen counter for him.

Alex,

 I'm at work. Do you feel like driving in for breakfast? I don't like the idea of your being alone. And please, don't get in another one of your moods. The brother's tumor made him sane, not insane!

               —Evelyn

On the porch, he sat down, dangling his bare feet above the grass, and read Velman's letter over for the third time, this time out loud.

 . . . But I do know one thing. New soldiers are sent down to the barracks to join the troupe with only the password: Volenti—and if one is dressed right, this is the way inside—simply show up at the barracks prepared to be a soldier and when asked who sent

you say, "Volenti." They don't expect new soldiers to understand the island, just a few basic rules, so everything else will be explained.

He sat in the café at the table that he and Iris had always taken. Evelyn brought him his food.

"I remember what you said to me once, that Iris had a sweet tooth that was costing you a fortune."

Alex smiled. But the name Iris had caught him by surprise. He hadn't expected it to come from anybody's lips but his own. He turned away from Evelyn and waited until she was gone.

It was a hot day. In the paper he read a follow-up of Marlin's story, a brief history with accounts by various islanders about his contribution to the community. "It baffles me," the police chief was quoted as saying. "Such a generous man and he never asked for anything in return."

Evelyn passed close by the table, the wind rustling the end of the newspaper. She dropped an order off and came back.

"Feeling better?" she said.

He stared at her, suddenly suspicious. Why was she so concerned about his mood?

"Maybe."

She leaned over and whispered. "I've got a boat, if you want to do it, if you feel like you have to do it, I've got a boat. Do you think you want to?"

He had no idea what she was talking about. He was about to say, What for?, but he stopped himself and looked at her eyes. Like Iris's eyes, Evelyn's had tiny crow's-feet at their corners. Now Alex saw Evelyn as twenty-seven, not nineteen.

"Yesterday you were talking about suicide," she said and turned to get an order.

"Why are you bringing that up?" he asked when she came back.

"Because you were."

"I wasn't just talking about it," he said.

"All right, you weren't just talking about it."

"I don't understand why you're so anxious to—"

She left to attend to customers. Finishing the paper, he got up, leaving a ten-dollar bill on the table to cover his small bill. Outside on the terrace he waved good-bye to her as she was taking somebody's order.

On his way up-island, at a corner on a rural road, a young man waved Alex to a stop. Alex saw that he was the same young man who had given him a ride to Verrehaven a year before.

"My car's stalled," the boy said. He wore a red T-shirt with the sleeves torn off. "Would you help me push it, at least out of the way?"

Alex parked on the shoulder ahead of the boy's car, then came back to help. Alex pressed his back into the trunk, straining to get the car moving, and the boy pushed from the open door, one hand on the wheel. Once it had rolled onto the shoulder the boy thanked Alex and asked him for a ride to Towson. In Towson, Alex dropped the boy off and went on to the town cemetery.

It was a small cemetery. Alex peeled a strip of bark from one of the red cedars near the gate in the white picket fence. Most of the gravestones were so old that the names had faded. In a short time he found the new section and the name Astley. There were two gravestones next to each other, Velman and Chester Astley's. Velman's said 1918–1991; Chester's said 1918–.

He knelt to read the inscription. May the Final Stage Be Blue. Under Chester's it said, Who Understood Life When His Brother Returned.

Alex stepped up to a collapsing, lichen-covered stone wall. He heard cheeping frogs and saw a freshwater pond with lily pads and long reeds. The water and the trees on the far side looked dark.

He heard footsteps in the grass and turned around. Evelyn

walked slowly toward him, pushing her blond hair behind her ears.

"How did you know I was here?"

"I got worried about you; I knew you'd gone somewhere."

She stopped close to him. Her face was close to his face, almost as if she were about to kiss him. Again he saw the tiny crow's-feet in the corners of her eyes.

CHAPTER **15**

$\mathbb{IN}$ Verrehaven they bought the
camping gear, the same equipment that Michelman had packed:
a tent, backpack, sleeping bag, an aluminum pot-and-pan set,
a knife with a spoon and fork on it, a canteen, a small propane
stove, six days' worth of canned and dehydrated foods. At the
checkout counter, Evelyn brought over a small inflatable pillow.
"You may find you're sleeping on rocks," she said.

In the yard at home, Alex set the tent up, lit the propane
stove, and cooked a can of beans as if he were camping. Then
he tried on Velman's uniform. Evelyn brought him a pillowcase
to use as a small carrying bag when he joined the army.

That evening they waterproofed the backpack by putting it
into large, heavy plastic bags and tying them securely. The air
in the large bags would buoy the pack in the water. They final-
ized plans; Evelyn would bring the boat as close to shore as
possible, and Alex would swim behind the pack, pushing it to
shore.

Alex studied the map and memorized the sketchy plan to join
Volenti's army. From the letter he could ascertain little about

the purpose of the army, and less about the purpose of the whole island. He kept thinking that it must be a CIA base or some secret military training ground. But each time he told Evelyn this, she said, "Definitely not."

They came up with a plan: once Evelyn dropped him off she would pick him up exactly ten days later, and if he didn't show up, she'd come back every Sunday afternoon for a month. If she saw a white undershirt hanging from a tree along the bluffs, she'd know he was waiting to be picked up.

Because the moon would soon be new, they waited two days. Alex sent a letter to Mr. Lovlor in New York.

Dear Mr. Lovlor,

I'm traveling and may be out of the city for a long time. Enclosed are as many rent checks as you might need. Please cash them on the first of each month until I return.

In the event that you see my wife, please let her know that I'm traveling alone and will be back soon. Please tell her that I will be thinking about her all the time and that I miss her terribly. Please tell her to wait right there for me and not to try to find me. I'll be back.

Thank you so much.

Alex Barton

Alex tried to write Iris a letter, thinking he'd send it to his apartment in case she got back. But every time he started it, he found himself so despondent that he thought he'd better not write anything. Lovlor would tell her what was in his note.

Circus World Museum, Baraboo, Wisconsin.

CHAPTER 16

EVELYN and Alex drove the outboard motorboat out of the harbor of Verrehaven, passing lanterns hung on the masts of moored sailboats. A small yellow light lit their bow.

Alex wore a swimming suit under a black bathrobe. The boat ride to the island was close to three hours long. Evelyn sat in the stern. After an hour she turned off the yellow bow light and Alex stared out at the dark water. Small waves splashed against the bow. He watched for land nervously without once turning to Evelyn.

High bluffs and tall dark trees rose up from the black ocean. Evelyn cut the engine, moved toward the bow, and picked up an oar, handing one to Alex and putting the other one in its lock on the gunwale. He pushed and pulled his oar in unison with hers. The water was calm; a dead stillness fell around them.

Then he could hear the waves on shore and a whiff of something sweet came to him from the trees, some kind of flower, maybe honeysuckle.

He told her he was ready to go in. He pulled the tight rubber fins on and took off his robe. She hugged him, pulling him hard against her, then he climbed over the gunwale and into the water. As soon as he was up to his neck in the cool water, he felt calmer.

Evelyn lowered the pack. Alex grabbed it and began to kick with the fins, pushing the heavy pack through the water. His calves became sore, but he kept moving, the swells lifting and dropping him. Vines hung from thick branches behind the white sand of the dunes. At the top of a cliff, a dead tree was outlined against the stars.

On the beach, he kicked off his fins, pulled the pack from the water, and carried it until he was safely behind the dunes. He rested, looking through the weeds at the water.

He could hear loud crickets. Behind him, in the darkness of the trees, an animal chewed on hollow wood.

He pulled the plastic off his pack, took out his flashlight, and shone the beam low on leafy vines and Spanish moss. After dressing, he climbed the steep hill through the vines and under-growth to the foot of a cliff and walked along its base looking for a route the rest of the way up. A path worn deep in the red earth led through boulders high above the starlit sea. He fell into the rhythm of the climb, straining and sweating against the heavy pack.

At the top, a breeze tickled his face, and he could smell the ocean again. The path, skirting the edge of the cliff, led up to a rocky pinnacle that overlooked the water.

He stopped. A faint breeze rustled the leaves behind him. Below, waves broke gently against the sand. In the distance, he began to hear a strange sound.

He held his breath to listen. It was a dog's howl. So faintly did it carry in the ocean air, from some place far away, that he thought it must be coming from some imaginary dog living in his own sad and yearning thoughts.

He walked on a little ways, then stopped. The yowling had grown louder.

It kept getting louder until he realized that the dog was running along the beach. Barks echoed off the cliff, and he thought he heard a car engine.

He rushed into the trees, blocking branches from his eyes. At the bottom of a hill, under the cover of vines, he stopped again. A stream trickled somewhere below him. He shone his light on the wide palm-shaped leaves on the ground and low on the trunks of trees, moving toward the water sounds.

He heard the dog again, this time much louder than from the top of the cliff. He ran, his feet slipping on the rocks of a stream so that he fell on his back against his heavy bag. Soaking wet now, he sloshed through the water, the dog chasing through the woods. He shone the light on the rocks on the bank, looking for a place to hide his pack. The water had carved hollows in the red earth. He found a dark opening under the roots of a tree, stashed his baggage deep within and ran on through the current.

When he came to a placid pool, he kicked off his shoes, tucked his light into his pants, and swam. The dog came to the edge of the water, barking ferociously, circling to the opposite bank. Soon Alex heard voices and branches breaking. Flashlight beams blinded him.

A deep commanding voice told Alex to swim to shore.

His trembling feet touched the stones of the bottom. A man pulled the dog back. Not knowing what to do with his hands, Alex raised them and climbed up a bank of grass under the trees. Someone tied his hands tightly behind his back, yanked a blindfold across his eyes, and gagged his mouth. Two men escorted him back toward the beach. The dog howled mournfully as if forlorn and in pain. The men exchanged short commands and questions in English, some with heavy accents.

The earth was soft under his bare feet, though occasionally he stepped on a sharp branch or a rock. They climbed the hill, then followed a path to the ocean. On the beach Alex was told to step up, and he climbed into an open vehicle, a jeep. Two

men squeezed in on either side of him. Other vehicles started
up around them.

The vehicles turned away from the ocean onto a dirt road.
The air was thicker; it smelled richer. They drove up and down
hills. After half an hour or so, they stopped. The two men flanking Alex escorted him out of the jeep, across some grass and
through a door.

They brought him down wet stone steps. The air became
cooler and damper. A door was opened and he was pushed inside, the men following. They untied his blindfold and then his
gag.

"What are you doing to me? Who are you?"

Two men held him, another untied his arms.

"I thought this was a public place."

They shoved him forward; his shins met the metal frame of
a bed. He fell down on a small mattress.

"You can't do this to me—"

The men walked quickly toward a door and Alex ran at them,
but the last man turned and shot his hands out, knocking Alex
flat onto his back. The door slammed shut and was locked. Rising to his feet, Alex grabbed the bars of its window. At the top
of the stairwell, the men disappeared through another door.

Alex turned. A pale lightbulb illuminated a room of stones,
slick colorful beach stones mortared into the walls. In one corner, he saw a tin bucket, in another, a cistern of smaller stones.
Water spilled over the edges, flooding that side of the room.

The lightbulb went out and left him in total darkness. He
yelled for help, yelled at the top of his lungs. Exhausted, he
turned and felt his way across the room to the cold metal bed
frame. He pulled a damp quilt over his legs as he lay down.

After a while he heard a creak. The stairwell door opened,
and footsteps came down.

Alex got up and started moving in the dark toward the footsteps. "Help me. Please help me. Open the door," he said.
"They've made a mistake. Please open the door."

The footsteps stopped just outside the stone room door.

"Hello, hello," Alex said. "I've just come to see Volenti. Mr. Volenti. I've just come to see him."

He grabbed the bars of the window in the door. "Please, whoever you are, whoever you are, open the door, turn on the light."

He could hear the man breathing behind the bars.

"Call the police, whoever you are, call the police," Alex said. "I don't even know what I'm doing here. I wanted to see somebody. I can't. Open up, please. Who are you? Are you there? What are you doing out there?"

The person shuffled his feet, then started back up the stairs in the dark.

"Wait, wait," Alex called.

But the footsteps kept going. At the top of the stairwell a short figure slipped out of the door. Alex shook the bars. "Come back, please, I need help!" he yelled.

CHAPTER 17

HE had been staring up into the darkness when the overhead light went on. At first he didn't register it as light, but as some huge physical change taking place within the room. He peeked through his fingers, letting his eyes adjust until everything was visible again. Water trickling down the side of the cistern had worn a vague, blue-green path in the cement and in the tiny stones. A kind of slot, like a mail slot, had been cut into the very bottom of the warped brown door. Kneeling next to it, he slipped his arm out up to his elbow. Water dripping over the bottom step drained beneath his door. He dragged his fingers through cold mud and slime, feeling for the drain. Then he pulled his hand out and stood up.

"Whose idea is this?" His voice vibrated and died among the walls. He called for help and kept calling until his throat was too sore, then the door at the top opened and a man's silhouette appeared for an instant in the bright white light outside the door. Holding the pipe railing, the man rushed down the steps, his left foot jerking forward at each step. The man wore tight black stretch pants and a black turtleneck shirt. His brown hair was cut straight across his forehead. Stopping short of the barred window, he yelled, "Get over by your bed."

"You can't do this to me," Alex said, stepping back. "It's against the law."

The man bent over to fit the key into the lock; Alex saw a larger, more muscular man coming down the stairs behind him.

The first man kicked the door in with his foot, knocking Alex onto the stones. Alex scrambled to get up, but the man approached him quickly, picked him up, and threw him down on the bed. Before Alex could move, the two men were on him, one holding his arms while the other went from wrists to ankles, tying him to the four corners of his bed frame. A blindfold was tied so tightly around his head that his eyes were pushed painfully back into their sockets.

He tried to struggle, but the cord burned into his skin.

The men left.

Alex yelled for help.

He kept yelling so loudly for so long that his throat dried and only air came out, no sound.

He heard the door at the top of the stairs outside his room squeak open and footsteps descend steadily.

"Help me, please, help me, help me," Alex said. "My God, whoever you are, whoever you are, loosen these ropes, they're cutting off my hands."

The footsteps kept coming down the steps. They crossed the stones of the room and stopped over Alex.

"Please, whoever you are, whoever you," Alex said, blindly. "Please, I don't know why—"

He felt a sharp pain in his ear.

At first he thought it must be coming from within his ear,

it was so sharp and powerful, then a wire penetrated the canal and something pulsed from it—an electrical current. It crawled and burned like acid through every crevice of tissue in his head.

The man pulled the wire out. Alex writhed, crying, "Get away from me, get the fuck away from me."

The man was still nearby.

"Don't touch me, don't touch me," Alex said. A bucket of cold water washed over him, caught him in the mouth, and made him choke. The pain in his ear was so intense that he couldn't tell whether the wire had been put back in again or not. The cold blade of a knife cut away his shirt, then his pants and underwear. Alex kept waving his head back and forth. "Please don't touch me!" he screamed.

A sharp point pierced his foot. He tried to kick to turn his body but it didn't work. He screamed out, "Help!" as loud as he could. The pain got so bad that he must have fainted. When he came to he felt water dripping over him; another bucket had been thrown on him.

The pain started on his foot again. This time it was hot, a flame. His leg twitched, but the pain stayed constant. He cried out: "Oh God, oh God, oh God help me, help me, help me." He kept saying "help me" long after the person had taken the flame away.

"He's not going to help you," the man said. "Nobody's going to help you. And if you start to think that he's going to help you, why then, I'll make sure, damn sure, he's not going to help you. Do you know who's going to help you?" The man pressed his hand down on Alex's chest. "Do you know? Tell me," he said. "Tell me who, tell me!"

"Nobody," Alex said.

The man pushed harder on his chest. "You lying sack of shit," he said. "You goddamn lying sack of shit, tell me."

"I don't know," Alex said.

The man lifted his hand from Alex's chest, then slapped something down on his stomach. It was a stick, the man beat him with a stick. When he stopped, Alex was screaming. "Somebody, please, somebody . . ."

CHAPTER **18**

ALL was quiet in the room when he woke except for the gurgling and dripping of water. He lay perfectly still, staring at the different colored sea stones that made up the walls, some white, some light gray, some yellow, all mortared together. Some were bigger than others; water had beaded on most of them.

One minute the pain that throbbed from every side of his body held his attention as if it were separate from him, as if he were looking out at it from a little circle, his real self safe inside his head. The next minute the pain went from an outer one to an inner one, the outer pain becoming minuscule compared to the swollen darkness that pulsed from within.

After a long time he managed to sleep, and he slept and woke with no notion of how many hours were elapsing during his sleeps.

Maybe one day, maybe two days passed before he so much as heard another footstep outside his stone room door.

He shut his eyes tightly. The person stopped outside his door, then went back up the stairs. Turning his stiff neck, Alex spotted a plate heaped with something by the slot of the door. He looked back up at the ceiling. An image of a plate of beans and rice rose up against the stones. He could smell them.

He stared at the ceiling for a long time.

He thought he should do something about them, but he wasn't sure exactly what.

Finally he pushed his good leg to the side of the bed and lowered his foot to the cold stones. Lifting his head, he propped himself up on his elbows. His tightened muscles ached with the movement of each limb.

He hopped on one foot, steadied himself against the wall, and urinated toward a drain where a trickle of water washed it away. Every hop closer to the door made him more fearful, fearful of the door, as if the electricity that had tortured him had come from the door itself. He kept his eye on the plate: a steaming white plate piled high with pink beans and white rice, a fork leaning against it. For an instant it crossed his mind that they might be poisoning him, then he scooped the food into his mouth with his hands, devouring it right down to the clean plate.

On his bunk, he examined his body. His veiny, purple-and-red wrists had swollen gigantically; his bulbous fingers and toes were numb. Touching himself, he felt his own hands against the skin of his thigh. They were not his hands. They belonged to another person, a person wearing puffy, leathery gloves. Welts had risen across his stomach; they too had the purple-and-red color. He did not dare look at the bottom of his foot.

CHAPTER **19**

HE had no idea how much time was passing. Every time he heard the footsteps of the person bringing the plate or the bowl he rolled over on his bunk and pulled the quilt up over his head and closed his eyes; his heartbeat quickened with the knowledge that somebody was nearby. The sound of the food slot opening was disturbing; anything entering his room penetrated him, like the electricity had penetrated his soul. After the meal was delivered, he'd find himself shaking as if he were freezing to death. Sometimes a great deal of time passed before he'd stop shaking, get up, and get his food.

He tried to learn to cope with certain aspects of the new conditions of his life. Each of the four corners of the stone room came to mean something different to him. The corner farthest from the door he thought of as the forest. The corner near the dripping spigot and cistern was the river area. In between these two were city streets. While pacing he could feel the differences between them. The bunk was home. Sometimes it felt good to leave home and visit the forest or walk to the river. He could even imagine himself swimming if he wanted to.

He didn't choose to play this game, or at least he couldn't remember choosing it. It just came naturally. Those places were as real as they would have been had there been real trees, real city streets, and a real river. But there were no people. He'd always take his walks alone and never meet a soul. Gradually he went on them less frequently and stayed near his bunk most of the time, focusing more and more on the food slot.

Then something else began to happen: his meals became smaller. They may have been getting smaller for a long time before he noticed it, but once they were down to less than half of what they'd been in the beginning, once he felt the intensity of his hunger pains increasing, and his satiation after mealtimes decreasing, he began to fret and worry again. When finally just a pea, a tiny scoop of potato no bigger than a teaspoonful, and a piece of steak the size of a penny came in, he picked the plate up, smashed it against the wall, then went back to his bunk and cried. He cried for a long time. And the next meal was even smaller. He smashed the plate again, jumped up and down, ran around his room, then lifted his mattress and tried to tear it. He screamed obscenities and broke into tears. For the next meal a bare plate was shoved through the door. He was so tired he fell right to sleep. When he woke up, he saw another bare plate had been shoved through the door. He didn't bother to smash it. Another bare plate came in at noon, and another at dinnertime.

He kept exhausting himself by crying. Finally, his hunger pains ceased, and he lost the energy to cry. He just sat on his bunk and drank occasionally, but after a while he stopped drinking and slept longer.

One time he woke up and saw above him the tips of pine trees coming together as if he were lying in a forest, white clouds crossing a sky as blue as the one Iris had disappeared under. Yelling for help, he heard his voice echo off valley walls. Birds circled high above, beautiful from a distance. As they got lower he put his hands over his face so their talons wouldn't scratch his eyes. Sometimes they'd perch just above his head. If he took his hand off his face, he'd see their yellow eyes staring down at him. At times he'd focus on them and notice their faces were human. They'd speak to him. "Nobody said you have to starve to death."

"It must really be a need of yours, a desire for attention. Why don't you see somebody about it?"

"Go upstairs, go on, they're waiting for you."

"Who is?"

"Don't play dumb, you know who we're talking about."

"I don't know who you're talking about."

"We're leaving, we're leaving without you. Bye bye, bye bye."

At the flapping of their great wings, he tried to move his arms. "Wait for me!"

CHAPTER 20

HE felt something on his lips; water poured down his throat. The water went down the wrong way and he began to cough and choke. He leaned over and opened his eyes. They'd carried him out of the stone room. The light was bright. He kept his eyes closed for a long time before opening them again. He saw his legs resting on a lounge chair. His feet were skeletons of feet, and his knees were swollen like baseballs. Loose flaps of wrinkled skin hung from his calves. He tried to move one of his arms. It felt like a weight had been wrapped around his wrist. Then he saw his hand. It didn't look human; the fingers were pure elongated lengths of bone with flaps of pale yellow skin wrapped around them. His wrist bone showed clearly and skin sunk into every joint of his arm. A blanket had been draped over him. He tried to move his mouth but the skin seemed to stick to his gums. A green color, reflected from what must have been grass, floated up around his chair, and there were dark trees, probably pine trees, below the slope of a hill. Over the tips of the pines he could see a watery blue light, the blue of the ocean. As he moved his head, shapes blurred together; a white, vaporous trail followed them. He was wearing a hat, he thought. He could feel its weight on his head as he turned his neck.

He sat there for many hours, his eyes focusing. Then he heard a voice and saw a person's shadow next to him. He turned his head and looked straight down at his skeleton legs.

The person put a bottle with a nipple before his face and told him to put his lips to it. He felt the bottle pressed against his gums and liquid pouring onto his tongue. The person told him to swallow, but Alex couldn't even close his mouth. The liquid ran down his lips and chin and dripped onto his chest.

"Put your head back," the man said and lowered the back of the chair so that Alex was looking toward the sky. The man put the bottle to Alex's lips and the liquid poured down his throat. Some went down before it caught in his windpipe and he began to cough and choke, struggling to breathe but unable to move his head forward to clear his throat. The procedure was repeated, and Alex coughed again. Then the person left him alone.

From tilting his head back to accept the liquid his neck was now sore; he didn't dare move it to the left or the right. He lifted one of his hands to examine it again. There were strange reddish spots on the yellow skin; his elongated fingernails were broken and curled. The one on his pinky had fallen off, and his thumbnail was split.

He was fed again later in the afternoon, then carried down to his bunk in the stone room. As they were carrying him, he saw a silver chain-link fence with razor-blade barbed wire at the top. On his bunk he fell asleep, thoroughly exhausted from the little motion he had been put through. He noticed that the sound of gurgling and dripping water had stopped. The air in his cell was drier. Somebody had shut the water off.

He tried to imagine who was doing this. Now that they had

decided to save him from starvation, he forgave them for everything, cursing himself quietly for ever having thought that they
were bad people.

They carried him up onto the lawn the next morning, and he
was fed again. A man told him that he had urinated on himself
and that the next time he should try to roll over. He nodded
his head at these words, but he was sure that he couldn't roll
over even if he knew that he was about to pass water.

Swallowing was a task with many different dimensions; he
relearned every one of them: opening his mouth to accept the
food while holding his breath, waiting for the liquid to build up
in the back of his throat, contracting then relaxing the muscles.

He said nothing, not even to himself. He could hear voices
in his head as if he were talking, but he could not vocalize. He
merely stared at the sky and waited for the people to do what
they would with him. Move him, roll him over, feed him. Somebody gave him a sponge bath.

After days of his being carried into and out of his room, of
his being fed with a baby bottle, somebody said, "My name is
Charles. How do you feel?"

He tried to turn his eyes to the person, but he couldn't. It
was like looking at the door when they'd kept him down there.
He couldn't look at the door, nor could he look at the people
who fed him. He wasn't even sure if it was the same person each
time. He looked up at the sky and heard the question again.

The next day they asked him, "Are you thinking?"

He turned toward the person who had said his name was
Charles and saw a man in a brown khaki army uniform, with
light golden brown hair falling across the top of his forehead.
He had small eyes, perhaps even kind eyes; maybe he was the
one who told them to give him food.

Even when they lifted him from his bunk and brought him
up the stairs, he felt exhausted. Being carried was exhausting;
being fed was exhausting. He slept most of the day and all night.

After a week he found he could move his head with ease and raise and lower his hands to scratch himself; he could also move his legs.

"Speak to us," Charles said. Alex turned toward him. Their eyes met for an instant, and he felt something shoot inside of him. He was being violated by another's eyes.

Alex stared at the clouds moving against the sky.

"Come on, say something." Charles touched his arm and shook him a little. A word came to his mind and seemed to enter his throat the way words do, but it stopped suddenly. The wire penetrating his ear made him afraid. If he spoke they might put it in again and turn it on.

In the stone room he was able to roll over and pull up his gown and urinate on the floor rather than on himself. After another week they lifted his arms and stood him up facing down the long hill of grass and the ocean. They supported him as he watched the water. A white sailboat tacked at an angle away from the island. Another boat far out on the water, probably a fishing boat, was trolling.

They told him to walk with them, and he began moving his legs, stumbling, leaning to one side, then to the other with the two men holding him. The muscles around his chest became sore, and he said, "Chair, please, chair."

The view from his chair became clearer and clearer. He was able to focus on the faint line where the sky and the ocean met. He could see the jagged branches at the top of the pines. Through an opening he saw the very tip of a telephone pole. In the morning the birds flew at an angle over his head away from him. In the evening they came toward him from the trees and the ocean. There were hawks, crows, sparrows, grackles, terns, heron, and seagulls, many seagulls. In the morning the smells were of the dew-covered earth, the grass, and sometimes when the wind was blowing right he could smell the pines. Midday the strongest smell was the ocean, but in the afternoon when the sun heated the field he could smell the grasses most strongly and hear the cicadas.

"What are you here for?" a man who was not Charles asked him the next day.

He turned and looked above the man's eyes to his forehead.

"Why did you come here? What are you doing right now?"

Alex shook his head slowly. "I don't know."

"Don't play games with me," the man said. "You came here for something."

"Curious," Alex said. "I wanted to know what it was all about."

The man was silent. Then he laughed. "How about another session?"

Alex shook his head slowly, then realized what he was referring to. He suddenly heard his own teeth chattering out of fear.

"Why did you come here?"

"I just came," Alex said. "I thought there was good camping."

"Camping?" the man said. "You can't be serious."

Alex nodded.

"You came all the way here to go camping? Camping?!"

A moment later the man held up the black butt of a whip.

"Ever felt one of these?" the man said.

Alex closed his eyes. "What do you want me to say?" he said.

The black leather strap slapped across his arms and stomach and ate into his flesh. Alex's body jumped and vibrated electrically. His mind leaped above him and he seemed to look down at what was happening to him. The man hit him again. Alex's body jerked, flexed, and vibrated. He could see his hand over his groin, protecting it.

"Are you ready to talk?" the man said.

A pool of blood had formed on Alex's belly. He stared at the man who was surrounded by water, a white cloud of tears.

The whip came down over the back of his hands and over his feet and legs, everywhere but his face. He fell out of the chair and began to crawl across the grass. The man followed him, beating his back until he fell into the grass and curled up into a ball. The man continued hitting him on the side.

"I have a good mind to kill you," he said. Alex felt another three blows. "But I'm going to save you. If you ask any questions, if I hear so much as a syllable out of you the next few weeks, you'll be finished." The man brought the butt end of the whip down on Alex's back, then left.

CHAPTER 21

LATER in the afternoon Charles and another man in khaki clothes came with a bucket and a sponge and cleaned Alex off. They treated his wounds with peroxide, then carried him downstairs and left him on the cot. The door was open, but he was too weak even to crawl to the door.

The next morning they carried him back out to his chair and gave him another baby bottle of food. An hour later he urinated on himself. They fed him again in the afternoon; his mind began to focus. He couldn't see his groin for the welts on his bloated belly. They fed him again in the evening. That night they carried him downstairs to the room and locked his door. The next day he asked Charles if he'd be beaten again.

"I heard them say that you'd make an excellent performer," Charles said.

"What does that mean?"

"Best you keep quiet. You're not to be asking me questions." He refilled Alex's bottle and handed it back.

His wounds began to heal. The swelling around his ear went

down. The welts turned into great long scabs. He did everything he could to keep from scratching them off.

He never had an opportunity to look in a mirror, but he could feel cavities under his cheekbones. The skin on his nose was tight, the cartilage perpetually sore. His joints were so swollen that sometimes in the morning he couldn't move his fingers.

Charles helped him walk again. This second recovery took longer than the first. He had become even weaker, though he hadn't thought it possible. Several times when he tried to walk by himself, he collapsed near his chair and couldn't get up again.

Most days the sun was out; only once did it rain in three weeks. Alex spent that day in the stone room, lying on his back.

A few days later Charles took him to the gate in the chain-link fence surrounding the compound. Here another guard in khaki clothes, a canvas belt, and high brown army boots laced halfway up leaned back on a lawn chair, holding a long blade of timothy grass to his mouth. Seeds weighed down the end of the grass. Charles asked him for the handcuffs, and the guard reached over to a small metal box and opened the door. Inside, two pairs of handcuffs hung from hooks. Charles held Alex's hand next to his own and the guard joined them at the wrists.

They walked through the pines at the bottom of the field to a path that ran along the edge of one of the clay cliffs. Alex could see out to the water. Charles climbed with him onto a large, gray boulder, polished by the wind. The beach below was all stones. Dark seaweed, rising and falling with the movement of the waves, clung to the big rocks offshore. The water stretched out calmly, only slightly lighter far out than close by.

It must have been the closeness to such rich blue water that made thoughts of Iris come to him once again. He tried not to think of her, only of the blueness which now rose from the calm sea like a vapor, surrounding him and hardening something inside him.

"Tell me, why did you come here?"

Alex looked slowly around at the man.

"To kill myself," he said. Then he turned and looked back out at the ocean. He could hear the round little stones on the rocky shore below rolling up and rolling back with every wave.

"I've never understood suicide," Charles said. A cormorant came around the bend of the red cliff, flying only a foot off the water, its long neck stretched forward, its wings beating short, quick strokes. "A person who wants to do that must have a reason to want to do it."

"No reason, just that things aren't worth it, not worth all the pain," Alex said quietly.

"Those are thoughts you get from being here, I'm sure. You'll start feeling better again soon. It's just the stage you're at."

"I don't understand why they had to do this to me."

"You came here. Somebody dropped you off. You can't expect to go snooping into somebody's backyard without being punished a little."

"A little?"

"Well, okay . . . All they really want is a confession out of you, a reason you're here. Not that you wanted to go camping, you shouldn't have told the men you wanted to go camping."

"But that's all it was. I wanted to explore the island."

"Then what happened to your partner? Where were your bags, your camping equipment?"

"I didn't come with a bag."

"Then you weren't camping. Come on, we've got to get back to your home."

Alex could hear Charles's footsteps as they climbed the path of clay and rocks and dust. The guard, still sucking on a long piece of grass, got out of his folding chair and unlocked the handcuffs from the two men.

In the compound, Alex turned to Charles. "All of this for

me. Do you really think I belong to some stupid organization or to a government? Why don't you check my tax records in New York? I'm poor. I'm nobody important."

"You're moving on," Charles said. "I'll report that you're moving on."

CHAPTER **22**

ALEX sat within the fence
outside his cell, watching the darkening water after the sun had
gone down. Fireflies came out, drawing short arced trails of light
against the trees.

The next morning, Charles woke him up and Alex came upstairs to the lawn for his breakfast.

"It doesn't matter what you do to me here. You're wasting
your time. You can kill me . . . I'll kill myself anyway."

"Something's missing in your life?"

"Yes, everything, that's what's missing, everything."

"Why did you have to come here to kill yourself?"

"I didn't want to do it where anyone who knew me might
find my body. I thought there were lots of woods here."

"And who dropped you off?"

"I hired a kid from Verrehaven, a kid with a boat. I told him
I was just having fun."

"And who was this kid?"

"He told me not to tell anybody who he was, it was part of
our deal."

"You know, we could punish you again for such obstinacy."

"You could but, like I said, where would it get you?"

"Punishing isn't much work for us," Charles said.

"I can get around it easily enough, too."

"You didn't get around it before. What makes you think—"

"How do you know?"

"You were down there crying your eyes out."

"I wasn't crying over being tortured."

"Then what were you crying about?"

"Just about life. I hate life. It's a big drag, you know. I hate it. Some people drink, but as for that method of killing the pain, I say, why bother?"

"I'm beginning to believe you."

"You'd better believe me. I tried to kill myself by swimming off of Verre; somebody tried to save me. I let him save me, but so what . . . I made him feel like a hero. Pretty soon I'll do it again, and he won't know about it."

"Do you want to go to the water?"

"No," Alex said. "I'll stay here."

"You need exercise . . . you're depressed."

Alex laughed. "Depressed, me?"

"Don't be so cynical," Charles said.

"Cynical? And your friend the torturer isn't cynical, just negative, eh?"

The man stood up, lifting Alex's arm. "Let's go, fellow."

Alex followed him out to the gate where a different guard stood up with a pair of handcuffs. They walked down the path to the water and sat down.

Everything that had happened when they'd first caught him had become mixed-up in his mind. Had they tortured him first? When did they decide to starve him to death? He'd seen so many things down in that room. But now the color of the water alone might drive him crazy.

"Why don't you let me go?" Alex said. "I'll jump head first onto those rocks."

"That's what worries me," Charles said. "I'm beginning to believe you. Maybe you did come here to commit suicide—an awfully long way to come to do it, but insanity doesn't know that."

"Do you think I'm crazy?" Alex asked.

Charles looked at Alex, and Alex tried to smile slyly.

"Maybe you *are* crazy."

"Then what's the use of keeping me if I'm crazy?"

"Do you want to get beaten again? I can arrange for it easily enough."

"You're a bunch of maniacs," Alex said. He stared at the blue water. It produced an emptiness inside him, a deep howling emptiness.

CHAPTER **23**

THAT night he sat on the
grass whispering her name to himself over and over and trying
to conjure up memories of her. For some reason, he kept thinking about a time when they'd been having fights almost every
day. The fights had been his fault, he thought. He had been
frustrated with his life, his unexciting job.

He'd become extremely disconcerted, living in New York.
All of the bad things that had happened to him there became
like pieces of a giant puzzle; as soon as the puzzle was complete,
he'd have absolute proof that New York was evil, but the problem was that the more pieces he found, the more he needed. But
she insisted, and he knew that she was right, that it wasn't New
York that was really causing him all the pain, it was something
inside him that New York brought out.

Iris had told Alex many times that she could feel something
holding him back, something frustrating him. It was a kind of
stage fright, a fear of expressing himself. His tendency was to
withdraw inside himself, to think of things from within a cocoon

of solitude. But the only time he was really happy, Iris reminded him, was when he was with people. He was certainly not a loner.

Charles brought Alex's dinner as the sun was low.

"I told them what you told me. I had to. I don't like all your talk about suicide."

"You won't be able to watch over me the rest of my life."

"We're going to bring you back to Verre soon."

"I'm to return now after my lesson?"

"It seems like you haven't learned it too well."

"I'm supposed to cherish living?" He held his plate up. "Cherish food, cherish those who bring it to me?"

"You're not very grateful, not very grateful."

"I came here to go camping. I get tracked by a dog—"

"Come off of it," Charles said. "You weren't camping, you knew what you were doing."

"I wish I knew."

Charles got up and Alex watched him walk back toward the gate and then through it.

After he'd finished he put his plate down and strolled around the grounds. The guard, who was also standing, watched him from the gate. From everywhere Alex looked, the man was facing him. Darkness fell; shadows filled the man's eyes.

Alex crossed the lawn to him.

"Would you do me a favor—just a small favor?"

"What kind of favor?"

"Shoot me between the eyes."

"Why don't you climb the fence, then I can shoot you, say you were trying to escape."

"I haven't the energy."

"Well, then, I haven't the energy to shoot you."

"Then let me shoot myself." Alex reached for the gun, but the guard didn't like the joke.

"Get away from the fence," he said.

CHAPTER 24

IN his cell, Alex began doing exercises. He wasn't sure exactly why he was doing them. He did every imaginable calisthenic, including lying on his back on the floor and lifting his cot. He did push-ups, deep knee bends; he jogged in place, skipped rope without a rope. If he heard somebody coming down the stairwell, he stopped and lay down on his cot as if he were sick.

His muscles grew in size, but he was careful to hide them and to make his shoulders sag as if he had bad posture. To Charles he continued to talk about suicide. Had there been another prisoner to distract the guard on duty, Alex could have climbed the fence and slipped through the barbed wire at the top. But the guard, who had only one person to watch, did his job well.

Then, one day, coming in from his walk to the water with Charles, Alex saw the second pair of handcuffs lying under the guard's chair, and the small key, which usually hung beside them on a hook inside the metal box, lying right next to them. As soon as his hand was released, Alex fell over backward, toward the chair, as if he had passed out. His head struck the pole violently. The impact must have convinced Charles and the guard that the faint was real. The guard stayed while Charles ran to get the jeep to take Alex to the hospital. When the guard turned to help, Alex grabbed the handcuff key and stuffed it in his pocket.

"I've always fainted, since I was four years old," he said as Charles lifted him into the back of the military jeep.

"You knocked your head."

"I'll be all right, just let me go." Alex sat up.

Charles stood back. "I guess you're used to knocks in the head," he said, quietly.

Three days went by. Each day Alex waited for the moment the handcuffs would be brought out of their little metal box on the side of the guard station. As he anticipated the pair that the guard would pick, fear bolted through him.

On the fourth day, the guard brought the second pair out. Recognizing them, Alex began trembling. After they were joined at the wrist, Charles asked him what was wrong.

"Nothing," Alex said. The thought that Charles might ask the guard to unlock the handcuffs sobered Alex. "I need to go for a walk, that's all. I have to."

They started down the red dirt path. Alex could smell seaweed from the rocks below the cliff. Out of the corner of his eyes he watched the side of Charles's head.

The path descended through bushes and short trees.

"Look," Alex said, stopping and pointing down.

"Look at what?" Charles said.

"A stone."

"So what, a stone? Who cares about a stone?" Charles said.

"A beautiful stone, a really beautiful stone," Alex said. He began to bend down.

"They're all the same, all stones are the same," Charles said.

Bending down, Alex reached for Charles's legs and tackled

him on his side. Then he jerked Charles's arm behind his back and pushed it toward the nape of his neck.

Charles cried out in pain. "They'll kill you, Alex."

"That's what I want them to do." Alex was kneeling on Charles's back, holding his arm against his neck. He got the key out and inserted it into the handcuffs. Grabbing the other hand he locked Charles's wrists together, sprang up, and ran down the path toward the ocean. Charles ran after him. Before the cliff, Alex turned toward the brambles, running through them, scratching his arms, his face, tearing his pants.

A path followed the edge of the cliff next to the ocean. Alex slowed his pace to a jog. After a while the path ended and he ran down to the beach and continued on dry sand, careful to leave a trail behind him for the dog to follow.

He came to the beach where he had first swum in. He took off his clothes, the gray pants and gray work shirt in which they had dressed him, left them in a pile above the high-tide line in the sand and ran to the water.

He plunged through waves and swam out beyond the swells. He did the sidestroke to conserve energy, turning one hundred yards out and swimming parallel to shore. A mild current helped him along. His eyes combed the crags and cliffs for people, but there were only rocks, fallen and broken clods of earth, shrubs and grass, and tall trees.

After passing a jagged escarpment flanking the white beach where his clothes were piled, he swam to shore, climbed out on the black, slippery rocks, and began moving from foothold to handhold up the cliff toward the woods. In the grass at the top he crossed the path on tiptoe, hoping that the dog wouldn't pass this way. Once in the woods behind the cliff, he made his way in the direction of the stream where he had left his pack.

The sound of water rushing through narrow chan-nels—splashing and tumbling over rocks, trickling into pools—led him through luminously green heart-shaped leaves to the cool stream. He sloshed through the water, barefoot and naked, looking for the bend where he'd stashed the pack. Then he saw it: the corner of a black plastic bag sticking out of a cage of yellow roots. He pulled the pack onto the bank. It had been untouched since he'd stashed it there long ago.

It was part of him. Something he'd lost and found again. He put his nose to it and smelled it. Then, fearing that the dog might have picked up his scent, he put it on and walked through the water upstream to the pool where they'd caught him that first night.

That night the pool had been dark and ugly. Now amber light came through openings in the trees, and he saw through the clear water to the soft red clay bottom. There were rocks and leaves on the bottom. The stream flowed out the other side and through the thick forest.

He climbed away from the water to the top of a rise in the forest, opened the pack, and pulled out all of his belongings.

He was exhausted. He didn't eat that night, but just barely managed to set the tent up under the cover of bushes and get into his sleeping bag. He didn't wake up until what he imagined to be well past noon. He didn't remember a single dream.

CHAPTER 25

HE stayed on the same rise three hundred yards from the stream for three days. There were no signs of dogs and search parties looking for him. Charles and the rest of his captors must have believed he had committed suicide after all. He ate the canned foods first, leaving the dehydrated foods for his hike. On the morning of the fourth day he packed up his belongings and began to walk toward the barracks near the mountain that Velman had indicated on his map for Michelman.

Everything assured him that there were no people in the woods. Startled deer stared at him curiously, their short white tails flickering timidly, before bounding off into the brush. Sometimes, though, he'd walk for hours without hearing a bird's trill, without seeing the soft yellow rays of the sun through the tips of the shadowy trees.

Before dark he came to a stand of cattails at the edge of a lake—the first clear space he'd seen since he'd started that morning and the first generous portion of sky for days. He looked at the clear beautiful lake through the tall, dead white trees of a marsh. There was no sign of a house or a person on it. Darkness was falling and he started walking around the edge of the lake. By the time he reached the other side, networks of dark insects skated over the reflection of stars. Mosquitoes came out. He set up his tent and got into it, zipping the door, then making his bed.

Despite walking all day he couldn't sleep at all. He found his shoes, climbed out of his bag, and put them on. At the lake's edge he sat down looking at the starlight on the water. A fish broke surface just offshore, its tail flipping, and then splashed. He heard another splash farther out.

The stars, perhaps because of a fine vapor rising from the cooling land, were not bright. He stared at them for a long while and felt himself getting smaller, shrinking on the log on which he sat.

In the morning, mounting his pack on his shoulders was difficult. His back and neck were sore, and so were his legs. After walking for an hour he found he was still exhausted from the night before. He hadn't really slept. He stopped, leaned his pack against a tall tree, got into his sleeping bag, and fell asleep much more easily now that it was light out. When he woke up he felt rested.

The sides of his feet were blistered from stepping on the uneven ground and the backs of his arms were crossed with scratches and scabs. He traveled along relatively flat land high up on the bank of a brook to a steep hill where the water came crashing down from rock to rock. Climbing the rocks, he saw a waterfall gushing over ledges into smaller pools.

Trees at the top of the hill were smaller than in the valley. He put his pack down, climbed one, and looked out over its branches to the mountain. The mountain was perhaps a little closer than a day ago, but it was still surprisingly far away. He looked the other way toward the ocean. He had walked at least twenty or thirty miles since the day before.

He climbed down the other side of the hill and walked through the dark green light of a valley to a small stream with fish facing into the current in shallow pools. In the leaves along the bank he found a large jagged rock. After searching the pools he spotted a trout big enough to eat. Alex brought the rock high over his head and threw it down with all his might. When the water cleared he saw the trout's white belly flashing as it darted between the dark green rocks. He lunged for it several times, then squeezed it tightly, and threw it into the ferns. It flopped feebly as he made his way up to it and grabbed it by the mouth and broke its neck. He used his knife to cut off its head and gut it, then he set up his propane stove and cooked it.

Late that afternoon he passed another lake, then walked for a long time without coming across water. Not seeing water made him worry. He didn't like to be right next to running water because the sound would block out other sounds and he was often afraid of something sneaking up on him, but he liked to know that drinking water and perhaps fish were nearby.

He became more and more afraid of darkness during his journey. One night he thought he heard a noise like somebody or something sneaking up on him. His fears built so in his head that he suddenly found himself shouting, "Get away from me! Get the fuck away from me!" He was certain that something was at the door of his tent, then he thought he could hear something breathing right at the mouth of his sleeping bag. He began shaking. Finally he pushed his head out of his bag and said, "Kill me! Kill me, go ahead, kill me!"

In the morning he got up and checked for footprints around the tent, but he found everything exactly as he'd left it. Even his dirty dishes, which may have attracted an animal, were in the same places as the night before. The next night he woke up in darkness and utter silence, a time when everything, both the night animals and the morning animals, were asleep, a time of such utter silence that it felt like he was the only one on the entire planet awake. He didn't think of Iris or of the past, only of the silence and the deadness of what lay around him.

He began to cry.

He cried until he fell asleep, and when he woke up it must have already been light out for hours, but he was still so tired that he could hardly move and getting the camp together again and moving on took him a long time. Late in the morning he stopped in a sunny spot, an opening in the trees where a meadow had grown up, and fell asleep and woke up in the afternoon in the shade, entirely rested now, but afraid that he wouldn't be able to sleep that night. He walked quickly the rest of the afternoon until dark fell, hoping to tire himself out, then he set up his tent and made a fire and sat feeding the flames for several hours. Before going to bed he took his flashlight out of his bag and began to walk through the dark. The thick, rotted trunk of a dead tree looked gnarled and nasty and had low brush around it. He stood behind the tree and said out loud, "You can kill me if you want, go ahead, do what you have to do to me. I'll be happy to die." Then he walked back through the brush and the low branches to his tent.

He woke up again that night: a person was walking through the brush. There was no question about it this time—it was not a dream, nor an illusion caused by fear. The footsteps were distinct and deliberate, they knew exactly where they were going. They were coming toward his tent. Alex jumped out of his bag and picked up his knife and his flashlight. He stood behind his tent in his socks and pants and shirt, and he held the knife in one hand, the flashlight in the other, but he didn't turn the light on. Instead he directed his eyes toward the dark where the person was walking.

"Who are you?" he yelled. "Don't come any closer."

The person stopped and was silent. Alex didn't turn on his light; he didn't want the intruder to know where he was. Then he heard brush breaking, and he knew that the person was running away. He flipped the light on, but saw only the top of some brush still shaking.

The rest of the night he stayed awake, sitting on a rock away from his tent with the sleeping bag draped over him. In the morning he fell asleep on the bare ground next to a tree and slept almost until noon. When he got up, he walked into the brush where he'd heard the footsteps. After combing the area past the dead tree, he found a shoe print. It had the same tread as his own, but it seemed a little bigger. He found another one where the man had obviously been running away. Alex looked around at the silent trunks of the trees, some light gray, others darker, then he looked up at the leaves that covered the sky.

CHAPTER 26

ALL afternoon he marched up the gradual slope. He came across rocks piled in a line and as he followed them he realized that the line was part of a collapsing stone wall at the base of a fallow field. He stashed his pack in the woods, climbed out to the border of the field, and stepped into the open. He could see over the hill to the mountain. It was far bigger than he had imagined it. The peak was above the timberline. There were patches of purple and blue and gray along its sides.

Below the field Alex saw a long house or a shed. He hid behind a stone wall and raised his eyes just over the rocks. He could see dark green army trucks in the yard on the other side. The building, probably the barracks that Velman had indicated on his map, looked like a long, dark brown warehouse.

A man came out of the back door carrying a huge kettle. Alex ducked out of sight, then sat up a little. The man poured water from the kettle over a wall, then returned to the barracks. He wore a white apron.

Alex went back to his belongings and took out the map and

examined it. He had definitely seen the barracks, but he thought he should investigate the area before joining the army. A dirt road ran behind the barracks, down into a valley, and up the side of the mountain. Alex rested, then put his pack on his back, circled the field and barracks until he was within sight of the dirt road, then followed the road keeping under cover of the trees. Twice he heard a car racing along next to him.

By late afternoon he reached the foot of the mountain. After climbing, he found a clearing with a view of the road. At the sound of another car coming down the mountain, he put his pack down and watched through the trees. An army jeep carrying three men in khaki uniforms passed quickly lifting dust.

Farther up the slope of the mountain, Alex came to the edge of a field. He could see a huge building that looked like a fortress or a château. The only visible opening in the tall gray stone walls was a black iron gate shaped like a church door that faced the valley. Keeping his cover, Alex skirted the field to where he had a better view of the medieval structure. There were men carrying rifles walking along the top of the walls; only their silver helmets were visible.

Alex heard the creak of metal and saw guards opening the black gate. A jeep came racing out followed by marching soldiers, at least sixty of them in brown khaki uniforms. Some held hats in their hands; others wore them. They followed the dirt road down the hill and through the field to the woods.

The rays of the sun grew long. The air was still. Alex went back into the trees to find a tent site and eat the last of his dehydrated dinners.

That night he could see the glow of the château lights over the treetops. He heard cars and trucks moving in and out, then all was quiet except the small animals and crickets close to him.

The next morning he moved around the château, peeking through leaves far across the yellow grass to the gray walls. Stone towers rose from all four corners. Two other entrances led into the sides; both were heavily guarded. Alex circled the building and when he returned to where he started he heard the sound of soldiers singing. The soldiers marched out of the woods on the dirt road from the barracks, dust lifting from their feet. They marched in a V formation, lifting their legs in unison and singing a song about a man—Alex could only hear the word *he* because it was the first word in the refrain. The gates opened and they passed inside.

Alex started through the woods for the barracks again.

Behind the barracks he found a secure place under a fallen tree to hide his belongings. He took out Velman's uniform and put it on, then gathered necessities—a change of clothing, his razor, toothbrush, and an extra pair of shoes—and put them in the pillowcase Evelyn had given him and climbed down to the dirt road.

He stepped onto the shoulder of the road. Over the lip of a hill, he could see the barracks' roof. He stopped and took a deep breath, then began to walk up the hill. He tried to lift his legs the way the soldiers had but after a few yards his knees began to feel weak and his hands were shaking.

He stepped back into the cover of the trees, climbed behind a rock, sat down, and closed his eyes. He tried to imagine the blue light he'd seen on the snow with Iris and what he'd said to her and the way he had felt then—*that's the way I must feel now,* he thought. But instead of calming down, his entire body went into a shaking fit and he could hear his teeth click together like toy windup teeth.

He got up again and began to pace between the leaves. His jaw felt numb to the touch, like it belonged to somebody else.

He became angry at himself, angry at his jaw for wanting to give him away. He forced his teeth together as hard as he could, stiffening the muscles so that they couldn't chatter. After a long while he let up. The chattering stopped for a moment, then commenced again.

He cut a branch from a beech tree, put the end in his mouth and bit down. He walked in a big circle under the trees, bearing down, tasting the juice from the sap. He could feel pain coming up from his jaw to his ear. He kept the pressure on the stick. His ear was aching, the whole side of his head throbbing. When he finally took the stick out, his entire jaw was so sore it was almost paralyzed. The chattering had stopped.

Crows flew off the side of the road as he approached the brown walls of the barracks where small square windows were covered with black wire mesh. He crossed a gravel lot and opened a screen door into a room with rows of bunk beds three high. The damp room smelled of soap. Most of the bunks were covered with brown blankets. Alex found a bare mattress and put his pillowcase down on it.

In the shower room that adjoined the barracks, water dripping from a leaking faucet echoed against the porcelain.

He found the door leading into the dining room. A man washing large gray pots in sudsy water glanced at him.

"Anything that I can do?" Alex asked. His jaw felt stiff and his voice sounded strange. It was the first time he had spoken to another person in many days. The man shut off the water and turned to him. He had a long Irish face. Dark greasy curls stuck to each other above his forehead.

"New here?" he asked.

"Just got in."

"You'll have enough to do once you get going."

"Where are the men?"

"Up on the mountain. They won't be back till supper time."

"You sure I can't do something?"

The man pointed out a sink of dirty pots and Alex started washing them.

At seven that evening the men began coming in through the bunk-room door. Their faces were dirty, streaked with sweat. They wore khaki shorts and tall boots, most carried a day pack, some carried canteens on their belts. They undressed and lined up for the shower. There were forty or fifty men but practically no conversation.

"Do you have my soap?" one man asked another man.

"I gave it back last night."

Alex lay in his bunk on his side watching the others. Nobody acted surprised that he was there.

Soon after they'd all finished showering, the dinner bell rang. A few men rushed out the door; others were still dressing. Alex crossed the mess hall and found a seat on a crowded bench. Eight men walked down the line of plates, scooping out potatoes and meat from pots on a metal cart.

"Did you report to the sergeant yet?" a soldier asked Alex after he was served.

Alex shook his head.

"You'd better do that before you get too far into your meal."

"Where's the sergeant's room?"

The soldier told him where the door was, and Alex left the mess hall. He found it: a pinewood door adjoining the bunk room.

He knocked.

"Who is it?"

"Brown, sir, new soldier," Alex said.

"Who sent you, Brown?"

"Volenti," Alex said. As soon as he said this one word, he realized his life depended on it. His teeth began chattering again and his hand went up to his jaw.

"Who?"

"Volenti."

"Just a minute."

The sergeant opened the door bare chested. "What's up, Corporal?" He was a middle-aged man with a powerfully built chest and a square face. His lower jaw jutted out slightly like a boxer's. He looked Alex up and down and laughed. "What the hell did Volenti send me you for? Does he think you can handle it?"

"It was my suggestion," Alex said.

"You sound awfully confident."

After dinner the soldiers made for the bunk room quickly, most undressing right away and getting into their beds. A few played cards. One man volunteered to help Alex get outfitted with a blanket, sheets, and clothes for the next day. After making his bed and putting his new clothes away, Alex got under the covers. He fell asleep almost immediately.

CHAPTER 27

A BUGLE woke him before the sun was up. The bunk lights came on; the men moved quickly, putting on running shorts, shirts, and sneakers. They gathered in rows five deep in the lot surrounded by army trucks. The sergeant, standing before them with a whistle in his mouth, led them through exercises. Then they sprinted down the wall of the barracks and out into the field in the back, falling into a line at the mouth of a path that led steeply down a hill through lush green trees.

Back at the barracks they were given breakfast and about ten minutes of rest. Soon they were outside again, marching down the dirt road. After several miles, they heard a jeep behind them and moved over. The sergeant passed them, tires kicking dirt high up in the air.

After a while the men began singing. *"We're off to see the flying man, the flying man, the flying man, we're off to meet the flying man . . . hello Mr. Volenti . . ."*

They came out at the bottom of the château field and approached the black iron gate on the dusty road. Guards stepped out of brass booths and opened the gates, and behind them Alex saw the sergeant standing in his clean khaki uniform with his hands behind his back, looking as if he had just eaten a big leisurely breakfast. He smiled at the men as they went in.

They came into a huge courtyard of white gravel surrounded by three levels of stone balconies. Everything appeared old and European. Gargoyles carved in stone, lion heads, and snake heads decorated the eaves and the balconies.

The men made for a statue in the center of the yard and began to drink from its streams of water. Before Alex drank, he noticed a disk-shaped object in the hand of the stone man.

He stared at it, then tapped a man who had wet his head and pointed at the object.

"What's that?"

"That?" the man said. He put his face right up to Alex's. "Where you from, lad?"

"A discus?"

The man slapped Alex's back. "Are you trying to be funny?"

"No." Alex continued staring at the object in the statue's hand.

After they had rested the sergeant led them into one side of the château and down a long dark corridor lined with paintings of large dark faces. They came into a kind of church with pews and high cathedral ceilings, and the soldiers spread out and sat down. On a raised platform in front of the pews where an altar might have been was a kind of pyramid. The pyramid consisted of successively smaller platforms stacked about eighteen feet high. Men stood on each level.

Once it was quiet the man at the very top opened a large black book.

"We're gathered here today as we are every day to pay tribute to that which is responsible for our very existence on this planet. But before I do that, I'd like to introduce to all of you some performers and actors of varying abilities.

"Though some of these men are better performers than others, all of you should be aware that every man standing up here is better than any single one of you. But all of these men started in the position you are in today: as foot soldiers.

"Not one of these men, myself included, were given any advantages in the beginning; we had only ourselves and our intuition to go by. Our first contact with the stage came in much the same manner your first contact with the stage should come, and that is with your feet facing down. It was only with the utmost patience and practice that we were finally able to achieve the positions you see us in right now. It is safe to say that you have all probably heard rumors about performers or actors who have shot to the higher stages, such as the one on which I am standing, and you probably believe that they were able to achieve these positions without going through all of the stages you see below me. Dispel these rumors from your mind. Even the Great Edward Volenti I of noble birth had to do exactly what you are doing right now. It's not an easy process, believe us."

The man paused and looked up from the book.

"You must be prepared to give your life when it is necessary to give your life. You cannot think of yourself as anything more than the platform on which you stand. Perhaps that platform will make demands on you, perhaps not. But you must be ready to obey it at any given time.

"It's not easy; it's not something you're used to. You've had no practice doing it. Look at yourselves, look at your neighbor: just an ordinary man who has come from an ordinary place, perhaps the suburbs, the city, or even a small country town." The man next to Alex started looking at him. Alex turned the other way; the other man on the other side of him was looking at him also. "He is not used to thinking that he himself is great, that he himself might even be a genius. He might have thought of himself as being very good at something, sports or business. But I am quite certain that he never thought of himself as great. And yet all of you can be great, not just the men who stand with me on the stage, but even you men, the foot soldiers."

The men were given a short break. Most took out cigarettes and sat around the courtyard. Some wandered around the château in pairs or alone. Alex put his foot at the edge of the fountain next to an old woman with dark, bold features washing clothes. She had wrapped a gypsy's kerchief tightly around her head. Gold hoop earrings dangled against her neck.

"Hot day," Alex said quietly. The woman looked up at him, then back down at the wet dress she pressed against the stone. Alex stood closer to the woman. "Do you speak English?" he asked.

"No," she said.

Alex took his foot down, turned, and walked away.

The men were gathering in a group on the far side of the courtyard. Alex joined them just as they were passing back outside through a side gate and into the hot sun.

They marched into the field of a hill, spreading out in a wide line. Dust lifted from their feet. Alex turned and looked behind him through the cloud of dust to the château. Guards wearing fatigues and holding automatic rifles were lined up against the wall watching the soldiers.

The hill the soldiers were climbing was bigger than it had looked from the bottom. The boots of the men raised so much dust that some of the soldiers put bandannas over their mouths. Most spread out so as not to be behind anyone. At the top, Alex could see back to the walkways on top of the château walls; at least thirty guards were up there, all carrying guns and wearing helmets.

On the other side of the hill, Alex saw down to a line of woods where objects with wheels, perhaps pieces of farm equipment, were parked. Closer, he saw that they were two-wheeled circular platforms, each with a long shank. "Our lovely stages!" one soldier yelled. Others began to laugh as if there were jokes among them about the stages. "Old Faithful, she's mine," one man hollered. There were also the Iron Horse, the Trojan War-rior, the Occidental. The men spread out, pulling pale red man-nequins from compartments underneath. The mannequins were faceless and hairless and stripped of clothes. Soldiers got on top of the stages, others handed the mannequins up. There were holes in the feet of the mannequins and holes on the wooden surfaces of the stages. Alex stood below, helping to hand the figures up. At last three of the faceless figures were bolted tightly to each platform.

Once everything was assembled, the men gathered around the shanks, two or three on each side, and silently watched the horizon of sparse dry grass at the top of the hill. A galloping horse appeared, ridden by a man dressed in full knight's armor who held a forked flag. A huge cloud of dust followed him. He stopped on the horizon; the dust caught up; for an instant just the horse and rider's silhouette appeared before the sky in the dirty air.

The knight dropped the flag below the neck of his horse, sig-naling the men to pull the shanks of the stages with all their might up the hill. As Alex joined in, a soldier ran ahead and waved for one group to pull harder, another to slow down, keeping them perfectly abreast of each other. Alex's arms and shoulders burned with pain. His mouth was parched, and the sun beat down on the back of his neck.

"Let's go, new guy!" the leader yelled at him.

Before they reached the top of the hill, the leader yelled, "About face!" The soldiers holding the shanks swung the stages around rapidly, almost knocking Alex onto his back.

"Heads down," the leader called.

With their eyes to the ground, they pushed the stages up the rest of the way. The sun scorched Alex's neck, and the wheels stirred dust around him. He felt the pressure of the shank lessen as they came to the top of the hill.

There was a command to halt. The men stopped, dropping the shanks, and lay down in the dust. Next to Alex a man buried his face in his arms, and Alex did the same. Soon he heard the horse's hooves galloping around the stages. The horse stopped near Alex, its hooves dancing near his head, then it galloped away down over the hill.

A whistle blew. When Alex looked up, the men were standing, holding their ends of the shanks again.

"Retreat!"

They walked the stages down the hill, leaning back against the weight.

In the courtyard, an army truck from the barracks was parked to one side. Next to it, a small tent had been erected on the white gravel. Oatmeal was served in tin bowls. Alex waited in line, then walked over into the shade with the other men. His arms and legs were so sore he could barely sit down.

After lunch the men appeared refreshed and ready for more maneuvers, but Alex felt dizzy. He dropped his bowl off in a barrel, found the soldier who had taken him to the supply room the night before, and asked him where he could find a bathroom.

Like everything else in the château the bathroom was designed for a king. Mosaics of hieroglyphic patterns had been laid into the floor with light blue and green tiles. Alex turned a brass door handle to one of the stalls and saw a toilet built high off the floor with light blue porcelain armrests on both sides and metal footrests like on a barber's chair. He closed the stall door, sat down, and waited until he was sure the men were gone.

Circus World Museum, Baraboo, Wisconsin.

CHAPTER 28

HE thought he would try to comb the château for evidence of Iris as systematically as possible. He started trying doors along the bottom floor hallways.

He quickly searched the halls on all three floors. Most of the room doors were locked, others were just storage rooms, a few were bedrooms. He rifled through a desk in an office and found two lists, one of men's names, another of women's. Iris's was not on the latter.

He continued on, stopping to look at the large portraits on the walls. At first glance they looked old, but on closer inspection the yellow light on the side of the subjects' dark faces had perhaps been made yellow on purpose and was not due to the effect of aging.

As he walked down the hall, a door opened and a short, plump woman with yellow hair backed out, pulling a tall trash can on wheels and a cart with a feather duster, sponges, and aerosol cans on it. She was jingling keys in her hand. Alex backed into an alcove built into the wood paneling along the hallway.

"Hey, Kala," somebody called from the end of the hallway.

"Yes, dear?" the woman said.

"I can't get this lid off."

"I told you to use my screwdriver."

"It just puts holes in it."

"All right, hold on." Leaving her cleaning implements behind, the woman walked down the hallway.

Alex slipped through the door she had come out of and hid just on the other side of a grandfather clock. After a moment, the short woman came back and locked the door.

He was in a den or a study with black leather furniture, dark red walls, and many bookshelves. A dark red writing desk stood before a fireplace with a musket hanging over the mantle. On the desk were beautiful lamps with lampshades of animal skins delicately decorated with circus scenes, a sword swallower, a juggler, a fire-eater. A birch bark cup held quills and a brass letter opener.

Alex picked up a brass plaque with a name on it and turned it around. Edward Volenti, it read.

As he stared at it the room that he was in seemed to darken. Looking up slowly, he saw the slitted face mask of a full suit of dark silver armor standing next to the fireplace. He had been half aware of it staring across the room at him. The knight held a spear adorned with striped feathers of faded colors. On the mantel behind it was a mounted eagle in flight, wings raised and claws extended, piercing yellow eyes, its sharply hooked beak open for prey.

The smells of the room became deeper, darker, more menacing, and more forbidden. Encroaching on him were the rich fragrances of oiled leathers, overripe tobacco, dry animal hair. He could smell shoes and dirty boots, a warehouse full of dirty boots. At his feet he saw a thick rug made from the skin of a polar bear. On the dark chestnut walls were masks from Africa, China, India, the Middle East. Mounted between them were shields of wood and silver, some with battle scenes carved into them, others with mandalas. High above, near the hand-hewn rafters of the room, Alex saw mounted dry and dusty animal heads. A hippopotamus, a gazelle, a water buffalo.

On a low iron table in one corner he found a collection of medieval torture devices, leather straps and whips, prods and pokers, crude chains for the ankles and feet. The table itself, Alex realized, was a stretching device with iron bracelets for the wrists and ankles.

Between the blades of two silver swords mounted on the wall, Alex saw a map of a circus and its grounds.

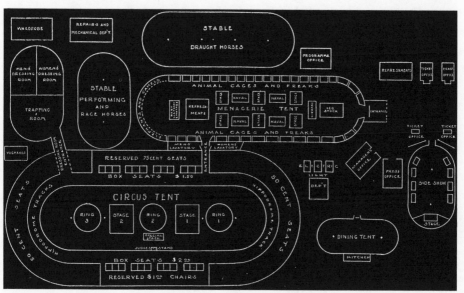

Circus World Museum, Baraboo, Wisconsin.

Moving farther along the wall, his eyes fell on a framed hand-written letter on crumbling yellow paper.

Edward Volenti,
*   Our generals have spoken so highly of your contributions regard-*
ing troop movement that we're at a loss as to how to thank you.
Currently, as you may have guessed, many of our campaigns are

born directly from the information you supplied. We feel that it's nothing short of a miracle that you're on our side. You're a great man.

Eleanor and I would be deeply gratified if you and your lovely wife would care to join us for a visit or for dinner or for whatever you wish.

Best,
Franklin D. Roosevelt

Next to this was a black-and-white photograph of two men. One was a circus acrobat, possibly a trapeze artist, the other looked by his vestments to be a Catholic priest. The trapeze artist was sitting on a swing about four feet off the ground, and the priest was standing next to him. In the background Alex could see a circle of people looking on. At their feet was a circus ring.

A carved wooden door opened into a closet. Inside he saw, hanging from the bar, circus costumes of varied styles and faded colors, most with tiny black moth holes and tarnished silver buttons. Bending down to the floor, he picked up a pair of silver shoes marked with a tag. The tag read: Perriot's Slippers.

Next to the closet, another door led into a bedroom with a canopy bed. Alex switched on an electric chandelier and crossed to the chest on the other side of the bed and opened one of the drawers. There were black socks in one. From the other he picked up a pair of old cotton underwear and shook the dust from it.

Under a lamp on the table next to the bed, he saw a black book, a photo album. When he opened it, his eye fell to a photograph of a young girl with curly hair and glasses no more than twelve years old. She was standing under a tree between a ragged rosebush and a fountain with a small pink statue of a naked boy in its center. The eyes of the young girl behind the thick lenses of her glasses looked studious and sad.

Alex held the album up to the light. The girl in the yellow, grainy, unfocused photograph looked exactly like Iris might have looked twenty years or so before. Alex laughed at the similarity of the young girl to Iris, then he turned the page.

He saw another picture of the twelve-year-old girl, but in this one she must have been at a Catholic school because she was among a group of girls her age all wearing the same white blouses and red skirts with insignias near the hem. He turned the page again and saw more pictures of the young girl in uniform with her friends. In each shot, the camera-shy little girl smiled out at him. He turned the page again and loose black-and-white pictures fell into his hand.

The photos, shot from random angles, were of people walking down sidewalks in New York. Shuffling through them Alex's hand stopped on a picture of a woman walking quickly down the sidewalk. Her legs and arms were blurred but her upper body and face were in focus. She looked exactly like Iris. Behind her he saw familiar glass doors, doors that he knew so well that he couldn't figure out exactly how he knew them. Then, behind the door's reflection, he made out a familiar man. It was Mr. Lovlor sorting through a handful of mail. These were the doors to his own apartment building.

Madly he shuffled through the loose photographs, dropping them on the floor as he went. One photograph after the next, haphazardly taken, showed Iris from a distance walking in or out of buildings. He remembered the dresses that she wore. In one photograph she had cut the curls of her hair short and he could remember the time she had come home with her hair short and straight like a boy's.

He scattered the photographs on the bed and crawled over them, lifting them up and dropping them.

They were candidly taken of her on the street. Somebody had been spying on her.

He turned around as if the person who had been behind the camera was standing right behind him. He ran to the door and looked into the empty den. Then he ran back to the photographs.

In one she was among many people on a crowded sidewalk in New York, perhaps Fifth Avenue. Also on the sidewalk were two white businessmen in suits, a black messenger, an oriental man, and an Indian in the crowd. Behind these people surrounding Iris a marker had circled a face. Bringing it up to the light, Alex saw his own face sandwiched between the shoulders of the pedestrians. The two businessmen engaged in conversation were sharply defined in the foreground, but his own face was slightly out of focus. If not for the circle he would not have noticed it. His mouth was open slightly, and his eyes were dark and out of focus.

Another photograph, taken from behind, showed him and Iris holding hands climbing the steps of a building that looked like City Hall. City Hall was where they had gotten married. He tried to remember what they were wearing that day, but couldn't. Again the photograph had been taken candidly, the angle tilted. He sorted through the rest of the pictures. He could not remember any single one of the random shots as a particular moment in time. He was either walking down a street or entering a building.

He began sweating and shaking with excitement. He kept picking up photographs. "Spying on us, Volenti was spying on us!" he said out loud. He threw the photographs down and picked them up, threw them down and picked them up. Then he turned and looked into the warlike den. He wanted to shout at Edward Volenti. "Now I know something about you. Now I'm beginning to understand you."

Turning back into the bedroom, he reached for drawers in a

tall chest. He opened one after the next leaving them open. But they were all empty. He ran to the doors around the bedroom. They opened into closets, most of them empty. In one he rifled through the pockets of a few large suits hanging from the racks. The dust from the fabric made him sneeze.

He moved back into the den. He rifled through the desk, but found it empty of articles except for scraps of paper, pencils with hardened erasers, and pens with dried ink. The urgency of his search mounted. He lifted rugs and the mattress of the bed, opened the bottom door of the grandfather clock, but he found no more pictures of people, nothing that would tell him anything about Volenti nor give a reason for the pictures of him and Iris.

After he put everything back into its place he went to the bookshelf and began flipping through the books. His finger stopped on one entitled *Edward Volenti I.*

He opened it to a random page. "Chapter Ten: Character Adjustments." A thin white sheet of paper protected a faint old photograph. Adjacent to it the text began:

Sometimes the performer will find he has taken a role so unsuited to his nature that every attempt to descend into that role, to become that showman, is foiled by some problem, hitherto unheard of by the performer (*see illustration*).

Lifting the protective paper, he saw a picture of a very large man in a long coat wearing a fedora and holding his left leg. He was standing inside a ring. The caption under the photograph read: "Performer in pain because of abrasive character role." On the following page, under another piece of white paper, Alex saw a picture of a large woman in a long gray coat, lying back on what looked like an operating table. Her feet in high heels hung from the end of the table. "Undiagnosed pain (possibly due to lack of character assertion)," the caption read.

A chapter further into the book was entitled "Sexual Energy." The text began:

> Although it is commonly felt that those performers who are most comfortable with members of the opposite sex are also those who are the most malleable, most suited to the profession of performance, we contend that this may be indeed a falsehood. In truth, the opposite is more often the case than the exception.

Flipping further into the book, he found a series of case studies conducted on a few of the apparently numerous members of Volenti's ancestry. In one case, a man stood with his hands at his sides and his feet close together. Directly over his head a tiny bird perched on a thin trapeze swing suspended from two very fine, almost invisible wires. The caption read:

> *Volenti did not merely find women disagreeable; he found it impossible to occupy the same room, the same house with a woman. But the ring was the one place he could open up (see diagram #2).*

The second picture, more faded than the first, was of the same man standing among five other women, all as big or bigger, with their dresses on, than he was. Under the picture it said, "Volenti: Fear of women overcome in the ring." One of his arms was raised like an Olympic athlete and a smile had formed on his face. "Triumph!" had been written in pencil in the margins.

He turned to another page.

> He was a twisted fellow, but he lived in twisted times. It is said that without the proper role model Volenti could not himself survive anywhere else but in the ring. His diaries at the time read as follows: "What a relief from the gray boredom of the chores of home life to step out into the ring. It's better than taking my life, it's even better than going to war. Well, I hope I meet a woman I like. I have found it too difficult to even look at a woman, let

alone talk to one. I'll get it right, someday, maybe in another life."

On another page there were line diagrams of Volenti from the side and from the front. There were waist, chest, leg, and arm measurements. Alex turned back a page. "The Physical Makeup of a Performer," the chapter heading read.

You must understand that everything that exists exists within time and space. The performer has no more of a right to claim physical immortality than other artists. It is hoped by some of the best performers that their acts will leave such a bold imprint on the spectators that their images will take on lives of their own, not unlike books or paintings, that their images will be passed from generation to generation. It is thought by the authors of this book that such a wish is folly. Even if such a thing were possible, it does not concern the performer, and should not concern the performer. The only goal of performance is to have no goal at all. To live fully in the present. The diagram on the following page shows the body of Volenti. It is thought by many that if his body had been an eighth of an inch wider, or thinner, or longer, then his capabilities as a performer would have been null and void. This is also folly, although of a different nature.

He turned to the final page.

EPILOGUE

We make no contention that Edward Volenti is a great performer, or even that he is a performer of high rank. But we will say that he is an unusual performer, one who is worth studying. The following is a list of questions. The student of performance would do well to write them down and memorize them. The questions are meant for both the amateur and the professional, the novice and the advanced.

1. Did Volenti ever cry in the ring?
2. Was Volenti ever generous to anyone in the ring or out?
3. Did he perform merely to get an effect?
4. Did he really hate women?
5. Did Volenti feel he was the only person to climb into the ring and sing?

Once having memorized these lines, the performer would do well to practice his part as if the questions didn't exist at all. The performer would do well not to mention these questions to any other performers or persons connected with the circus. The performer would do well not to discuss the name Volenti in the company of anyone but a master performer. It has been predicted that master performers are a dying breed, that master performers will not be around forever. If that is the case, then the following instructions may be followed by the student of the future. While in the ring, do not think of your friends, do not think of anyone who is neutral to you. Think only of your enemies. Do not try to befriend your enemies. Keep them as far as possible from you physically, but do not hesitate to fight with them in your mind. Use this method of discourse to distract yourself from the task at hand. Nothing can be said about the task at hand. Indeed, the task of the ring is none other than the task of the ring. It does not refer to anything else than what it is.

He put the book back onto the shelf. Once more he returned to the photo album and sorted through the pictures. He still could not think of a reason for them.

A photograph fell from the pile into his hand, one that he hadn't seen before. It showed a telescopic close-up just of Iris's face. He put it into his uniform shirt pocket.

After pressing his ear to the door to listen for people, he unlocked it, turned the knob and slipped out.

He thought he should get back to the barracks. But soon he heard footsteps, and a thin woman with long dark hair and black sunglasses rounded the corner of a hallway quickly. Alex turned his face and pretended to be looking at the paintings. After she passed he followed her.

"Excuse me," he called.

She stopped, swung around, and looked at him. He had no idea what her face might have looked like behind such dark glasses.

"Briefly," Alex said. "I'm looking for a woman named Iris. She may be with Mr. Volenti, I'm not sure."

He opened his palm and showed her the close-up photo.

"What's your name, sir?" the woman said, looking up at his face.

"Brown."

"Are you with Sergeant Berringer?"

Alex nodded. "Yes, of course, but I just need to know if she's here, that's all. I have no intention of contacting her or anything. Just curiosity, you know."

"Your first name, Corporal Brown?"

"Alex. Please, couldn't you tell me if she's around? I have a message for her, actually."

"Wait here, Corporal, until I contact your sergeant." The woman turned, and Alex could see her vague reflection on the shiny dark tiles of the hall as she walked quickly for a door.

Once she was gone he ran downstairs, crossed the courtyard to the gates and called through the black bars to one of the guards. Several of them came over.

"I'm sorry. I was in the bathroom—I'm new here—I couldn't leave the john—I've been sick—I've got to get back to the barracks."

He was so scared that he must have looked pale and sick. The guards let him out and he started down the hill, following the dirt road through the field to the woods.

As he lay on his bunk he heard trucks pull up outside the barracks, doors slam, and soon the men were coming into the bunk
room and undressing. Alex rested, looking up at the bed board
of the bunk above him.

"Sergeant wants to see you," somebody shouted in his ear.
He saw the slightly gleeful face of a big soldier whose name he
had already learned was Blair. He was a soldier whom all the
others admired and followed. "He's in his rooooooooom!"

Alex got up, went to the pinewood door, and knocked.

"Come in," Berringer called.

Alex opened the door.

"Ah, Corporal Brown, you're here." Berringer was sitting on
the corner of an office desk that faced the doorway. There was
a neatly made bed to his left. Pine boards paneled the walls
behind it.

"I'm sick," Alex said. "Sorry I couldn't stay with the other
men."

"You've got a lot of nerve, Corporal. I've had a report that
you've been asking for a woman."

"I'm sorry." Alex looked down.

"Who were you asking for? I heard you were asking for a
woman by the name of Iris."

"Iris?" Alex said, his voice trembling. "She must mean
Irene—that's who I said, she's an old friend of mine."

"You've got a friend here?"

"Yes. I'm pretty sure she's here. I thought she was here."

"If you ask for her again, you'll be punished—severely punished. Do you understand what that means or should I give you
a demonstration?"

"I apologize," Alex said again.

"You're a soldier now, soldier." Berringer raised his voice.
"But if you don't watch out, not only might you be severely
punished but you might be out of the army on your ear. On
your ear!"

"Yes."

Berringer got up from his desk and waved for Alex to follow him. They went outside along the back wall of the barracks to a small wooden structure that looked like an outhouse. A board rested across the door and Berringer lifted it. The door swung open.

"Step in, soldier."

There were no windows, just air holes in the rear and on the ceiling. Alex started to ask how long he'd have to stand in here but Berringer slammed the door shut, dropped the board across it, and walked away, leaving him in darkness.

The walls that Alex was pressed against were as sturdy as brick. Finally he tried to make himself comfortable, but there was no way to sit down and hardly enough ceiling room to lean back—he was already crouched over. He tried to slump, but his knees pressed into the door in front of him; standing up and keeping his head bent would be the only tolerable position.

In front of the box he could hear a vent fan whirring on the barracks' wall. Trucks came in and out of the yard, and doors slammed. Then he heard the footsteps of a man who may not have known somebody was in the box. "Tuna," the man kept saying to himself. "Tuna, tuna, tuna."

Later Alex heard him come by again. "Marlin," the man said.

"Marlin?" Alex called. "Do you know a man named Marlin?"

The man's footsteps came toward the box. "Who said that?" the man said.

"In here. Do you know Marlin?"

"Is somebody in there?" the man said, slapping the boards of the box.

"Do you know Marlin?"

"Flounder is a much better dish," the man said. Laughing to himself, he walked off.

After a while the dinner bell rang. He could hear the men going into the dining room, then a door must have been closed because there was silence except for the vent fan. Through the air holes Alex could see that the sun was down. Not only were his neck, back, and knees in pain but he felt extremely hungry.

Long after dinner must have been over, footsteps approached his box. The wooden crosspiece was lifted and the door opened. The sergeant was standing there with a cigarette in his mouth. He took a drag, dropped it into the grass, and stepped on it, then turned and walked away.

CHAPTER **29**

DO you love the stage?" the man on top of the pyramid of stages asked the congregation of soldiers the next day in the château. A different set of performers were standing on all the different levels. "If you don't love the stage you have no business in uniform. If the first thought that came to your mind was anything else but 'I love the stage' then you're doing something seriously wrong.

"I ask you now to trust us; we are not your enemy; all you have to do is speak the truth and we'll be able to help you. Believe me, we want you to succeed, for only then will we succeed."

The third soldier down from Alex stood up. His hands and legs trembled as he grasped the pew in front of him. The speaker in the robe nodded his head as if to acknowledge the man. "Come forth," he said. The speaker's voice echoed. The soldier was so nervous that he stumbled as he made his way past the other soldiers and into the aisle. The speaker called, "Somebody help the man."

Two soldiers propped the man up from under the arms and led him down the polished aisle to the bottom stage. The speaker came down the stages and whispered something in the man's ear, then pointed toward the top stage. The speaker looked out into the audience. "You see, the power of the stage calls this man." The two supporting soldiers left the soldier near the speaker. The speaker whispered again to the man and pointed toward the top stage. The man fell to his knees, crying, and laid half of his body on the bottom stage. The speaker climbed the stages to the top stage, turned, and looked out into the chapel. "Our soldier is confused. There is room on this island even for those who are confused; there is a place for everyone in the compound, everyone."

The soldier sobbed against the bottom stage. The speaker went on with his speech; then, as if the man's sobs were part of his speech, he stopped speaking and let the sobs take over. The soldier's sobs grew louder and became more hysterical. They reached a crescendo, then died down. When all was quiet, the speaker seemed to bow.

"You must understand your role here as foot soldiers is to love the stage, to worship the stage, to be willing to exert yourselves physically for the stage, to be willing to kill for the stage."

The man was silent. The word *kill* echoed against the stone walls. The man raised his arm. "Is it necessary to hurt people to progress as a performer? It may be necessary to hurt people to progress as a performer. Is it necessary to inflict wounds on other people who would otherwise be close to you? It may be necessary to inflict wounds on other people who would otherwise be close to you. If you've chosen the profession of performance, is it safe to assume that you are a person of little or no love for others?

"Please listen to these words. They are important words. If your love for the stage doesn't supersede everything that you value in life, then now is the time to admit it to yourself and to others. There are others who want your places. I assure you, you won't be exiled from this great island; all we'll have to do is find out what you really desire."

———

The sun in the courtyard was bright. Alex sat near the men, not next to them but close enough to hear what they were saying. They were smoking and laughing, speaking of the stage, speaking of it as if it were a person.

They started across the field and up the hill, the dirt and dust rising into the air, the sun getting hotter and hotter. Alex heard snips of conversation about the stage and man's duty toward it. They got down to the shanks of the stages resting in the tall grass at the edge of the field, made themselves into teams, and started hauling them up the hill.

CHAPTER 30

AS the days passed, Alex used every free moment to inquire about Iris. During breaks he'd quickly stroll to various wings of the château and peek into rooms. If a group of men and women were passing he'd try to follow behind them to determine what they were talking about.

But he learned nothing more than he had learned the day he got into Volenti's chambers. He kept the picture of Iris with him at all times. Moments alone he took it out and stared at it. He wondered who had taken it.

"How do you like it here?" Berringer asked him one night as he was returning to the bunk room from the dining room.

"I like it enough," Alex said.

"Have you got a future in it?"

"A future? Yes, pretty much."

"You're looking forward to the future?"

"Yes, but I'm anxious to meet Mr. Volenti. I've heard talk of him, but where is he?"

"You see, you're overstepping your bounds right there. Who says Mr. Volenti wants to meet you? You're a soldier now, soldier. You start thinking of those other things then you're going to lose it, lose everything that you have here."

"But where is the old man?"

"Are you doing this on purpose, are you taunting me?"

"No. I just was curious, that's all. I just don't understand why I can't know who I'm working for."

"Follow me, Corporal." The sergeant pinched his shirtsleeve and led him from the bunk room to the box outside. "Get in there."

Crouching down, Alex got in and the door was closed.

"Some just never learn," he heard the sergeant say as he walked away.

That night long after lights had been turned off, Alex lay awake in his bunk unable to sleep because of the sore neck and shoulders he had gotten in the box. He stared at the plywood board under the mattress of the bunk above him and thought of his wife. He heard the creak of wooden planks. Two soldiers filed through the door to the yard, and Alex recognized the silhouette of Blair and Blair's best friend, Fletcher, a slightly thinner man with a long, narrow closely shaven head.

The next day he overheard a conversation about a hospital and understood that the two men had been there visiting the nurses the night before. During a rest stop on the way back from the château, Alex whispered to Fletcher, "Are you going tonight?"

Fletcher was taken aback.

"I'll come," Alex said. "Are you leaving tonight?"

"Yes, tonight."

He kept himself from falling asleep by exercising his memory, going over things he and Iris had done together in the city. He'd take an unmemorable night, such as a night at the movies, and try to recall every single thing they had done on the way there: who had been sitting across from them on the bus, the weather,

everything they'd said to each other before and after, even what
he was thinking during the show, perhaps what she had been
thinking. But his thoughts kept coming back to the photographs
he had seen in Volenti's chambers.

Boards creaked as Blair and Fletcher crept from their bunks.
Alex got up, following them out the back door into the moonlit
yard. Hearing Alex's footsteps, Blair sprinted into the woods
with Fletcher following. Alex crept from tree to tree, whispering, "It's only me, Brown."

They went back to the sergeant's jeep at the edge of the clearing. Blair took it out of gear, while Alex and Fletcher pushed
it across the clearing onto the dirt road and then down the hill.
Far down the hill, away from the barracks, Blair turned the key
and popped the clutch. Soon they were moving very quickly,
hanging on tightly to the seats and roll bar.

At the bottom of the hill, Blair turned sharply onto a road
that skirted the edge of a swamp. The jeep lunged in and out of
puddles. A chorus of frogs filled the air in great waves. Finally
the road narrowed to a logging trail overgrown with seedlings
and grass, walled in by pines. Alex turned his back to break the
cool wind and watched the ground rushing away under the red
glow of the taillights.

They drove over a collapsed stone wall, stopping and shutting
off the jeep at the bottom of a field. It was safer to walk from
here, Fletcher told Alex, the hospital was just over the crest of
the hill.

Alex's shoes and pants quickly became soaked by the long
wet grass of the field. Over the hill's crest he saw the hospital,
a small, white cement-block building, rectangularly shaped,
adorned only with chimneys and crooked silver vents on the
roof. Puffs of silvery blue steam issued from the vents into the
moonlight.

Alex jogged to keep up. They crawled through a hole in a tall
wire mesh fence into the backyard of the hospital, then descended steps to a basement door propped open with a shingle.

A pale lightbulb illuminated a dirty brown boiler room. Blair went ahead, climbing a flight of wooden steps to the floor above.

"They're all starved to see men, especially soldiers," Fletcher whispered to Alex. "Just pretend you're a patient. Go to any floor, wander around, you'll see. If they like you, they'll take you in. But be back here in an hour."

Blair came down the wooden steps with three white hospital gowns, the kind that are open in the back. They changed into them, draping their khaki army clothes on dirty chairs and pipes around the damp, musty basement, then climbed the stairs into the fluorescent light of a linoleum and cement-block hallway. Alex could smell medicines, antiseptics, clean sheets. A woman's voice crackling from a loudspeaker paged a doctor. Nurses in white uniforms and caps pushed a cot on which lay an elderly patient. The three soldiers stepped aside to allow them passage. A nurse with rich brown hair and scarlet cheeks glanced up and smiled at Blair, who smiled back, then turned to Fletcher and winked.

Blair and Fletcher started down the hall, feigning wounds. Blair limped conspicuously; Fletcher hid his arm under his gown as if it hung from a sling. Alex twisted his foot around as he stepped.

They passed a nurse carrying a clean plastic bedpan, another a handful of linens. A doctor, a young man with glasses, strolled by, studying figures on a clipboard, unaware of the soldiers who peeled off into rooms one at a time until Alex, limping alone, stopped and pressed the silver button of an elevator. On the second floor he limped down another identical hallway.

Somebody caught his elbow from behind—a young nurse with long dark hair and silvery white skin. "Turn here." She pointed to a bed in a deserted hospital room.

Alex sat on the white sheets. The nurse closed the door behind them. "You're a soldier?" she said. "What's your name?"

"Brown, Corporal Brown," Alex said.

"Mine is Ava." She had a bright white smile and beautiful

dark moist eyes. She walked over to him, her arms to her sides as if to give him her body. "It's not every nurse who gets to talk to a soldier as handsome as you."

He smiled; he had not been called handsome by a woman other than Iris in a long time. Hearing these soft, salubrious words, he suddenly felt that they were words that had not been spoken to him in many years but that he had desperately and secretly desired for a long, long time.

He stood up and went to the window, looking through his dark reflection to the mountain. A few yellow lights speckled the valley mostly covered with dark trees. The mountain's purple slopes reached up into the night sky, the moon settling over its peaks. "How long have you been here?" he asked. He could see her reflection next to his; she was still sitting on the bed.

"About a year," she said.

"Do you like your job?" he asked.

"Why do you ask?"

"I don't like mine."

"Don't you like being a soldier? I thought you had to like it."

"No," he said. Her white reflection disappeared into his as she got up and came toward him. Turning from the window, he looked into her face; there was an eagerness in her countenance, a desire to please him, but there was something else too, some sadness that Alex felt was distancing her from him. He looked for the malice he had seen in the others' faces, for the animosity he believed to be in the expressions of everyone on the island, but all he saw was her soft white skin, her beautiful dark wet eyes, and the gleam of her black hair.

"Aren't you afraid of telling somebody that?" she asked.

"Not you," he said. "You don't seem like the type to turn somebody in."

"You happen to be right, but be more careful," she said. He felt guilt rising up in him; he'd been looking at her too long; her beauty was taking him over.

"I'd like to ask you a question," he said. "It's just something I've been curious about for a while. Have you ever heard of a woman named Iris Barton? Is she on this island?"

"Is she somebody you like?" she asked.

"I have a message from somebody on the outside who knows her."

"I think I've heard of her—she's an actress, isn't she?"

"That's the one," Alex said.

"From New York?"

"You know her?" He placed a trembling hand on the window sill to steady himself.

"I don't know if she's here. I saw her in a play in New York a long time ago."

"You haven't seen her here?"

"I just know her name, that's all." Ava took his arm. "Are you all right?" She brought him over to the bed; he placed his hand on the clean white sheets and looked back at the window. He could see only himself in the reflection.

"She makes me curious," he said, composing himself again. "I've read a lot about her."

"You've read a lot about her?"

"You know, as an actress," he said. "You see, I—" His words stumbled out of his mouth. "I . . . I had a dream about her once." He had not wanted to speak of her even like this. He tried to laugh to show how ridiculous he knew it was. "One time I dreamed we were lovers, that we lived together in New York, and that we were going to have a family." He turned to Ava. She waited eagerly to hear his story. "I dreamed that we were in love and nothing could separate us, nothing in the world; it was us against the world and I dreamed about holding her every night and falling asleep and waking up and kissing her and smelling her skin. Her skin smelled like clean sand from a beach cleared by dark waves from a tumultuous storm." He stopped and looked at her. She was nodding her head gently. "A family, we were going to have a family, a real family, a real live family.

That's what I wanted. That's what she wanted. That's what we wanted. We wanted a family, because we hadn't had a family, we'd never had a family, neither of us had. Not a real family . . . We were both—you know, we hadn't had one, we were brought up without one." He stopped when he couldn't utter another word, when he felt that if he uttered another word he'd break down and cry in front of her.

After silence, she said, "Are you sure you want to meet her?"

"Oh, yes."

"If you dream so strongly about a person then she'd probably not match up to your expectations."

"Oh, expectations. I haven't any of those," he said. He almost started to laugh. Ava looked at him curiously. "No, no. Not anymore," he said.

"I'll look for her for you then," she said quietly.

"You'll what?"

"I'll look for her."

"Would you?"

"Yes. I'll help you find her."

Alex looked down and saw the glowing face of his watch. Somehow over an hour had already gone by. He got up in a panic, turned to her before he left, then ran to the door.

The field outside the hospital was wet from the dew. A mist hung in the tall grass. Sitting down on the backseat of the jeep, he felt moisture from dew soak into the seat of his pants. He heard footsteps and turned. Blair and Fletcher were running quickly over the hill. They split up before the jeep, one climbing up the hill through the tall dead grass, the other leaping a stone wall, crashing down through the brush. Alex jumped from the jeep and ran through the briars. In a small clearing, he lay down.

It was quiet. His stomach was wet now too. His breathing

slowed. After a long while, he heard somebody in the brush behind him. It was Blair.

"What was it?" Alex said.

"One of Berringer's pals."

"Did he see you?"

"We don't know." They waited at the jeep for Fletcher to come back. Finally, Blair called out for him. "Hey, clown, let's go!"

After a while, Fletcher appeared in the silvery mist, taking long dark steps down the hill.

Alex shared the front passenger seat with Fletcher. He kept looking over at Blair, who was driving, and whose face shone in the soft green light of the dash. Alex had never seen him like this. He was usually very confident, but now his jaw stuck out and he appeared to be gritting his teeth. As they drove through the cool night air of the pine forest, Alex brought his hand up to his hair and felt the moisture that had gathered from the mist. They passed the swamp, then turned onto the dirt road and started up the hill toward the barracks. In the darkness ahead of them, before the headlights, Alex saw a flash of red light like a taillight. Blair must have seen it too; he turned the jeep off the road and slammed on the brakes.

"Let's go," he said. He and Fletcher took off running through the woods. Alex followed. Thirty yards or so into the dark trees he tripped on a stick and bashed his knee against a jagged rock. When he got up again, the other two were way ahead of him. He followed their sounds, the sounds of branches breaking. The hill became steeper. He stopped. In the darkness, he saw a large gray boulder as big as a house. He ran to the back of it, and felt the soil beneath it in various places. He found a soft spot to one side and lay down in it, pressing himself under the side of the rock and covering his body with leaves.

He heard the sound of footsteps, men running by him. He lay still, listening to their sounds, and listening for the sound of dogs. More men went by, and more men, but there were no dogs. Silence fell around him. Far away on the side of the hill, he could hear the shouts of the search party. He got up and started through the woods, parallel to the road, heading toward the barracks. At the edge of the woods, he saw the barrack lights; both the indoor and the outdoor lights were on. He circled the camp and came out into the meadow behind it. Leaves and twigs stuck in his hair. He brushed himself off carefully, then put his hands in his pockets.

"You there," he heard. "Who are you?" An armed soldier stood in the shadows in the back of the barracks.

"It's Brown," Alex called out.

"What are you doing out here, Brown?"

"I was just taking a walk."

"A walk? At two-thirty in the morning?"

"I couldn't sleep."

"You'd better tell that to the sergeant."

The soldier brought him through the bunk room and into Berringer's bedroom and office. Berringer sat at the edge of his unmade bed in a T-shirt and pajama bottoms. A dark shadow coursed the contours of his jaws.

"Well, Brown, where the hell have you been?"

"Taking a walk."

The sergeant laughed. "What time is it?"

Alex was standing in front of him. He looked at his watch. "Two forty-five. I couldn't sleep."

"Couldn't sleep?" The sergeant laughed in disbelief.

"I went down the path to the lake. What's going on here?"

"You really couldn't sleep, huh?" The sergeant slipped one foot into a black slipper, then the other and sat on a corner of his desk, crossing his arms. He nodded his head. "So you've got trouble sleeping. What's bugging you, soldier?"

"My neck . . . from standing in the box. It's too low for me," Alex said.

"I'll build you a bigger one next time."

"Yes, sir."

"What do you mean 'yes, sir'?"

"I mean, no, sir. The box is fine."

The sergeant's jaw hung down; his mouth was open, doglike; there was spittle on his lips. "Go ahead, get back to bed," he said.

From his bunk he heard the first of the search party come in. They'd found the jeep and heard the men running through the trees, but hadn't been able to catch them. After the lights were out again, Alex lay in the dark wishing he could talk to Fletcher and Blair and convince them not to tell on him.

CHAPTER **31**

IN the morning Blair and Fletcher's bunks were still empty. After the men were dressed and lined up outside for their morning exercises, the sergeant came out, now clean shaven and wearing dark sunglasses, and made a short speech. He told the men that Blair and Fletcher would soon find their way back to the barracks. "And when these clowns do come back," he said. "I'm going to demonstrate an antic on them which should make you all not want to do what they've been doing. You'll all be dying to behave."

That night Alex went to bed early and slept through all the noise in the barracks. The next morning the men told him he had been snoring and saying something loudly in his sleep and that a soldier had sat on him and he had restlessly rolled over without waking up. He felt better the rest of the day, despite a splitting headache. During the stage maneuvers, they had to cut roads or paths through the woods and push the stages through them. "Show us that you can push these stages anywhere," the sergeant told them.

Before dinner that evening, they were told that a treat was in store. They were going to a theater where there would be a performance and the soldiers could mingle with performers and chat. "A kind of reception," the sergeant said.

After dinner, a yellow school bus stopped in front of the barracks driven by a man wearing studded leather bracelets. His arm muscles rippled and swelled from a sleeveless sweatshirt. They were as big as the calves of most soldiers. He looked like a circus strong man.

The men were excited during the drive; many jokes were circulating. They stopped at a round, single-story building built on the side of a hill. The walls had been painted like a circus ring, with large red and yellow interlocking triangles. A sign hung above the entrance, which Alex stopped to read: Theater of the Sea. Under it, a small sign said: In Every Ring There Is a Stage, and under that was the definition of the word stage:

stage ('stāj) n. 1. A raised and level floor or platform. 2. a. A raised platform on which theatrical performances are presented. b. An area in which actors perform. c. The acting profession, or the world of theater. Used with *the: The stage is her life.* 3. The scene of an event or a series of events. 4. A scaffold for workers. 5. A resting place on a journey, especially one providing overnight accommodations. 6. The distance between stopping places on a journey; a leg: *proceeded in easy stages.* 7. The height of the surface of a river or other fluctuating body of water above a set point: *at flood stage.* 8. a. A level, degree, or period of time in the course of a process, especially a step in development: *the toddler stage.* b. A point in the course of an action or series of events: *too early to predict a winner at this stage.* stage v. staged, staging, stages. -tr. 1. To exhibit or present on or as if on a stage: *stage a boxing match.* 2. To produce or direct (a theatrical performance). 3. To arrange and carry out: *stage an invasion.* -inter. 1. To be adaptable or suitable for theatrical presentation. 2. To stop at a designated place in the course of a journey.

Alex ran up the steps and inside. The men were already seated
in a small theater with closed curtains. Programs had been laid
out on the cushions. Alex picked his up as he sat down. "The
One and Only Stage Presents the One and Only Mrs. Vespers."
Under it was a drawing of a woman standing on a stage with a
circus ring around it, her hands raised as if to a god above her.
Tiny print below the picture read: "Also Featuring the Infamous
Mr. Meep."

Berringer stepped onstage as the men were looking at the programs and called for silence. He had rolled up his sleeves. He
clenched his fists and held them to his sides.

"You guys are to pay attention to what you see up here in
the next fifteen minutes. There will be a party afterward. But
remember something: this isn't just fun." He pointed to the
stage. "This is not fun!" he shouted.

He stared from face to face. His own face appeared to be
changing. He was tightening his jaw muscles, flexing his neck
and chest, his uniform was bulging. Veins popped out of his
forearms as if he were lifting a huge weight and his fists seemed
to swell.

He turned and walked offstage.

The theater went completely dark. The curtains opened and
a spotlight came on. A woman was standing midstage behind a
podium. She had curly hair, an oval face, and canary-blue horn-
rimmed glasses, pointed at the ends. She poured water into a
glass from a pitcher, took a sip, then shuffled the papers in front
of her. Finally she bent the microphone down to her lips, stared
out over the soldiers to the back of the theater, and began speaking slowly. Her voice was amplified to an almost deafening level:
"It is not I *I I*"—her voice echoed as if in a great hall—"who
is speaking tonight *tonight*. No, it is not I *I I I* . . . It is
the stage *stage stage* . . . Why is the stage speaking tonight? *tonight?* . . . because the stage is master of our emotions, because
everything *everything everything* we could possibly strive for is
within it *within it within it* . . . already, *already, already.*"

She looked down, then up. "The words of the stage are not words . . . They're not symbols representing meanings *meanings meanings* . . . They're pure effects *effects effects* . . . utterances that give rise *rise rise* . . . to nothing but utterances *utterances utterances* . . ."

As her voice faded, the lights dimmed and the curtain closed.

Then the curtain opened again and a spotlight shone down on a man getting up from a wooden chair, a chubby little man with rosy cheeks, light brown hair, and small dark eyes behind glasses with perfectly circular lenses. Tucking his hands in his pockets, he casually strolled up to the edge of the stage, the spotlight following him.

"Hello, men," he said.

The men were silent.

"I said, hello men," the man repeated. He tucked his shirt in and pulled his pants over his round little stomach.

The men were still silent.

"Has the cat got your tongues? I said, hello, men!"

"Hello," said one soldier. Then a few others said hello, and finally the room was filled with the voices of soldiers greeting the man on stage.

"That's better. I'm Mr. Meep, the infamous Mr. Meep as the person who prepared that program would have you believe. The infamous Mr. Meep." He paced up and down the stage patting his chest, then he stopped and put his hands over his ears. "Boy, did that little speech hurt your ears, or what?"

He resumed pacing. "Have you ever heard of that woman before—a Mrs. Vespers, a Mrs. Hildegard Vespers, no less?"

The company was slow to answer him.

"Have you?"

The men started shaking their heads. One man called out, "No."

"Lucky you, look at your programs. Do you see where she's

standing? She's standing where I'm standing: on a stage. But do you know where she thinks she's standing? In heaven, or someplace like that." The man kept pacing back and forth on stage, his round little belly showing in profile.

"So I'm here to warn you about her and about a lot of other people like her. Fools, I call them, stage fools, fools of the stage. You see, quite frankly, if you haven't already heard enough about 'the stage' you soon will. And what you're going to hear is a lot of nonsense. You'll hear that the stage, for example, is made up of all kinds of fantastic materials, that to walk on it is not like walking on anything else. You'll hear myths about this plain ordinary structure. Idiotic myths. But what is it really?" the man said, stopping and staring out at the audience.

The men were silent.

"It's lumber, nothing more than lumber, assembled into a structure for a very practical purpose: displaying the actions of performers.

"But let me warn you. People here will come to you with all sorts of wild stories about it. They'll tell you it's the center of the universe, that it's an equation, one of the most significant equations ever discovered by humankind.

"Come over here." The man pointed to a soldier in the front row. The soldier got up. "Put your hand on the surface. Look at the platform right now carefully and tell me exactly what you see," he said. "Go on."

"A wooden platform," the soldier said.

"Fulfilling what purpose?" Meep said.

"Displaying performers to an audience," the soldier said.

"Very good. Now let me ask you, why is there such a grand hurrah about this plain pile of boards?"

"I don't know," the soldier said.

"Take my word, people like Mrs. Vespers have nothing better to do with their time. Indeed, they might have deified anything else inside the ring. Like this for instance." In the spotlight he flipped a nickel and dropped it into his pocket. He called over his shoulder. "Chandelier, please."

A chandelier over the soldiers began to glow. "That might have been their god," he said, pointing. "There's nothing special about the objects in this room. Those curtains, for example, they're made from ordinary material that could be purchased in an ordinary store, those ropes, those pulleys, everything you see, you yourself could have gone out and bought." He told the soldier to sit back down, then called backstage again. "I'll take a performer.

"Please, soldiers, when this man shows up, pay no attention to where he is. If you like, imagine that he's standing on a city street, or in a kitchen, or that he's waiting for a train."

A slightly round and puffy-faced man in black pants and a black turtleneck shirt with hair cut straight across his forehead came out and stood at center stage. He brought his hands together, closed his eyes and inhaled deeply several times. "I'm a man of the stage," he said. He paused for another deep breath.

"You see," Meep said. "He's trying to create a sense of his own importance by linking himself with this concept of the stage. But, as I said, the stage is nothing."

"I do not fear what other people fear, for the stage is my partner. Where I go, the stage will follow. Where the stage goes, I will follow. I have seen the stage in the woods of this property. I have seen the stage under the bed in my room. The stage is the most important element in my life," the man said. "It's more important than these." He lifted his shoes and showed the bottoms to the soldiers. "The stage is not just a friend, and it's not just an enemy. The stage is something else altogether." The man fell to his knees, put his hand over his face and began to cry.

The curtain closed and Mr. Meep stepped out in front of it.

"He thinks he is possessed by something outside of himself, but he's only possessed by himself. Mrs. Vespers will soon be out, so please be careful."

The theater darkened and the men heard somebody running across stage. The curtain opened, the lights came on, and Mrs. Vespers, her sharply pointed glasses sparkling in the light, was leaning over catching her breath.

"Was there a man here just a moment ago?"

The soldiers were silent.

"Was there?"

"Yes," somebody said.

"I tried to get here before—what was he talking about, not the stage, I hope, oh, not the stage."

"He was," a soldier said.

"What was he saying about it?"

"He said it was an ordinary structure," another soldier said.

"A what? He said it was a what? An ordinary structure?" The woman stamped her foot and turned away from the men. "An ordinary structure? The stage an ordinary structure? What kind of a mind would say something so sick?"

"He said it was just lumber," another soldier said.

"Lumber?" she said. She laughed. "Lumber? Just lumber? That fool, that dirty, nasty, lying, rotten—" She took a deep breath, turning her eyes away from the audience.

"If it were lumber, nothing but lumber," she said, "why would the greatest performer in the world think about it, obsess about it? Why would an entire army be built around it?"

Darkness fell on the woman as she looked out at the soldiers. The curtain closed.

A spotlight shone on the curtain. Mr. Meep put his head out. "Did you see what I was talking about, men?" he said. "Did you see? According to her, everything is a matter of the stage: the stage this and the stage that. Whatever anybody does has to fall into one of two categories: off the stage or on the stage."

Stepping through the curtain, Meep made a sweeping gesture with one hand, then pointed at the men in the front row. "Call me anything you want, call me a father figure, call me a preacher, a pundit, a pugilist. But know that I'm a straight talker just coming here to tell it like it is," he said, "to speak to you man to man. I'm just coming here—" he stamped his foot, "one man talking straight to another, one level-headed man talking as straight as an arrow to another and trying to set you right before she sets you wrong. Understand? I'm being honest, forthright, perfectly frank. I'm trying to cut right through it, right to the heart of it, right to the truth of it. I'm just trying to show you in as clear a light as possible what's going on so as to give you a little clarity, a little guidance, a little sprinkling of knowledge, a little something to go by to help you along with your lives. Do you follow me?" Meep said. He pulled a sheet of paper out of his pocket. "The stage," he cried, "is nonsense!" He threw the paper down. The lights dimmed.

When the lights came on again, Mrs. Vespers was walking across the stage. She passed the paper that Meep had thrown, stopped, and came back to it.

"What is this?" she said aloud. "Ah, a letter written by Mr. Meep to somebody off the island. A letter that will tell us exactly what he really believes."

She began to read:

Dear Susan,

Every day is a constant struggle with the stage. It is like a struggle with the sea. There are days when it is pleasant, calm, warm, soothing to swim in, to lie near, to listen to. Other days the surf is raging, one cannot even stand on board one's own ship, one is in a constant battle with the sea, begging it off you.

I feel so lucky to be here where the stage is recognized. A walk through the woods in the most remote part of the island can turn

*up a stage born of the ring, well camouflaged, ready for war with
other stages born of the ring, that is if you know what you're
looking for. I am comforted to know that others share my concerns.
I'm not merely alone, struggling in the dark with a problem. Above
all else, there is the great Volenti, whose conduct and acting techniques have been an anchor and a light. You must come here.*

Much love,
Meep

"I hope that puts the matter to rest for us for now," the
woman said. "There's nobody here, that man included, who
doesn't believe in the stage."

The lights went out and the curtain closed. Alex could hear
soldiers whispering to each other.

A spotlight came back on. The man was standing at the very
edge of the stage with a sheet of paper in his hand.

"That piece of paper in my pocket was, in fact, a letter, but
it did not read as Mrs. Vespers read it to you. I did not stop
her; she would only have lied about something else. Here is
the letter the way she found it in my pocket." He adjusted his
spectacles to read.

Dear Susan,

*I am very bored and very tired. There are many eccentrics here
on the island. All of them claim to be possessed by something they
call the stage and they'll do anything to bring it up in conversation.
A careful study of their speech patterns reveals them to have over
two thousand definitions for the word, many of the definitions
contradicting each other. The stage seems to fill some gap in their
lives, that's what they feel, but it doesn't come close. The true gap
in their lives cannot be filled by a silly concept. Most of them need
to learn the old values again of family and friends, the old circus*

values, quite frankly. They come here from those despicable urban areas throughout the world. They come to impose their ideas on the good old ring. Many of them, despite their alienation from every person and every object, despite their alienation from themselves, truly believe they're communing with the ring through the vehicle of the stage. They say the stage contains all human feelings, there is nothing beyond it. I wish you'd come here. I need a companion to keep my head level.

Once again darkness fell.

The curtain parted. Mrs. Vespers was standing at the podium again.

"One more thing, good men. I must think of a question to awaken you to the magic of the stage. I must think, think very hard, very hard."

She turned away from the soldiers to think, then turned back again. "I've got it. The perfect question: if the stage were a book, soldiers, yes, that's it, if the stage were a book, what would that book say?"

She scrutinized the audience, shook her head and began pacing. She stopped. "Ah, another question to awaken you." She bent over and faced the men.

"Has anybody ever given birth onstage before?" She started to smile. "And if so, was the child born alive? And, soldiers, what were the child's first words? Did the child, in fact, ever speak of the stage again? If the child was born onstage, was the mother a person or an object? Later in life, did the grown child feel privileged or deprived?"

She looked up and stood very still as if frozen in place. The lights went out and the curtains closed.

The lights came back, and the men clapped. Berringer stepped out after the applause and told them to exit through the door at the rear and join the actors and performers for a party.

Alex followed the men into a room of stages piled on top of stages—anywhere one stood inside one would be on a stage, and on all the different layers of these stages were men and women in the tight blue bodysuits of performers.

The countenances of the performers were similar; their faces were round, their hair straight, and they spoke with very clear voices. Their androgynous outfits made it difficult to tell the men from the women. The soldiers were given drinks, and Alex lit up a cigarette and looked among the performers for Iris.

"You want to be a performer?" a round-faced performer asked him.

Alex nodded without speaking.

"You're on the bus," the man said. "You're on the right bus."

Alex tried to turn away, but the man followed him.

"Come back here, friend," the man said in a soft voice. "You're shy. We should talk a bit about your shyness." Alex kept moving through the other men whose tongues, due to the cocktails they held in their hands, loosened rapidly. Soon conversations centered around two things: the stage and women, the definition of one mingling with the other, making it impossible at times to figure out whether a woman or the stage was being referred to.

Alex himself took several sips of a cocktail and immediately noticed its high proof.

The same man who had approached him before kept following him up and down the stages, through the party of men and performers. Finally, Alex turned to him and said, "I can't for the life of me remember her last name, but I was wondering if you know a woman named Iris."

Clearing his throat, the man said, "I guess you're not as shy as I thought. Why do you ask?"

"I'm just curious. Her name is Barton, yes, Barton, that's the

name. I heard she's a very good performer." Alex handed
the man the photograph he had taken from Volenti's room.
The man held it up to the light, then gave it back to him.

"I've seen that face. She's inside the mountain."

"Inside the mountain?" Alex asked.

"Yes. Have you been to the mountain yet?"

"No."

"Well, there's a lot there that you'll see when your sergeant
brings you in."

"I'll see her?"

"It depends which part of the mountain he brings you into."

"But which part is she in?"

"My, my, we are anxious tonight despite the festivities."

"Well," Alex said. "I'd just like to know where she is, I mean
where I might expect to see her."

"Expect to see her in the ring."

"Which ring?"

"In the mountain . . . but you ask your sergeant, not me,
where that is."

"He doesn't allow us to ask for women."

"Then you'll just have to wait and see. For now, you should
just be paying attention to the stage. Marry the stage, so to
speak."

The man walked away. Alex followed but soon lost him
among the many similar-looking performers. Moving up and
down the levels of the stages, he noticed that the performers
were trying to separate soldiers from each other and question
them alone. A caterer kept coming by with new drinks, but
Alex held onto his first and sipped from it cautiously. The other
soldiers were slurring words and falling over themselves. Some
soldiers bragged about operations they'd performed; others
laughed at their own jokes. But the performers themselves remained sober and upright.

Some of the soldiers lay down and curled up to fall asleep.
One man threw up on a stage. Alex himself was feeling a little

dizzy just from the few sips he had taken. One soldier bragged about drawing the Iron Horse through swampland without the aid of ropes to hoist it up a steep cliff. He told of storm clouds that had moved over them, dumping a heavy rain.

Another soldier kept shouting: "What would it be like to live on the highest stage? Can you imagine building a house up there? What would that be like? Can you imagine?"

After a while, the men, all of whom were sleeping, were carted out of the theater and put in the back of the trucks. Alex himself, feigning sleep, was carried in a stretcher by three men. The men who carried him were the caterers.

CHAPTER 32

THE next morning the bugle played inside the barracks, and the sergeant walked through the bunk room, dragging people into standing position next to their bunks. When everyone stood at attention outside on the grass for exercises, he explained to them all that their performances the night before had been abominable and that all of them but one were guilty of bragging, which according to him was about the worst offense a soldier could commit against the stage.

After the morning's lecture at the château, Alex began to understand some of what was meant by the strange party. The head performer in the lecture hall had talked about not talking, about how important, how crucial it was, not to speak.

"You are all the time in the ring," he said. "When you go home at night and sleep in your barracks, you are in the ring. When you run down the path and go swimming, you are in the ring. You are always in the ring!" he shouted. "And the only thing that should speak when you are in the ring is the stage. Are you clear on that point?"

The treatment the soldiers were given that day was twice as brutal as before.

They had to push the stages over chasms without bridges, across swamps, and up steep embankments using ropes and pulleys and only breaking briefly for lunch. Alex felt exhausted and sore.

Several times the sergeant called to them through a megaphone: "Just be glad you're not Blair and Fletcher. They'll be back, don't you worry. The hungry dogs will return to the pack."

The next night after dinner at the barracks, Alex was approached by a soldier holding a bundle of letters.

"Corporal Brown?"

"Yes," Alex said.

The soldier handed him an envelope with a cellophane window. Corporal Brown, Hunt's Barracks, Cea, it said. It looked like a paycheck or a bill. He tore it open. There was a handwritten note. For a moment he thought it was from Iris. The script was similar, but Ava had signed her name.

Dear Corporal Brown,

I've been thinking about you. Things have changed since I met you. I don't know what it is; I can't put my finger on it. Maybe you just came at the right moment. I'd like to see you again. Please—

At the bottom she had written:

(No luck yet finding her. Please get rid of this note and the envelope as quickly as possible. If anyone asks, tell them it's about your blood test during admissions.)

He lay down in his bunk. The other soldiers were lying in theirs, looking at photos and rereading letters. Alex kept hearing the drop of the dice on a backgammon board behind him. He closed his eyes, hovering close to sleep.

The letter was pulled from his hand; he looked up. The narrow, beady eyes of an old soldier, a soldier who looked like he'd been in the army since the day he was born, read it over. The soldier handed it back. "I know the one," he said. Alex could smell his bad breath. "You did good." Alex sat up, shaking his head a little to wake up. The gray-haired soldier touched him on the arm near his shoulder. "You got lucky, mate. She's a gem."

On the part of his mattress facing away from the room, Alex cut a tiny slit, then stuffed the envelope in.

The next day during their break at the château, Alex went upstairs and strolled through the halls. For the first time since he had found the photographs, he saw Volenti's door open. He stopped and looked in. The room had been rearranged. The rug had been removed and a round table placed in the middle of the floor. Six men dressed in black suits were seated around it, most with briefcases open in front of them. He looked from face to face, as if he were certain he would recognize Volenti. But all of the men were alike and no one of them seemed to be leading the meeting. As he stared, he realized a guard's harsh eyes had fixed on him. He turned and walked away.

"Hey, soldier, come here." Alex glanced back and saw the guard's face, strained under his tight collar, coming toward him. "Where are you going, pal?"

"Nowhere."

"What's so interesting about this room?"

"Nothing."

"You look awfully curious."

"We're on break. We're tired; I was just staring into the room."

A young soldier named Stern was strolling by with a hand in his pants pocket. He stopped behind the guard. "What's the problem here?" he asked.

"No problem," the guard said. "Just your mate here was spying."

"Him spying? No way."

"Then what was he doing?"

"I don't know. What were you doing, Brown?" Stern said to Alex.

"Looking in, that's all," Alex said.

"He can look in if he wants to," Stern said to the guard.

"Why don't you come along with me," the guard said to Alex. Alex looked to the young soldier.

"Where are you taking him? He's on his break," Stern said.

"I thought he'd like to speak to the board members."

"Well then I'll go too. How does that sound?"

Alex followed the other two to the threshold of the door. One of the men in black brought his fist down on the table and said, "That's sheer nonsense!"

He stopped as the guard came in. "This man seemed to have an interest in what goes on in board meetings," the guard said. The man looked over his shoulder at Alex. Alex lifted his hands and said he was just looking around.

"What do you want to know, soldier?" the man at the head of the table asked.

"Nothing," Alex said.

"Have a seat, soldier," the man said. "Who's your friend?"

Stern came forward next to Alex. "My friend here was just walking by," Stern said. "Your guard stopped him."

"It doesn't matter. Have a seat," the man said.

Alex and his companion sat down at the table with the six other men. The faces of these men, though older, perhaps squarer and heavier boned, were similar to one another the way the performers at the party had been similar.

"As I was saying," one man went on, "it's possible, damn possible, to have too many performers. Soon we'll have diminished the audience to such an extent that the only people watching us will be the ushers."

"You're crazy. A member of the audience is a perfectly valid part for a performer to play; we just have to create a role!" another man said.

"How so?"

"Well, look at these fellows," he said, pointing at Alex and his friend. "How do you two feel about being anonymous?"

"Anonymous?" Alex asked.

"Yes, a number, one of a thousand." He lifted a few stapled sheets of paper from his briefcase. "Well, one thousand and twenty-nine at this very moment. How does that feel?"

"We're proud to be soldiers," Stern said, his chest out. "We don't think of ourselves as numbers."

"How can that be?" asked another man at the table. "You dress alike. You're made to do the same dreadful things every day."

"Yes, but we're all different. Look at my friend, Brown. He rarely talks, but I talk all the time. I think out loud sometimes."

"But underneath it all," the man went on, "underneath it all, you must feel a bit like a number."

Stern looked toward Alex. "How do you feel?" he asked.

Surprised by such a question, he looked to Stern for an answer, but Stern only stared back at him.

He looked at the others in the room. They had all turned toward him and stopped moving. One man had been about to put a sheet of paper in his briefcase; his hand holding the paper appeared frozen in midair.

"How do I feel?" Alex said.

He suddenly felt as if he were onstage, as if whatever he said would have to be important. He began mumbling. "Well, well . . . I'm just getting used to all the . . ."

Alex looked around again. The faces of the men looked extremely tense, as if they were holding their breaths.

". . . all the . . . exercise."

The men burst into laughter, laughter so loud that it hurt Alex's ears. Stern stared at him amazed, then he too began to laugh, slowly at first, slapping Alex's back, knocking him forward. Soon all of the men were bent over double, laughing, and Alex heard the guard, who had dropped to his knees, coughing, trying to catch his breath. Alex went to the door. The others were laughing so hard that they hardly noticed him do this. He looked back into the room. Two men had crawled under the table. The guard, in his double-breasted uniform, was lying on his back with his feet up in the air crying for help, one hand over his heart, the other slapping the ground.

"What was that guy's name?" Alex heard somebody say as he walked outside along the balcony. Below him he could see the other soldiers gathering at the gate of the château, ready to file out into the field. He ran down the stairs and across the courtyard to join their ranks. The gates opened and he went out with the soldiers and started up the hill.

The sun in the field was hot, hotter than Alex had ever felt it. The dust from the men in the front line rose up into the faces of those behind. Alex turned and looked behind him toward the château; guards had lined up along the front of the wall, their guns resting on their shoulders. As he turned back to the marching men, he saw a man, an older man, fall to his knees, then fall face forward into the dirt. Almost as soon as he went down, four other men picked him up, one for each arm and leg, and started carrying him up the hill. Five minutes later another soldier went down. Four men picked him up too. Once they were marching again, a third soldier, another older man, started slowing down, staggering a little, then went down. Alex rolled him over. His eyes were closed; he was breathing hard, the sun shining into his wide-open mouth. Alex took off his own hat and fanned him. Other soldiers gathered around him, reached down and picked him up. Twelve men were now carrying three others.

They went over the top of the hill, then down the other side toward the stages. The men burdened with the sick stopped and put them down to rest and fanned themselves. They were sweating violently. Finally, they reached the stages, lowering the three sick men next to the wheels in the shade. Alex sat down in the dust and looked along the stone wall to crows perched on the dead branches of a tree. They were big black crows; he counted six of them, all facing the same direction.

Then, at the top of the wide field, Alex could see a man running toward them. He held his hat in his hand and his shirt was soaked with sweat. It was Stern. He was laughing, still laughing. He sat next to Alex. "Very good," he said. "That was really something."

"I have no idea what was so funny," Alex said.

But the soldier kept laughing, thinking of the incident, and then laughing again.

The men who had passed out woke up one at a time. "Where am I?" the older man said.

"Look behind you," a soldier said to him.

The old man looked up and saw the stage. "My Iron Horse, such a good friend," he said, patting the tread of the huge black rubber wheel. "I couldn't have landed in a lovelier spot."

"Nor I," another man said, awakening.

After a while the men got up, brushed the dust off each other, and went to the shanks. They started pushing the stages up the hill, moving more slowly than usual. The sick men stayed behind. As usual a soldier went out ahead and directed the teams, keeping the stages perfectly abreast of each other.

At the top of the hill, one of the soldiers got on the shoulders of another soldier and began waving his own hat and his partner's hat at the château. There were half a dozen people on the fortress's walkways, but Alex couldn't see at whom he was waving.

"It's too hot for them," one soldier said.

"They'll be here shortly," another said.

Three stages had been dragged to the top of the hill. Alex saw the crows flying high above.

Then the gates of the château opened and horsemen came out, two at a time, riding at a full gallop, one hand securing their hats, the other on their reins. The soldiers lay down on the ground, putting their faces into their arms.

"Here goes," one of the men said.

The horses danced around the men. Dirt kicked up onto Alex's shoulder. He kept his head snugly inside his arm. Every time he breathed in, dust and dirt came into his mouth. Then he heard the sound of the hooves on the stages. Somehow the men had ridden the horses onto the platforms. The horses whinnied; they were prancing on the wood. Alex could smell their sweat mixed with his own sweat. The horses calmed down; the noise of their hooves seemed calmer. There were moments of silence. Cautiously, he brought his head up and looked to the side where a soldier had been lying. The man was gone. All of the men next to him were gone. Alex looked on the other side of him. The men on that side were gone also. He turned his head and glanced up at the stages. He saw a horse and quickly put his head back into his arm. As he lay covering his eyes he began to think that the horse he'd seen had been riderless. The reins of the horse hung untied.

Alex lay with his face in his arms for a long time. The horse snorted occasionally. Finally he turned his head again. On the stage right above him a sweaty black horse stood looking toward the château.

Alex stood up and turned toward the other stages. Horses were standing on each stage. There were no men around. He brushed himself off, put his hat on, then walked down the hill toward the barracks.

CHAPTER 33

BEFORE dinner Alex lay down in his bunk to rest. He dozed off and woke later to find Stern sitting by his legs. Stern laid his hand on Alex's forehead and the other hand on his own forehead as if to test for fever.

"Are you okay?"

Alex let him rest his hand on his head.

"Do I look sick?"

"You've been yelling in your sleep. You keep saying some-body's name."

"Whose name?"

"The name of a woman."

"Well, I have a lot of dreams, sometimes," Alex said, sitting up. "What's today?"

"Today? It's the eighteenth, what for?"

"What day of the week?"

"Friday, why do you ask?"

"No reason," Alex whispered.

Alex noticed that Stern's eyes had fallen on something across the room. The soldiers in the bunks were suddenly quiet. Alex turned just in time to see Blair and Fletcher come wearily through the doorway into the dormitory with a heavy growth of hair on their haggard faces; their pants were ripped in places; scabs and cuts streaked their arms. They looked deeply ashamed of their absence. Without saying a word, they lay down on their bunks and rolled over, turning their faces away.

The dinner bell rang. The two wayward soldiers remained where they were. But when Alex came back from eating, he noticed that their bunks were empty and that the door to Berringer's room was shut. He went into the bathroom to brush his teeth, then came out, and lay down on his bunk.

He heard from behind Berringer's door a muffled noise that sounded like an excited woman or child: it was high-pitched, not a scream, but something else, somebody in great pain. Alex looked around. Moments before, other soldiers had been in their bunks, but now, as if they had known something that he hadn't known, the room was deserted. He started to get up. He heard more noises, feminine almost, as if somebody were trying to say something, trying to express some awful pain but just couldn't find the words, any words. He looked to the door of the bunk room that led outside. He didn't think of covering his ears, just of getting to the door and outside. But as he crossed the room the sounds came again. They were sexual now, as if one of the soldiers were being seduced by death itself. The soldier, Blair or Fletcher, sounded like he was about to ejaculate. The pain could have been construed as pleasure had it not evolved into another ghastly sound—a begging sound. As Alex moved for the door, he tried to lean into his gait to make himself run, but his legs seemed to fold under him like rubber and the doorway shrank farther away, as if the noises of torture were sucking him backward. By the time he was outside he was out of breath, his heart racing, his fingers trembling, clutching each other. He turned and kicked the door closed behind him and walked to the dirt road.

Darkness was falling among the trees; the sky was a deep

purple, a fringe of red fading at the horizon. He tried to speak to himself, to get something else into his mind beside what he'd heard. Pushing his hands deep into his uniform pockets, he hummed something he remembered from the family he lived with during his childhood, a tune they'd sung at Christmas. He pictured the family Christmas tree: the ornaments, the silver and gold ornaments that the mother had made herself.

In the cobwebs of darkness that gathered under the pine trees, he saw groups of soldiers. He stopped at one of the groups, and stood just far enough away to hear their voices muttering quietly.

"Why didn't somebody tell me?" he said to the men. As if awakened from a secret conversation, they turned and looked back at him. The gleam of their faces, some with cigarettes glowing from their mouths, were all that he could see of them in the descending darkness. They watched him with eyes as fearful as deer's eyes.

"How did you all know?" he said. After a silence they turned back to each other and began their muttering again as if he were a ghost.

After a while, they all came back up the hill, walking abreast slowly, stopping to hear if Berringer was still at it. Alex could hear water trickling from a stream that came down off the mountain and ran along the road, then under it. The tiny bells of crickets rang out in the darkness.

Blair and Fletcher were lying in their bunks, their faces turned away from the other men. Next to Alex's bunk a letter had fallen to the floor. The envelope was familiar, his name showing through a cellophane window.

I still haven't found her. But when can I see you again? I don't know what's happened to me, ever since that night, ever since then . . .

He lay on his bunk and stuffed the envelope in the tiny slit on the other side of the mattress.

CHAPTER 34

LOOK in there," Berringer said to the men. They were standing on the side of the mountain, looking up narrow railroad tracks that disappeared into a cave-like opening between the boulders. Guards stood on the chiseled gray rocks on either side of the tracks, resting their guns against their shoulders, staring straight out over the hill. From where the soldiers stood they could see nothing but darkness. Then they heard a squeaking sound, a sound of rusted wheels.

A flatbed railcar appeared, rolling out of the darkness. Two men covered with sweat and layers of brown and black dirt stood in the rear, one man operating a lever, apparently a brake. The railcar—about half the size of a flatbed on a normal rail-way—rolled to a stop at the threshold of the entrance. A third man was sitting on a footstool next to a black lunch box eating a sandwich. The brakeman locked the lever, jumped off, and walked back up the tracks, disappearing into the darkness.

Berringer went around the side of the flatbed and spoke to the man who was eating his lunch. The man nodded, then Berringer came back.

"Soldier, step forward," he said to Alex.

It took Alex a brief moment before he realized he was being summoned.

He stepped forward on the rocks.

"What is that?" Berringer said, pointing to the flatbed.

"A railcar."

"A what?" Berringer said. "A what? That's a what?"

"It's a stage," another soldier said.

"A stage, do you understand that, soldier?"

"Yes," Alex said, stepping back in line.

"That's a stage. I hear you call that anything else but a stage, you'll be fired, like that!" he said, snapping his fingers. "Now follow me, and don't touch the walls of the tunnel."

Once inside Alex could not see a thing, not even the shapes of the men in front of him. He put his hand out and rested it on a soldier's shoulder and felt the hand of the soldier behind him on his own. As the pack moved along the railroad bed, Alex saw a soft, shapeless green light ahead of them. He couldn't make it out clearly, but he could tell there were other colors within it too. The temperature kept getting cooler. The men stopped, then moved on. As the light became clearer, Alex saw a room carved out of one side of the tunnel. This room had laminated hardwood floors and white plaster walls, and was furnished with beautiful antique rugs and green-and-gold couches with wooden legs carved like a cat's paws. On the dark mahogany tables, Alex saw lamps with blue flowers painted on their shades.

The soldiers stood in the green light, having taken their hands off each other's shoulders. Berringer walked across the room and disappeared through a green door with a pattern of narrow gold lines crisscrossing it.

With Berringer gone, the men relaxed, venturing into the room. Alex stepped up to the lampshades to examine them more closely. Within the flowers he could see the backs and the faces of women contortion artists striking their poses on pedestals.

Paintings hung from the walls, narrow paintings of old ship-
yards, harbors, faint blue-and-green skies. In one very old Flem-
ish or Dutch painting, Alex saw three large sailing vessels
moored in a harbor, their sails down; tiny specks of gray and
white paint represented men on their decks. Crates had been
stacked on a dock. A dog on one of the crates was barking. Men
worked in white shirts, their sleeves rolled up to the elbows,
unloading the crates from a sloop. At the end of a cobblestone
street behind the dock, Alex saw a park or square and in the
park between the tall pale green trees was a stage. The stage had
a shank and large black wheels like the stages the soldiers used.
There was something on it that he couldn't quite make out. He
brought his head back to get a different perspective. It was a
horse, a ghost white horse standing proudly in a bright shaft of
sunlight.

Staring at the riderless horse, he heard the squeaking sound
of a flatbed coming down the tracks that ran alongside of the
room. Everyone turned to face the dark tunnel where the noise
was coming from. The sound was a painful, creaking, iron-
against-steel sound, the aching sound of a flatbed rounding a
sharp corner. Then the railcar itself appeared and on it stood a
workman in a blue shirt, and Berringer steadying himself against
a pile of dirt. The workman's thick forearms were covered with
dirt. He pulled back on the brake. The squeaking sound became
louder as the flatbed slowed and finally jumped to a halt.

Berringer hopped down, slapping his hands together to clean
them off. His face was red from walking or running. As he
crossed the living room, the flatbed started up again. Berringer
opened the green door and waved for the men to go through.
There were little blue lights, no bigger than Christmas-tree
lights, strung along the walls of the narrow dirt passageways.
The men climbed up a kind of winding staircase; boards had
been laid into the dirt for steps. After following a long straight
hallway, their shoulders touching the narrow walls occasionally,
they heard men shoveling, nobody talking, just shoveling. They

came into a huge room lit by the brilliant yellow flames of torches hung at intervals along the walls. The room, twice the size of a football field, had a dome-shaped ceiling. The dirt walls were brown, and somewhat rough with indentations where dirt had obviously fallen out. To one side, where the railroad tracks came to an end, flatbeds were lined up, twenty or so, some of them loaded high with dirt. The flatbeds were made of iron and had been pushed up on a slight trestle erected so as to give the loaded cars enough momentum to roll out of the room. To one side of the room another track came in, divided into sidings by switches.

The men were given shovels, pickaxes, and wheelbarrows. Alex took his shovel and buried the blade in the earth near one of the gas torches. He could hear gas rushing through the lines. In the bright yellow light he could see his shadow: the shadow of a man holding the handle of a shovel, lifting great shovelfuls of dirt into a wheelbarrow.

The wheelbarrows were pushed up a ramp and dumped onto the flatbeds. When full, the flatbeds were rolled out of the room and probably unloaded outside the tunnel alongside of the track; three men were sent with each flatbed. All of the workmen were stronger than the soldiers, bigger boned, healthier, but grimmer.

That night the men showered and so much dirt washed off them that the shower floor became covered with mud. After dinner Alex lay in his bunk. Every time he turned his head, he could hear the creak of the iron wheels as if the creak itself were in his muscles.

CHAPTER 35

NOW Alex was no more tired than the rest of the soldiers at the end of the day. He had noticed his muscles were getting bigger; he was far stronger than he had been when he first came to the island, stronger than he had been since boarding school when he had worked one summer unloading boxes in a freight yard.

One night Alex had a dream in which he saw Berringer across a bleakly lit room, his back turned, writing something furiously at a desk.

"The stage is nonsense," Alex said as he approached him. "It's part of your system of insanity, and you're trying to indoctrinate me with it. Indoctrinate! Indoctrinate!" he called out like a child learning a new word. He could hear Berringer's pen against paper as he scribbled. "Did you hear me? Indoctrinate, that's what you've been up to. But it hasn't worked, has it? I'm still me. I'm still Alex. You can fuck with me for a while, but not forever." Berringer still didn't look up. "Hey," Alex called out. In this dream he was so physically rugged that he had to hold his arms out from his torso like Popeye. Every time he glanced down at himself, he seemed to get bigger. "I'll kick your ass even without a can of spinach," Alex said to the preoccupied Berringer. "I'll kick your ass clear across the seven seas!" Berringer kept scribbling. "What are you up to, you indoctrinator, you? What's cooking? Writing some more speeches for your insanity?" He laughed at the word insanity. God that was a funny word, one of the funniest words he'd ever heard. If one man is insane, every man is insane, he'd heard somebody say once. That might be true, Alex thought. But then, there are degrees of insanity.

He heard footsteps behind him, turned, and saw in a clear, yellow light a messenger no taller than a midget coming toward him. The buttons on his little blue uniform glistened like jewels. A round flat cap sat on top of an almost perfectly round head. His slender white hands held an envelope up to Alex. "From your wife," he said. Alex opened it and read the fine handwriting at the top of the sheet: "Darling, is it making you sick? It's making me sick. How could it happen, you and I, I thought we were forever—"

"Berringer, do you see this!" he yelled. Approaching Berringer he tried to turn him by the shoulder, but Berringer shrugged him off and continued scribbling. "Look, can you believe this?" Alex begged. But Berringer kept on.

Tears came to Alex's eyes. He fell to the floor and began to cry. He cried like a baby and then read on. "Why are we apart? Could you tell me, is there one reason—"

Somebody was shaking him. His open eyes flooded with tears, real tears streaming down the side of his face.

"You want to go?" somebody said in the dark. Through the water in his eyes Alex could see Blair, squatting next to him in the dark, his hands on Alex's shoulder.

"Where?" Alex whispered. He was exhausted from the dream.

"Shhh, you're going to wake everybody up," Blair said angrily. "Come on, get dressed."

"Are you crazy?" Alex whispered. But Blair was already heading for the barracks door.

Alex lay there without moving. Blair had gone out. Alex couldn't believe that he was going to break a rule, any rule, after his punishment. Blair came back in again.

"She's working tonight," Alex heard him whisper. Alex started to ask who. "Your jewel," he said.

"I'm too tired."

"Listen, I need you to push the jeep."

"You're crazy," Alex said, but Blair interrupted him.

"We didn't tell on you," he said. "But it's not too late."

"What?"

"I need help, man," the soldier said. "You'd better come outside. Besides, she's working tonight. Your little friend is working tonight."

Blair went out through the door again. Alex sat up and dressed. His legs and arms were sore. He'd push the jeep for him, that would be all. That was enough of a risk.

He opened the door and slipped outside. It was a cool evening, no moon, just the stars. The grass across the meadow was white with dew. He could see the jeep parked under the trees. When he got to it, Blair came from around the side. "Let's go, we'll both push."

Alex got behind the jeep and pushed. They rolled it across the grass to the dirt road. Once the jeep started rolling on its own, Blair jumped into the driver's seat. "Let's go, Brown."

"No," Alex said.

"Get in here. I'll fucking turn you in."

"What for?" Alex said. He was jogging alongside of it.

"Because I saved your ass once already. I had to lie to cover up your ass."

Alex let the jeep get ahead of him. Blair was turning around, talking louder and louder. "Get in here, come on," he said. "Don't try me. Don't fuck with me. I'll show you."

Alex sprang forward and got on the bumper and then climbed into the back.

"You'd better not leave me behind," Alex said.

"Nobody's going to leave you, soldier. Don't worry about that."

They turned onto the road that ran along the swamp. The sound of frogs, tiny high-pitched frogs, grew louder and softer in waves as the jeep rushed by them. Then they could smell the sweet dampness of the pines and hear the sound of the jeep echoing in the cavelike tunnel of the trees.

After killing the engine at the edge of the field, there was a sudden silence. Then crickets started up around them, one at a time.

"They're on to us, you know," Alex said as he followed Blair over the hill. "They'll notice the jeep gone. They know we took it once."

"Keep thinking that way," Blair said. Alex's legs were wet with dew; he could see the blurry whiteness of the hospital in the moonlight.

In the musty basement they put on their hospital gowns. Alex found a stethoscope hanging from the caved-in seat of a dirty wicker chair, shook it free of dirt and put it on.

"Yeah, they'll think you're a doctor," Blair said.

"Are you serious?" Alex asked.

Blair took it from him and held it up. "Think on your feet, Brown. You're a patient now. What the hell would a patient be doing with a stethoscope in his hand?" He threw it into the corner by the boiler. "Wait until you get a doctor's costume," he said. "It'll still be there, don't worry."

They mounted the shaking wooden stairs to the hallway. Alex went right to the elevator, taking it to the second floor. As he walked toward the reception area, he felt somebody take his hand.

"You there," she said. "I knew you'd come back."

Ava brought him into a room, locking the door behind her. She held his hand with two of her own and pulled him toward her.

"You're nervous," she said.

"They tortured the other soldiers."

"I know. Sit down," she said.

As they sat on the hospital bed she put her hands between his hands. Her hands felt like Iris's, perhaps slightly smaller, slightly cooler. Alex looked down at her bare knees under her white dress, but she lifted his chin with her hand. "What's the matter?" she said.

He glanced from her to the window. There was something different about the window. A blue light was coming through the glass. It was a different blue light than the other one, the one he had seen with Iris; this one was darker. It came from the stars or from the moon, flooding the tiny hospital room. Alex looked around him. There were television monitors, plastic tubes, and wires hanging from a robotlike machine on wheels. All of the equipment lay dormant under the blue light.

Then he could feel Ava move closer to him; he could feel her hand against his shoulder, then its warmth on his neck. She was pulling him down to her, pulling him down to kiss her, and, with his eyes closed, he bent over toward her and felt her lips against his. They didn't feel like Iris's lips. They were a little bigger, a little softer. He pulled his face away from her.

"What's the matter?" she asked.

He saw the blue light still resting on her shoulders, softly resting on the windowsill, on the table, and against the wall. He could feel her breath against his cheek; she was so close. "I can't stop thinking about you. Thinking about you day and night," she said. "I can hardly do anything I've been so excited about seeing you. You appeared then disappeared, but you know how people are; they always assume the worst. I couldn't let myself believe that you would reappear, but here you are."

He closed his eyes again, feeling her lips against his. He wasn't going to be able to tell her how he really felt, what the blue light reminded him of. He pushed her back from him just enough to stand up. From the window he looked out over the valley and into the blue sky. "Is it usually this color?"

"Do you see a color?" she asked, coming toward him, her hair pushed around the side of her face.

"Yes," Alex said.

"I do too," she said. "But I was afraid to say anything."

"You've never seen it before?"

She put her arms around him. He knew he must have appeared strained. He put his hand into the light and looked down. His hand was blue.

She pulled on his waist, bringing him over to the bed and sitting down next to him again, taking his head in both hands. "What makes this blue?" she said.

"I thought it was only the color of dreams."

"Yes," she said. "That's what it is."

Her lips came up against his lips and this time he let her kiss him, then push him back against the cool sheets and climb on top of him, kissing his neck, up the side of his face, running her hands through his hair. He opened his eyes and now the color was a deeper blue, a darker blue that seemed to fill her face, fill her eyes and mouth, fill her cheeks and nostrils. "You there," she kept saying, rubbing her lips all over his face. "You there."

She pushed her tongue into his mouth. He tasted her tongue, tasted her clean mouth and brought his hands up along her ribs. He could feel every one of her ribs, then he could feel her breasts, the tautness of the skin, the heaviness of the sides; he let his hands go farther. She breathed heavily and whispered and kept whispering, "You there, you there."

Suddenly she stopped and moved her head back and looked down at him in the blueness. "Do you have somebody else?"

"No," he said.

"You're sure?"

"Yes. But I have to go."

"Already?"

"I'm afraid. I don't want to get caught."

"Please," she said, bringing her lips down to him again. This time she rolled over and drew him on top of her. So afraid was he that he kept his eyes closed, unbuttoning her shirt in the dark, lowering his mouth down to her breasts. She was moaning, pulling at his hair, quietly breathing, her chest rising. He put his mouth to her breast and sucked. He kept sucking, wishing that something would come out—milk, a blue milk. He moved his head down, kissing her stomach. He opened his eyes. It was still there, the blue light. It lay all over her body and all over his hands. He pushed his hands into the elastic of her skirt and pulled it down over her thighs, pulled it gently, feeling the shape of her naked thighs, feeling the shape of her naked behind, then tasting the hairs at the bottom of her stomach, the stiff, curly hairs. As he licked down through these hairs, thoughts pressed in on him.

But then his tongue touched moisture, he tasted salt, and he heard her moan louder and grip his hair tighter so that it almost hurt him. He stayed here, licking her, rubbing her buttocks, rubbing her legs, the inside of her legs, then the outside, then slipping his hands under her back and lifting her so that he could press his tongue down farther into her. She was calling, "Help help I need you I need you you're so beautiful so beautiful please, corporal, please!"

Then she got up and pushed him down against the sheets. Untying his gown, she pulled it out from under his back, then dragged his underwear down his legs. Then she climbed on top of him so that he slipped into her.

Her breathing was slowing down. Her soft breasts pressed against his chest. With his hands he searched her face, the eyes, the nose, the mouth, such a gentle mouth, so wet and open.

You're not her are you? he thought. *You're still not her either you're somebody else and so am I that's what I have to learn I'm someone else not Alex anymore not him he's back with Iris in New York you been there to New York? Of course everyone's been there. Lived there? It's too hard to live there—no trees not as many birds as I like to see. Birds? Yeah, I love birds, don't you? Ever get tied up with a place? Tied up? I mean you can't seem to leave either way, maybe because of somebody? It's happened, everything's happened. Nothing is new. No, nothing is new.*

She was shaking him gently. "It's still here," he heard. He opened his eyes; he'd been dreaming.

"What is?"

"Look," she said. She sat up a little and he could see her body, such a perfect body in the strange blue light, the soft, sensuous blue light, the light from the otherworld.

Then he was out in the hall, all the final words between them still inside him. *Write me, please write me . . . But they'll open it . . . I'll understand you, don't say things directly . . . I love you, love you, love you. I love you, love you . . .* He took the elevator one floor down and went to the door where Blair had said he'd be and knocked.

Blair opened it just enough for Alex to see a slice of the high cheeks of his long Irish face. "Clown, you're too early."

"We've got to get back," he said. "What if they check our bunks?"

"Clown, go wait for me in the basement. I'll be down shortly."

He started down the basement stairs, then turned around and came back up to Blair's door. He knocked lightly, then waited, strolling along with his fake limp so that nobody would notice him. Behind him the door opened a crack and Blair stepped out, closing it behind him. "Asshole."

"I didn't ask to come here," Alex said.

"Let's not get into that," Blair said. "Wait outside for me."

"Why should I?" Alex said.

"I'll kick your ass, you fairy bastard," Blair said.

"Bastard, you say?"

"Bastard." Blair backed him against the wall; Alex tried to push him back but he couldn't.

"Leave me alone," Alex said.

"Get down in the basement and hold tight until I'm back, asshole."

Blair pushed him to the side and started walking down the hallway. Alex came up behind him.

"Give me the keys," he said.

Blair turned around and threw his fist at Alex's face, but Alex blocked it and swung back, hitting the top of Blair's jaw near his ear with the side of his fist. Blair came at him cursing. He swung and Alex blocked another punch, and this time threw one back directly into Blair's ear. The punch stunned Blair for just a moment, just long enough for Alex to bring his knee up against his stomach. "You give me the fucking keys," Alex said. *"Give me the fucking keys!"*

He was speaking too loudly. He heard footsteps, doctors, nurses running down the hall. "I'll kill you," Blair said. Alex got up and ran for the basement door. Downstairs he grabbed his clothes, put them under his arm, and ran outside in the white gown through the wet grass. He changed behind the jeep. Soon Blair, who had already changed, came over the hill.

Alex faced him with his fists raised.

"Give me the keys," he said.

"You've already fucked up, asshole," Blair said. "We're both going to get shit now anyway."

"Give me the keys," Alex said.

"Do you want to drive or something?"

"Give me the fucking keys!" Alex said. "I'm tired of being kicked around by assholes like you! Give me the fucking keys!"

Blair went around to the passenger side. As he climbed in, he threw him the keys, and Alex got in and drove.

"Do you think the doctors have contacted Berringer?" Alex asked.

"You'd better believe it, soldier."

The jeep moved quickly down the hill and into the pines.

"How are we going to do this?" Alex asked.

"You're the boss now, pal," Blair said.

The jeep was bouncing through the pine forest, the sounds echoing off the tree trunks. Alex turned the jeep onto the dirt road.

"Just go for it, gun it up there," Blair said.

Alex drove up the long hill, getting enough speed to cut the engine and roll into camp, stopping under the same tree where they'd picked the jeep up. He handed the keys to Blair, and Blair reached over and pulled the emergency brake. The lights were off in the barracks. Blair walked alongside Alex, then stopped, and Alex could see him breathing heavily, staring at the barracks as if he knew they were waiting inside for him. Alex went on and opened the door quietly. As he tiptoed through the barracks, he could see the shapes of the men in their bunks sleeping. He undressed and got into his own bunk. His knuckles hurt; they ached; his fingers seemed to stiffen on both hands, as if he'd broken something. He kept his hands away from his body, resting them on their palms. Just as he was falling asleep he heard Blair come in, the pine boards creaking under his feet.

The next morning after breakfast, the men started their long trek up the mountain to the cave. In the tunnel they put their hands on each other's shoulders and walked toward the green light of the room. They passed the first room, following the tunnel all the way into the dome where the other workmen were already shoveling. A wheelbarrow load of dirt had been dumped on one of the flatbeds.

When they broke for lunch, all of the soldiers were loaded on a flatbed. A brakeman loosened the brake and the railcar

started down the ramp through the dark tunnel. Outside in the
sunlight, it stopped and the soldiers got off. Two soldiers who
had carried the lunch up from the barracks in backpacks were
waiting with pots and dishes spread out on the rocks. The men
sat on the side of the hill and ate, looking over the valley toward
the sea.

They were tired and irritable that night. Alex wasn't woken
up by Blair; perhaps Blair had found somebody else to go out
with, or maybe he didn't go himself. Alex's knuckles hurt so
badly that if he moved his hands in the night, the pain colored
his dreams like dye. During the day he could hardly hold a
shovel.

All week they worked at the tunnel, piling the dirt on the
iron platforms and rolling it out to be unloaded down the mountain slope. The dome was extended by seventeen feet on one
side. Men worked on the ceiling with ladders, hacking away at
the dirt. Berringer himself helped out, though often enough he
seemed to have office work to do.

At the end of the week, the sergeant called Alex into his office
in the barracks. "I hear you're quite a fighter," he said to Alex.
He was seated behind his desk, turned sideways, resting one
elbow on the back of his chair, the other on his desk.

"Who told you that?" Alex said.

"Word gets around."

"Who told you?"

"Why do you care who told me? You know who you
whipped."

"I didn't whip anybody."

"That's what I like to hear—humility," Berringer said. "A
good fighter has humility. That's the beauty of a good fighter."

"I'm not a good fighter."

"You're a damn good fighter," Berringer said, getting up from
behind his desk. "There's no question in my mind that you're
a good fighter." He quickly reached down and lifted one of
Alex's hands and looked at the knuckles. They had become ugly

since the fight. They were purple and swollen. Alex wanted to pull his hand away, but there was nothing he could do.

"How did you get these?"

Alex shook his head. "I don't know, sir."

The sergeant stepped up so that he was less than an inch from Alex's face.

"You're lying, Corporal, you don't lie to a sergeant, Corporal!" he shouted, spraying Alex with saliva.

Alex kept his chest out, his arms by his side. His eyes were blinking, but no other part of his body moved. He could smell cigarettes on Berringer's breath. Berringer walked around to the door, slid the bolt across to lock it, then returned.

"Did you lie to me just now?"

"Yes, sir."

"Why did you lie to me?"

Alex could feel that something bad was coming, something really bad.

"Don't say you don't know," Berringer said. "Don't play dumb with me, Corporal."

"Because I didn't want to fight," Alex said. "But I was made to."

"Who made you?"

"The person I fought, Blair," Alex said.

"You don't like him, do you?" Berringer said.

"No," Alex said. "I don't."

"But you kicked his ass once, do you think you could kick it again?"

"I don't want to," Alex said.

"That wasn't the question."

"Maybe I could."

"You've got a week to get ready for it."

"What do you mean?" Alex said.

The sergeant smiled. "Now get out of here!"

CHAPTER **36**

THE next day in the big dome, a flatbed was pushed off the main line onto a siding. The wheels were blocked so it wouldn't roll and two soldiers were assigned to work on it. As Alex pushed wheelbarrows full of dirt up a ramp onto the railcar, the men hammered and sawed away, securing four posts with holes drilled through them to suspend ropes. Alex realized what they were doing. They were building a makeshift boxing ring. When Berringer left the dome, Alex walked over to Blair and pointed toward the ring.

"Did he tell you we're fighting?" Alex said.

"It's your fault," Blair said. "They saw us up at the hospital."

"What's he want us to do?"

"One of us is going to get the shit beat out of him," Blair said. "You'll see."

"He's done this before?" Alex said.

"It's better than what happened to me in the office, so I'm happy to go into the ring with you, Brown." Blair smiled, drove his shovel deep and threw a pile of dirt into a wheelbarrow.

Later, Alex asked Berringer when the fight would be.

"I told you a week."

"And when am I supposed to get ready for it?" Alex asked.

"Do you want time off?"

"He's twenty pounds bigger than me," Alex said.

"You should have thought about that before you went on your little date with him."

While pushing a wheelbarrow up one of the ramps, Alex noticed his strained arm muscles were much more defined than they'd been two weeks ago and he started thinking that maybe it wasn't luck that had allowed him to win the fight the first time.

"The men are bored, they need entertainment, besides, it will be your first chance to work on a stage," Berringer told Alex that night after dinner. Alex had been heading from the mess hall to his bunk room. He stopped and stared at the sergeant, who reached into his shirt pocket, pulled out a gold cigarette case and flipped its lid with his thumb to offer one to Alex. On the underside of the lid, Alex saw a tiny picture of a man in a blue suit doing a flip between trapezes. Berringer held it before his eyes.

"I don't smoke," Alex said.

The sergeant lifted a cigarette from the open case to his lips. "In this fight you're going to have to fight fair, you know," he said, lighting his cigarette. He walked around Alex to the door.

Alex followed. It was just getting dark outside; Berringer walked through the long grass of the meadow in the back toward the dark line of trees.

"Give me more time," Alex said.

Berringer turned around, bringing his cigarette down from his lips. "Do you really want more time?"

"Yes," Alex said. "I need time."

Berringer turned again and Alex followed.

"I'm getting in better shape," Alex said. "The match will be more even in two or three weeks. If you want entertainment—"

Berringer stopped at the edge of the meadow. Darkness was gathering in the trees. He exhaled and smoke drifted slowly up and over his head.

"I do want a show, a performance," he said. He seemed to be thinking of something. "Maybe you have a point. It will be more interesting in two or three weeks." He turned to Alex. "That is, if you're not lying. But I have noticed you're stronger. Where were you before this?"

"Before the island?" Alex said.

"Yes, before the island, what did you do?"

"I was an actor," Alex said.

"Ah, an actor," the sergeant said as they walked back to the barracks. He dropped his cigarette into the grass and stepped on it. "An actor, in New York?"

"Yes," Alex said.

"There you have it. When I first saw you I mistook you for a turkey. I thought Mr. Volenti had sent down a Thanksgiving turkey early. But then I saw that you actually had the nerve to break a few rules. Turkeys don't break rules." Berringer stopped in the darkness, far enough away from the barracks so his voice wouldn't carry in. "Now, let's see if you have it in you to follow through."

Once the flatbed with the ring was finished, it was pushed off onto a track siding and left alone. Neither Blair nor the sergeant nor the rest of the men mentioned the fight. Three days later a letter came from Ava.

In some ways, it's made things worse. I think about you so hard that sometimes I think you're going to appear, magically appear before me, right here in the hospital. At night, I feel like I'm going

to turn around and see you all at once. Other times, like in bed,
I'll wake up and feel for you across the sheets.

Alex put the letter into the mattress. He didn't want to think
about her. He wasn't mad at her, he just didn't want to remember the night at all. Besides, it was Blair's fault that he had been
unfaithful. *I had everything under control until that night,* he
thought, *even if I had already kissed her, but so what? What's
a kiss? People kiss their friends good-bye. I wouldn't object to
Iris kissing somebody good-bye, or even kissing somebody because she liked him though I must admit I wouldn't be very
happy about it.*

CHAPTER **37**

THEY were building a giant arena in the mountain. There were tunnels with strange rooms, ancient dressing rooms, ancient set rooms, tiny vertical passageways that you had to climb a ladder to get up, passageways leading into bigger and bigger rooms or smaller rooms, rooms of different colors, the blue room, the red room, the green room, the gold room, the orange room, the room of silver light, and the room of no light at all. The room of darkness.

The hard work during the day put Alex into a deep sleep at night, otherwise he probably would have been up all night every night thinking about Iris. During moments of optimism he would think of the fight to come, Blair coming at him in the ring, punching at him. *So what if he knocks me out*, Alex thought. *It will be good to tell Iris about how mad I was at him and mad at myself for going with that other woman. I'll show her my scars.*

Another letter came from Ava.

I know from what happened and I know from your silence that you're thinking about somebody else. I don't want to interfere

with you until that's over, if it's ever over. Your questions about
Iris Barton, weren't they to cover up something? Is there another
woman you love here? Sorry for the tone of this letter. It's just
that you've changed something inside me ... I'm still hoping
that you don't have to fight that soldier. If you do, I'll pray
for you.

One afternoon during work in the mountain a soldier came
up to Alex and told him that he had the rest of the day off.
"Feel free to wander around the island but tonight you have
to come up here and fight." Alex leaned his shovel against a
wheelbarrow.

"Who told you?"

"The sergeant."

"He's really making me fight?"

"Maybe you and Blair can strike up a bargain."

Alex followed him over to Blair who was throwing dirt on
top of a full wheelbarrow, yellow light reflecting off the sweat
on his bare arms. The soldier told him what he had told Alex
and Blair started to smile.

"Where are you going to go?" Alex said to Blair.

"I'm going to hit the bag some more."

"You've been hitting a bag?" Alex said. He followed Blair
out of the big room and up a stairway of packed dirt. "Why
didn't anybody tell me about this bag?"

"You should have asked. You're a rookie, but you're too
damn cocky."

They came into an exercise room with a rounded dirt ceiling,
a universal gym with various weight presses for the arms and
legs, back muscles, and stomach muscles, and, off in one corner,
a punching bag. Blair went to the bench press, lay on his back
and lifted a stack of weights repeatedly. When he got up, Alex
lay down. He moved the stack up and down even faster than
Blair had. Standing before a mirror afterward, he looked at his

biceps. It was the first time he'd really looked at himself. He was much stronger than he'd ever been before. Even his neck was thicker and his face more defined.

Alex returned to the bench press, lifting the entire stack in one burst of energy before the eyes of Blair, who remained silent.

"Do you want to fake it?" Alex said, getting up.

"Do you want to know what will happen if we do, by any chance?"

"What?"

"We'll both be brought into the sergeant's office and the doors locked."

"What did he do to you?"

Blair began hitting the punching bag, hitting it so fast that the punches blurred into each other, making a constant humming noise. When Alex stepped up, he hit it once but couldn't hit it again until it had almost stopped moving.

"There you are."

Alex turned. A man, hardly taller than a midget, strode across the floor wearing knee-high boots and a vest. A long, stringy white beard, the coarse texture of a horse's tail, dangled to a point just below his chest. In his hands were two pairs of boxing gloves.

He stood in front of Blair. "It's our day," he said to Blair. "Our day to *remove* him."

He handed Blair a pair of gloves and helped him put them on. Then he put on his own pair, turned to Alex, and asked him to lace and tie them.

"How do you feel?" he said to Blair, while Alex threaded the laces.

"This is our man right here," Blair said.

The man didn't seem to hear Blair. "You are going to *remove* him from the living, aren't you?"

"He's lacing your gloves right now."

The man turned to Alex. His face was covered with baby oil or greasy lotion, beaded with sweat.

"*You?*" he said to Alex, then turned to Blair. "Tell him to leave. He'll learn our moves. Go on," he said to Alex. "Go practice with your own coach."

"Nobody gave me a coach," Alex said.

"Then go do some shadowboxing, just don't hang around here."

Alex looked at Blair. "I've got to practice with the bag. I haven't practiced with the bag," Alex said.

"Not now," the man said.

"Why not? It's not your weight room."

The short man put his gloved hands up and began punching quick hard jabs into Alex's chest. Alex jumped back toward the door. "Get out of here, go on," the man said. "The room will be free in two hours."

"How come they gave you a coach?" Alex called over the man's head to Blair. Blair had turned and was hitting the bag.

He walked out of the cave entrance. A vague haze hung in the immense space of the valley below the mountain. To one side, far below the rails curving around the side of the mountain on a trestle, he could see the walls of the château, the whiteness of the gravel in the courtyard. The eyes of the two guards stationed at the tunnel entrance peered over at him; the guards didn't move their heads.

Alex started down the tracks. Half a mile below the tunnel, he saw a small fallow field of brambles and long grass. He crossed a stone wall, pushing his way through the spiny branches on which he saw raspberries, most of them unripe, but others bright red, and he plucked these off. Scores of birds were squawking and chattering in the trees and field around him. Red-winged blackbirds hovered overhead making a clucking noise, protecting their nests. With a handful of berries, Alex found a spot in the sun and lay down and looked at his watch. He had all afternoon still before the fight. He ate the berries one at a time, breaking them open in his mouth, the fresh wild tang bursting on his tongue. An ant crawled along the folds of cloth on his pant leg. He put his finger in front of it and lifted it and watched it crawl around and around making its way to his palm.

Circus World Museum, Baraboo, Wisconsin.

CHAPTER **38**

FROM inside the ring he
looked out at the cheering faces of the men, who were tightly
packed, pressing against the bottom of the platform; something
had come over each and every one of them; an eagerness shone
across their pale faces as if Alex's actions now took on an importance far beyond any other actions in his life, as if he was tempo-
rarily given a place high up in the world, and he was now being
tested in that place. As long as he didn't slip up, he'd be allowed
to keep it.

A heavy fog of tobacco smoke obscured the arena. Beers
popped open; men laughed and cursed and spit yellow tobacco
juice onto the dirt floor, and Alex felt naked in front of them.

Then the roar of the crowd rose. The men parted, clearing a
path all the way to the ring for a man in clown makeup wearing
boxing trunks and boxing gloves and a purple and silver jacket.
It was Blair. Over whiteface, he wore a pathetic, thickly painted
red V-shaped smile, a round rubber nose held on by an elastic
band, and black wrinkles painted around his eyes. Climbing over
the ropes, he sat down on his low stool in the corner and leaned

forward for the short white-haired, bearded man to massage his
neck.

Behind the men Alex heard a bugle and saw the company
bugler standing at the tunnel entrance where tracks came
through. All of the men below Alex turned. Like thunder, the
loud creaking, rumbling noise of a rolling flatbed broke out into
the arena, silencing the men. Pink rugs had been laid over its
surface to make it look like a stage. Red-and-white banners hung
from its sides. In its center, high on a green pedestal, were two
purple thrones. On one of them sat a woman dressed in a sparkling purple bathing suit holding a silver staff. As the stage jerked
to a halt behind the men, she stood up, steadying herself against
her chair. A banner hanging from her shoulder across her shapely
chest said, Natasha, the Mermaid. She wore large false eyelashes
and her painted cheeks were crimson. Lifting her white gloved
hand, she waved delicately. Yellow-and-brown smoke drifted
around her. The men cheered. Alex looked over at Blair the
clown, who craned his neck, staring like a child at the woman
across the arena. Behind him, the bearded man slapped the side
of his head with a damp towel.

"Not yet!" the man yelled in a scratchy, agitated voice. Alex
had hardly loosened himself up for the fight. He wore a heavy
cotton sweatshirt. His boxing gloves were tied tightly on his
wrists.

The men standing below and behind him were shaking their
fists and calling out: "You ready for this?" Alex couldn't tell
whether they were jeering or cheering him on. He looked over
at his opponent. Blair's neck was still craned to get a better look
at the woman, who was now seated in her throne, her knees
pressed tightly together, her gloved hands resting on her legs.
She was half hidden in smoke as were the tall flames of the
torches licking at the walls behind her.

A man crawled up into the ring. He appeared to be a performer, one of the men dressed in blue from the party. A silver
whistle hung around his neck and in his hand was a megaphone.

Raising it to his lips, he called, "Gentlemen! Gentlemen!" in a tinny piercing voice. The crowd hushed slowly. "Quiet! Let me have your attention before our show begins." The performer waited until the room was quiet. "I want to thank the two soldiers, Corporal Blair to my left and Corporal Brown to my right, for donating their time and their talent to this spectacle here tonight. All of you have worked hard in the creation of this arena. As you know, we have a great deal of work ahead of us still. But as a reward for the good work that all of you are doing so far we give you this night of entertainment. These two men, we believe, are fairly evenly matched. More beer and more cigars will arrive shortly, so drink up."

Alex felt such butterflies in his stomach that he wasn't sure he'd be able to stand once the bell went off. He closed his eyes for a moment, put his gloves over his ears to lessen the noise, and thought of Iris. He spoke to her as if in a prayer. "I love you, darling. I love you. Please, darling, know that I love you." He kept saying this out loud, his lips moving; he didn't care if everybody was watching him. The performer went on talking, but Alex went on speaking to himself. A bell sounded—a loud, decisive bell—and with it came a deafening cheer, a cheer so loud that it hurt his ears even as he held his gloves over them.

Blair got up and danced from corner to corner around the ring and around Alex. His quick movements made Alex dizzy. Then Blair stopped, punched himself on the side of his face, and fell down. Laughter exploded from the crowd. Blair got up again, hit himself on the side of the head and fell down again. He did this over and over, drawing louder and louder laughter and cheers.

Alex stood with his gloves up, watching the man's performance. Because of the painted smile he could not tell Blair's true expression. But suddenly Blair, getting up from one of his antics, began staring at him, and he knew that it was getting serious, deadly serious. He closed his eyes as Blair approached him. *For you, Iris,* he thought, *for you and only you.* Then he saw a flash of red, then black.

He came to seated against the pole in his corner. Men slapped his back. "Get up, get up."

Blair bounced up and down on the mats, his naked chest and arms glittering in the strange yellow light. Men kept slapping at Alex until finally he got up. He was still dizzy. As he swung his head, his vision of the crowd moved in a great blur, a blur of yellow smoke, of brown uniforms and blue work clothes, of black hats. Laughter pierced his ears. He looked down at the mat. There were Blair's black boxing shoes dancing before him. He felt a punch on his forehead. The crowd roared. He fell back toward the rope. Again, looking down at the mat, he saw Blair's feet, and then he heard his gravely voice.

"Come on, you son of a bitch, come on, I'll knock your head off." Alex looked up. The punch came at him like a blackbird diving from the sky. He held onto the rope as his knees melted beneath him, watching the bottom of the referee's pants, then his feet. The crowd was yelling Blair's name. Alex was propped against the rope. The referee began counting; he counted down from one hundred. It was an act, no doubt, for he kept counting and counting and counting. There was no end to it. Alex tried to get up, but he couldn't. Then the bell went off and the referee dragged him back into the corner. Looking up at the dirt ceiling, at all the strange shadows on the dirt ceiling, he thought he could see the birds again—the same ones with stern human faces he'd seen in the cell.

The bell sounded again. "Get up," somebody behind him yelled. But Alex sat there, leaning back on the post. "Get up, or he'll kill you." Alex got up, but Blair was standing right in front of him. He hit Alex again, this time on the side of the jaw and Alex sat down again. Blair circled the ring, away from him, holding his gloves up. "She's mine," Alex heard him yell. "All mine, this wimp couldn't handle her anyway." He was yelling this at the top of his lungs. "If he's this bad in the ring, think how he must be in bed. He must be macaroni in bed."

Blair swung around, his gloves high over his head, and came toward Alex who was now standing up, holding onto the ropes behind him. "Are you ready for this?" Blair said. Alex's eyes focused first on Blair's shoes, then on his legs.

"Yes," Alex said. "Knock me out."

"You're a chicken shit," Blair said. "Do you know that?"

"Yes," Alex said, inhaling deeply. "I'm that, too."

"We don't need men like you in this army, I hope you realize that."

The crowd began chanting at such a pitch that Alex could hardly hear what Blair was saying.

"I've wanted to weed you out for so long. What a wonderful moment this is, wonderful moment to be onstage and performing with you, you dirty rotten no-good faggot!"

The crowd was chanting and the noise was deafening.

Blair went on. "I would bet any money you've never ever satisfied a woman. My guess is that pussies scare you. Terrified of them, aren't you? Scared of that dirty hole, aren't you?" He started dancing around Alex, tapping him on the side of the head, in the temple, on the forehead, then on the other temple. Alex put his gloves up. Blair danced in front of him.

"Let me make you a wager. I'll fuck any woman that you've ever fucked and get them to love me. I'll fuck your nurse friend Ava until she's screaming, screaming my name out into the night. And this week when I'm fucking the Mermaid we'll both be thinking of you deep in the ground in your black box. Deep in the ground in your black box!" he yelled. "And then you know who else I'll fuck? I'll fuck that woman you keep talking about in your sleep, what's her name?" He knocked Alex on the head, but Alex didn't feel it because he was staring at Blair's clown face, staring through the makeup and into the eyes, then at the thick red V-shape around the mouth. He could see spittle in the paint, beads of sweat dripping down under the plastic nose.

Blair's mouth was open just a crack, just enough to let air in and out, just enough to breathe and curse. "I can't remember her fucking name, hold on," the lips said. Alex saw him walk to the edge of the stage and bend over to speak to Fletcher who stood puffing madly on a cigar. Then he came back and danced in front of Alex. "I'll tell you who I'll fuck, I'll fuck your friend Iris. I'll fuck your friend Iris!"

Alex's fist shot out for Blair's clown mouth, shot so hard and so fast that when it hit he heard a crunch, the crunch of teeth. His glove had penetrated the opening. Blood splashed across the Blair's whiteface all the way up to his eyes. Alex's other fist went into motion, a rapid-fire motion of fists pounding into Blair's stomach, and slowly Blair bent over. Alex's fists came up to the clown face and hit repeatedly, so fast that the motion felt completely separate from him, as if somebody had attached somebody else's arms to his shoulders, arms with superhuman strength and speed. His fists kept pounding and pounding into the face, driving the face backward. Then he felt the referee grab his arms, then others grab his arms and he heard the shouts, the screams of the others that he would kill Blair if he kept it up. But he broke free and went at him again while he lay on his back on the mat, striking the clown face until the men yanked him away.

Now he was shaking, his arms and hands becoming his own again, vibrating even as the others held him. They pushed him back, but Alex's eyes remained fixed on the men who surrounded Blair. "You won, you son of a bitch, you won," a soldier yelled into his ear. "Now leave him alone. Leave him the hell alone."

Alex's eyes were fixed on where Blair lay. Men stood around him. He couldn't see him, just the chests of the men who stood in front of him. "You trying to kill him? You trying to kill Blair, you bastard?"

Even through the cigar smoke he could smell sweat, his own sweat and the sweat of the men around him. He saw them bring a stretcher up into the ring. They put Blair on it and started to carry him away. Alex pushed through the others. "Get back, son of a bitch," the men said, "or we'll go at you." They were sliding the stretcher through the ropes, three men holding the ropes apart and four men carrying it. Alex could see blood all over Blair's feebly rising chest and over the makeup of his face. His eyes were closed. Alex lifted his own gloves and saw that they were red, so were his arms and shirt, and then he became aware of the blood on his face. Two soldiers pushed him back to his corner. "Sit down," they said. Sitting, he watched his gloves twitching on his knees, his arms twitching.

The arena was clearing out quickly. The referee with the megaphone called to the soldiers. "Our winner is Corporal Brown."

The referee lifted Alex's shaking arm and Alex pulled it back down. Somebody yelled, "You'll pay."

Alex's hands were shaking so hard he couldn't clench the brown laces of his gloves. The referee untied them for him, and Alex dropped the gloves in the ring, took a towel from the rope and cleaned himself off. He could see the empty chair next to the Mermaid. "Get going," the referee whispered. "Get on there with the woman and get the hell out of here."

He crossed the arena and climbed up next to the woman. A soldier who was supposed to work the brake for him jumped off, cursing under his breath at Alex. Alex released the brake himself and the stage rolled across the arena and into the dark tunnel.

CHAPTER 39

THE flatbed, carried by gravity, rolled out of the tunnel and into the night air. Alex leaned against the brake, the steel brake shoes squealing out over the valley. The Mermaid put a robe over her shoulders, her eyes and teeth glistening in the silver-blue night.

They rolled for almost a mile down the steep mountain incline. Had Alex let up on the brake, the steel vehicle would have taken off down the rickety rails. By the time they reached the bottom, the palm of his hand was blistered and his muscles cramped.

He had never been to the base of the tracks. In the darkness he saw flatbeds on sidings, a giant train yard of rail cars. Beyond the sea of flatbeds were little houses with soft yellow lights shining through simple four-paned windows with curtains. The houses were made of logs, like Lincoln Logs.

"Here?" he called to the Mermaid.

She nodded, flashing her white smile in the darkness. Alex pulled all the way back on the brake. The vehicle halted and he locked the lever in place. The Mermaid sat with crossed legs, the robe over her shoulders. Alex hopped off the platform onto the little stones of the railroad bed, turned, took her by the waist, and lifted her down.

"This is where we're supposed to be?" he asked.

The starlight reflected off the surfaces of the flatcars. Some had cargo on them, chains, garbage pails, giant rusted springs, a pile of moldy work shirts and pants probably to be used as rags. On the ridge around the switchyard were the sleepy yellow lights of tiny cabins, each glowing with a strange uniformity.

The Mermaid slipped—she wore white clogs—and Alex stayed next to her to give her his shoulder for support. Above them, the purple mountain rose like some fantastic memory of an event that one could never return to. "You're sure you know where we're going?" Alex asked her.

They were in a kind of basin. Rickety wooden stairs led up to the cabins at the rim of the basin. Each step up, as Alex followed the woman, shook the stairs. At the top, the woman rested, and Alex saw a tall round building, like a control tower at an airport, rising over the switchyard behind them. In the top window a red lantern blinked every two or three seconds. The silence of the train yard seemed to hum with the memory of the sound of the fight. Alex could still hear the cheering.

A car with dark windows waited for them on the road at the top of the stairs. Alex opened the door and helped the Mermaid in. A driver sat in front, a cap down over his eyes, a cigarette glowing. Mist had formed on the outside of the windshield.

Alex closed the heavy door. A throbbing, aching feeling penetrated the joints of his wrists. He turned to the Mermaid and saw light reflecting off her cheeks and eyebrows. The car started down a hill, only the slightest trembling coming up through the springs from the dirt road. He pressed himself against the window, looking out through the tinted glass.

He saw a lumber mill, sawdust piled high under a tarp behind it, huge saw blades through the open doors of a shed. They crossed a track for transporting the flatbeds back up the hill; cables with hooks running down the middle must have been

used to draw them up like a ski lift. Farther on there were buildings with giant dirty engines inside, one of which was running.
Behind a large storage tank, Alex saw the back of an airplane
hangar and a long narrow landing strip.

The car came to a small village with yellow streetlamps and
glittering sidewalks. It was a town perhaps for the workmen and
their families. Many in leisure dress passed in and out of shops
that sold T-shirts, ice cream, and fudge.

The taxi turned onto a white gravel drive that circled under
the portico of a hotel. Two men dressed in navy blue bellhop
uniforms stepped out from the lobby and opened the door for
Alex, who turned to help the Mermaid out.

In the lobby behind a large white reception desk across a glittering green rug, Alex could see a man with a narrow face and
wire-rimmed glasses. His thin pale hands rested on the desk.

"You're Corporal Blair?" he asked.

"No," Alex said. "Corporal Brown."

"Corporal Brown?" the man said. His thin face quivered.
"I'm so sorry."

"I won the fight," Alex said.

The man handed him a black pen. "Sign, please," he said.

They followed a man in double-breasted attire to a silver elevator. At the top floor he opened their door, gave them keys, and
asked if they wanted anything. "Champagne?" he suggested.

Alex looked at the Mermaid, who didn't respond either way,
then turned back to the man and shook his head.

Alex limped through the fresh-smelling room and stepped out
onto the balcony. He saw the dark silhouette of the mountain,
its peak high above the tree line. Directly below him, fifteen
floors down, pale moonlight glittered on an immense oblong
lake. Canoes had been drawn up on a white beach beyond the
terraces of the hotel. A dark figure, tiny from this height, stood
at the edge of the water.

The Mermaid took clothes out of the open drawers of a dresser
and went into the bathroom. She came out dressed in black jeans

and a black cotton shirt with a collar. The shirt hung loosely down from her chest, but her jeans were tight.

Opening drawers to different dressers, Alex saw men's clothes, a pair of khaki pants, a light green chamois shirt. In the bathroom he looked at his face in the mirror. Black-and-blue rings had formed under his eyes. An open cut had not yet scabbed above his left eye. His lips were swollen and bumpy. They felt smooth to his tongue and tasted of blood.

This is really what I look like, he thought. *I really look bad. I'm ugly; I'm as ugly as an ugly clown.*

In the bedroom he saw the Mermaid sitting back against the pillows of the bed reading a novel.

"Talk to me," he said. She put the book down and stared at him.

"You weren't expecting me to win," he said. "Did you want Blair?"

She kept staring.

"I would have let him knock me out . . ."

He brought his legs up onto the bed, lay down, and breathed in and out slowly; there was pain in his chest now. After a long while he fell asleep.

When he woke up it was dark in the room except for moonlight that came through the curtains. He could hear the Mermaid's long, steady, almost silent breathing. She lay on her back in a white nightgown, her chest rising high as she inhaled, then sinking slowly down. Her wrist rested on her stomach, and he could see a bracelet with a strange design on it. Moving closer, he saw engraved in its silver a sword swallower performing his act.

He got up—all his muscles hurt as he moved—and went outside to the hall, pressed for the elevator, and waited.

Downstairs he crossed the lobby toward the desk clerk, who looked up from a small yellow reading lamp, the neck of which was bent over his book.

"Is there any way I could get some food?" Alex asked.

The young man looked back at his book, marking a place with his finger, then putting a bookmark in and closing it. He stood up.

"Our kitchen's closed, sir. There are vending machines down that hall, though."

"I don't have any money."

The young man stared at Alex.

"You're with the army, right sir?"

Alex nodded.

"I'll give you some change, then add it to the army's account."

"Thank you."

Alex crossed the lobby, looking down at the glittering green rug. Glass windows of small shops faced out into the lobby. The shops were closed.

He heard the humming of a refrigerator and saw a red soda machine and two other vending machines. He put quarters into the one for candy and pressed for a chocolate bar.

On the way back to the elevator, he saw posters hanging in the hallway. There were several theater posters of actors dating back to the nineteenth century, including a framed circus poster.

When he woke up in the morning he saw the Mermaid standing on their little balcony, the wind blowing her dark hair against her shoulder. He watched her out of one eye. She stood looking out at the view without moving for a long time.

Behind the lake, the steep mountain rose far above the timberline, its clifflike slope covered with dark green trees and long streaks of rock slides. On one of its stone precipices Alex could see a tiny flat rooftop that looked like a hiker's hut.

He got up and went into the bathroom. When he came out, the Mermaid was still in the same position, leaning against the railing.

"Hey," he said from the door. His jaw hurt from uttering this one syllable.

She turned slowly and looked at him.

"I saw a poster with your name on it. Are you a circus performer or something?"

She stared at him quietly.

"Is there a circus around here?"

She kept staring.

"Do they need an ugly clown?"

She turned and looked out at the view. He stood next to her.

"I know there's a circus around here. There must be one."
Almost every part of his body ached, especially his neck.

"Are you hungry?" he asked finally.

She seemed to nod, then she turned and walked into the room.
He followed her to the elevator.

During breakfast in the prow-shaped dining room, Alex became dizzy and went into the bathroom to vomit. Bracing himself against the mirror, he saw strawberry marks all over his face.

The Mermaid was standing by his food when he came back.
He was so dizzy that the dining room swung back and forth
like a rocking ship. She held his arm and walked him through
the lobby and up to his room.

The view from the room was still astonishing. As he looked
out at the long, thin blue lake his stomach contracted. He lay
on his back on the bed. The Mermaid stood above him, staring
at him, her gaze wide-eyed and strange.

She went into the bathroom and dressed in the suit she'd
worn the night before: the blue bathing suit with reflective scales
over it. She put on her robe and white clogs. Carrying a handbag,
she left the room.

He became feverish that morning. He tried to think of the circus
poster as if this one-hundred-and-seventy-year-old picture
would save him. But images of Blair kept playing before his
eyes. It was as if the images themselves were responsible for
his illness: the bloody, toothless face; the crooked, anguished,
childlike expression that begged for life as Alex pummeled it out
of him—yes, thinking back on it, he had really wanted to kill
him, to exterminate, abolish, remove him from the face of the
earth, this undeserving, inhuman beast.

Blair's image became the chimpanzee in the painting behind
Evelyn's house. Like the manlike face of the ape, there had been

more than mere physical pain in Blair's expression as Alex hit him. There was something else afflicting him, something interminably sad, something black and unforgiving.

The thought crept up on him that Blair was not well, that Blair might not make it.

He slept from late afternoon into the evening. When he opened his eyes, the Mermaid was there leaning over him.

He tried to sit up, but the pain made him drop back to the mattress.

"Tell me," he said, "about your role in the circus."

"A strange coincidence has happened," she whispered. "My best friend is Ava. It is strange because, you see, I love Ava, I love her more than I love myself, and I know what it must do to her to think about our sharing the same bed. She's asked me to tell you something." Behind her he could see light from the stars and the moon. She still wore her strange suit, and now her hair hung on either side of her face, uncombed, casting a dark shadow across the sides of her eyes. Her face was right above Alex and she was whispering. "You have two more nights here before going back. Once you're back the soldiers are going to attack you, this she knows from what the other nurses have learned." Alex was still hardly awake. "Blair is going to die."

"Die?" he screamed, jerking his body out of sleep. An excruciating pain shot from his neck into his shoulders as he sat up. "That's impossible, impossible!" His shouts died without the slightest echo.

The Mermaid left the next morning before Alex woke up. She did not return that next evening. Two days later a car picked him up and delivered him to the barracks just before dinner.

CHAPTER 40

DURING dinner Alex ate at
one end of the table, away from the other men, keeping a steak
knife concealed at the side of his plate. Before Alex finished,
Berringer summoned him outside. Walking past the men, Alex
heard curses; somebody turned and spit at the floor near his
boots. He caught up with Berringer in the meadow. Darkness
had fallen almost completely; cigarette smoke trailed around the
side of the sergeant's face as they passed through the grass toward
the dark trees.

The sergeant stopped and turned, and Alex could see just the
shadows of his eyes and his chin.

"There are certain times when a man needs help, when a man
can't do it all on his own," the sergeant said, quietly. "The men
want to kill you, and there are seventy of them in this troop and
only one of you. You can't handle this on your own, Corporal.
Tomorrow you're not to go to the mountain, but to the château
and see a man named Jean Courier. You'll be talking to him for
a few days."

"Talking to him? What about, what for?"

"He's a performance counselor; he's new," Berringer said, looking down. "I don't know much about him, but I hear he's good."

"Counseling for what? Why do I need counseling?" Alex said.

Berringer took a deep breath, biting his lower lip and exhaling through his nostrils. "He died this morning," he said.

For a second Alex didn't know who he was talking about.

"Died?" he said, not quite believing it. "He's dead?"

"The men don't know about it yet. I'm not going to let them know until tomorrow morning, until you're safe from them inside the château. After a few days, after the funeral, you may be able to come back." Alex walked around Berringer toward the edge of the darkening woods and looked up into the trees.

"You did the right thing," Berringer said, coming up behind him. "You did what you had to do."

Alex turned around; he felt as if he were going blind, as if the darkness of the trees were swallowing him. "What if they find out tonight? I can't sleep in there tonight."

"How will they find out?"

"They sneak out at night. They might sneak out and find out. They'll kill me in my sleep."

"You'll have to stay awake then. You're not leaving the camp until morning."

"I'll sleep outside," Alex said. "I'll take a blanket and sleep in the woods."

"I've told you how we'll handle it."

As Alex stepped into the lighted barracks, all of the men, as if sensing what Berringer had just told Alex, looked up from their playing cards and board games. A man shaking dice in a cup stopped without tossing his roll. Players dropped their cards before the others. Even those who had seemed neutral a short while ago were now intensely hostile.

Alex lay in his bunk, his hands behind his head, and tried to appear at ease. But as soon as he closed his eyes, the image of Blair lying on a white cot with a sheet pulled over his face came to him. The sheet moved and the name Iris ushered from beneath it into the room.

"Your wife!" somebody shouted.

Alex sat straight up in his bunk bed. The men had made a semicircle in front of him, and Alex wasn't sure whether they had said it or whether the sound had come from a dream. He jumped up to face them. "What do you want?"

Five or six stood ready to square off, their fists at their sides; a row of men stood behind them.

"Blair had better recover," a chinless, red-haired man said. Alex could hardly remember his name.

"He'll recover," Alex said.

The men moved closer.

"Not here, not here," somebody in the back said. Fletcher stepped in front of the men. "Go back to bed, Brown. Have a pleasant sleep."

The men and Fletcher turned and walked away.

That night, after hearing the men sneak out the door, Alex went to the window. He watched them push the sergeant's jeep to where the road sloped away. They were off to the hospital to see how Blair was doing. Alex returned to his bunk and lay down. After a while he got up and quietly crossed the hall to Berringer's door, knocking gently so as not to wake the men. The longer Berringer took to get to the door, the more urgent became Alex's need to see him. He kept knocking, tapping steadily louder, but Berringer didn't answer. Finally he turned the knob and opened it.

The bed was still made, the room empty.

He heard the jeep roar up to the grounds and stop. He ran to the door to get outside, but the men saw him and yelled, waking all the other men. Alex ran along the side of the building toward the meadow, but soon he could hear their footfalls behind him.

He ran into the pitch darkness of the trees, keeping his hands in front of his face for branches. At least one person crashed through the underbrush close behind. Alex came to a boulder field leading up the side of the steep hill. He tried to move more quietly to throw off the man who was following him only by sound. Alex pressed himself against the underside of a large boulder, and felt around the ground, digging a loose rock from the leaves. The man ran by, stopped, and came back. Alex heard the click of a blade. He lifted the rock over his head. He couldn't see who the man was, only that he moved forward, a faint glistening of steel visible for a second in the darkness.

He lifted the rock high. "I don't want to hurt you, Fletcher," he said.

"It's Stern."

"You're a young man, Stern," Alex said. "I don't want to kill you."

Stern moved toward him slowly. Alex threw the rock down at his chest as hard as he could. He heard a thump and then Stern falling into the leaves.

Alex turned and ran through the trees.

At daybreak he found himself in a grove of young trees, pale sunlight coming through the slender trunks; the chattering of freshly awakened birds began. He felt exhausted. Under a dense bush in a shallow declivity, he fell asleep for a long while. When he got up, he climbed a steep hill under green cover, trying to orient himself. Through an opening in the leaves, he saw the mountain, and realized he was toward the rear of the barracks. He descended the hill to where he'd hidden his pack before joining the army.

Everything inside was intact. After pulling the circus tickets from their plastic bag, he sat down and examined their design and hand-drawn letters carefully. *"The child will follow,"* he said to himself several times.

That night, though he hadn't eaten since the day before, he set up the tent in the forest below the field, the same forest he had hiked through, and fell to sleep quickly and deeply. Before dawn, though, his eyes opened mysteriously and he found himself alert, staring toward the roof of the tent into pitch darkness. A branch rustled, a stick broke. He pushed his head out of his bag to listen more carefully. Dry leaves crunched, a twig snapped. He grabbed his knife and flashlight, pushed through the tent door, and pointed the beam at the noise.

Two disk-shaped eyes reflected the light: a raccoon was standing on its back legs pawing at the air. It turned and ran off through the ferns.

The next day he moved deeper into the forest he'd crossed months before as he looked for the stream where he'd killed the trout. Eventually he came across a section of it and began to hunt up and down its pools for fish. There were fewer trout than he remembered; he saw only one large one in water shallow enough for him to kill it with a rock. He found a rock and threw it at the fish. When the water cleared, there was no sign of it anywhere.

He tried many times before he stunned one, a small one, which he quickly cooked and ate. But after he'd finished he felt even hungrier than before.

During the second day he made his way back toward the fields behind the barracks, hoping to find some berries. But he had no luck. The few that the birds had left were too green to digest.

After dark he stashed his pack and made his way down to the road that led to the hospital. Around midnight he reached the hospital, entered through the basement door, climbed the stairs, and then took the elevator to the second floor.

He moved quickly through the hallway, frightened that he'd turn into a room and see the body of Blair covered by a sheet as in his dream. But soon he saw a group of nurses standing in the reception area. One nurse turned and came toward him, and Alex saw that it was Ava. Ava did not seem at all surprised to see him. Taking him by the arm, she led him into an empty room and locked the door securely, her eyes filling with tears. By the bed she helped him off with his clothes and under the covers, then lay on top of him, resting her head against his chest, as if she needed confirmation that he had been alive all along. After a long time she told him that she would disguise him as a patient by wrapping his face in bandages. She'd lie to each doctor separately and make each one think that another doctor was taking care of him so that no one would bother him.

Alex told her how long it had been since he had eaten. Soon she brought in a tray with dinner. Before leaving her shift she wrapped gauze over his entire face, leaving openings for his eyes, nose, and mouth. Later another nurse came on duty, fed him again, and reassured him that she was Ava's good friend and that she would take care of him as well as Ava had done.

Evenings and nights, Ava took care of him. In the daytime her friends took over. It had been a long time since somebody had cared for him the way Ava did then. He found himself speaking to her in more and more detail of various aspects of his strife on the island. But he left out one important detail: his real reason for being there.

Sometimes she talked about her life as a child on a farm in the middle of wheatfields in Kansas, where she had lived happily into her twenties until one day something happened to her. "I became crippled with a fear," she said.

Alex took her hand and looked up at her dark eyes. "A fear of what?"

Ava whispered so quietly that he could barely hear her. "Vanishing . . . Do you know what I mean?"

Early in the morning before dawn on the fourth day, while she was sitting next to him on his bed in the half-light, he spoke words that sounded strange to his own ears. "You see," he said, "I'm not supposed to be here. I'm sort of a spy, I guess."

He watched to see if she would be alarmed, if she would turn on him, but she wasn't even slightly surprised. "I've been looking for somebody," he said.

"A woman?"

"My wife." He looked into her soft, dark eyes. They were moist, but there were no tears.

"I'm sorry. I miss her, you see, I miss her terribly."

"Yes," she said.

"We were together on the Island of Verre and we went to a circus," he said, sitting up next to her. "That's the last I saw of her. I never saw her again . . . I was so in love with her that I went into shock. When I look back at that year after she was gone—last year—I see nothing but cold gray rain. I wanted her back more than I wanted my own life. I would gladly have—"

"Shh." She put her hand over his mouth, then reached around his back and untied his nightgown and pulled it off him. She took off her blouse and pushed him back on the sheets. Her bare breasts trembled as she brought them down to his mouth. Then he was inside of her and she was above him, pressing his shoulders back against the bed.

"Please, get dressed, I have something to show you, please follow me," she said.

She checked in the hall for the right moment for him to leave his room. They went downstairs and pushed through an exit door. The stars were beginning to fade. Over the tips of the pine trees at the edge of the parking lot he could see the faint light of dawn.

Ava squeezed his hand and brought him onto a trail through the pine forest. It was dark under the trees. As they passed a clearing, a meadow of long grass, Alex saw reddish light brightening the sky.

After several miles, they came out at the edge of a cliff over the water. Crimson light had gathered on the low clouds of the horizon. Waves broke crisply and whitely below them; gulls called overhead.

They climbed down a clay cliff and crossed a rocky beach. At the edge of the water Ava stripped off her white clothes and waded out, staggering on the slippery rocks. Alex stripped and followed her, stepping and falling on the seaweed until he was deep in the water, which was warmer than he'd ever remembered ocean water. Ava swam ahead of him, kicking up white foam.

Far out, she stopped, waited for Alex to catch up, then turned toward shore and pointed.

Faint red rays of the morning sun struck the side of the mountain. Entirely visible, the mountain seemed to rise up out of the sea itself, towering like a great wave. Ava rolled onto her back, lifting her hands over her head as she floated, then stopped and treaded water close to Alex, touching him and finally wrapping her arms around his neck.

They held each other tightly and went under. When he opened his eyes in the salt water, he could see her face next to his, her cheeks puffed out. Just as his lungs were ready to burst, she let go of him, and he followed her up to the surface, blowing out air.

After she caught her breath, he heard her choking and saw that she was crying. He moved close to comfort her, but as he touched her, she turned and pointed to the mountain.

"Volenti's circus is in the mountain . . . The entrance must be somewhere in the château . . . I know because we take care of their sick . . . Your wife must be in there if she was stolen by a circus, that I'm sure of."

A rising breeze blew small, choppy waves at the back of their heads as they swam in. The light on the water changed. It was harsh. The sun had come up over the horizon and daytime had arrived without the full transition of dawn. The ocean felt colder, and he was sure they were too far from shore to make it back. Foam caught in Alex's lungs. He swam slowly, staying next to Ava.

Before they got to shore, Ava slowed down, and Alex put his arm around her chest and dragged her in by kicking. On the stony beach, Ava lay exhausted on her side on the rocks, and Alex saw her body looked thinner and weaker than it did at night.

CHAPTER **41**

IN Alex's hospital room, Ava covered his face carefully with gauze, kissed him, said good-bye, and left her work shift. That morning he fell asleep and dreamed he'd returned to the arena where he'd lost Iris. Once again, as in the other dream, he was at a circus and he had been called up onto the stage by the man in blue who swung a pendulum before him. Alex watched the pendulum. He heard tropical birds and saw lush tropical plants on the stage, then he began climbing the railroad tracks into the darkness of a tunnel.

But this time before reaching the green light at the end of the tunnel, he heard a voice calling him, and he turned into one of the mountain rooms, a green room where a man sat with his arms tied behind his back in a straitjacket. The man, in his late sixties or early seventies, had luxuriantly flowing white hair that hung down his back. He begged Alex to untie him, and Alex did, unknotting first the sleeves in the back, then a cord around his ankle.

"Are you Alex Barton?" the man said.

Alex nodded.

"I'm your father."

Alex stared at the man's wrinkled face, at his great nose and high cheekbones.

"How do you know you're my father?"

"Your mother's farther inside the mountain. I tried to follow her in, but Volenti tied me up here. He doesn't want me to go in after her. I have some things to settle with her."

"But how did you know who I was?"

"I heard that you were on the island. I heard from the Great Volenti. He thought you escaped, but I knew better. I knew that you'd never leave."

"What are you doing here on this island?"

Alex touched his father's hand. A tingling sensation ran through his arm.

"This is as far as I was able to make it inside. Your mother is farther in. Volenti is at the center. I know what he's done to you. I wanted to tell you, but I couldn't, you see. I wanted to get to the detention camp where you were and set you free, but I couldn't leave the mountain. Once you're in here, it is almost impossible to get out. The only way out is through the château or down the railroad tracks, or through one of the vents."

"You left me, didn't you," Alex said. "You didn't take care of me when I needed help, you left me to the state!"

"I did the best I could for you."

"Go to hell, die . . . See if I care . . . I don't want to go any farther, anyway," Alex said. "Why do I want to go farther? I don't care about Volenti—I don't care about Volenti, I don't care, I don't care, I don't care about performing, either, I don't care, I don't care, I don't care about performing!"

When Alex awoke the bandages covering his face were soaked with sweat and tears; his throat was sore from yelling. Sitting up, he smelled ammonia. After pulling the bandages off his face, he felt his crotch. He had urinated on the mattress.

CHAPTER **42**

THAT morning he wrote a note:

Dear Ava,
I know we will meet again, but meanwhile I'll love you and miss you always. You've meant more to me than anyone can ever know.

A. B.

In the afternoon he left the hospital and surrendered himself at the gates of the château. The guards had been given orders about what to do with him when he came. One of them escorted him into a basement hallway between small bedrooms to a locker room and shower and gave Alex a bar of soap, a towel, and a change of clothes. After Alex was clean and dressed, the same guard led him up three flights of stairs to the highest balcony encircling the white courtyard and knocked on a glass door. A man called to enter.

The guard stepped in, saluting rigidly. "Good afternoon, General Thumb, I've brought Corporal Brown."

General Thumb's large bald head reflected the gold light of the room. He sat behind a carved wooden desk in front of a wide hearth. He wore a monocle with a silver chain dangling across his shoulder and smoked a long thin, crooked cigar. There were two lamps on the desk, both decorated with tigers leaping through hoops of fire; dark red leatherbound books and a cup of quills stood between them.

The guard backed out of the room. Alex saluted the general, who rose from his chair and came around his desk. He was a very tall man wearing high black boots and long white leather gloves with frills at the cuffs. As he walked, he kept one hand behind his back, while the other steadied his monocle. He stood before Alex, carefully examining him through the lens, moving his sharp chin up and down, his long legs slightly apart.

"Corporal Brown," he said, nodding as if to confirm Alex's existence. "You've gotten yourself in some deep trouble here, I understand. Rumor has it that you've murdered a man."

Alex stood with his hands stiffly to his sides.

"I didn't murder him. We were boxing."

"Let's hear your side, Corporal." The general blew dark purple smoke into the room. Taking the cigar from his mouth, he cleaned his lips with his tongue. "Let's hear it from the beginning, the very beginning." He turned and went to the windows of the door.

Alex began. "Well, sir, some of the soldiers, myself included, have been leaving the barracks at night to see nurses in the hospital."

"Without permission?" The general spoke with his back turned to Alex.

"Yes, sir, without permission."

"Are you aware of what the punishment such a breach of conduct carries?"

"No, sir."

"I will have the sergeant inform you. Go on, Corporal."

"Well, I made only one trip to the hospital before realizing that I didn't want to break the rules here."

"That should have been a realization that you'd come to before you set foot on the island."

"Yes, I know, but after I had decided to abstain from the hospital, I was forced by Corporal Blair to go—"

"How did he force you?"

"By blackmail—I had gone out the one night when he was caught and he told me that he would tell on me if I didn't go with him. Anyway, I told him I'd go with him to the hospital but only for half an hour, but after half an hour, I knocked on the door of the room he was staying in and he told me that I should wait for him—he had the keys to the jeep."

"You got there by jeep, Corporal?"

"That's correct, sir."

"Does the sergeant know this?"

"Yes, sir. Anyway, Corporal Blair and I exchanged words and one thing led to another—"

"This was over when you should get back to the barracks?"

"That's correct, sir. I didn't want to be there. I wanted to get back. We ended up in a fistfight in the hospital hallway. The hospital personnel then informed the sergeant of our presence in the hospital."

The general nodded his head. "And?"

"As punishment the sergeant set up a boxing match between Blair and me. He thought it would be entertaining to the men. He also thought it poetic justice that we should have to fight as punishment. Well, I must have swung too hard . . . I killed him."

"I see," the general said. "But the referee informed me that you didn't stop when he blew his whistle."

"I did, but it was too late."

"You killed him on purpose," the general said. "It wasn't in self-defense."

"General Thumb, I was only trying to win the fight."

"The men want to pay you back, you killed their man, their leader."

"But I didn't want to . . . it was all part of the fight."

"What did he say to you? I heard he said something to you?"

"He said I wasn't worthy."

"Worthy? Worthy of what?"

"He said I was a fake."

"We don't have any paperwork on you, none at all. We've been trying to determine who you are exactly—who are you?"

"I'm a soldier."

"But who were you before you came here?"

"I lived in New York—"

"The sergeant tells me there's something wrong with you . . . you're different than the others. What makes you different, Corporal?"

"I don't know," Alex said. "I don't stop where others stop, that's all."

The general examined Alex, nodding his head. "We've got a hell of a mess on our hands, you know. What if it gets out that one of our men died at the hands of another man?"

"I'll tell them what happened."

The general smiled. "You'll tell them? The accused will absolve himself?"

"Well, there's no reason to suppose that . . ."

"Legally, you're a murderer, legally, we're harboring a criminal—we're guilty unless we act on this. You threw punches even after they tried to restrain you." The general wanted to silence Alex. "They'd put you in jail anywhere else."

"But I was fighting against my will. Blair was trying to kill me."

"He was following the rules. What's the difference between what you did and if you had shot him?"

"But they should have stopped me earlier."

The general shook his head. "That won't hold up in court.

Tell me, Corporal, what's in it for you here? Are you just here to defend the island against intruders?"

"I like wearing a uniform. I like the routine of being a soldier. It's a good profession provided there isn't intensive combat."

"And if there were combat?"

"Believe it or not," Alex tried to smile. "I'm not sure who the enemy is . . . I'd like to know who I'm fighting against and who I'm working for, you know."

"It should have been made clear that that's a question you don't ask as a soldier . . . that's not a decision for you to make. An army is an army, Corporal."

"But I'd like to know what kind of army—"

"Corporal, must I repeat myself?"

"But there must be a philosophy behind it . . . if it's at war with another one. They must have differing philosophies."

"An army is no different than anything else. It has interests, Corporal, territories. We're not into crusades or the like. We're soldiers, and like everybody else, we must survive . . ."

"Then what is it all about—the stage?"

The general put his hands behind his back and began to pace. "The stage is a fact of life. There is no need to defend it. It has nothing to do with a philosophy!" he shouted. "Now, Corporal, unfortunately I must absent myself from the island for a while. I haven't had time to examine your performance and ponder your fate . . . you'll have to await my decision. I've heard that otherwise you've been a good soldier—a model soldier in many ways despite your idiosyncrasies." He stopped and raised a gloved finger to Alex. "I will take it all into consideration." Then he began pacing again. "While I'm gone, you're to see our performance counselor; he will interview you and give me his recommendation."

The same guard who had brought Alex to the general escorted him down a flight of stairs to a dark, richly finished door marked with a shiny new brass plaque saying Dr. Jean Courier. The guard knocked for Alex, and a voice told him to come in.

Behind a wide oak desk under the glow of a mild yellow lamp sat a man with a friendly, perhaps even understanding, face. He wore glasses with oval lenses, a dark Italian suit, a narrow tie, and many silver and gold rings, three or four on each finger.

He bowed his round head. His hair was thin, not gray, but reddish and slightly yellow. Rising to his feet he strode quietly around his desk and shook Alex's hand firmly and patiently, making him relax.

The office smelled faintly of antiseptic, like a doctor's office but with a trace of incense. Courier offered Alex a seat on a dark leather sofa and returned to his desk.

He smiled and said, "I'm here to help you." Alex became faintly embarrassed as if the man were looking into him, as if the man had already seen into his dreams. "You probably haven't slept well for a few days."

"No," Alex said.

"A lot has been happening to you." The man began writing on a yellow legal pad with a gold fountain pen.

Alex noticed a painting across the room: it was unmistakably one like Michelman's. There were no animals or people in this one, just the sea, a green hill, and in the center of the hill a stage. On this stage lay a red velvet cloth in a heap and in its shadow a tiny striped beach ball. In the other corner a large thorn lay on its side and at its tip, as if it had fallen from the sky, a droplet of blood. The sight astounded Alex. He gripped the leather arm-rest of the chair and focused on it.

"You've had your own war going with some of the men," Courier said.

"Yes," Alex answered distantly. He was lost in thought.

"Do you want to talk about it?"

"You've probably heard it all." He turned to the man.

"I haven't heard it from you; I'd like to hear your side of things."

Alex was silent. After a while, Courier said, "That's all right. I just want you to know that I need to hear your side. It's not just that I want to hear it."

"Why?" Alex said.

"*Because it's your side.*" His eyes rose to meet Alex's and he smiled as if embarrassed by what he'd said.

Alex smiled back. "What do you mean?"

"I just mean to tell you that your situation, or at least what I've heard about it, interests me."

Courier's smile was still one of embarrassment.

"Corporal Brown—do you mind if I call you Alex? You've killed a man, Alex, another soldier. You fought him; it was not your choice to fight him, you were even prepared to let him win if not kill you, but he said something to you that transformed your entire personality for a moment or maybe two, just long enough for you to beat him, breaking the rules of boxing, and kill him."

Courier looked down at his pad, his pen poised over the paper.

"And now, you must feel responsible for his death, do you?"

"No," Alex said.

"You're sure?"

"Maybe I do."

"It must be a lot of responsibility to bear."

"Yes," Alex said.

"You see, responsibility is the hardest thing of all. You see, there's a saying in my book, it's not 'those who travel alone, travel the swiftest,' it's 'those who travel without responsibility or real morality, travel the swiftest.' Everything in this world seems to emphasize swiftness, or immorality over morality. But these people are not fully human; their lives pass before their eyes like a blaze of white light.

"Alex, we need to talk, to really talk for a few days. I've come here only recently. You know a lot more about this island than I do, so I may need your help occasionally when you're talking about what goes on. Nevertheless, I'm here to help you. Soon,

I think, you'll find yourself becoming extremely depressed. You're going to wake up and realize that you're not the same person you used to be, you're somebody else. This new person is a foreigner to you, understand?"

Courier wrote something down.

"All right, I'd like to learn a little bit about your history, where you're from, what kind of a family you grew up in, then we can get back to the problem of the death of Corporal Blair."

"I have no memories from before I was twelve, a few vague images, that's all."

"We'll start with those. What are these vague images?"

"Come to think of it, I really don't have any," Alex said.

Courier again wrote on his pad. "You must have some."

"I don't."

"Please, Alex," Courier said, putting his pen down. "You, like many of the artists on this island, have been ignored since birth. That's what inspires you to be artists. Nobody has ever really heard your voices, acknowledged your true actions. That's why you want to be performers. Logically, it's going to be very difficult for you to trust me, but you must learn to trust me. I'm going to help you. I want to help you. I know what you've been going through here—I have some idea, anyway. But I'm not like the others. Tell me what you remember from your childhood, go ahead."

Alex was thinking of the painting again. So these people did go to Verre to buy Michelman's paintings. He looked back at Courier. "Crying," he said suddenly, surprising himself. "I remember crying about something. I used to throw tantrums, but I don't remember what they were about."

"Was there anybody there when you were crying? Your mother or father?"

"I didn't have a mother or father," Alex said. "I'm an orphan." He gripped the sofa armrest again, wondering what his physical reaction would be to telling somebody again that he was an orphan.

"Did you have foster parents?"

"For the first part of my life . . . after fourteen I was transferred to a school."

"What was your foster home like?"

"I wasn't adopted by the nicest people. I always had trouble with people. My problems here with the men were not my first problems."

"Tell me about the first person you ever had trouble with."

"I had this older brother who was jealous of everything I did. If I got close to my foster mother, he'd beat me up."

"What did he do to you, exactly?"

"Control me. Boss me around, and when I wouldn't obey him, he'd do horrible things to me."

Courier continued writing things down. Alex told him more about his past, but as he did, he felt himself sinking into his chair while his suspicion of Courier's motives for asking him questions rose.

"What's the last really bad thing that happened to you?"

Alex wanted to change the subject, which was upsetting him so much that he didn't want to talk about his past at all. But the first thing that came to his lips was, "My wife—I thought she died—over a year ago. We were in love."

Courier nodded slowly, staring at Alex kindly.

"Do you want to talk about it?"

"No," Alex said. "Not now. I can't now."

Courier led Alex out into the hall and showed him to a small bedroom off one of the big balconies of the château. Tapestries hung from the ceiling and walls of the room. A small dark wooden desk with a letter pad and pen rested in one corner. There were two chairs, one for reading and another for writing at the desk. The room didn't have windows, though it had a vent in the ceiling. Another man showed Alex the mess hall where guards and workers at the château ate. A bathroom with a shower was located five doors down along the balcony.

Alex spent the first evening doing what Courier suggested at the end of the meeting. He wrote a letter to himself about what had happened the last few weeks, about the fight and about hearing that Blair was dead. He wrote that he had no feelings for Blair's death. "I don't know him. I even asked him if he didn't want to fight."

CHAPTER 43

EVERY day from ten until noon, then from two until five he saw Courier. The meetings for the first few days concentrated on both Alex's past and his feelings about the death of Blair. After a few days, Courier told him that he seemed surprisingly comfortable with having killed a man.

"I didn't like him," Alex said.

"But even if you didn't like him."

"He was trying to kill me; it wasn't like he wasn't trying to do me in."

Despite what he told Courier, he had become increasingly upset about Blair's death and Courier's questions agitated him. On the one hand he felt the death had been his fault; unless he was certain that Iris was here, he really didn't belong on the island; but on the other hand he felt so angry at whoever had tortured and humiliated him that Blair's death seemed suitably retributive.

After a meeting with Courier he'd go back to his room, lie on his bed, and think about Iris. There were few signs of a circus anywhere in the château. Everyone appeared busy, even the guards who paced back and forth on the walkways along the top of the walls and sometimes on the balcony in front of his room. Sometimes men and women would come out into the courtyard and practice shooting arrows with bows into targets set up against hay bales. From his balcony, Alex saw a man with mules come in during the morning and allow his animals to drink from buckets near the fountain while he dropped off what looked to be a pouch full of mail. Most of the men and women held their heads back arrogantly and self-consciously whenever they made an appearance in the château.

Of everyone at the château, the cleaning and maintenance people were the most friendly, especially Kala, the woman assigned to clean Alex's room. Kala was only slightly taller than a midget or a dwarf. She was plump with curly yellow hair stuck through with bobby pins and clips. Her face was wide, and, because she was always squinting, her eyes were crested like a cat's.

One time, as she entered with a broom and dustpan, Alex asked her who had been staying in his room before him and she told him a picture painter named Peter.

"Did he look like me?"

"I thought you were him, my dear, when you first moved in."

"Was his name Michelman?" Alex asked.

"Oh, yes," she said. "He's working with the old man now, that's what they say."

"Which old man?"

"The old man of the island, Volenti."

"Who is Volenti?"

"He's the old man of the island."

"He owns it?"

"He's retired, dear. His son is taking over . . . The old man and Peter left together . . . Peter was always talking about a patron, you know, and I think Volenti rather liked his paintings. The old man himself wants to be a writer. He couldn't write here. Could anyone? So he left."

"Where did they go?"

"Off the island somewhere . . . his son is coming here to take over. His room is in mothballs right now."

A few days later, Alex called her into his room again. "Kala, would you have any idea why the old man would collect photographs of people? Does he spy on people?"

Kala laughed as if Alex had asked a ridiculous question. "He's not a collector of photographs, he's a collector of people."

"Of people? Does he kidnap people?"

"He's not like that, oh, no. He's a very nice man. Oh, he wouldn't do something like that."

"Have you ever seen this face?" Alex asked. He handed her the photograph of Iris. Squinting her eyes, she brought it close to her face, then far away.

"I'd swear it was familiar, but I couldn't put my finger on it. Maybe she lived here long ago."

During the time of his meetings with Courier, Alex had many dreams. Some were of swimming away from the island to freedom, others were of coming across a circus on the island and finding Iris in one of the acts. Most of his dreams followed the pattern of the latter. He told Courier the dreams when Courier asked, but always excluded the most important part—finding his wife.

Whenever Alex walked into Dr. Courier's office, he felt a very strong sensation, which at first he thought was because of the trace of antiseptic in the air. But the feeling definitely came from more than just an odor. Dr. Courier was not merely interviewing him; he was studying him, monitoring him. Like a scientist Courier remembered everything that Alex said verbatim as if he'd been reading his notes between meetings. Fortunately, he never judged Alex and only drew the scantiest conclusions from what was said. Often he nodded his head while writing things down, then looked up from the gold light cast by the antique lamp at the edge of his desk and repeated back what he had heard.

Though Alex felt important when he was in the office, there was also a less pleasant feeling. These interviews, he felt, were the preliminary steps of some kind of operation or perhaps some kind of treatment. There was something extremely cold about Courier. Perhaps he would be ruthless in his administration of the treatment, perhaps what appeared to be acceptance of Alex—the doctor's nodding—was confirmation that Alex was sick and needed to be treated. Alex had no idea who Courier was nor whether he was really interested in him or interested in completing some performance.

Nonetheless, there was something in Courier that he found he trusted, maybe due to the doctor's promise to keep everything he said absolutely confidential. Alex cried during the meetings. Memories came mysteriously to his lips as he was speaking. He had run away from home when he was twelve—something that he'd completely forgotten until he was telling Courier about trips he'd taken with the family. He couldn't quite remember why he'd run away, only that while he was used to conflict with his brother and father, when his mother had turned on him as well there was nothing to do but run away. The police had found him hitchhiking only a few miles from his home.

Alex had always considered his mother the one island of sanity in his family. But as he examined his relationship to her more closely with Dr. Courier, he found that while his mother had been extremely kind to him most of the time, she had been unpredictably wrathful at other times. As a child sometimes he would call her from his room; he wanted to show her a picture he'd drawn or he'd lost something. But her response would be an angry "What do you want?" or he'd hear her cursing to herself, "Damn these brats."

"But you were very independent for a boy your age. You managed alone."

"I built tree houses. I had an entire world of my own by the time I was eight. I knew a lot of bad stuff was going on, but I was happy because I had this world."

"Are you sure you were happy?"

"Yes," Alex said.

"But then what happened? Why did you become unhappy?"

"My wife. If she were alive—" But before Alex finished he remembered thinking how unhappy he had been even when he was with her. In truth he was dedicated to her the way a survivor of a shipwreck might be dedicated to a floating board or a life raft. The moment she was out of his sight, he worried that he might not see her again, however irrational that fear was. And when they were together, he fretted over the next time they would be apart.

"Maybe I wasn't as happy as I thought," Alex said.

Everything that had happened to Alex throughout his entire life appeared to be more and more of a nightmare. Alex wondered *how did I survive it?* as if he were no longer in that nightmare. But then he'd think about where he was now: inside the château, talking to a man with unknown motives, a man who might well discover who he really was: a person without the slightest sympathy for the society he'd joined.

"Do you trust me more than you did a week ago?"

"Yes," Alex said to Dr. Courier. "But I don't know why I'm seeing you."

"You killed a man, remember. Killing another man can destroy you if you don't watch out, even if it was just an accident."

"Are there any other reasons I'm seeing you?"

"Well," Courier said, dropping his pen and pushing back

away from his desk. "Sergeant Berringer noticed something different about you, that's one of the reasons he sent you to me." Courier put his hands on the back of his head; his elbows stuck out. "He said you weren't engaged. He thought something was eating at you. Besides that, we couldn't find your papers; we've lost your paperwork somewhere in the admissions department, and we don't know your history, why you're here."

"But I've been coming a week. Have you found something else out about me that makes you want to keep me here longer?"

"We're working on things together. We're breaking ground, it seems. I also feel a certain affinity with you, as if things could have happened to me the way they happened to you with only the slightest twist of fate. I believed in my mother as if she were a god . . ."

Alex stared across the desk at Courier's round face and head.

"And for a long time," Courier went on. "I wanted to be a performer, but I backed away from it because I didn't feel I could be one—or perhaps I was luckier than you, I didn't feel I had to be one. So, instead, I became a doctor and I've come here to see what it's like to be among performers, to see if my choice of careers was really so bad. I also came in order to try to be of help to those who are more talented than I."

"I'm not a performer; I have no talent either," Alex said.

"But you're here," Courier said. "Everyone here has to be a performer, an artist."

"Being in the army makes you a performer? Being in the army is one of the most regimented, repressive things a person could get into!"

"Maybe that's what the sergeant saw was going on with you. You weren't enjoying yourself."

"But how about the others—they're tortured, they moan every morning, afternoon, and evening. They hate their leader, or fear him."

"But, Alex, they must get something out of it."

"Did anyone you know ever try to commit suicide?" Courier asked him one day. The question was unexpected.

Alex nodded slowly, watching him carefully.

"What did you think of it?"

"What did I think of it?"

"What did it make you feel about that person?"

"Angry. I felt angry at him. I'm always thinking that life is just the way you look at it, that if life's bad, you're looking at it the wrong way and I was angry he didn't change his view because I thought it would be easy to change your view, to give up your expectations of yourself or whatever it is that makes you do it."

"How about yourself, did you ever look at life wrong? Did you ever find yourself in a position where you really had to change your view, drop your expectations?"

Alex hesitated a moment.

"Once," he said.

"What happened—what made you look at life wrong and what made you change?"

"Well, something bad happened to me."

"Your problem with your wife? The fact that you thought she was dead?"

Alex hadn't mentioned her since the first meeting. "Yes," he said.

"How long did you think she was dead?"

"I didn't know if she was dead for a long time, but I really thought she was for about a week."

"What did you do during that time?"

"I tried to do myself in," Alex said, looking up at Courier who placed his pen down on his paper and held his hands together neatly.

"It didn't work or did you decide against it?"

"I . . . both. It didn't work, but then I decided against it."

"So you did change your view?"

"Well, I began thinking she might be alive."

"Do you still think that she might be alive or do you know?"

"She might be—I don't know. I haven't seen that she's dead or that she's alive. I haven't seen anything of her."

"If you found out that she wasn't alive, would you try to do yourself in again?"

Alex waited a moment, then nodded slowly.

"Then have you ever thought that you still might be looking at life wrong?"

"No," Alex said. "This is different. I have reasons . . . it's not a matter of viewpoint . . . it's something else altogether, another reason."

"What are your reasons?"

"They're private."

"I respect that, but can you at least hint about what they might be?"

"Well," Alex said. "Sometimes . . ." There was a long pause during which Alex looked only at the back of his hands. "That's what love is all about."

"I don't quite understand."

"That's what it's all about, you see, that's what it's about."

"I don't understand this island," Alex said the next day. "You say that all of the people here consider themselves performers or artists, but how are they different from other people in society? Performers and particularly artists are people who explore different parts of themselves; they don't exploit just one part by becoming a soldier or a guard or whatever else these people are."

"Everyone has to play a role; everyone has to take on a point of view."

"But an artist has a flexible point of view and a soldier a fixed one."

"But even an artist has to decide that he's an artist. The artist or performer is a role in itself," Courier said. "These people have chosen their roles for now. They've given up responsibility for now, that's all. When you're working on a painting, a book, or a play, you must dedicate yourself to it—you give yourself up to it. You're working on this book now or that play now. You must concentrate."

"But when are these soldiers going to graduate?"

"When their role destroys them. When they're nothing but soldiers, then they move on. The sergeant said you were getting further and further away from this. You resisted like few people he's ever seen resist before. But we're beginning to get to the bottom of it. Your dependency on your mother, your fear that there is nothing outside of her, that the world is an ice-cold place outside of her. You say it's not a point-of-view problem, but I think it is. I think you have to learn to change your point of view whether your wife's still alive or whether she's dead. It's not a question of her. It's a question of you. You're hurting yourself every day, every moment, by keeping this point of view."

"What if I told you I want to go back to New York?"

"Then I'd say you're crapping out of what we've started here in this office."

"But what if I told you that the only reason I'm here is because I think my wife is here."

"I've known that for quite a while."

"How so?"

"There could be, from what you've told me, no other reason for you to be here. Why would you be here unless you were hoping that she was here?"

Alex shrugged, admitting that that was why he was here.

"If you go back to New York before sorting out these things, it's all going to come up again, all of the same stuff. Besides, what evidence do you have that she's here?"

"I have a lot of evidence."

"But tell me what you mean—you're not telling me every-thing."

"The fact that everyone here is a so-called performer."

"You mean because your wife is an actress?"

"No," Alex said. He looked down at the diamond patterns in the red carpet. "More than that." He looked up at Courier sitting behind his wide, comfortable desk. "It's a long story."

"I'm here to listen to long stories."

"She was taken from me by performers."

"What kind of performers?"

"Circus performers."

Alex studied the doctor's face to see if the word circus had taken him by surprise, to see if he might be concealing some-thing. But the face remained earnest and compassionate.

"Can you tell me more?"

"I can't really."

"Why not?"

"I don't know," Alex said. Suddenly, he felt tears pressing against the back of his eyes and he had no idea why.

"Come on, you must know."

Alex broke out crying. "Do you want some kind of confession out of me?"

"I'm just trying to help you."

"How? How are you—you're trying to get me to tell you something, you think I'm hiding something from you, don't you? You think I'm crazy or something. I'm here to find her, doctor, to get her back. It's as simple as that. I don't want to be here. I don't even want to be here and I can't seem to find her, I just can't."

That afternoon, Alex decided that, because he felt an almost compulsive need to tell Courier intimate things about himself, sooner or later he might confess even more about his illegal sta-tus. For this reason he thought he'd better plan a way out of the château whether he ever had to use the plan or not. He had never tried simply asking the guards to let him out, perhaps lying to them, so he went down to the front gates and told them that Sergeant Berringer had told him he could go back to the barracks. The guards shook their heads and told him that they had strict orders not to allow him out of the château. They didn't know why, they said, but until they were told differently, Alex was to remain within the palace walls.

"Who gave you these orders?" Alex wanted to check to see if Courier was the one who had given them.

"The general," they told him.

He went into the basement of the château, wandered into the guards' shower room and began opening locker doors until he found a uniform that he thought might fit him. He put it back. If necessary, he might be able to pose as a guard long enough to get free. In a storage room he found rope and picked up a coil to confirm in his mind that he could take it at will and lower himself down the outside wall of the château. He was not entirely confident of these escape plans, but they gave him some reason to hope that he could get away if it became evident they were going to haul him back to the cell and do whatever they had planned on doing with him before.

When he saw Courier again that afternoon, the doctor seemed exceptionally calm and kind to him.

"Last meeting we really got somewhere," he said, happily.

Alex wanted to ask him why, but he only nodded and said, "Yes."

"Now I know that you've kept a few things from me partially because you've been feeling that they might make me look down at you or even that I might report you to the military as having ulterior motives, as not really wanting to develop your performance capability or some such thing. But let me assure you, and I don't know how to do it, Alex, except to say it to you over and over, I'm not here to render a judgment on you—I will never even judge you in my mind, though I might admire you.

And I will certainly never report my findings in this office to anyone outside of this office. Never, okay?"

Alex nodded slightly.

"All right," Courier went on. "I can almost see what you're thinking, but right now there's nothing else I can say to you. If writing down my promises to you would help, I'd write them down, but I don't think it would, so let's get on with the other issues that we've been working on.

"We've talked about your past, about your mother in particular, and I've been meaning to ask you something for some time now. Have you any memories, any recollections of what might have happened to you if she died? I know one time, when she turned on you, you ran away; everybody was against you then. But think back, tell me the first thing that comes to mind if you like."

Alex began to think about his mother; there were some memories, but first he wanted to know a little more about why Courier wanted to hear them.

"You told me that she seemed the one island of sanity in your family—you must have been deeply dependent on her. You were an orphan—where would you have ended up if something happened to her? It sounds like your father really didn't think of you as his son."

Alex nodded, feeling a heavy weight inside him from what the doctor had said. He was silent, and he could smell the medicines in the strange room as if smelling them for the first time. "I did think about Mom's death."

"What did you think would happen to you if she died?"

"Well, I thought . . . I couldn't think of what would happen to me. I just thought about her, how unhappy I'd be."

"Did she seem fragile to you?"

"She'd given me everything. She was the most generous person in the world; I loved her," Alex said.

"What would you have done if she had died?"

"If she had died, I would have felt so sorry for her that I

might have killed myself, I'd definitely thought of that before. But—"

"But what?"

"But I can tell you want to relate this to my wife."

"Maybe," the doctor said, smiling. "Is that all right?"

"But it was different with her. I'd made a promise, I said the promise out loud. I told her that I would kill myself, but in a way I wasn't even telling it to her but to something else."

"To yourself?"

"To a color," Alex said.

Courier laid his pen down again slowly.

"To a color?"

"Yes," Alex said. "One day, one night, a color surrounded us—we were in bed—and I made a promise to it."

"I don't understand—tell me from the beginning, what happened."

"The beginning? The beginning was a long time ago if you want to know the truth."

"Start there, Alex, start at the beginning."

"Well," Alex said, thinking for a long time of where to start. "I guess I told you I was sent off to school when I was twelve . . . that's because the bank foreclosed on the farm owned by the family who had adopted me, but my mother made sure I was sent to a good school, a private Catholic school, a boys' school.

"And I had this desire when I got there and that was to be an actor—my mother loved theater, I think that was one of the reasons," Alex laughed nervously. He thought he was going to cry again. "You know, I haven't told but one other person that since that time?"

Courier nodded and smiled and Alex thought he heard him say, "Thank you."

"But I didn't get along with the drama teacher at the stupid school that I went to, he hated me, and when I tried to get in a play he told me I was too ugly. So, to get experience in front of an audience, I joined the debating club. But you see, our first debate was at a girls' school and I didn't have much experience with girls—I was scared of them, really scared. And when I got up before them, I couldn't think, I couldn't even speak, I began to stutter; I mumbled a bunch of half sentences; I said something weird even—a couple of words which I . . . which I . . ."

Alex had started breathing quickly.

"Which you what?"

"Which I don't remember," Alex said. "Which I can't remember."

Courier got up, walked around his desk and took Alex's hand.

"Are you all right?"

"Yes," Alex said.

"Tell me some more," Courier said after a few moments. He turned and went back behind his desk.

"All during high school I was desperate to get away from that school, desperate to get away from anybody who knew what I had done before the audience. So once I left the high school I was careful never to bump into anybody from there again and I never told anyone else about this until . . . my wife . . . and I didn't tell her until I knew her for a while and until she one time asked me about it."

"And how did she react?"

"She seemed to know about it already." Alex paused.

"Somebody had told her?"

"No, it's just that that's how understanding she was . . . she knew that I had gone through something bad just from knowing me. She set out to cure me . . . she got me to take some acting lessons, and then she got me into a play. You see, it happened again, and this time I hallucinated and saw only girls like the first time and I got scared and I . . . ." Alex's heart was beating quickly.

"And you what?"

"I mumbled something in front of everyone again."

"The same thing as before?"

"I think so."

"What were you saying when you were mumbling?"

"I don't know."

"Are you sure?"

"I'm pretty sure," Alex said. But a phrase began to come to him. He didn't know from where.

"Try for me, please," Courier said.

"The child . . ." Alex started to say.

"The child?"

"The child will . . ."

"The child will what?" Courier asked gently.

A knock came at the door. Apologizing to Alex, Courier crossed the room and opened it. A guard waved him outside. A moment later, Courier stepped back in. "Alex," he said. "I'm so sorry to tell you this, but the general is back and I'm afraid he wants to see you right now."

Alex got up.

"I'm sorry," Courier said again. He patted Alex on the shoulder. "I'm so glad we've gotten to this point. It's helped me, Alex."

The door opened and the guard was standing there. "General Thumb is waiting," he said. Alex followed him out and along the balcony and knocked on the glass doors. He heard the general call for him to come in.

"I've had some time to think about what I'd like you to do," the general said, looking at Alex. He was standing with his hands behind his back. "You are to leave the island in an hour. We'll drop you off at Verre and you can catch a flight to Boston."

Alex stared back at him. He was in shock; he felt heavy and immobile as if his feet were glued to the floor.

"You see," General Thumb said, turning his back to Alex and standing next to the curtains of the tall windows opening to the balcony over the courtyard. "There's too much at risk. Your case is not the only one . . . another man on the island has broken the law . . . if any of it ever came out, the privacy of

this island would be threatened, we would all be in jeopardy."
The general clasped his white-gloved hands behind his back.
"As it is, you've killed a man. If you were to be prosecuted,
you'd go to prison and if I were to allow you to stay on the
grounds, I might go to prison, too, and so might your other
superiors." The general shook his bald head and turned to
Alex. "We can't risk it. It would be better for you if you simply
got off the island . . . if you want to change your identity,
that's up to you. But if you stay here, there will be nothing
but trouble. Do you understand?"

Alex nodded his head at the word *trouble,* knowing the word
meant something entirely different to the general than to himself.

"Then it's decided," the general said. "Of course, you know
that everything you've learned about our island is strictly confidential. Don't talk about it . . . and we, of course, won't talk
about you, that's to be understood, right Corporal?"

Alex nodded.

The general opened the door. "A guard will stop by your
room within fifteen minutes. A boat will be waiting."

Circus World Museum, Baraboo, Wisconsin.

CHAPTER **44**

ALEX stepped outside on the balcony and looked down at the bright white sun reflecting off the white stones of the courtyard. The words that the general had uttered were catching up to him slowly, their meaning becoming real. He went quickly along the walkway to Courier's office and knocked. But there was no answer. He knocked again, then tried the door. It was locked. He ran farther along the balcony, stepped into an office, and asked a secretary where Dr. Courier had gone. The secretary looked at her watch. "He's not here, can I help you?"

"I need to see him."

"He's gone for the rest of the day."

"What!?" Alex shouted. "He was just here. I'm leaving in fifteen minutes. Where is he?"

"He's flown off to see a traveling performer."

"That can't be. He didn't say anything . . . I'm leaving; I've got to talk to him. I've got to . . ."

Alex ran downstairs to the front gates. A guard was facing him. Alex begged him to let him go, but he kept shaking his head. He ran back upstairs to his room, closed his door, put his desk and chair against it, ran to his bed, and started shaking his head and crying.

Rarely had there been a moment on the island that he wouldn't have welcomed, at least on one level, an opportunity to go home. But now that the opportunity was at hand, it was making him sad, overwhelmingly, unfathomably sad and afraid. He buried his head deep into his soft pillow. The smell of the clean sheets reminded him of his foster mother and he began to cry. He cried so hard that he had trouble inhaling, he was coughing everything out of him. He heard somebody knocking on the door . . . they were coming to take him away, to bring him back to New York, to that horrible, horrible world without Iris, to that cold, cruel emptiness without Iris. The person kept knocking, then the person turned the handle and tried to push the door open against the desk. He could hear feet sliding on the stone floor as they pushed, then a nervous, chattering laugh. The door had opened just far enough for fat little Kala to slip in with her broom. She closed the door behind her.

"Bring what you have and come along," she whispered at the door. "There's somebody who wants to see you."

"They're sending me away."

"Quick, I heard. We have no time." She grabbed his arm and pulled him up. "Come, come, cry later, there'll be plenty of time later, but not now. Vera, the contortionist, wants to talk to you."

She pulled him up from the bed by the arm. "Come, I'll come back and get your clothes. Follow me. It's your chance."

Alex followed the woman past the desk and chair and through the door. They climbed down the steps to the hallway, then through the chapel doorway and down the aisle between the pews to the pyramid of stages of the altar. On the lowest stage she opened a low door leading into another hallway, this one flanked by tall dark portraits of portly men with sallow faces.

The floor was dark and shiny. Alex could suddenly hear Kala's and his own footsteps.

Kala stopped at a painting the frame of which reached to the floor. Waving Alex back, she unlatched something behind gilded wood, opened it like a door, and went through into darkness, closing it behind her. Alex examined the portrait. Over the shoulder of the man, in the distance, he could see a wooden stage inside a ring covered with a black fishing net that stretched in a narrow line over the dunes behind it and into the placid blue sea. A huge pile of silvery blue and yellow fish lay in the center of the stage, their obscene eyes staring widely up at the sun.

The portrait opened a crack and Kala stepped out. "Take off your shoes," she said. "And take three steps inside and don't move. Be very careful in there. It's very dangerous if you don't remain still. You'll understand."

The little woman pointed down at Alex's laces and he got down to untie them.

Shoes in hand, he passed through the picture frame into pitch darkness, the door closing behind him. The silent room smelled of freshly washed linen; his feet rested on something soft like a rug. In the distance a light came on over a circular stage with a circular canopy of white curtains surrounding it. The stage appeared to grow as if coming toward him and under the diaphanous canopy, Alex saw pillows, colorful pillows.

He did not recognize it at first, but among them lay the body of a person folded up like a pillow: a small, frail white-haired woman in white tights. She was resting on her chest, but she had folded her body backward, arching her pelvis out so that her buttocks nearly touched the back of her neck, her legs folded over her shoulders, and her knees touched the stage. The edge of her silently moving vehicle stopped right in front of Alex and a spotlight shone directly above him.

Slowly the woman lifted her legs back over her head and came out of her pose, finally sitting up cross-legged.

"Corporal Brown?" she said. Her image floated before him in the darkness: a short, squat face with wide-set eyes and a wide froglike mouth and hair as white as the sun.

"Yes."

"Ah, welcome. Kala has spoken well of thee." She spoke in a gravelly voice. "She says thou desirest to join our family, to work with my son, to be a follower of his ways, to be a brother to him, is she right?"

Alex hesitated before saying, "Yes."

"Then take off thy shirt," she said to him.

Staring at the strange, drifting image of the woman, Alex reached for a button on his shirt and slowly, almost absent-mindedly unfastened it.

"Faster," she called. "Please!" He hesitated, then kept going until all of the buttons were open. "All the way!" the woman called. He pulled it off. "Thou art beautiful, beautiful enough to be a son, beautiful enough! Now kneel down."

Her face was powdered white. Layers of white gowns floated around her tiny body. She sidled over to the edge into the white light surrounding Alex. "Thy body," she said quietly in her scratchy voice, "is very beautiful. Come to me."

He stood up, his chest near the front of the stage. The old woman pulled herself by her hands, dragging her withered legs behind her through the white mesh curtain to the very edge of the stage. She raised the back of her hand, waiting patiently for him to oblige her.

He held it to his lips and kissed it.

"Ah," she said to him. "I am certain that thou wilt learn what thou must learn and conquer what thou must conquer." The musical cadence of her voice rose in pitch at the end of her phrases.

"Now, Corporal," she said. "Touch the stage. But I warn thee to touch it lightly, touch it lightly, Corporal!"

Alex put his hand down and touched the rim of the stage. He jerked his hand back. It was red-hot.

"You see how difficult it is, you see?" she said. "It will not be easy. Look." She pointed to her side. Turning, he saw on the other side of the room another stage light up, revealing the profile of a man standing with fists held low. The man punched rapidly out from his stomach. "Your brother's disciples will be no smaller than that man, only they're much faster. And there will be no less than twelve of them, Corporal, no less than twelve, including yourself."

High up, so far away that it looked tiny, he could see the underside of a stage bordered by yellow footlights. As it descended it became bigger. Alex could see a woman on the platform, a woman who resembled the Mermaid. She wore a bathing suit of shiny scales, her hand held a silver staff. She did not move her head. Her body looked perfectly formed. Her long black hair rested on her shoulders.

"Ah, and your sister will be as beautiful as she is, just as beautiful as she and she will be fierce, Corporal, and dangerous, just as dangerous as he is!" She pointed to the boxer. "Look at her, Corporal, see her beauty, see its danger!"

The woman, standing with one leg bent slightly in front of the other, gazed upward like a picture of a saint. Her stage began to rise. It rose high up, disappearing into the darkness.

When Alex looked down, the boxer's stage had disappeared too.

"You are to follow my son because my son is the son of a circus. But that is nothing to be happy about, young man. The circus he was born of is a circus of darkness as well as light, that's all thou needst know about it. Now I must go."

She rolled onto her back, bringing her legs over her head, bending at the torso, then folding her knees against her stomach and chest so that she compressed herself once again into the size of a bedroom pillow.

Then her stage retreated, becoming tiny in the distance of the long dark room. Because he couldn't see the walls it looked as if the stage had shrunk, but he knew it had traveled far away from him.

He could hear wheels turning and a voice calling commands—a stage appeared to be coming at him from an angle and on it sat a violin player: a woman pressing a violin between her head and her shoulders, her bow up and ready to play. The stage stopped, she drew the bow down, but her arm stopped moving before she'd made a sound.

The sound of a trumpet came out of the darkness behind her. The trumpet played a very sad tune as the stage the woman was on backed away, and Alex listened to the singular, mournful notes carving a clear, brass sadness into the darkness, becoming fainter and fainter as if traveling farther away. Then Alex felt himself lifting off the floor ever so slightly; he must have been standing on a platform with a hydraulic lift. He traveled through darkness, squatting for stability, a barely detectable breeze hitting his eyes and face. His platform stopped and lights gradually came on, lights from the ceiling.

He was in a black room padded with thick carpeting on the ceiling and on the floor, standing on a very small stage, no bigger than the lid of a garbage can. He stepped down.

Light rushed in through a door that was partially ajar. After putting his shoes back on, he pushed it wide.

CHAPTER 45

A HUGE space lay behind the door. He stepped into an auditorium with a ceiling so high that it gave one an impression of walking under the sky. Circus rings divided the dirt floor, twenty or thirty of them, in which troupes of performers rehearsed every imaginable circus act. Nearest Alex, a man, standing before an elephant, had lowered the length of a sword down his own throat. Releasing the handle, he motioned to the elephant who stepped forward, wrapped its trunk around the handle slowly, and drew it out inch by inch. Cages encircled four or five rings, and behind their bars animal trainers snapped whips at black and brown bears, Bengal tigers, and African lions on pedestals. The popping noises sounded like firecrackers. In the ring nearest Alex, children bounced high off trampolines, attempting stunts, their guardians standing by at the edges ready for their falls. Alex heard a noise just behind him like a rush of wind and felt a sudden burst of heat. Turning, he saw three women with long, shiny black hair, wearing silvery purple bathing suits, hold lighted torches to their mouths and blow three enormous flames above their heads in unison.

As he turned back to the rest of the acts that went on cease-
lessly, as if they had been going on for an eternity, their implica-
tion seeped into his blood, inebriating him like a strange,
powerful drink.

A man juggled black bowler hats like Frisbees, throwing them
toward the wall of the underground building. The hats, illuminated by the lapping tongues of torches set along the walls, traveled in a silent circle as if floating. Alex began to move slowly
from ring to ring.

A bareback rider, balanced on the back of a large, galloping
horse, threw himself up into the air backward and landed firmly
on another horse galloping just behind.

Behind silver bars an animal trainer with tall black riding boots
lay on a dirt floor under the bellies of two lions, slapping the
butt of his whip in the dirt to induce a third to lie across his
stomach too. On pedestals at the edge of the ring, two tigers
and a bear sat on their haunches while three grooms—all of them
women dressed in jumpsuits—watched from the edge of the
cage, their hands on the wire mesh. The lion paced back and
forth, growling and roaring at his vulnerable master.

High up in the arena above one ring covered by a net, Alex
saw a family of trapeze artists working. Men and women hung
upside down from swings, their hands dangling below them.
Two adults and a child crossed from one person to the next,
flipping through the air, catching hands and forearms. Music
came from across the arena. A band kept starting up and stopping erratically, practicing several refrains.

Two rings of clowns caught his attention. A midget with a
giant squirt gun was robbing a cardboard bank. The teller kept
adjusting his wig. Clowns were bouncing off a trampoline into
a pile of hay, diving and flipping. In the confusion Alex hardly
noticed at first a woman clown on a unicycle riding in his direction. He turned quickly away from her and walked for an exit
ramp that led out of the big room, but the woman caught up
and held onto his sleeve.

"Keep walking," the woman said. "We're going to the clown's locker room."

"I'm here to see somebody," Alex said, turning away from her again.

But the woman held onto his sleeve. "Alex," she said. "Come with me."

"Who are you?"

"Come with me quickly."

She got off her unicycle and led him up a flight of stairs into a bunk room with colorful wigs and clown costumes hanging from the walls. She closed the door and quickly yanked off her plastic nose and her wig.

The face Alex saw underneath the makeup was so familiar that he tried to say her name but couldn't; it just wasn't possible.

It was Evelyn and she was smiling, her tears blazing paths down the white makeup below her eyes. She moved toward him, wrapping her arms around him. He grabbed her around the waist, squeezing her tightly and lifting her high in the air. Then he put her down and touched her waist, felt her cheeks and eyes and nose and drew his hand through her hair. Stepping away from her, he looked at her from a distance. "It's you, you," he kept saying. "It really is you."

Finally, he began to tell her some of the things that had happened to him since she had dropped him off in the water near the beach. Some time later, Evelyn told how she had gotten onto the island through an admissions center in Massachusetts. She described a strange test she had taken that tested her belief in circuses.

"They asked me questions about circuses and examined the expressions on my face while I listened and answered them. I thought of Michelman's paintings the whole time. I pictured them right before me, and I could feel them. I think that's why I passed."

She told him how they had given her a tour of the island when she first got on it and before she was brought into the inner circus, as it was called. In various places she had seen Michelman's paintings, but had no luck locating Michelman himself. Alex told her what Kala had told him about the painter being with Volenti.

"You mean old Volenti, Volenti Senior?

"Yes."

"But he's not on the island anymore."

"I know. That's what Kala told me."

"Then Michelman's not on the island."

For a long while she kept asking Alex questions about his short conversation with Kala, then the fact that Michelman wasn't on the island seemed to sink in and she had to sit down.

"Do you have any idea where Iris is?" Alex asked her.

Still stunned, Evelyn shook her head. "No, I don't know. But I've looked almost everywhere on this island. I don't believe she's here. I don't know, but I don't think so."

Instead of allowing this news to cripple him, Alex began asking Evelyn questions about the island: why had they tortured him, why was there an army, who was old man Volenti, and why had he been spying on him and Iris, who was his son, and what did these people plan on doing with their militia?

Evelyn knew only a little of the history of the place. Mr. Volenti had come from Europe during World War II to assist the United States military. In Europe he had owned twenty-nine circuses and was an expert at moving thousands of men, animals, and hundreds of tons of equipment quickly and efficiently by rail or by truck. He came to America to flee the Nazis, but when he learned that Hitler had placed spies in Ringling Brothers and Barnum and Bailey circus to study their methods of moving shows, he offered his own knowledge to the Americans.

After the war, he and his wife had a child to whom Volenti became deeply attached, but this child was kidnapped from him during a theatrical performance in New York. The child was never recovered, and Volenti never got over his loss.

"He's had more children and, now that he's retired and gone off, one of his sons is taking over, Volenti Junior."

"So what is this circus in here?"

"Circuses have always been the Volenti family's life. Most of the people here are old performers. In the tradition of his father, Volenti Junior will return from abroad just in time for auditions, and, as his father has done for years, he'll pick a show that will travel with him for a five-month tour. Everyone will be chosen in a different way, and he has a strange attitude toward the clowns," Evelyn said. "Like his father, he's interested in laughter only in so far as it carries with it a few tears. He has a very strange laugh. It is both very sad and very happy, bold and fearful. When you hear it, it will mean something to you. It transports you back in time, back to the original circus. Our group leader, Tara, has told us that most of our routines will merely fill in the gaps between performances, but even these routines should aspire to do to Volenti what he is able to do to us."

Alex looked around the colorful dressing room.

"But you haven't even heard Iris's name mentioned?"

"I actually met a woman named Iris, but she wasn't your Iris, not the Iris that came to the restaurant with you."

Alex told Evelyn how, just before the officers were going to deport him, Kala and the contortionist had admitted him through the room of stages.

"I doubt the officers meant merely to deport you," Evelyn said.

"What were they going to do with me?"

"Oh, they don't just return people to the mainland. It's never that simple. They're never that kind, that's why Kala took pity on you."

She left the room and came back with a polka-dotted clown costume. Stripping to his underwear, Alex tried it on and looked in the mirror. Evelyn pulled a wig of red hair over his head, then sat him down and began to paint his face. She painted his face white and drew red and blue stars over his eyes.

Evelyn told Alex that to join the clown troupe he should introduce himself at dinner to the head clown, Tara, as a latecomer from the clown school. Because Tara was disorganized and never checked records, nobody would suspect Alex's real reason for joining the clowns.

The tube-shaped mess hall accommodated five hundred performers and workers. Food was dispensed from silver carts wheeled between the long tables and benches. After the meal Evelyn brought Alex over to meet Tara—a short, light-haired woman with plump shoulders and eyes so small they made her face look enormous. Alex was still in his clown disguise.

"I couldn't come until today because of my illness," he told her, as Evelyn had suggested.

"Nobody told me that there was somebody left behind."

"He was in our class," Evelyn said.

Tara winked at Evelyn. "You'll take care of him, won't you?"

CHAPTER **46**

THE clowns were given more free time than any of the other performers. The only obligation they had to fulfill was presenting their routines or short acts to Tara once or twice a week. Most days were spent practicing gags, tricks, stunts, alone or with one or two partners. Alex spent all of this time with Evelyn.

Evelyn seemed to concentrate on whatever she was doing, but Alex's attention would often drift. He felt he had to use all of his spare time to explore the inner chambers of the mountain for Iris. But the passageways that Alex found leading out of the arenas either came to inexplicable dead ends or turned back on themselves and brought him into the circus arenas or into the menagerie, a huge room high above the central area.

Among the many animals quartered in the menagerie were horses, llamas, camels, zebras, monkeys, doves for the magicians, performing dogs, and house cats. Tigers, lions, and bears lived there in cages on wheels. In the morning and evening elephants were harnessed to the cages to pull them back and forth from their respective rings. Because the vents had not been

properly designed, the menagerie was hot and smelled strongly
of dung and urine and facilitated the spread of disease. Five men
using sleds pulled by horses were digging a second tunnel out
to the surface of the mountain to complement the ventilation
system.

After three days, Alex saw men in army uniforms searching
the rings for a defector. He and Evelyn were playing clown
baseball. Alex was pitching and Evelyn was swinging at the ball
with a huge bat, missing, and falling on her back. The men
watched them, then went on.

Sometimes a large crowd of performers gathered in the big
dome room for a lecture.

"We are the circus at the end of the tunnel. We are the circus
of the ring and of the womb. We are the circus of light as well
as darkness, the circus of ignorance as well as knowledge, of
devilry as well as enlightenment, of love as well as hate.

"There is only one direction you should be taking in the circus
and that is the direction downward inside the ring. You should
be diving down inside the ring inside yourself. You should be
diving down into the tunnel of darkness inside the ring, into the
tunnel of sadness inside the ring. You should be returning to a
former self, a former life, a former century, a former epoch.
You should be returning to a place that existed before the earth
itself was born. In doing that you will be getting closer to the
mother of all things, the mother of the earth, the mother of the
air."

Alex worked with Evelyn on his routines. She kept telling him
that even a clown must use material that means something to
him. "Do something based on a true incident about yourself,"
she said.

"But that would give me away," he said.

"Dig into your past. What happened to you when you were
younger?"

"I've already gotten into that too deeply." Eventually, he tried to remember things he had done to make his class laugh in high school. This brought back memories of that time.

"When you're growing up," he said to Evelyn, "it takes a long time for you to realize that you're different, that something is different about you. On one level, you know there's something strange, but on another, yourself is the only thing you ever knew. It seemed to take me forever to understand it. Even after I was in boarding school, after I was really aware of being an orphan, I still didn't understand that my life wasn't normal."

Alex befriended a midget named Mr. Manis. Mr. Manis helped Alex learn the basics of the art of clowning, like juggling. "Juggling is to us what tattoos are to sailors," Mr. Manis said. "If you were a sailor, it really wouldn't do not to have a tattoo."

As time went on Alex learned to juggle balls, then pins, then Frisbees and hats, and these led to other stunts, which he began on the trampoline with some of the children. After three weeks of long practices and guidance from acrobats, he could do a back flip from the floor and land on his feet, and he started enjoying juggling, looking at it as useful exercise for toning his muscles.

One day while pacing back and forth on a stage inside a ring, Manis said, "Do you feel like you're finally home here in the circus?"

"A little bit," Alex said.

"You remind me a little of myself," he said. He was dressed like a musketeer in baggy red knickers and pointed shoes. In one hand he held a plastic sword that he used as a walking stick but also swung around freely like a pointer. "As a boy at night there were two things I prayed for: that a circus would never come to my town and that I would grow taller than the second shortest person in my class, Muriel Voighter.

"For a long time, my first prayer was answered; no circus came to my hometown for years. But then one day when I was fourteen I heard whispering among my schoolmates that one had just arrived. The next afternoon, a Saturday, most of the town including my parents went to the show, but I stayed home and sat in the basement watching television until somebody started banging on our front door.

"I opened the door. Muriel Voighter stood there and I understood why I had been staring at her for so long: not only was she almost as small as I, but she was beautiful. At the time she wore a white silk blouse and her long brown hair was cut evenly at her shoulders, and she had large round eyes and soft lips.

" 'I knew you wouldn't be at the circus,' she said. My face must have changed color, but she stepped in and shook me. 'Oh, God, I'm a midget too, don't be mad. I like being small, but you always look like you're about to get sick in class when somebody mentions height.'

"Then she put her arms around me and began to kiss the side of my face. The next thing I knew I had my arms around her waist and was kissing her. Then we went upstairs to my room and made love. Afterward I felt so desperately attached to her that the thought of leaving her for even a moment made my legs and arms shake.

"Arm in arm we walked outside through a field, crossed a stone wall, and the next thing I saw in another field was the circus tent.

"Had I not been so attached to her, I would have run away. But she coaxed me in, and once she did, once I was in the scariest place in the world, my only hope was that a midget wouldn't be among the clowns.

"But sure enough, after the lights went off a spotlight found a very short clown in whiteface with a red dot on his nose. I prayed he was a child, but by the confidence with which he crossed into the ring, I knew he was a midget. And as if my very worst fears came true, he looked right up into the bleachers at me and began beckoning me to come down to him. I saw what he wanted me to do. He wanted me to open the door to a small car so that out would come the rest of the clowns.

"I shook my head, but he marched right up to me, the spot-light following him, grabbed my arm, and began to pull.

"It would have been worse at that point to refuse. Besides, Muriel had gotten up and was helping him to pull me.

"I knew the eyes of many of my schoolmates were on me. I turned and started to run, but I ran right into the arms of Muriel, who picked me up and hugged me tightly.

"We both opened the door to the small car and clowns of all sizes fell out. Finally a giant slid out, reached down and lifted me high above his head as if I were some kind of animal on display. I saw most of the kids from my high-school class laughing and pointing at me.

"When the huge man finally lowered me to the ground I ran blindly out of the arena followed by the howling laughter of the audience. I didn't run home. I started to hitchhike.

"For days I didn't sleep, I just took rides from strangers. After a week, a ride left me off at the edge of a field. Across the field I saw a circus tent. I walked toward it.

"And there at the door of the tent was the midget who had pulled me down into the arena. He kept looking at his watch. 'My word, you're late . . . you were due half an hour ago . . . Muriel's been fretting about where you've been. My word, and look how nonchalant you are about it all.' He broke out into cackling laughter."

One afternoon Alex visited a knife-thrower in his ring and asked him for lessons. The thrower was a quiet, mild-mannered Chinese man named Reynolds. "It's good even for a clown to learn knife throwing," Reynolds said.

He was throwing his daggers at the outline of a woman, the knives piercing the black lines in perfect succession. Alex did not know what he would do with this skill if he acquired it. It just seemed like the right thing to do.

The first lesson Mr. Reynolds gave him was an exercise. "Stare at the target until you see yourself in the target. You must become your target."

The exercise lasted a week. Alex practiced it at night when Reynolds was not in his ring. He stared at the outline of a woman and imagined himself becoming her. After a week, he told Reynolds that he had finished the exercise.

"You are quick, very quick," Reynolds said. "Maybe you are better equipped than most?"

"Maybe," Alex said.

Reynolds put the blade of a knife between two of his fingers. "Who is holding the knife? Are you holding the knife or is the knife holding you? When the knife doesn't know you are there and you don't know it is there, then we'll go on."

After a week, Alex threw his first knife and after another week his skill was improving greatly.

He had dreams during this winter of Dr. Courier. He'd be in the doctor's office explaining the circumstances of the death of Blair, explaining why he had to bend over him and hit him while he was down. One time he woke up Evelyn and told her he needed help. Stepping outside into a hallway, he told her that he was a murderer, that it was the one irrefutable fact he would never be able to run away from no matter how many tricks he learned.

"For God's sake, Alex, a murderer is not somebody who kills somebody in self-defense."

"He was on the mat." He slapped the dirt floor.

"He had been trying to kill you. He said he was going to kill you—he said that, didn't he?"

CHAPTER **47**

AFTER two months he had explored every room in the mountain until he was quite sure that Iris wasn't on the island. His hopes rested on Volenti Junior, whose return would somehow bring her back. Maybe she was traveling with him. Alex waited for him as anxiously as did the other performers.

One Saturday night in the middle of the winter, a night when all of the circus people had parties and many got drunk, a weather report told of high winds and severe cold outside on the mountain. Evelyn and Alex entered an empty arena with a six-pack of beer and a pint of whiskey and climbed onto the bleachers. They drank and talked and gossiped. After a while, Evelyn led him by the hand down from the seats. In the center of the arena she put her arms around him and started kissing him.

In his mind he told Iris that of everybody he knew Evelyn had worked the hardest to help him find her. She was her ally as well as his. But the truth was that Alex was so comfortable with and dependent on Evelyn that becoming physically close was inevitable. In the morning they walked through the tunnels to the mess hall and sat down together without speaking.

The more time Alex spent inside the mountain, the closer he became to Evelyn and the more he wished that the spring would come and the tour would begin so that he could escape from the island.

He spent many hours practicing his knife throwing. His aim was quite accurate for somebody who had begun so recently. But he still wasn't accurate enough to throw with a living subject standing against the board.

"Only after many years, not many hours," Mr. Reynolds said, "will you forget that you are a knife-thrower, forget you are a performer, forget you are in a circus in a ring. Only then can you throw with a person standing against the board. For now you must meet the Flying Man. Knife throwing is small. The Flying Man is great!"

Reynolds brought Alex to the dark blue, circular arena where he and Evelyn had spent the night together. It was slightly warmer and more humid than the other ones.

"You wait here for the Flying Man," Reynolds said. "Just be patient."

After Reynolds was gone, a strange disembodied laugh, half animal and half human, filled the arena. Its echo made it seem as if it were coming from all of the walls. Soon a tall, lithe young man in whiteface and silver slippers crossed the room gracefully.

"You must be the clown that Mr. Reynolds told me about," he said, approaching him. He had a slender, sweaty face with a long nose and narrow-set eyes. He spoke in a quick, nervous, chatty manner. "Ha! Mr. Reynolds has spoken highly of you. You have passion, he told me, and you'd like to be a different kind of performer."

"I would," Alex said.

"Then we'll do it. Don't worry about talent. I am living proof that there is no such thing as talent, only passion. I've always wanted to fly like my father. So here I am," he said. "I am probably no more talented than the average. Do you want to fly?"

"I wasn't thinking of flying. I'm scared of heights," Alex said.

The young man laughed. It was the same cackle, half dog and half man, that had filled the arena moments ago. "All the better. I would never teach a man who was not scared of heights to fly, never. Those who are scared of flying are the only ones who are ever really able to fly. We will start on the tightrope tomorrow morning. Is that all right?"

The next morning, Alex followed the intricate passageways that led to the Flying Man's arena and opened the door.

In center ring, the man was setting up a short wire only a foot off the ground.

"How is your balance?" he said, just as chattily as the night before. He laughed. "Come on, step up."

Alex stepped up. He took three steps along the wire before twisting his arms back and forth and finally falling.

"Stop, stop, take a breath. Look at the wire. What does the wire say? A straight line is the shortest distance between two points, right? That is what it's saying?"

"Maybe," Alex said.

"It is really not saying much any way you look at it. It is you, you are the one saying so much." He laughed. "You must not say so much when you walk on the wire. Keep silent. Up here," he said, touching Alex's head.

Alex took several deep breaths and stared at the wire. It was not unlike staring at the outline of the woman in Reynolds's ring. Then he got up on it and walked calmly across it.

The Flying Man clapped, his white gloves making a soft,

patting sound. "Where are you walking?" he said. "You're walking on the ground? No. You're walking on a wire? No. You're walking on the air. Yes. Remember that. When the wire becomes the air, then you are ready to move it up higher and higher. Before you go to bed tonight, hit your head seven times against your pillow and each time say: the wire is the air. Say that now. The wire is the air."

"The wire is the air," Alex said.

"And remember this word: *flying*. Do you know what it means to fly? To fly is to live, remember that. It's the same thing."

That night Alex did as the man said, hitting his head against the pillow seven times and saying, "The wire is the air."

The next day he returned to the arena. The man had moved the wire between its posts so that it was two feet off the ground instead of one foot.

"I'm leaving soon, we must work on this very quickly . . . I need to know why you want to be a performer."

"You're leaving?"

"Yes. But I'll be back. I perform in Italy every year."

"Where?"

"On the street. I have a circus that's all my own. Do you know why it's all my own? Because I'm the only one in it." The Flying Man nearly fell over backward laughing.

"Where do you sleep when you're here? I've never seen you before."

"Never mind where I sleep. I sleep up there," he said and pointed to a high perch. "If you are a flying man then you know you have your best dreams up there. That's why I'm up there to begin with. It's good for the dreams and dreams are good for life, they're good for living. Dreams are good for living. Now, why do you want to be a performer?"

"No reason," Alex said. "Just to be up there."

"That's stupid. If you have no reason, you'll get hurt. There must be some reason."

Alex thought for a while. "For food," he said.

The man looked at Alex very seriously. Suddenly he laughed so hard that he fell over backward.

"That's perfect! You see, you have a goal. You are not such a drifter. You want to go up there to eat something. What do you want to eat?"

"I don't know."

"Ah, you must like something, chocolate?"

"No," Alex said.

"Fruit?"

"Well, some," Alex said.

"What do you like?"

"Well . . . I like . . . macaroni," Alex said.

"That's perfect," the Flying Man said. "It's like you're reading my mind. That's my favorite dish too. How do you like your macaroni?"

"Hot."

"Hot macaroni! The audience will see the steam rising. It will make them hungry too. We have work to do . . . I'm leaving tomorrow . . . We have work to do."

He asked Alex to look at a straight line he had drawn in chalk across the ring. "Look at it for a long time," he said. "Stare at it until it's no longer a line, until it's a *path*."

Alex stared at it.

"Now, remember your breathing," he said. "You want to pay close attention to your breathing. You want to be as light as air, so you must pay close attention to your breathing. Every time you take a step you want to become lighter and lighter. If there are heavy things up here," he said, touching Alex's head, "then it can be very dangerous. Now follow the path."

Bending his knees, Alex followed the chalk line.

"No, no, no," the man said. "Do not pretend you're floating. No, don't pretend. You must really float, you must soar . . ."

The young man demonstrated for Alex.

They worked together the rest of the day. The man kept demonstrating movements and giving Alex advice. "Move the wire up higher every day . . . just spend time up there getting used to the height, that's all," he said.

Before they quit that evening, the Flying Man sat on the ring curb with Alex.

"Macaroni, do you mind if I call you Macaroni? Now listen, Macaroni, remember this, when you eat up there, the food will taste very good. I've tried it, believe me. It is like no other food you've ever had before. But remember this, you must taste every bite and every bite must be as good or better than the first bite. That is the trick to staying alive. If you forget what you're eating, then you'll die, you realize that, don't you?"

"Yes," Alex said.

"Never forget what you're eating on the tightwire."

"I won't."

"Don't tell me you won't just like that and then go up there and forget. Hold up your hand, make two fingers like a V for Volenti. Say: on my soul, I will not forget that I am eating macaroni when I am high up."

Alex held his fingers up. "On my soul, I will not forget that I am eating macaroni when I am high up."

"That's good," the Flying Man said. "That's perfect. I could tell by the way you said that, you'll never forget. But just in case you do, don't forget to do plenty of push-ups and pull-ups."

"What for?"

"Muscles are not necessary for flying, but they're nice to have in case you forget why you are flying."

The next day, Alex returned to the Flying Man's ring. A net had been set up across the ring and a note was on the curb.

Macaroni,
   Use my arena in my absence. Just remember: to fly is to live!
<u>*Buon appetito!*</u>

                                    —*The Flying Man*

Alex was on his own. Every day he practiced walking back and forth across the low tightwire, until he could run, stop, hop on one leg, hop on the other, back up quickly, touch his toes, spin around on one foot, jump with both feet, and even lie down on the wire. He practiced for so many hours that he learned to balance on the wire while sitting in a wooden chair, its back legs resting on the wire, and eating an entire plateful of macaroni.

The more time he spent with Evelyn the fonder he became of her and the less he talked about Iris. He wasn't sure whether this was because he was thinking less about her, or whether he knew it would make Evelyn uncomfortable. He talked to Evelyn about this, telling her that she must understand what his mission had been all along.

The only time he truly felt free of the conflict of seeing Evelyn was while performing tricks that endangered his life. He enjoyed climbing up to the Flying Man's perch. Sometimes with the aid of the net and sometimes without it, he'd walk the tightwire high above, and after a while he realized that it was the only place in the entire mountain where he could truly relax. Often when he was up on the high wire he simply didn't want to come down. Eventually he brought his chair up with him and practiced his act—sitting on the chair and eating his macaroni.

Everyone began calling him Macaroni and, partially because of this nickname, he became very popular. Whenever he entered the mess hall, the performers would call out, "Hey, Macaroni! How's it going Macaroni?"

Often during a speech or gathering, a performer would call out: "Let's hear Macaroni's opinion on the subject!" and everyone would cheer him on, knowing that he was too shy to speak publicly. Even Evelyn began calling him Macaroni and eventually Macky.

Alex enjoyed being with the different types of people. There were people with obscure but necessary jobs like the two full-time butchers who were needed just to cut the meat for the tigers and lions. They drank beer all day and were always in a raucous and merry mood. Every time Alex passed their refrigerator truck—a truck that went back and forth from the boats every few days—they called out "Macaroni!"

Alex practiced his act as often as possible. Often at dinnertime one or two spectators would stand at the door to the Flying Man's arena as Alex balanced on the back legs of the chair high above the net.

Alex took greater and greater risks. Sometimes he noticed an old man watching him from the arena door. The man's name was Joseph and he wore his makeup all the time. A few times the old man followed Alex to the mess hall and sat across from him. Each time this happened, Alex ate quickly, dropped his plate off in the dish line, and went back to the bunk room without staying and socializing with the others as was the custom.

He told Evelyn about him. "He's like an undertaker, isn't he?"

"He's a magician and a mind reader. He can make an elephant appear in the ring with the snap of his fingers. But he also can read a person's mind like a book."

One time while Alex was sitting next to him, the old man asked him to pass the butter and when Alex reached his hand across the table for the butter dish, he noticed his knuckles were the same ugly, purple-and-red color they'd been when he'd fought with Blair. Alex glanced at the old man's great big eyes, but the man took no notice. When Alex looked back at his knuc-kles, they were normal.

One afternoon Alex went to Tara's room door and knocked. The dome-shaped ceiling of her private bedroom was covered with dark red tapestries. On the walls were paintings of the Madonna and child, crucifixes, and candles. Tara was sitting at the edge of her bed in the red light of a lantern; apparently she'd been taking a nap.

Alex told her why he'd come to see her. "Could you ask him not to be there when I present my act to Volenti? Just knowing he might be there would make me very nervous."

"I can ask him, but I can't make him stay away."

In the hallway on his way out, Alex saw the old man coming toward him. The old man held a walking stick but he seemed to dodge at him like a boxer. Alex put his arms up over his head, as if the man were striking him. But as soon as Joseph had passed, Alex couldn't figure out whether he had so much as raised a finger to him. Maybe he was just imagining it.

Another time while Alex was walking by the ring in which Joseph practiced, he saw him levitating a woman, passing his cane under her and over her. For a moment, the woman, who had definitely been a woman with long blond hair and fair skin, turned into a woman with darker, curly hair, who looked just like Iris. Her appearance scared Alex so much that he stopped. Not only had he seen something strange, but he felt somebody breathing down his neck. He was sure a man was standing right behind him, a dark man like the old man. But pivoting around he saw nobody there. When he looked back at the old man again, his subject was the blond woman again.

More and more often Alex would sleep with Evelyn in the ring. The Flying Man's arena was warm and with a blanket beneath them, their bed was soft. They would lie awake most of the night talking and laughing and staring up into the arena at the intricate patterns of wires, ladders, trapezes, and ropes.

Then one day Evelyn wheeled one of the circus stages out into the arena. Lying down on the stage with Evelyn, Alex thought he could hear voices. One time he heard a baby crying. The sound was so distinct that he thought that Evelyn was making the noise, but she denied it. Another night Evelyn asked him if he had ever thought of a woman giving birth on a stage and Alex said, "What do you mean?"

"Have you ever thought that the stage is blind? Have you ever wanted to follow the light of the stage?"

Alex didn't know why, but the words made him feel like crying.

Every night after the performers and workers were asleep, they'd slip through the winding tunnels to the Flying Man's arena and turn on the lights. Sometimes Evelyn made the room green, other times she made it red, another time she made it yellow and blue. Sometimes she'd ask Alex to sit high up on the circular benches and look down at the ring and imagine himself already in her arms. Other times she would hold his hand tightly and say to him: do you hear that?

Alex did hear things. He couldn't deny it. Once he heard faint flute music, another time he heard a violin, another time a trumpet. The simple notes of these instruments made Alex look toward the ceiling of the arena as if the music were coming from up high. And the music changed depending on the color of the lights Evelyn had selected. If she left the arena dark, Alex would hear the crying of a baby or sometimes the shouts of fighting men and women.

One time Evelyn turned the lights on right away, locked the doors, and walked around the benches of the large arena looking for the source of the sounds, then she turned off the lights and crossed to the stage in center ring. Climbing up on it, she took off her own clothes and helped Alex off with his. Alex put his arms around her. He heard high-pitched laughter coming from the upper regions of the arena. It was the same laughter, half dog and half human, that he had heard before and it went on and on as they got down among the props on stage.

Soon they were making love.

Circus World Museum, Baraboo, Wisconsin.

CHAPTER 48

THEN one day everyone was assembled on the seats of the big arena. The band played and a ringmaster announced the arrival of Volenti Junior. The lights went out. A spotlight searched the trapezes and found a man dressed in blue moving from swing to swing alone. He was high up and it was difficult at first to see that he was flipping and twisting faster and more gracefully than Alex had ever imagined possible. The clear notes of a trumpet, punctuated by drums and cymbals, accompanied his agile flight.

He stopped for a moment against a pole and put his hand out. The performers clapped and yelled wildly, standing, whistling, drumming their heels on the hollow bleachers. Volenti crossed a tightwire, running quickly with bent knees, each foot pointing outward. He stopped. The lights came on below in the sawdust arena, and Alex saw a large woman wearing a plumed hat—similar to the one he had seen on the woman who had first led him and Iris to their seats in the circus. She held a drawn crossbow and pointed the arrow up toward Volenti. The band became silent. The arrow flew. A second later, Volenti held it in his hand. The woman loaded another arrow and shot it; Volenti caught it. She shot more until he held an armful.

Dropping the arrows, he dove from the wire, catching a trapeze and continuing his stunts. Finally he returned to his perch high up and called out:

"Children, I'm so glad to see you again, so glad."

The performers had taken out handkerchiefs and waved them up at him; some were crying. They gave him a standing ovation.

That night an elaborate meal of crabs and steak was served. Volenti was not at dinner, but a schedule of performances circulated. Everyone's name was on it. Macaroni was scheduled as the second clown.

The arrival of Volenti made Evelyn nervous. Maybe she knew that it meant that Alex was closer to finding Iris than he had ever been before. Alex noticed that she tried to distance herself from him, sitting with others, and talking to him less frequently.

Alex became more nervous about his audition, but he tried to think of it less as a show for a large audience, than a simple dialogue with a single man.

The day of auditions came. After the crowd gathered in the bleachers of the arena, Volenti came out to the edge of the ring on a white horse. Evelyn told Alex that it was the Volenti family's custom to watch acts while mounted on such a horse. The ring had been polished, fresh sawdust scattered around it, and new rubber mats laid down. The elephants, horses, llamas, and camels were paraded out in full regalia.

After the first clown act, Tara stepped into the ring holding a plate with a silver lid. She held it up toward Volenti and announced, "Ladies and gentlemen, children of all ages, Mr. Macaroni will ascend to the tightwire strung as high as possible in the arena. Carrying a plate of his favorite meal, macaroni, he will cross to the center of the tightwire, make himself comfortable, and enjoy his dinner."

Alex got up from Evelyn's side and climbed down into the arena, a spotlight picking him up right away. Tara lifted the cover off his steaming dish and handed it to him. He thanked her and walked for the ladder.

"Macaroni," somebody yelled, "Macaroni, why do you want to eat your meal so high up?"

Alex looked to the man in the audience who had spoken. "Because that's where it tastes the best," he said.

A woman stood up and yelled, "Are you as in love with macaroni as people say?"

"I'm in love," Alex said, "but not only with macaroni." He could see Volenti far away on his horse at the entrance to the arena.

"Would you give up things for your love?" another woman asked.

"I would give up many things," Alex said, continuing on.

"Would you give up your life?"

"Many things."

"*Buon appetito,* Macaroni," a woman yelled.

The physical exertion from climbing helped ease his fears. At the top of the long ladder, he stood on a perch, looked down through the blinding spotlight toward Volenti on his horse, and tried to focus on him as if he were the only one in the arena.

Holding the hot plate in one hand and a chair he had left on the perch with the other, he began to walk out on the wire, one step at a time.

In the middle, he fitted grooves in the back legs of the chair over the wire. Straddling the chair was the most difficult part of his act. It required balancing on one leg and taking a high step over the chair. Lifting his left leg, he took the step and placed his right foot on the other side. Slowly, he dropped his rear end to the seat, then threw out his legs and arms to keep his balance, all the while holding his meal level.

Taking a deep breath, he picked up the fork and, keeping his eyes on the macaroni, he began to eat, tasting the warm, salty cheesy noodles.

The sound of the crowd was faint from this high up, but he knew they were clapping wildly. As he continued forking the nourishment into his mouth, he heard a faint voice rise up from the din.

"Don't think of her, Mr. Macaroni. Pay no attention to her!"

Turning to look below him, he saw Joseph in his black tuxedo standing among the crowd on the bleachers, waving his cane and shaking his head. Tara was running toward him, her arms raised.

Alex turned back to the plate of noodles. He lifted a forkful to his lips and tried to taste the thick yellow cheese.

"Macaroni! You're thinking of her! If you think of her, you'll die!" Joseph said.

Alex rocked back and forth in his chair, throwing his legs and arms out to catch his balance. The macaroni slid off the plate, he threw his fork away. His body became as stiff as a board.

He kept tipping back and forth, unable to find his center. Each time he thought he'd go over, he'd catch himself just in time, but there was no end to it.

Finally, he went over backward and his arms shot up for the wire, one hand snapping against it, the force of his fall practically jerking his shoulder out of joint.

He grabbed on with his other arm, his whole body swinging helplessly back and forth. The crowd roared louder and louder. People were screaming.

He began to move down the wire toward the perch, sidling, one hand sliding and burning down the wire behind the other. Then he stopped. The blood had gone out of his arms. Alex tried to kick, to get himself to swing. But he was stuck . . . He couldn't move from his position below the wire. He closed his eyes and prepared himself for the fall to the ring.

Then he heard a peel of cackling laughter. "Macaroni!"

Above him on the wire, he saw the Flying Man's narrow face, his sharp eyes and hooked nose.

"Grab my forearm as I grab yours, Macaroni," the Flying Man said.

The Flying Man gripped Alex's forearm.

"Oh, Macaroni, let go with the other!" the Flying Man said, still laughing hysterically.

Alex let go. The powerful grip of the Flying Man pulled him right up to the platform next to the wire.

Alex fell back against the pole that supported the platform. His arms and legs were shaking.

"Too much up here, I thought I told you." The Flying Man pointed at Alex's head. "Too much up here and it's very dangerous, Macaroni."

Alex leaned over and looked straight down. Directly below him was the bare back of the white horse that Volenti Junior had been watching the show from. Alex looked back to the Flying Man.

"Where is Volenti?" he said, catching his breath.

The Flying Man squatted next to him, breathing and sweating. He watched Alex with a serious expression on his face, then said, "You didn't know who I was?" He began laughing again. "I thought you knew! Macaroni, I thought you knew!" He held his hand over his slender stomach and shrieked with laughter, his laughter echoing against the walls of the arena.

Finally, Alex got up and the Flying Man got up facing him.

"Where is Iris Barton?" Alex said.

"Do you know her? Who are you?"

Alex grabbed the man's shirt and pushed him against the railing at the back of the platform. "I don't want to hurt you, tell me where she is!"

"Macaroni! Calm down," the man said. "She's not here, not here."

Alex tried to shake him, but the man slipped so quickly and

gracefully from his grip that Alex nearly fell over the side himself.

"I'm telling you the truth, Macaroni. Believe me. She is not on this island!"

The Flying Man instantly thrust his arms under Alex's arms from behind, and pressed his hands behind his neck, putting him in a full-nelson headlock.

"Where's Iris . . . Where is she?" Alex said.

Struggling, his chin pressed against his chest, Alex realized that the Flying Man was cutting off the flow of blood to his head. More pressure was applied to the back of his neck.

"Give her back!" Alex said, but the pressure increased and he felt himself collapsing . . . collapsing slowly into the Flying Man's arms.

CHAPTER 49

HE woke up propped between two guards, his arms held firmly behind his back by a strait-jacket; a vicious pain pierced his head behind his eyes. He was on a flatbed stage, which was vibrating and jolting along the rickety tracks down the steep side of the mountain. He could smell the salt air, the earth, the pines and weeds along the tracks and he could see out over the side of the mountain, across the forests and valleys below, all the way to the sea. He had not been outside now for over six months. The winter had come and gone and it was spring again. The tree leaves had blossomed and the clouds were light and misty. Behind him he saw a soldier, nobody he recognized, operating the brake of the flatbed.

They rode down the long hill. At the base, a car met them and Alex was ordered to sit between the two guards. They rode on dirt roads for a while, the guards and driver quiet, Alex looking straight ahead. Finally they came to a small town of stone buildings and cobblestone streets and a long pier extending into a harbor protected by a jetty. The two guards escorted Alex down the wooden pier to a boat similar in shape and size to a commercial fishing troller; they told him to get in. Alex hesitated, but one of the guards pushed him. "We're not going to kill you," he said. "We're taking you back."

"Back where?"

"To Verre, that's where you came from, that's where we're dropping you off."

Alex got down onto the backseat of the open deck. The guards climbed down beside him and signaled for a tattooed man wearing a tattered black beret and smoking a stubby cigarette to lift the ropes. The man threw them on board, then jumped on and joined the captain. A cool wind hit Alex's hair as they opened the throttle outside of the small harbor. Three hours later, Alex could see a long strip of green, the Island of Verre he had left months before; he turned and looked behind him at the open sea, believing that if he watched the island he would never get there.

After a little while the men untied the sleeves of his straitjacket and he slipped out of it.

"Mr. Volenti asked us to show you this note," one of the guards yelled over the sound of the engine.

Dear Macaroni,

I do not know any more about the whereabouts of Iris Barton than you do so I cannot help you with your search. You are wrong, though, to think that she is here. Please don't talk about our island to others. It is really quite a private thing, you know.

You were soaring beautifully before you fell . . . Oh, well, better dining next time. Buon appetito!

—The Flying Man

One of the guards took the note back and put it in his pocket.

The captain cut back on the engines as they entered the harbor—the same harbor Alex had departed from with Evelyn. Alex could see boaters in bright clothes standing and sitting on the decks of moored yachts and sleek sailboats. A young boy rowed an inflatable dinghy toward one of the many piers; a dog sat on the bow.

The captain reversed the engines and the boat bumped up against planks. Rising, the guards motioned for Alex to get off first. As soon as he stepped on the planks, the boat backed away from the dock with its crew and guards. Behind them the island ferry, its rails lined two deep with tourists in colorful costumes, glided into the harbor, cutting and parting the still water, then bumped against the pilings of the landing. The boat on which Alex had ridden turned around in the ferry's wake and headed out of the harbor.

Alex ran down the long pier, jumping over a cement barrier into a parking lot. He followed a heavily trafficked road through the small town to the main street, dodging tourists and a group of children on the sidewalk. Tripping over the leash of a dog, he got up without apologizing, then climbed a steep hill high above the town, passing the cemetery where Evelyn had taken him.

A few streaks of white clouds in the bright blue sky rose from the distant trees. He made several turns on small crooked streets to make sure he wasn't being followed. From the top of the hill, he could see sailboats, mostly white, some black, some red, moored in the silky blue waters between the jetties of the harbor. A flock of white seagulls sat along the jetties' rocks. It was low tide, almost noon. Blanched green seaweed and clusters of barnacles clung to the big stones exposed by the ebbing waters.

He walked on back roads surrounding the town. Bathers wearing flip-flops walked along the edge of the road. Some rode bicycles, their bright beach towels heaped high in their baskets. Children peered curiously out of the rolled-down back windows of cars; some put their hands out, making an airplane of their fingers in the rush of wind from the car's motion. Alex kicked at sand on the side of the road, kicked it out onto the hot pavement. Hearing a lawn mower, he stopped to inhale the smell of cut grass rising pungently over the dry, baking pavement smell.

Ladders, paint pails, speckled tarpaulins decorated the sides of houses. A young red-haired boy wearing a white painter's cap and speckled white pants lay on his back next to a picket fence, holding the brush above him and stroking lazily.

Alex got in a cab and asked the driver to take him to Evelyn's address. Below her house, at the foot of the hill, he asked the cab driver to wait for him.

The front door and windows were locked. Alex peeked in at the dark rooms, knocked, but the house was uninhabited. He went around to the back of the house, found a window with a broken latch, opened it, and entered. The small bag of his extra clothing was still here and a coffee can with money and a bank-card. He had left all of his identification in the backpack on Cea. He changed clothes, taking the bag. Back at the cab he directed the driver to King's Beach in Towson.

After traveling down the long dirt road past the town, they came to the edge of the field. Alex walked through long, dry pale green grass and patches of purple flowers. The stage was no longer standing, just the jagged ruins of cement blocks stick-ing out of the earth in a circle. It looked as if a great wind or some other force had ripped the stage away. Kicking around in the grass in the center, he found chips of the floorboards, a rusted curl of wire, and a rotted strip of yellow canvas with a tiny red stripe running down the middle.

He ran across the field to the top of the dunes and looked out at the water. The waves slapping the sand were no bigger than the waves from a small motorboat; the ocean was calmer than he'd ever seen it. There were two people far away in the lines of heat rising from the white sand, one standing, the other lying down. Their naked bodies were the color of the sand.

At the airport in the center of the island, he paid the driver and went inside to buy a ticket to New York with money he had withdrawn with his bankcard. The attendant told him that he would have to spend the night in a hotel room in Boston because his flight from the island would arrive too late for a connection, otherwise he could take a train.

He bought an island newspaper and read through it while he waited. There was no mention of Evelyn, no mention of anyone or anything that he knew about, just an article about curtailing ferry service during the off-season in order to bring the ticket price down.

As his plane took off, he moved to a window seat facing the east in hopes of getting a view of Cea. The air was clear, there were no clouds, but even high up he couldn't see land east of Verre.

In Boston he stayed in a Holiday Inn, watching television, piecing together the stories on the national news to gather what had happened since he'd been gone. In the night he got up, turned on the heat, and looked out the window at the parking lot below his room. A man with a long screwdriver was prying open a car door, perhaps breaking in. The man worked avidly and nervously for a long while without concern for being seen.

In the morning Alex woke late. Most of the cars, including the one the man had been trying to get into, had already been driven away.

During the flight to New York he realized he'd been doing something he'd stopped doing for a while. He was thinking, anticipating, dwelling on meeting Iris as if the very motion of the flight forward was for her. She'd be in the apartment when he got back; if not, she'd be somewhere in the city.

He read magazines, and, while reading them, he thought of what she would say about the articles. A stewardess with a long neck reminded him of her, and he kept waiting for that stewardess to come through the curtains in front of her service station.

New York was buried in yellowish brown smog. Stepping down the airport ramp and up into the crowd of waiting people, he could feel the frenetic energy of the city. Even in the

handwritten signs for passengers held by limousine and taxi drivers, a certain desperation could be detected. He looked for a
familiar face looking for him. "It's New York, anything can
happen in New York."

He ate a meal in an expensive cafeteria, watching the clicking
second hand of a clock on the wall. After busing his tray, he
started across the busy lobby for the glass doors behind which
taxi and limousine drivers waited. His knees began to tremble;
his legs wobbled like a clown's. He thought maybe it was just
a relapse, but then he felt himself sinking with every step. Suddenly, a pain wrenched at his chest as if a hand had burst from
his heart and was pulling him inside out. He fell to the floor.

He woke up slowly from a milky, dreamy sleep of soft shapes
and gentle hands. He thought he was floating above the floor,
supported by whiteness, perhaps by pure willpower or lack of
willpower. He looked to a plastic bag of pale liquid hanging
from a metal pole, then to a pale blue ceiling framed by white
walls. He became aware of a steady, computerized beeping
noise, a noise he realized he'd heard in his dreams for days,
perhaps longer.

"You had money and a bankcard, but nothing with your address on it," the woman said.

"I don't know where I am," he said, the words coming out
slowly as if huge bubbles had to slip out with them.

"You've had a stress attack."

"I have? Me?"

"Yes, you, sir. What happened to your wallet?"

The room moved each way he turned his head and kept moving even after he'd stopped. "Am I on a ship?"

"You're in New York. You were in JFK. You collapsed."

"I did? But I was fine."

"You weren't. The doctors believe from the condition of your
heart that you've been going through a lot of stress. Stress."

Alex slept and woke and slept for almost two days. On the morning of the third day he was staring up through the liquid haze of his eyes at the ceiling when a doctor holding a clipboard stepped into sight and spoke to him. The doctor's voice was as young as his own, sharp, knowledgeable, and understanding.

"We've given you a sedative to relieve the stress," he said clearly.

As Alex blinked his eyes, the image of the doctor was squashed. His eyes were watering and there were tears.

"Do you have a doctor in New York you can see when you go back this afternoon?"

Alex nodded his head.

"I'm going to prescribe a number of pills just in case. We'll put you in a taxi later this afternoon."

On the Brooklyn Queens Expressway the traffic ahead of the taxi slowed down and then stopped, and Alex could hear the gentle idling of the engine. Faint salsa music came out of the cabbie's radio. A sign on the Plexiglas divider said Thank You for Not Smoking.

The traffic was stop and go all the way into Manhattan. Every time the cab jerked forward, Alex kept thinking about her.

Gravity pulled him deep into the backseat of the cab.

From the rear window, he looked up at the tall buildings, as if seeing the city for the first time. After paying the driver, he crossed the sidewalk and pushed the Lovlors' buzzer. He held a bag with the clothes he'd picked up at Evelyn's and another smaller paper bag with the bottle of pills for his heart. Mr. Lovlor, a tall, gaunt, high cheekboned man in his midseventies, came out into the lobby. He wore a pair of black slippers and a robe over brown corduroy pants.

He stared through the glass door at Alex, as if he didn't recognize him, then he pushed the door just hard enough to unlatch it and Alex stepped in.

"Where've you been, friend?" the old man said. "We didn't know what to tell people. Nobody knew what to do, where to get ahold of you."

He shook Alex's hand.

"In the hospital for one," Alex said. "I just had some kind of heart problem."

Lovlor brought Alex into the apartment. Mrs. Lovlor, a heavy-set woman in a faded dress and orthopedic shoes, got up from her tattered easy chair.

"He's here, Catherine," Mr. Lovlor said.

"We're glad to see you. I hope you've been all right. We were very worried, very worried about you. Where've you been?"

"Looking for Iris," Alex said.

Both the old man and woman, slightly hunched over, dropped their jaws and stared at him. Lovlor held onto the door handle.

"I thought she was—"

"It was in my head," Alex said. "She isn't."

The Lovlors gave Alex the extra set of keys to his apartment and he went out to the elevator.

Mail had been piled just inside his door. He went through it carefully in the hall light, then went in. Moving from the living room to the bedroom, he examined his belongings. As far as he could remember, the year before when he went to Verre he had left everything the way it was now.

He went out to buy some groceries. On the way in, Mr. Lovlor waved him over to the door of his apartment. Mrs. Lovlor stood just behind him in her worn-out orthopedic shoes.

"Some time ago, a whole bunch of people came looking for your wife again," Mr. Lovlor said.

"People were looking for my wife again? What do you mean again? Who were these people?"

"They'd been by here years before, almost two years before."

"You mean when she first disappeared?"

"Yes. We didn't think much of it then. But they got to be quite a nuisance, this year."

"One man," Mrs. Lovlor said, "couldn't have been but yay high." She put her hand down below her waist. "And then a woman came, a woman with a lot of makeup on and long eyelashes, very gaudy. Then a big heavy man, really arrogant, really rude."

"We wondered who they were," Mr. Lovlor said. "They wouldn't leave any names." He caught his breath. "One day they came here and Catherine had her camera ready. I answered the door, swung it wide and she snapped a picture of them . . . They got really uppity. They tried to force their way into our apartment. But I got the door closed and Catherine went to call the police. Then they fled, like a bunch of animals."

"Just like a bunch of animals," Mrs. Lovlor echoed.

Mr. Lovlor handed over a blurry snapshot of three people. Alex slowly began to recognize them behind the milky white haze. They were the three who had answered the door of the first trailer Alex had knocked on the night that Iris had disappeared: the burly ringmaster with his great paunch; the long-faced dwarf clown and the woman with the long fake eyelashes and the layers of makeup. The ringmaster, he noted, still wore his gold-buttoned suit.

"The original circus," Alex said while examining them.

"Weather-beaten as a pack of pirates," Mrs. Lovlor said.

"They were really looking for Iris?"

"Yeah, they were looking for her," Mrs. Lovlor said.

"They meant to find her, too. They tried to break in up there, you know."

"My door?"

"Your neighbors phoned the police, they made such a racket. We didn't know what they were doing."

"Do you have any idea where they came from?"

"I had a talk with that lady," Mrs. Lovlor said, pointing to the photograph. "She was a good bit friendlier than the two rude ones. She told us where they were from. They were from a circus."

"Which circus?"

"Their car had Mississippi plates on it," Mr. Lovlor said.

"What did they want?"

"They wanted to know if we'd seen Iris and when we said no they asked where you were. But that's the trouble with just up and leaving like that, Mr. Barton. A lot of people can be looking for a man who just leaves like that."

Alex examined the photograph. The flashbulb had whitened their faces like ghosts. They were all turning their heads away. "You can keep that, Mr. Barton."

CHAPTER 50

HE hardly slept that night. He kept hearing the word *circus* as if somebody were standing in the dark near his bed and whispering it to him over and over. That morning he paid his telephone and electricity bill and went to the bank to cash in a savings account certificate.

Later in the afternoon, he took a taxi uptown to the Library of the Performing Arts at Lincoln Center and began a search for names and addresses of circuses playing in America. The only comprehensive list of circuses he found was compiled in a book written in the 1950s. He photocopied the staggeringly big list of names and took it home, reading the names over to himself.

Atterbury Bros. Circus; George F. Bailey Circus; Mollie Bailey Circus; Al G. Barnes Circus; Barnett Bros. Circus; Batchelor & Doris Circus; Clyde Beatty Circus; Beers-Barnes Circus; Benson Bros. Circus; Buckley & Weeks Circus; Buffalo Bill Wild West Show; Campbell Bros. Circus; Carson & Barnes Circus; Christy Bros. Circus; M. L. Clark Circus; Clyde Bros. Circus; Cole Bros. Circus; Famous Cole Circus; W. W. Cole Circus; Coop & Lent Circus; Cooper &

Bailey Circus; W. C. Coup Shows; Christiani Bros. Circus; Dailey
Bros. Circus; Orrin Davenport Shows; Sam Dock Shows; Downie
Bros. Circus; J. H. Eschman Circus; Flatfoot Shows; Adam Fore-
paugh Circus; Adam Forepaugh-Sells Bros. Circus; Franconi's Hip-
podrome; Garden Bros. Circus; Gentry Bros. Circus; Gollmar Bros.
Circus; Mighty Haag Circus; Haagen Bros. Circus; Hagenbeck-
Wallace Circus . . .

Twice more he questioned the Lovlors for information about
the visitors.

"You're sure those were Mississippi plates, Mr. Lovlor?"

"I know they were."

Over the next few days he planned a trip to the South. Beginning
in Mississippi, he would interview people about circuses, show
them the pictures, find circuses, and ask them about other circuses. *They must know about each other,* he thought. *And when
I find the right one* . . . He didn't know quite what he would do.

Once again he said good-bye to the Lovlors.

"Another journey, Mr. Barton?"

"No. Just business."

"What should we tell people who come calling on you? Where
will you be?"

"Tell them I'm on business," Alex said.

After flying to Jackson, he picked up a rented car, then bought
a small tape recorder and began his search. In his first hotel room
he drew a picture with colored pencils of the forked flag he had
seen on top of the original tent, then he put this picture, several
photographs of Iris, and the Lovlors' snapshot of the three circus
people into a photo album to show to people during interviews.

Quickly he moved from the city to the rural areas where
people seemed to have a lot more, if not too much, to say about
circuses, but few were ever able to supply consistent details.

On one rural drive, around midday, he stopped in front of a
shack, its yard of long grass cluttered with rusted cars, refrigera-
tors, ovens, chicken wire. On the porch two men in their late
sixties or early seventies fanned themselves. One smoked a pipe.

On closer view, Alex saw that they were twins. They were dressed differently, but the aged lines in their faces were remarkably similar.

Alex showed them the picture of the flag in his album and asked them if a circus had come through flying its design. One man began shaking his head, but the one with the pipe nodded.

"Do you remember the name of it?" Alex asked him.

"Gentleman Brothers Circus," he said.

"You got that wrong," the other said. "General Brothers the name of it, ain't no such thing as Gentleman Brothers."

"You say they had a flag like this?" Alex asked the other one.

"Hell, yeah," he said, sucking on his pipe and nodding.

"He didn't see no flag," the second one said.

"Hell, I saw a flag."

"If you saw it, where'd ya see it?"

"On top of a pole," the other twin said.

"What do they need a flagpole for? They got tents, don't they? This fella here said it was atop the tent." He turned to Alex. "Don't listen to him. He don't know no better."

Alex stopped and asked anybody who looked like they had the time to talk. Eventually he came across circuses and interviewed their performers and workers.

But the circuses he found were suspicious of people looking for circuses and gave out information sparingly.

"They in deit to you?" one manager asked after a show.

"In what?"

"In deit."

"No, no debts, nothing like that."

"Then why are ya so anxious to find 'em?"

"I'm studying circuses."

"Hell, how come you don't study us? Cause we don't owe you no money, right?"

He tried different approaches with different shows.

"I'm a circus historian," he said to a ringmaster of another small show.

"You don't have to tell lies, friend. I know what you're here for. If you boys would show up when I call you, you'd catch your man."

"But I'm looking for a woman."

During his search he stopped into barbershops, beauty salons, and drugstores in every small town. His questions and pictures sparked stories about extraordinary circuses, unusual circuses from foreign countries, circuses from exotic lands arriving mysteriously at night in isolated pastures or forests. One old woman told him that the flag belonged to a circus of Chinese midgets who had a freak show that only cost a quarter. "Inside they had a normal-size human being. Just normal size, I tell ya."

After three weeks he had come across four circuses in Mississippi and two in the neighboring state of Alabama. He had spoken to many performers, managers, roustabouts, and spectators.

As he traveled an insidious fatigue crept up on him. At first he thought it was the humid weather, then he thought it might be the food he was eating. He began checking into hotel rooms in the afternoon. Sometimes he'd sleep all afternoon, through the evening until morning, dreaming about wild circuses of flying men and women, naked centenarian contortionists, bizarre underwater acts viewed in a giant aquarium in center ring with crocodiles and naked young boys with little scuba tanks. In one dream a Seeing Eye dog led a blind man across a tightwire, the Seeing Eye dog putting one foot carefully in front of the other, the blind man feeling the air with his stick.

Perhaps, he thought, the dreams themselves, being far richer and more colorful than any he had ever experienced, were using up his waking energy.

At times, while watching these acts in his dreams, he could hear the roaring of the ocean and see surf washing in under the tent's flaps.

CHAPTER 51

ONE evening, he woke up in a hotel room completely disoriented. For a few minutes he groped in the dark for the light switch, having no memory of where the light had been when he went to sleep.

He looked at his watch. It was nine-thirty in the evening. Hunger pains contracted his stomach.

Recalling a restaurant he'd seen at the end of the forlorn little town, he got up and walked along a street of deserted brick buildings, listening to the quiet crackling of streetlamps. A cloud of moths surrounded the yellow globes.

There had been people on the streets earlier and he wondered where they had gone.

Grass and weeds grew through the cracks in the sidewalk. The restaurant door was locked; a Closed sign hung from inside. The hours said 6 A.M. to 10 P.M. His watch said it was only nine-forty.

Continuing on, he soon came across a boarded-up railroad station with graffiti on its peeling red walls. Somewhere across the tracks on the other side, perhaps from a field, he heard the notes of a trumpet.

The tune was crisp and clear. He thought he had heard it in the contortionist's room of stages on the Island of Cea.

Then in the darkness a bright yellow flame rose violently up into the sky. It rose so fast, so high, that it seemed to come out of the darkness itself.

Following the sound of the music, he stepped over rusted rails and through long grass onto a playing field and then across the dry dirt of a pitcher's mound.

The flame licked up into the sky again, this time higher, making a faint sound like damp sheets unfurling in the wind. Its source was the mouth of a short man in a worn-out black tuxedo and a crumpled top hat. He was standing in a circle of a hundred or more people.

Alex pushed toward the center of the crowd until his feet stopped at a small wooden red-and-yellow circus ring. Inside the ring the fire-eater was lighting torches stuck into the ground, their light glistening off the sweaty tattooed arms of a strong man in a tattered leopardskin suit, his chest thrown out and his hands on his hips. A large gold hoop earring tapped against his veiny neck. Near him squatted a woman in a skintight suit of reflective blue scales holding a drum. An old gray-haired dwarf in whiteface and bright red tights blew a polished brass trumpet.

The fire-eater doused his fire stick and picked up a balancing bar with the strong man. They lowered the bar for the woman to climb on, then raised it to shoulder height, lifting the balancing woman so high up that the crowd pushed back away from the ring to give her room for her act. Closing her eyes, the woman put her elbows out and her hands together as if in prayer and swallowed slowly.

The dwarf, seated in the ring, rolled the drum.

Silence fell in the still night air.

The woman sprang from the bar. She rose high up, her body

becoming pure body, pure flesh in motion, arcing in a perfect circle, a perfect back flip, and landing feet first on the flexible bar. Before descending to the grass, she returned her hands to the prayer position.

The crowd clapped and whistled as the four performers bowed at the edge of their ring.

"We rely on your gracious and generous contributions to survive," the fire-eater called.

Alex heard change clanging against tin. At the edge of the ring, he saw a white monkey with yellow eyes darting back and forth in the light of the torches. It held a tin pail and reached out for the bills, climbing right up to open wallets and purses. As Alex took a five-dollar bill out of his wallet, the monkey hopped across the ring toward him quickly, rocking back and forth on its little legs, its long tail curled up behind him.

After the crowd left the field for the town, the four performers set up camp. The fire-eater piled sticks into a campfire. The woman began making dinner while the dwarf and the strong man erected a sleeping tent behind a small trailer and car. Alex watched from the grass nearby, then approached the fire-eater who had doused the wood with kerosene.

The man's red, weather-beaten face glistened in the torchlight. He struck a match to the kerosene, then watched the flame as if mesmerized by fire.

"Hello," Alex said.

The man turned from the flames.

"Could I ask you some questions?"

"We're tired, come back in the morning."

The woman, a robe draped over her shoulders, cut meat into chunks, dropping them into a pot on the hood of their car.

"You'll be here in the morning?"

"Of course, who are you?"

"I'm a historian."

"A what?" the man said.

"A reporter," Alex said. "I'd like to do a story on your troupe."

"Well, come by in the morning. You can speak to us in the morning."

"Just a few questions?"

"I *said* in the morning."

The next morning, Alex got up early. Carrying his recorder, he strolled along the abandoned railroad tracks, looking out over the field to the small ring, the burned-out fire with the pot hanging over it, the tent, the trailer, and the old baby blue rust-eaten Pontiac. A white coating of dew crested the grass.

Strung between two bamboo poles and leaning against the car, a tattered bannerlike sign read Circus of Yellow Dogs.

An hour or so later, the strong man and the woman came out of the tent, crossing the field toward a restaurant. A few minutes later, the dwarf and fire-eater came out of the trailer.

Alex intercepted them as they crossed the field.

"Are you going for breakfast?"

The fire-eater's black jacket and crumpled top hat looked filthy in the daylight. He looked at Alex suspiciously.

"About that interview," Alex said.

The dwarf reached into his blue jean pocket for a cigarette.

"You're from a newspaper, are you?" the fire-eater said.

Alex nodded his head.

"You're always too late. You run your stories after we leave."

"Well, we could offer you some money for the interview."

The man pointed toward his trailer. "Let's go," he said to Alex. The dwarf went on toward breakfast, and Alex followed the fire-eater who opened the door of his trailer and told Alex to step in and take a seat in one of the folding chairs in front of the sink.

The smell of soiled linen and animal hair hit his nostrils. The monkey crouched on a dresser busily eating nuts and fruit from a bowl. There were two beds covered by colorful quilts. Above one hung a rectangular painting—for a moment Alex thought it was one of Michelman's paintings, a stage on green grass before the sea, but actually it was merely the face of a yellow cat sitting before a pond, butterflies in the long grass behind it. Alex took his eyes off it as quickly as possible, smiled at the man, and turned on the recorder.

The man introduced himself as the Great Tintorelli.

Alex opened the album with the pictures of Iris, the performers, and the flag he had drawn.

"Have you seen this woman?"

The fire-eater looked up. "You're a detective?"

"No . . ."

"Then what are you really here for if you're not a detective?"

"As I said, I'm a reporter, but I also happen to be looking for this woman."

"You should have shown me the picture last night. I don't know her, never seen her."

Alex showed him the picture of the performers. "Any of these faces familiar?"

The man shook his head.

"How about the monkey? Where did you get him?"

The question seemed to take him by surprise. "Sebastian? Why do you want to know? Another show gave him to us."

"Which show?"

"We camped near them one night. A young boy came up to us, woke us up in fact, and offered us him. He's got a temper. But he can smell a five-dollar bill a mile away."

"How long ago did you get him?"

"A year and a half, at least."

"Did you see their show?"

"The boy came over with the monkey because we had accidentally crossed into their territory. They didn't want to fight us. It was just a kind of gesture. They were giving us a monkey in exchange for our leaving their territory."

"Where is their territory exactly? Did you find them in Mississippi?" Alex asked.

The monkey turned its emptied bowl upside down, looked to the fire-eater, and began chattering loudly, so loudly that Alex could barely hear the man answer. "Young man," he said. "I know why you haven't found what you're looking for. It's because you don't even know what you're after."

"I have an idea," Alex said.

But the fire-eater shook his head and put his hands together on his tight stomach. "No, you don't. I can tell by your questions. Did you find them in Mississippi?" the man laughed. "You don't have the slightest idea what you're looking for if you think that way when we are talking about territories."

"What am I looking for?" Alex said.

"You'll have to pay me, my friend."

Alex opened his wallet. The monkey hopped across the floor onto Alex's leg, took a twenty from his hand, and brought it over to the fire-eater.

"All right," Alex said. "What am I looking for?"

"How can I say?" The man looked at the ceiling and Alex could see the whites of his eyes. "To start with, you're looking for a race of people, not merely a group of people who perform under a tent."

"A race of people. What kind of race, from where?"

"A traveling race. A nameless race that includes all races, black, brown, yellow, and white. A race that is defined by something that people outside of the circus cannot understand, a race that is defined by the ring."

"Tell me about the ring, please," Alex said.

"It's nothing I can simply talk about, nothing that I can explain. But know that women in this race give birth within its boundaries and their babies are nursed in it. The ring, they believe, has supported them for years, given them food and clothing. Without it, they believe they would die or even worse, they would vanish." The man's small, squat face sharpened like a cat's. A faint gleam of sweat appeared on its dirty surface. "They're scared of it, believe me, Mr. Barton."

"Of the ring?"

"Of vanishing, every race is afraid of vanishing, but this race is very afraid of it, terrified of it."

"Why?"

"Oh, that's something that's hard to explain. They're on the brink of vanishing all the time. They live on the edge of it, you see.

"It's like this, my friend. Imagine what it's like to go through the motions of worship, of praying, chanting, repeating amen, or singing, or kneeling, of genuflecting, of watching the man in vestments read his speech and gesture to the great unknown. Even if you do not believe in God one gets something out of these motions. Well, it's the same with our business. Perhaps it has no meaning, perhaps it is only for physical survival, but we don't look at it that way nor do they. We see it as something profound, something quite honestly, terribly profound and terribly sad." His voice softened considerably. "The ring has to do with loss, everything to do with loss."

"Why?" Alex said.

The man was practically whispering. "Because one loses something every time one performs. One loses a part of oneself. Each performance marks the passage of time. An hour is more than just an hour, you see. But, if done right, every time one steps out into the ring one allows a certain something, perhaps the eyes of the spectators, to eat away at the flesh. One comes close to death, very very close every time, and one does not return altogether intact."

A strange cadence in the man's voice exhausted Alex the way his dreams in the hotel had exhausted him. He could hardly focus on the speaking lips of the fire-eater. He fell into a daydream, a daydream that became more than just a daydream. Once again he was approaching the army from the forest for the first time, only this time everything—the trees, the barracks, the trucks, the hills—was bathed in the soft blue light. *How dangerous,* he thought.

He was not sure how long he had been lost in these thoughts, but when he finally looked up, the fire-eater looked out of breath from talking. "Ah," he said. "Perhaps you'll see it when you watch our little show."

Suddenly the man reminded Alex of something so melancholy that he felt he might break down and cry. He closed his album, turned off the recorder, and staggered to his feet, bumping his head on the roof of the trailer. A lump in the back of his throat was making it hard to swallow, his eyes were watering. If he so much as mentioned Iris's name one more time he'd lose it.

"I must say good-bye."

"But you're coming to see our performance tonight?"

"Not tonight."

The fire-eater took his hand. "You'll find her, rest assured, my friend."

"Find who?" Alex said.

The rest of the morning and into the afternoon he lay on his hotel bed. He kept the television on, trying not to dream. He said out loud to himself that he was sick of everything, sick of this stupid, pointless quest. The elusive words of the fire-eater made him realize clearly that finding her was just the hope of a dreamer. As the sun outside his window was setting over the roofs of the little town, he rewound his tape and began playing it again.

He began to hear things that he did not remember the man saying, ". . . there's an emptiness, a yearning inside all of us that only the ring can eliminate. It won't eliminate this yearning forever, but it will appease it long enough for you to make it until the next time you're in the ring." There was a long pause, a pause during which Alex heard the chattering of the monkey. "There are people all over the world who were born in the ring.

One time or another they will find themselves coming back to it. Maybe they will go to the theater every available night or maybe they will find some television show into which they will step every time they see it." Alex heard the man laugh, a maniacal cackle, so shrill that he wasn't sure whether it was the man or the little monkey. "There are people like yourself who come to me all the time, begging for a chance to step into the ring. But what do they have to offer the ring?" The same shrill half-human laugh seemed to force itself out of the tiny speakers of the recorder. "Can they stand on their heads? Can they walk a tight-wire high up above the heads of an audience? Can they work in a cage with tigers or bears? Are they fearless? Are they willing to be homeless? Are they willing to travel week after week? Are they willing to live for months without a moment's security? Can they make people disappear? Can they disappear themselves? What good are they if they can't? Are they performers? Do they belong with us? What separates them from those in the audience? You see, that is crucial, the boundary between the two. Crossing the boundary can take a man's life, this is for certain. Crossing that boundary is exceedingly difficult, but if you are born in the ring, you want to cross it, you will cross it, you have no choice."

There was another long pause and Alex could hear the sound of the monkey chattering, a chair, maybe a door opening and closing. Then he heard a voice. It was his own voice and yet he didn't remember speaking at all.

"I need help," the voice said, weakly.

"I can see it in your eyes," the man responded.

"Will you help me?" the voice asked quietly. "I'm desperate. Dreams are taking over my life . . ."

The monkey continued chattering. He thought he could hear somebody crying, perhaps himself; he heard a cough, and the man clearing his throat.

"Do you know what's getting you down?" Alex heard among the noises. "I know what's getting you down. What you're seeking is among the very saddest things in the world, sadder than what you see right here. Can you stop looking for it?"

The crying sounds went on.

"Then let me explain. What you're looking for is not connected to the written word or to any kind of record. The only thing that holds it to this earth is water."

"Water?" It was strange hearing his own voice when he had no memory whatsoever of this conversation.

"Yes, water."

"But what kind of water, what do you mean water?"

"Any kind of water. Even the water of your tears. But think of something bigger. Think of *rivers*. Now you see, I can only give hints to you of the world of which we are all a part. Or perhaps you can see it when you watch our little show."

There was another pause.

"I must say good-bye," Alex said. He heard his chair slide back as he got up.

"But you're coming to see our performance tonight?" the fire-eater said.

"Not tonight."

"You'll find her, rest assured, my friend."

"Find who?"

The tape clicked off at that moment.

Alex got up from his bed and ran outside his hotel room. The sky above the horizon where the sun had gone down was glowing a light red. But the air over the town was already dark. He crossed the empty streets of the town past the railroad station. In the dark he ran across the field, expecting to see the yellow flame rise up again. But they had packed up and gone. All that was left was the charcoal of a burned-down fire and a yellow circle where the wooden ring had smothered the grass.

CHAPTER 52

FOR days Alex followed roads that ran along the banks of the Mississippi River. He worked his way south, sometimes crossing back and forth on bridges in order to cover both banks, until one day, on a country road that had meandered away from the water, he turned at a rusted yellow sign that said Boat Launch. The road ended in a parking lot strewn with beer cans that sloped down to a dilapidated pier. At the end of the pier, three boats were moored, cargo ships of some kind, with sharply peaked bows and sterns of warped planking. Black algae dripped from heavy ropes slung over the stanchions of the rotting pier. A ramp bridged the water between the opening of a door at the stern of one boat and the muddy bank of the river.

At the foot of the pier a black man sat on a low stool whittling a white oblong piece of wood. At one time his filthy, squashed hat had obviously been red but now it was brown and black. His clothes were of roughly woven material like burlap patched with heavy white threads. Through the layers of dirt, Alex could see colors, red and yellow. One of his long pointed shoes sagged at the tip from the weight of a round bell. On the muddy bank next to the disheveled man, Alex saw piles of horse dung, smaller pellet-shaped dung, and hoofprints.

He crossed in front of the pier's sagging boards and looked across the ramp into the dark mouth of the huge ship. He could smell animals and hay. Above one cabin, he noticed the tattered remains of a flag drooping from a dirty white flagpole. The flag's thin vertical stripes were yellow and black. It was the same flag he had seen at the first circus.

"That's their flag," Alex said, then he turned to the man. "Is this a circus?"

The man looked up for a second, then went back to rocking.

"Is this a circus?" Alex asked again.

The man continued rocking and whittling.

Alex turned and ran along the guardrails. He saw more bits of brown dung and small hoofed tracks along the shoulder, the tracks of ponies.

He ran back to his car, got in it, and drove to the first intersection. On the other side he saw a dirt road covered with animal tracks, mostly horse and pony tracks.

Alex drove up a steep hill and stopped on a ridge above a valley of fields. Disappearing over the opposite side was a wagon train of animals and carts rocking back and forth over the ruts. Through field glasses he saw trailers, cars, carts pulled by teams of horses. Huge bundles had been strapped to the backs of elephants; men and women straddled their swaying necks. Behind the elephants were camels and llamas and behind them draft horses pulled the caged animals, the tigers, lions, bears, and chimpanzees.

An old pickup truck rumbled at the rear, blue smoke mixing with red dust.

It was hot out. Just standing in the sun made Alex sweat. In his car again, he followed behind them at a distance, sunlight flashing through the trees onto his hood.

Children and adults came to the picket fences at the edge of farmyards and lawns to watch the circus train pass.

After five miles along rolling hills with wide fields and broken-down farms, after passing tangled scrub and trees covered with Spanish moss, they came out onto a paved road that led steeply down a hill into a town. Half a mile past the town, they turned onto a grassy road behind a farmhouse, crossed a field, and disappeared behind a line of trees. Alex parked his car below this field and crossed it to the woods. On the other side of the trees he saw another field, this one bowl-shaped and protected by woods on all sides. The circus people had spread out in a circle to erect the tent.

Sitting on a rock camouflaged by the foliage, Alex watched the circus set up, first the big top, then the other smaller animal and wardrobe tents. He focused his field glasses on everyone in the show, looking for Iris's face. They were the same people he had confronted after she disappeared. He saw the ringmaster and the dwarf working together. A lion kept growling so loudly that Alex could feel the sound deep in his chest.

Returning to his car, Alex drove to a highway and followed it until he found a mall. In the toy section of a large department store he bought a clown kit, a box painted colorfully with stars and moons. In it was a wig, a plastic nose, eyeglasses with black eyebrows, and a pair of white gloves that were too small for him. On the way out of the toy section he saw a basket of squirt guns. Reaching in, he shook a black gun free of the others, put it in his pocket and went down the escalator and out into the mall parking lot without paying.

On a back road he pulled off onto a dirt turnaround and applied the whiteface and the lipstick, then put on the wig, the nose, and the glasses with the black bushy eyebrows.

He drove on, back up to the site of the circus, and parked his car on the side of the road. Before getting out, he put the squirt gun in his pants pocket, then climbed on the grassy road right up through the trees and down the hill to the tent site. He knocked on a trailer door, the same one he had knocked on after Iris had disappeared. As he waited, he fingered the handle of his squirt gun. The burly ringmaster, the man whose picture he had traveled with since New York, opened the door, his tumescent belly straining the buttons of his dark red jacket. The dwarf, dressed in paint-speckled dungarees, pressed against the ringmaster's bowed legs, straining to see who had knocked.

"I'd like to work for you," Alex said.

The ringmaster looked Alex up and down carefully. "We're not looking for a clown," he said.

"I'm more than a clown," Alex said. "I'm an acrobat."

"We already have clown acrobats," the man said, shaking his head.

"Well, I'm a real acrobat. I'm as good as any acrobat you have. I walk the tightwire," Alex said. "I sit on a chair on the tightwire and I eat a meal."

The ringmaster stared down at Alex's hand in his pocket and did not take his eyes from it. "Just what is it that you eat up there on the tightwire, my friend?"

"What do I eat?"

"Yes, what do you eat, what kind of food do you eat?"

"Macaroni."

"Macaroni?" the ringmaster began to smile. "*Macaroni?*" Slowly his smile grew. He laughed from his belly up and turned to others inside the trailer behind him. "Macaroni!" he said. "This man eats macaroni on the tightwire!" Alex heard people behind the ringmaster laughing. At the sound of their laughter others came out of their tents and trailers to find out what it was about.

"Macaroni!" the ringmaster was yelling. "He eats macaroni on the tightwire!"

But suddenly the ringmaster's excitement vanished. "Very

good," he said, soberly and brusquely. "But we're not hiring a clown and that's final."

"I don't expect to be paid much," Alex said.

"Go on. Get lost," the man said. He started closing the trailer door. But Alex put his hand up.

"Please," he said. "I'll work for nothing."

"Go find yourself another circus," the man said and pushed the door closed in front of Alex.

The performers behind Alex had dispersed. There was nothing but the trampled grass and the burning white sun. Everyone seemed to have gone back inside. Alex walked to the big tent and stepped through a canvas flap. At first, he saw no one on the bleachers, no one in the ring. Then high up near the tent's crown he spotted a man in whiteface wearing a black tuxedo with white socks, white gloves, and a tall black top hat. Holding a fly swatter in his hand, he stepped gracefully along the nearly invisible line of the tightwire, then stopped suddenly and began swatting at a fly. He swatted his shoulder, then the top of his hat.

He spotted Alex far below him and looked down at him, not moving, frozen and silent. All at once he let out a loud, shrill laugh.

The laugh ended abruptly when he began to lose his balance. He teetered dangerously from one foot to the other, his arms making a flying motion, like wings, to compensate for the pull of gravity. He leaned backward, then forward, then backward. Just as it seemed he would fall, he caught himself.

Tipping his hat to Alex, he walked on calmly.

As Alex crossed the inner grounds, he heard a whip crack behind him and turned. The ringmaster was dragging a long black lash through the trampled grass.

"Didn't I tell you to beat it, clown?"

CHAPTER **53**

THAT night, having cleaned
his makeup off his face and changed his clothes, Alex drove
behind pickup trucks and cars full of old and young people going
to the show. A ticket booth had been erected at the mouth of
the tent. In it sat the same old woman who had refused his
twenty dollars on Verre. Alex stayed close to the crowd at all
times, finally climbing high up into the bleachers.

He recognized the faces of some of the workers. Every once
in a while a person crossed the ring whom Alex vaguely remembered to have been in an act. He focused his field glasses on the
women in particular.

The same arrogant, paunchy ringmaster was ordering workers
around, preparing for the opening act.

The night with Iris two years ago, they had not been admitted
until after the first few acts. The third act Alex watched he re-
called vividly. A man stumbled out into the ring, apparently
drunk and rowdy, and tried to mount a swaybacked horse, finally falling upside down, dangling against the ground with one
foot caught in the stirrup. Attempting to get up, he slapped the

horse's flank. The horse took off, galloping around the ring, dragging him by the foot. He knocked and bumped his head against the ground. Miraculously, during all his drunken fumbling he bounced up, landing backward in the seat of the saddle. Soon he was standing on the horse's withers, dancing and flipping back and forth.

As each act came on, Alex began to anticipate seeing Iris. She would appear in the ring with the tigers or high up on the trapeze or riding a horse bareback. He gripped the front of his seat tightly. Sweat beaded on his face and dripped down the side of his neck.

Finally the lights were extinguished and the ringmaster announced the disappearing act.

Alex breathed deeply. It was as if he had forgotten all along that there would be a disappearing act. *Now she'll appear,* he said to himself, *now I'm going to see her.*

Instead of announcing Father Fish, the magician, the ringmaster introduced the Amazing Mr. Surf.

When the lights returned, Alex saw that Mr. Surf was much shorter, much stouter than the tall, thin Father Fish. Despite a thick covering of powder, his catlike face looked almost identical to the fire-eater's. But all the other elements of the act were unchanged. A stage was wheeled into the arena, and on it a coffin stood upright with its open door exposing its plush interior.

"Ladies and gentlemen, the Amazing Mr. Surf asks for a woman volunteer from the audience. He does not ask for just any woman, he asks for a woman with the spirit of adventure in her, with a love for the unknown, with a curiosity for uncharted waters. An uninhibited woman, a fearless woman, a woman with tremendous faith, faith in the invisible. All women with faith in the invisible please step forward!"

The hushed crowd looked among themselves for a volunteer. Alex stared at the heads. He was almost sure that Iris would stand up. *Please stand up,* he said to himself. *Please, Iris, stand up.*

"Come, come, dear people," the ringmaster called. "Never having vanished is never having lived. It is a simple art and you'll never be happier and more secure on your journey than tonight with the Amazing Mr. Surf."

At last, partway around the arena from Alex, a woman stood up. She did not look at all like Iris. She appeared to be in her mid thirties with long, straggly, sandy blond hair and an oval face. She wore a light blue sleeveless dress, and she was holding the hand of a young man with neatly parted brown hair who must have been in his early twenties.

As the woman climbed down through the bleachers slowly and carefully, the crowd clapped wildly. Alex saw through his field glasses that her cheeks glowed healthily. Her loose dress was hiding a pregnant stomach. Holding her enormous belly with one hand, she climbed up onto the stage.

The lights in the arena dimmed to a dark, watery blue. Mr. Surf held the pregnant woman's hand, lifted his top hat, and bowed in several directions, each time grinning at the audience.

Through the binoculars, Alex saw the woman was gazing straight ahead, as if spellbound, not moving her eyes.

As soon as the man snapped his fingers in front of her, she fell back into his arms. Then the man let go of her, pulling his arms away. The woman levitated before him, her stomach showing in profile against her dress. It was the same thing that Iris had done. *But she's not Iris,* Alex kept saying to himself.

Collapsing into the stout man's arms, she returned to a standing position and, with the same trancelike look on her face, stepped back into the coffin.

After covering it with cloth, Mr. Surf lit a corner of the fabric. The fire took a long time to spread, burning a little, smoldering and smoking, and then burning a little more.

Alex turned his glasses to the bleachers and found the thin young man who had been sitting next to the volunteer. He wore a light-green button-down shirt with a collar. There was something softer, more sophisticated about him, even in the way he was sitting, than in the hard crowd around him.

Before Alex looked away, he noticed the young man's face sharpen sternly and remembered the dark feelings he himself had experienced watching Iris.

The flames had grown. Black smoke leaped up into the arena. Men held buckets of water ready in the darkness at the ring's edge.

The flames rose higher and higher. The coffin collapsed, one side at a time, embers and ash scattering and breaking on the stage.

Alex looked back at the young man. He was even more tense, gripping the bleachers with both hands.

The men tossed their buckets of water on the now smoldering coffin. Plumes of steam whitened the dark smoke.

"Ladies and gentlemen, our volunteer has now exited the world of the living and is traveling through the world of the invisible. She is now walking on water. Do not fear for her. Our Amazing Mr. Surf has never failed to bring a subject back from such an exquisite journey."

"*Never failed*," Alex said out loud. He began to laugh a little, but his laughter stopped as tears came to his eyes.

A new, shiny black coffin was carried out into the ring and set on end. The Amazing Mr. Surf opened it and turned it around for all to see the cushioned lining inside. Then, closing the door, he knelt down in front of it, placing his hands carefully together to pray.

Focusing on his face, Alex saw his eyes were closed. His lips mumbled something rapidly, like a priest's Latin rituals. Sweat rose and streaked through the powder on his cheeks, dripping and staining white his black tuxedo.

The audience sensed the power of his praying and became silent.

All at once relief flashed across Mr. Surf's face. He opened his eyes and looked toward the peak of the dome, spreading his arms as if to thank God for an offering.

Smiling, he climbed to his feet, turned, and opened the coffin.

The pregnant woman stepped out, holding her hand beneath her belly. She looked slightly dazed, but also relaxed, like a person returning from meditation.

But why didn't this happen to us? Why didn't this happen to us? Alex said to himself.

Applause rose from the bleachers as the young man made his way down to her.

"*Bastards,*" Alex said.

"Good night and thank you!" the ringmaster called. "We've enjoyed this show with you!"

Alex stood up. He wanted to start shouting madly at the circus people. *I hate you, I hate you, you bastards, you dirty bastards.* But instead he followed the crowd down from the bleachers onto the grass, keeping his eyes on the young couple who were now holding hands.

In the grassy darkness outside the tent, the couple split from the crowd and crossed through a field of parked cars. Alex caught up from behind. But suddenly they stopped and began kissing.

It was a long kiss. Alex waited for them to stop, but their embrace grew tighter. The young man's stomach pressed against the woman's swollen belly. He was rubbing the woman's back, the woman was holding the man's head.

In the dark, clear of the circus people, Alex watched the couple's silhouette. He could hear the traffic exiting the field. Then he followed them to the door of their car. There again they started where they had left off, ardently massaging each other's bottoms, finally falling backward into the front seat of their red Buick convertible. Alex found his own car and got in it. He could see them through his windshield.

Finally, they sat upright. Their headlights illuminated the field and the young man began to drive. Alex followed them on a dark and hilly road. But less than a mile away they stopped at a run-down motel along the entrance ramp to a highway. After the couple opened their room door, Alex went to the front desk and asked for the room next to theirs.

By the time he had filled in the check-in forms, the couple's curtains were drawn, their lights were out.

He stood at the door to knock, but heard lovemaking noises coming from behind it.

Through the wall in his room, he could hear a bed squeaking, moans, and a word, a word he could barely make out as they spoke it over and over to each other. *Nadir,* he thought they were saying, *nadir, nadir.*

As Alex lay on his bed, his dreaming began. Despite his attempts to keep himself awake, the images of red-and-yellow tents, blue costumes, faded props, and rust-colored wagons forced their way behind his closed eyes.

CHAPTER **54**

HE woke to the sound of the young man moaning as if he were being strangled, as if his life were about to end. At first Alex thought it was a last desperate call to fend off the darkness of death. But then it sounded like a cry of ecstasy. When it stopped, Alex heard the sobs of the young woman.

The sobs went on until dawn slipped through his curtains.

An hour later he heard their door open and went to his window. The young man, dressed in a pressed shirt, his healthy brown hair parted neatly to the side, drove off in the rusted red car alone.

After dressing, Alex stepped outside to the next door and knocked.

He heard the latching of the inner chain and then the door opened partially. The young woman with the bulging stomach looked out through her scraggly blond hair. Alex could see rings around her eyes.

"Hello," Alex said. "I saw you and your boyfriend in the

circus. I was wondering if I could ask you a few questions about it."

"We quit last night. Last night was our last night," she said in a deep voice, then started to close the door.

"You were working for them?"

"That's right. They paid us."

"Where are you going now?" Alex said.

"Jason will be back soon. You can speak to him," she said, closing the door.

Alex paced up and down the crumbling cement sidewalk that ran just outside the buildings until Jason drove the car up to the room. Alex walked in front of him, turned, and looked directly at him to see if he would be recognized. But Jason passed him and went into the motel room.

Alex waited a minute and knocked on the door. Jason opened it.

Alex smiled. "I just told your friend—"

"My wife—"

"Your wife that I saw you two in the circus. I've got some questions."

"What kind of questions?"

"Not about you. About somebody else. You might know about her, you might not."

The woman had put her hair up and was wearing wire-rimmed glasses. She leaned against the headboard of the bed studiously reading a book.

"Come in," Jason said. He twisted open a Coke. "Have a seat." Alex sat down. Jason sat at the end of the bed and introduced himself and his wife, Lois.

"What do you want to know?" Jason asked.

"I'm looking for somebody, somebody who may have run away with the circus."

"This show doesn't take runaways; they're more or less a tight family. We're the only ones not really part of them," Jason said.

"Do you know of a woman named Iris Barton?"

Alex looked at their faces. They were not necessarily innocent faces, but earnest ones. Their expressions didn't change.

"She was in this circus at least for a while two years ago," he said.

"Well, we only joined less than a year ago."

"Have you heard of her?"

Alex handed them the photograph of her he had taken from the album. They both examined it, but handed it back shaking their heads.

Alex thought a moment. "How long have you been working for them?"

"Almost nine months."

"Did you ever hear them talk about kidnapping somebody?"

Both Jason and Lois shook their heads. "Why, was somebody kidnapped?"

"Possibly," Alex said.

"Are you a cop?" Jason said.

"I'm looking into this on my own. I'm a schoolteacher, that's what I do for a living. I hope you don't mind my asking all these questions."

"I've never heard of anything like that. But we quit because they were beginning to make us nervous," Jason said.

"We're broke but we quit anyway," Lois said. She closed her book and Alex saw its cover—*Dictionary of Saints*.

"We're not totally broke, but it was getting to be too much," Jason said.

"What was too much?" Alex asked.

"Everything. But why are you coming to us?"

"You looked like two people I could talk to."

Jason stood up. "If you want to talk, let's go outside. I've got plenty to say about that stupid circus."

Lois turned on the television with the remote. Jason leaned over the bed and kissed her.

Stepping out into the sun, they followed the shoulder of the busy road in front of the motel and turned onto the first country lane, a lane that ran through a valley and over a bridge across a stream. The sound of the freeway came from the hill behind them.

"Who are you working for?" Jason said.

"Nobody. I teach grammar school. But I've taken time off. This person I'm looking for is a friend. What did you mean the circus was getting to be too much?"

Jason stopped, sighed, and took a deep breath, then he looked across a field to a line of willows along the meandering stream. "The whole thing was giving me the creeps. Somehow I had this feeling that if we'd stayed another week we might have been in there forever." He turned to Alex and started walking again. "There's no way you can understand what I'm saying."

"I might," Alex said.

"I know I sound crazy, but this last year, ever since we joined the show, I've felt funny. Like I've been dreaming. Like I've been living in a dream, a dangerous dream, but somehow it's my own dream.

"And I've got this idea that it all started right when Lois volunteered for the act. Right then, that was the beginning."

"What started? The beginning of what?"

"Things got crazy right then."

"Crazy in what way?"

"In every way."

"But like what? Tell me exactly."

"I can't tell you."

"You can tell me. I've had trouble with that circus myself. They've done a job on my life."

"All right," Jason said and stopped. "First of all, that first night, right? We went crazy in bed. We didn't use birth control. We went at each other, not like two people. Like animals. We tore at each other like animals. And do you know what? Neither of us have been the same since. We've been fighting. Fighting like dogs and making up, fighting and making up. We can't seem to stop it. Lois has been crying so often that sometimes she cries during the act. She's threatened me constantly. One time she told me that during the act someday she'd put a gun to her head and disappear for good.''

"She threatened suicide?"

"Yes."

"And what did you do?"

"What did I do? What could I do? I tried to ignore it. I kept acting more and more like a big man. Like I was going to save her and save us in the meantime. I kept thinking that during the act I'd get up and run down into the arena and pull her out of that flaming box, carry her to safety, then come back and decimate the show, animals, and people. One big pile of dead circus, you know." Jason laughed a little. "But guess what?" He looked at Alex and smiled. "That never happened. No. Just the opposite. I just sat there during the act sweating and crying to myself, yearning like some little baby. Come out, please, come out of that box, I'd say. Oh God, please bring her out, please, I'll do anything for you if you let her come out, please God, please God.

"And when she did come out, each time I'd run down into the arena and hug and kiss her and . . . it was like we fell in love again. God, I love you, I'd say. God! I love you!"

"Did you ever talk to any of them about this? Did they know?"

"They didn't give a hoot about us. Hey, we could have killed each other and they probably wouldn't have noticed."

"Didn't somebody say something?"

"I hardly wanted to talk to them about it. But one time after the act, Mr. Surf stepped up to me and whispered: 'Jason, keep your eyes open.' He wouldn't tell me any more than that. But something began to click. A day later a pregnant acrobat who had gone into labor was brought into the tent and put on a stage in the ring where she lay until Mr. Surf helped to deliver her baby.

"That night the baby and the mother slept together on this little stage. Don't ask me why. But it scared me. Scared me so badly that I started thinking we should get out, get the hell out."

They climbed the opposite slope of the valley, passing into a stand of trees alive with bird song. On the other side of the trees, they stopped at the foot of a hill of cornfields and pastures crisscrossed by deeply worn cow paths. Against the soft blue sky, high on a ridge, Alex could see the watery silhouettes of a herd of grazing cattle.

"I've got a proposal," Alex said. "Do you think you might return to the circus for me to find out where this woman is? I'll pay you. All you have to do is to ask around . . . You must have some friends in there."

Jason had put his hands in his pockets.

"They're probably pissed off that I left, that I took Lois with me. Are you sure you've got the right circus?"

"Everything's the same except the magician. It wasn't Mr. Surf, but a tall thin guy named Father Fish."

"A priest?"

"I don't know. Couldn't you ask them, at least? Bribe them? I'll get money from a cash machine. I'll give it to you. Take what you want and use the rest to bribe them."

"You're serious about this, aren't you?" Jason said.

Alex nodded. "They must need money."

"We need money, that's for sure. We're broke. But I'd better ask Lois."

They returned back down the hill to the motel. The lights were off in Jason's room. Lois was sleeping. Jason turned to Alex and told him to wait outside the door.

A few minutes later, he slipped quietly out again. "She says it's okay. She even has an idea whom we might ask."

CHAPTER **55**

THAT night there were no lovemaking sounds through the wall. But every time Alex woke up he heard Lois's quiet sobs.

The next morning he knocked on their door. When the couple came out, they both looked tired and disoriented, though Jason had once again put on fresh clothes.

After breakfast, Jason suggested they walk to a field near the circus where Alex and Lois could wait while he went ahead to the show. He was not sure how long it would take to get certain people alone so that he could question them.

Lois brought her *Dictionary of Saints* and a yellow blanket. The three of them walked along the lane that Jason and Alex had been on the day before, crossing the stream, crossing the ridge with the cattle, until finally Jason stopped and pointed across a wide field.

"They're on the other side of those trees."

Lois spread the blanket in the shade near a stone wall.

Alex gave Jason money he had withdrawn the night before. "Take what you need for yourself," he told him.

Jason crossed the roughly cut grass of the spacious sun-drenched field. Soon the heat that rose in wavering lines distorted his figure, bending his body in places, making him appear watery. Soft white clouds gathered in the hazy blue sky. Far away, he crossed a stone wall and disappeared into the trees.

After a while Alex turned to Lois, who was sitting up, her arms around her knees. "When is the baby due?"

"A week."

Alex looked at her soft but serious gaze from the side.

"Jason told me something that I'm not sure I understand. He said that joining this circus was like joining a dream. Is that right?"

She leaned back on her elbows, her heavy stomach arching up as high as her chin.

"A dream?" she said. She thought for a while, looking through her delicate glasses at the place where Jason had disappeared. "That's pretty accurate, but the dream started for me before I joined the show."

"How do you mean?"

"A few months before. In Rome."

"What were you doing in Rome?"

"Trying to get my first husband out of my mind."

"You were divorced?"

"I had gotten divorced, yes, and it was devastating. By the time it was over I didn't even hate him anymore. I didn't feel anything for anything or anybody. I thought I was finished with life, to be honest with you. In Italy I began visiting churches, praying to God for a sign, for some connection to myself. But it didn't work. By the time I reached Rome I was at the very end of my rope.

"But then I walked out of a church into a small square where I saw a crowd standing in a heavy downpour of rain and looking high up to a man riding a unicycle on a tightwire between two buildings, without a net below. He was looking up in the air. His mouth was open, and he was catching raindrops with his tongue, swallowing and wiping his lips with a napkin. After he'd had his fill, he started to laugh. It was the strangest laugh I had ever heard. It was half human, half animal, neither sad nor happy, and it seemed to go deep into me and mesmerize me. That's where the dream began."

"Why did it begin there?"

"Because that's when I first started to feel different. And soon afterward something strange happened, something that I still can't believe really happened to me. I mean, I think I did see this performer. But I'm not sure if everything that happened afterward really happened."

"What happened?"

"After the act was finished and the crowd had gone away, I was still staring up at the wire, as if the act was still going on when I heard a voice near me. 'I'm here.' I looked down and saw a soaking wet man about your age standing in front of me, waving his hand. He looked serious and intense. 'Are you all right?' he asked. He was obviously the man who had been on the wire.

"I couldn't speak. I just stared at him. A smile came across his face, slowly.

" 'Are you thinking about going up there? What are you staring at? Can't you talk? Has the cat got your tongue?'

"He began to do things to make me laugh. He followed somebody down the sidewalk, walking on his hands with his hat resting on his shoes.

"Finally he came back over to me.

" 'Can you cry, at least?'

"I kept staring.

" 'Are you alive, at least?'

"He poked my ribs with his finger.

" 'That's it. That's your problem, you're not alive. That's what it is,' he said, slapping his knee as if I had told him the answer to a riddle. 'You have no life and that's not an easy thing to find.' He laughed again.

" 'A life is not an easy thing to find. First you must learn to fly. Do you know how to fly? Once you learn how to fly, it's easy.'

"Thinking back on it, I might have dreamed the whole thing. I can still hear his laugh but it was like no laughter I've ever heard before and every time I hear it in my mind I feel like I'm in another reality, like I'm dreaming.

"Well, listen. After standing out in the gray downpour talking to me and trying to cheer me up, he told me that I should meet a friend of his father. The next thing I remember is following him through intricate and ornately decorated halls. I don't remember entering the Vatican but that is the only place I can think of that could have been so beautiful. Whenever we were stopped at a checkpoint, he would say to the guards that we were going to see *the vicar* and they would smile and let us through.

"After passing along many grand hallways and through rooms with high domes, we began to ascend a circular staircase of stone. At the top we passed down a very narrow passageway that seemed to make a circle. Finally, we came to one of the most beautiful wooden doors I've ever seen, elaborately carved with vine leaves, blades of grass, sheep, saints, and angels. As I stared at it, I noticed a little gold plaque with letters barely big enough to read. It said The Pope Lives Here.

"Before the Flying Man knocked, he put his finger to his lips and whispered.

" 'He is a very strange man, this pope. Perhaps he will speak to you. And if he does, and you happen onto the word *circus*, be very careful when you say that word.' He turned and knocked.

"The door, unlatched from the inside, swung open crisply, like the door to a castle treasury. Inside I saw magnificent paintings, tapestries, and statues, angels and vines carved into the stone of a huge fireplace. Standing next to the door was a short man, almost as short as a midget. But then I gradually came to recognize his gentle, gentle face. Closing his eyes, he bowed his head slightly as if he had been expecting me all along. His pale lips mumbled some nicety.

" 'Come in, come in, child,' he said.

"So mesmerized was I by this man after stepping inside his gentle aura, that I did not notice the Flying Man had left my side and backed away.

"Entering his chambers was truly like entering the passage-ways of a dream. There I was flying for the first time."

Lois was sitting up again. Her squinted, reminiscing eyes appeared to be moving back and forth as if she were reading.

"Circus," she said clearly and slowly. "Circus . . . circus."

The word remained in the air and then faded sadly away into the sounds of crickets.

"As this man spoke to me about circuses, he kept wiping tears from his eyes. At first he seemed to be reciting from Genesis. 'In the beginning God created the heavens and the earth,' he said. 'The earth was without form and void, and darkness was upon the face of the deep; and the Spirit of God was moving over the face of the waters.' But then without skipping a beat he was talking about circuses. 'And after many years the Great Circus rose from the depths of the ocean and walked upon the land and gave birth to the Great Religion and for many years the Great Circus and the Great Religion lived in harmony and there was peace on earth. But then the strength of the Great Religion grew and the strength of the Great Circus diminished because it was away from water. And forgetting whence it had come, the Great Religion waged war against the Great Circus, and in time the Great Religion won out and the Great Circus was driven back to sea from whence it had come.'

"He spoke about the history of the Great Circus and the divisions of the Great Religion, but finally he began telling me a personal story about himself. Many years ago when he had first become pope, he was in the midst of a terrible personal crisis. He felt that he was even further away from God than he had been before. All this work and all this prayer only to be even further away from God than when he had started. He was deeply depressed . . . his depression went on for years. He was sad, so sad, his world was as gray and lifeless as the smog over Rome, but he could not for the life of him cry. 'Had I shed my tears,' he told me, 'I would have been rid of them at least for a moment, but I could not shed a single tear.'

"Then, one cold winter afternoon he saw from the window of his motorcar a crowd gathered around a street performer and asked his driver to stop.

"Climbing out of the car, he walked unescorted through the small crowd that seemed not to care who he was. His feet hit the edge of a small, pathetic ring, painted sloppily. In the ring was a famous trapeze artist, the father of the man who had brought me to him. The man was doing pantomime like a clown. The pope was on the verge of a nervous breakdown, perhaps a heart attack, and somehow he knew that he was not bound for the circle of heaven. In the cold of that small crowd of bundled spectators, he no longer knew where to turn for help. His knees were weak, his breathing shallow, and he felt himself fainting. Just then the trapeze artist for no apparent reason began a dance of mysterious gestures. They were ritualistic gestures, gestures expressing the unknown, gestures expressing the invisible. Perhaps they were like the ritualistic gestures performed during Mass. Whatever it was, it sent laughter through his body that felt like electricity. His body convulsed with hilarious laughter and out of his eyes, like water from stone, came tears, tears such as he'd never seen before . . .

"His laughter seemed to be something inside him communicating with the performer. It was not merely laughter that issued from his lips, but a language, a language of humor. The artist would gesture, he would bend this way or that, and the pope would answer in the tongue of laughter. You're making me sad, the pope seemed to say to him. You're killing me with sadness. And the artist's strange response communicated to the pope through gestures was—it's okay to die of laughter, it's okay to die of tears.

"The artist, having read about the pope's then famous insomnia and unhappiness, begged him to go to the circus where he would be performing. The pope attended later that evening. Nothing in the show struck him as remarkable. But as he sat there, he noticed a sensation in his knees. It was the same feeling he had gotten as a child when he had first started kneeling in prayer, a time in his life when he had not been full of false, stereotypical ideas about where to find God. It was a time in his life when he had worshiped purely. By the time the show was over, he began to feel God once again, *feel* him as he had felt him when he was a child.

"After that night the pope began to discover what he called private circuses, personal circuses that come up out of the earth like strange, mysterious, and secret plants growing between the rocks, like cacti or weeds climbing through the cracks of sidewalks in some broken-down alleyway."

Lois paused, breathing for a moment and thinking. "As I told you, all of this must be a dream, I couldn't have met the real pope, but I just don't know."

"You could have met him."

"Whether it was a dream or not, before I'd left his chambers I started thinking that I didn't really know what a circus was. I thought he might just sort of mean the practices of a 'nonbeliever' or an 'atheist,' so I asked him, 'What is a circus?'

"He started to tell me that a circus was merely a place of performance, but then he changed his mind and said, 'No.' Then he started down another line of thought. 'Circuses are a form of insanity.' He stopped again, laughed heartily. 'What am I talking about?' he said. 'They're just the opposite, circuses are sanity, pure sanity.' But then he stopped again and said, 'No, circuses are something that your eyes become.'

" 'Your eyes become a circus?' I asked.

" 'Yes, you see, it is only after your eyes become a circus that you can see your life as it really is. Like colors, you cannot really see colors until your eyes become a circus.

" 'Before the circus,' he said, 'I'd never truly seen the true color red, that is the red of the earth, and because of this I'd realized I'd never seen the true color of blood and because of this I'd never really seen the blood of Christ and because I'd never seen the blood of Christ, I'd never tasted it, never felt it, never smelled it, never touched it.'

"He told me not to confuse Christ with the circus. 'Christ is not a circus,' he said."

Lois turned to Alex, she was gently shaking her head, her hair tapping her temples. "No," she repeated. "Christ is not a circus."

Neither she nor Alex spoke to each other for a long time. They sat there looking at the heat rising from the yellow field.

"Soon afterward I met Jason and came across this circus. When they needed a volunteer for the vanishing act, I stood up, inspired by something the pope had told me before I left his room. Something he told me in such a low whisper that the whisper itself seemed to signify some insidious conspiracy taking place in the Vatican. Only later was I able to piece together the various bits of what had been said. 'Vanishing is to the circus,' he had said, 'what fasting is to God.'

"I always assumed there were trapdoors, but because Mr. Surf mesmerized me each time, his trick remains a secret from everyone including his subjects. I tried to stay conscious for it once, but he knew it and the ringmaster announced to the crowd that Mr. Surf's powers were in remission."

"You have no memory of what happened to you during the act whatsoever?" Alex asked.

"I would try to remember things after the act, but all I could remember was being suspended in space and crying."

"Crying?"

"Yes, crying. I'd be in a place that was nowhere and I'd be crying. There were no coordinates in this place, no tree next to a pond, or field next to a sea, no colors next to each other. There was not much I could do about this place. It was not a place you go to. It was a place that comes to you, a place that you must submit to," Lois said. "It was as if you were stationary, but the place moved into you the way a baby moves into you when you're pregnant. Sometimes I think that my child is actually the place that arrived in me when I performed the act."

Tired from talking, Lois lay back on her pillow, looked at the sky, and closed her eyes. Alex got up to stretch his legs. He had noticed crows pecking at something in the grass. The crows flew up to a tree as he approached. The pulverized body of an opossum lay on the ground. Beetles moved in and out of the spotted flesh. When he returned to the yellow blanket, he saw Lois was sleeping deeply. Sitting down, he flipped through her *Dictionary of Saints* and read a few of the entries.

Dark rings had grown around Lois's eyes, then tears dripped from their corners. Her lips were moving. She was mouthing the words *I love you* over and over without actually uttering them. On Lois's calves below the hem of her maternity dress, Alex saw red marks, as if somebody had drawn their fingernails along her flesh.

He reached over, gently putting his hand on her swollen stomach. At first he thought he could feel her heart beating, then he realized that it was not her heart, but the movements of the baby.

CHAPTER 56

THE border of the shade in which they sat moved across the roughly cut field. Alex could hear crickets and cicadas. Through the lines of heat, he saw the figure, small at this distance, of a man running toward them across the field. The man tripped and fell to the dirt.

He did not get up for a long time. When he lifted himself to his feet he appeared to stagger like a drunken man. After waking Lois, Alex dashed toward the figure who appeared to be losing his balance again.

As he got close to him, Alex saw that it was Jason. Jason fell to his knees and then onto his back. He held his ribs as he squirmed and writhed against the dirt in pain. His face was beaten and bruised.

Lois screamed when she got to him.

"Help us, Alex! Help us!"

Alex ran across the field and turned down the road to a house where he had seen a white-haired woman hanging sheets from a line. He found her behind the house coming out of a shack, carrying a grayish blue carton of eggs. She told him where to find the telephone and he ran in and called an ambulance.

He returned to Lois and Jason in the field. Lois was kneeling near Jason's face. She had calmed down and was speaking quietly to comfort him. Alex told them he would wait for the ambulance at the entrance to the field.

When the ambulance came, Alex rode with them over the rough field to where Jason lay. After Jason was loaded into the ambulance, Lois got in the back with him. The red lights and siren came on as they left through the opening of the field.

As Alex jogged back to the motel to get his car, he saw the old woman coming toward him along the road, wiping her hands on her white apron.

"What was he doing in that field?" the old woman asked.

"He fell, that's all," Alex said.

He left her staring across the field, squinting her eyes. "Fell?" she said.

Lois sat in a plastic chair in a waiting room with families. A child was playing on the floor with a doll with a green face. Lois was holding a paper towel to her eyes and crying.

"Whatever they did to him, he can't speak," she said.

Alex put his hand on her neck to comfort her. He could feel her crying.

After a while a doctor holding a clipboard came out and stood near Lois, who stared at the floor and cried. The doctor told her that X rays showed a hairline fracture of the skull. They believed that Jason was suffering from temporary head trauma and that his speech would come back shortly.

Alex followed Lois into Jason's room. Bandages were wrapped around his head. His eyes were closed, and his lips were turned up at the ends, almost as if in a smile. A plastic intravenous line curled down to the inside of his arm. Lois knelt next to him and held his hand. His eyes remained closed.

Alex stood behind her for a few moments, then whispered that he would be in the waiting room. There he sat down, watching the door for Lois. Beneath his feet the little boy held the green doll up to the leg of a chair and spoke to the chair leg as if it were another doll.

When Lois came out, she told Alex that the doctor had said that the medication was keeping Jason from waking up. The doctors would allow her to stay with Jason until ten o'clock.

Alex met her in the hospital room just before ten that night. Jason had not moved at all since earlier that afternoon.

Alex drove Lois back to their shabby motel. In bed before turning off the light, he heard Lois's crying through the wall. It sounded no different than it had for the past two nights. The next morning he waited for her outside by her red Buick, finally knocking on her door for a long time. When she came to it, he saw that the rings around her eyes were darker, the wrinkles deeper.

At the hospital, a nurse told them that Jason had been moved to another room on the floor above and to speak to a doctor before visiting him.

Lois rushed to the stairs and up the single flight. The receptionist did not give out Jason's room number. "Dr. Morris wants to speak to you."

"Is he all right? Is he all right?"

"Dr. Morris wants to speak to you," she repeated.

"But is Jason all right?"

When the doctor finally came, Alex stood behind Lois, who had placed paper towels once again to her eyes.

The doctor spoke in a quick, low mumble. Jason was experiencing a kind of dementia, he was speaking a little but he was having hallucinations. He told her not to be alarmed by this. "His mind is healing itself," he said. "He'll be better soon."

They went into the room. Jason's eyes were partially open. Kneeling next to him, Lois held his hand.

"Oh, God, Jason, what did they do to you, what did they do to you?"

Jason was looking toward the ceiling.

"Is the pain terrible? Are you all right? Is it terrible?"

His eyes focused on the ceiling, Jason lifted his hand and pointed.

Lois looked up to where he was pointing, then looked back at him.

"What do you see? . . . But it's in your head, it's in your head."

He kept his arm up.

Lois stood up and tried to hold the hand that was pointing, but he kept moving his hand away.

"Fire," he said.

"What fire? It's in your head, darling, it's in your head. There's no fire in here."

He moved his hand in a circle. "All fire," he said again.

"No, you're seeing things." She broke out into tears. "It's not fair, it's not fair, why you? It's not fair . . . I love you."

But he kept moving his finger in a circle and saying, "Fire, fire."

"Why did they do this to you? Is it because we left? Is that why?"

Jason kept pointing and saying, "Fire."

Finally, Lois turned to Alex and asked that he leave them alone for a while.

Alex waited near his car in the parking lot outside the hospital. After a while Lois came down the hospital steps. But instead of coming toward him, she turned and walked to a barbed-wire fence strung tightly between cedar posts. Beyond the barbed wire was a wide grassy field. Holding her belly with one hand, she tried to climb one of the posts, balancing herself with her other hand. After tottering a little, she got down in the tall grass on the ground and crawled under.

Alex watched her walking across the grass toward a line of trees. After climbing the fence himself, he followed her from a distance. In the farthest corner of the field, under tall slender oaks, she got down on her knees and pulled at the grass. Closer, he noticed that she was uprooting grass in a circle as if to make a ring of black earth. He called to her to let her know that he was coming, but she kept on without looking up.

Dirt and yellow grass stained her fingers and knees. The sun at Alex's back cast his shadow across the uneven ground.

Finally, she got up and stepped from the black circle, her fingers dirty.

"Jason told me why they beat him up," she said as she walked back toward the hospital with Alex. "He mentioned a church that we had been wondering about."

"What kind of church?"

"One that's been destroyed, but one they visit frequently. Nobody would tell us why. But the ringmaster and his friend have been going there for several months."

"Where is it?"

"It's in Everly, Mississippi. It's boarded up. There must have been a fire there. When Jason asked them about it, they attacked him."

"What for?"

"They must have thought he knew something. He's lucky he got away."

Crows began coming up over the dark tips of the tall oaks, crossing the white sky. He began to count them.

At the fence Lois got down to crawl through the long grass while Alex held up the wire for her.

In the parking lot, she turned to him again.

"You have business to take care of with them. Go there," she said.

CHAPTER 57

IN the small town of Everly, Alex found the church with its fire-blackened walls and boarded-up windows. Parked in front was the rusted old circus pickup truck with its rounded hood, big fenders, and tall, thin wheels. After parking his car a few streets over, Alex returned and stood near the stoop of a small brick building and watched the church's front door.

The ringmaster and dwarf stepped out, turned, and locked the big wooden door, then climbed down the crumbling steps and started walking along the sidewalk away from their truck and away from Alex.

Alex went to a locked black iron gate and climbed over into an alleyway, then followed it into a small overgrown cemetery in the church's rear yard. Short eroded gravestones dating back to the seventeen hundreds stuck crookedly up from mounds of moss-covered earth. A white tree limb had fallen and broken in the long, dead grass. In one corner, against a rusted iron fence, a torn baby carriage without wheels was smashed on top of a metal shopping cart.

Red plywood boarded the back door of the church. The basement windows at ground level were covered with heavy wire mesh, which had already been kicked in and pried away. Alex tried pulling on each window, until finally one opened.

He slipped through, feet first, lowering himself down onto a stone floor. A familiar smell, the smell of wet stones, came to him, as he groped in the dark for a light switch.

His feet knocked something over, perhaps a dish. He stopped. He heard something through the wall. A muffled sound.

He went on, stepping over crates full of china, his knees bumping into objects that felt like the backs of chairs. Finally, he found a switch and flipped it up. A bare yellow lightbulb behind him came on.

The room was full of circus props. Giant papier-mâché faces, old elephant harnesses, a wooden section of a ring, a broken bullwhip. Religious icons were piled among the rubble. White plaster statues of saints, their arms and legs broken. Folding chairs had been stacked high along the wall near the window. At Alex's feet was a box of brass candlestick holders.

The noises were coming from behind a wooden door that Alex tried to push open but found locked from the other side.

Footsteps crossed the church floor above him. After flipping off the light, he crept quietly past the boxes to the window he had come in by. Under the window, he crouched and listened, holding his breath.

A light in the opposite room came on; yellow stripes and bars of light fell through the cracks in the door onto the pile of plaster saints. Footsteps of two men climbed down the stairs into the opposite room.

Alex heard the gruff voice of the ringmaster, then the sudden heavy breathing of a man.

A feeble voice spoke. Alex could not make out any of what it said except the word *blind*, which it repeated emphatically.

"*Vittles*," the ringmaster said and laughed. Another man laughed too.

A few moments later, Alex heard their footsteps and the light went out.

He turned on the storage room light again, used the leg of a chair for a lever and pried the door until the latch itself pulled through the soft wood.

In the wan light from the storage room he could see a thin, frail middle-aged man, his lips pulled sharply back by a gag, a yellow handkerchief. The gag forced his lips so far back that it looked as if he were smiling.

He was seated in a wooden chair, his hands tied behind his back and his chest pressed against a table. He wore a priest's vestments; a cross hung from his neck. On the table before him on a paper plate was the large cooked drumstick of a fowl, and next to it a glass of red wine.

Nodding his head, the man began to whine. There was something familiar about the huge, exhausted eyes that bulged from his head like those of a fish out of water.

Alex untied his gag. Wheezing and gasping for breath, the man turned toward Alex, and Alex stared at him.

As he stared, he remembered the watery light that had played over them the night of the circus, he remembered the tuxedo with its fish's tails, but most of all he remembered the eyes. From a distance, the dark shadows under gaunt cheeks and sunken eyes made the man look old. But close up Alex saw that he was probably in his early thirties.

"You're the one," Alex said quietly.

The man looked up at him slowly. "Which one?" he whispered, hoarsely. His big eyes in their shady sockets searched Alex's face slowly. His swollen lips rose slowly into a feeble smile. "Which one am I? Tell me, which one am I?"

"You're Father Fish."

The man nodded his head slowly. "And I'm starving," he whispered.

"You made my wife disappear."

The man continued to nod. "You're her husband then? You're

her husband? Do you know where she is? Please tell me. If you know you will save me."

"That's what *you* are going to tell me," Alex said.

The man was so emaciated that he could hardly hold his head up. Closing his red, wrinkled eyes, he whispered, "Not you too, not you too." His chin sunk against his chest.

Alex lifted the man's head back up and stared into his blood-shot eyes.

"Exactly what are you saying?" Alex said.

"Do you think I would be starving if I weren't blind and ignorant?"

"Where is she?" Alex demanded.

Father Fish closed his bloodshot eyes. His breathing quickened. "Please untie me, please."

"No, you tell me right now what you know."

Father Fish kept shaking his head and looking down. His sharp shoulder blades stuck up from under his robe. His thin neck did not look capable of supporting his swollen head.

"You just tell me what you did with her that night," Alex said.

"That night? Yes, that night." Father Fish raised his eyes. "Do you want to know? Do you really want to know?" His face became red with blood. His pupils dilated. "She *vanished!*" he yelled.

"*Vanished?* That's a lie!"

"We lifted the lid of the inner box after our trick and she was *gone.* Do you hear me? *Gone!* Do you hear? *Gone!* There was *nothing* in the box. *Nothing! Nothing!* Do you understand me? Do you hear me clearly? *Nothing!!* And now they think there is some power in my arms, my eyes! But I am as blind as they are! I am blind! I don't know where she is!" He closed his eyes and shook his head and cried.

"You're lying!" Alex said.

"Can I help that she's gone?" Father Fish said with tears in his eyes. "And do you know the man who hired us, the man who was going to pay the money, was going to save us from starvation, was going to save our lives, he got mad. He promised to kill us all. We have no right to live. If we don't get the woman back we have no right to live. Not only will we die, but all of our animals will perish. We will burn like in hell! And this man he has an army of disciples, he has an army that will burn us all to death! Wipe us clear off the face of this earth so that nobody, nobody will ever hear from us again. He'll destroy us with his wrath, simple as that!"

Alex grabbed the man's frail shoulders and began to shake him. "Tell me the truth, goddamn it! Tell me the truth! Was the man who hired you Edward Volenti? Was that his name?"

Tears fell from the man's bloodshot eyes. "Maybe," he said, feebly. "Maybe."

Alex kept shaking him. "Tell me, Father, where is Edward Volenti now? Where is he? He's not on his island. Where can I find him?! Tell me before I hurt you! Tell me!"

"He told us nothing, nothing."

"Tell me who can tell me!" Alex said.

The man's eyes searched the room. "There's a man I know . . . a man I know . . . maybe he can help you . . . he's a friend of mine. He knows the old man . . . he knows him . . . Michelman."

"*Michelman!?* Peter Michelman?"

"Yes," Father Fish said. "Yes, yes, yes, a painter."

"Where does he live? Where can I find him?"

"Trinity."

"Where?"

"A town up north."

"Where up north?"

"New Hampshire."

Alex reached down, untied the priest's hands, ran to the back room, and slipped out through the window.

CHAPTER 58

YELLOWING paint flaked from the tattered shingles of Trinity's sunken little houses. Along Main Street the maple leaves were falling gently to the sidewalk and a line of school children kicked through them. The children carried lunch pails decorated with cartoon characters and movie stars.

There was no wind when Alex stepped from his car, but the air, streaked with morning sunlight, seemed to shimmer with an unexpected chill, a chill he did not remember since before he had entered the circus inside the mountain almost a year earlier. He crossed the porch of a country store with dark wood siding and a paint chipped, rusted white sign that said Feed Store above the door. The clerk, a round woman in a dirty baby blue turtleneck, told him that the painter Peter Michelman lived on North Road just past the library. His mailbox said Volenti and was decorated with flying yellow sparrows.

A line ran down the center of the winding road. The weeds next to the pavement were blanched and dry, their narrow, jagged leaves withering and folding in. Alex passed a meadow of long yellow grass. A silver bucket hung from a maple tree that grew alone in the very center of a field; behind the field, the slope of a mountain began, pine trees standing one above the other up to a ridge.

In thin letters on the mailbox Alex saw the name Edward Volenti. The box itself was crumpled as if a rock had hit it. Long pine branches swept against Alex's windshield as he drove up the gravel driveway. At the top, under the majestic limbs of giant fir trees, he saw a salt gray house with a glass roof of seven pyramid-shaped skylights covered with pine needles.

Alex knocked on the front door, then opened it. Inside, under mottled light from the sky, he saw a dozen gigantic paintings fifteen feet high or higher leaning against wooden support beams. The large paintings cast shadows onto the speckled cement floor and against the wall. Alex walked through the shadows.

Perhaps Michelman had further perfected his technique or perhaps the size of these paintings rendered them more real, the wounds of the animals more ghastly. Each showed a circus ring in green grass before a calm blue sea. Mayhem had taken place inside and outside these rings. Blood poured from gashes in the flesh of horses and elephants, llamas and zebras. Scattered in the melee were the bodies of strong men, bearded women, Siamese twins, lion trainers, trapeze artists, midgets, and acrobats. The blood on their chests and backs looked vulgarly real. In all of the canvases, seagulls sat calmly and obliviously on the bodies of the dead.

In one giant canvas a chimpanzee stood firmly in center ring. He was the only living animal besides the gulls and the occasional fish whose fins could be seen far off in the blue water behind him. Dressed like a soldier in camouflage, he leaned forward slightly, holding an automatic rifle across his chest, his glaring yellow eyes staring straight out into the room.

On a table covered with curled tubes of paint, Alex saw a black book and opened it. Inside were charcoal and pencil studies

for the paintings. Under one sketch he read a note in flamboyant handwriting: *"Night of water, night of tears . . ."*

Alex looked up and saw an old, framed circus poster on the wall with a handwritten note on it.

"Michelman? Are you back?" Alex heard. In one corner of the studio, Alex saw a man under the blankets of a bed pushed against the wall. "Is it you, Peter? Are you back?" The man lifted his head from his pillows. He was an old man, his hair as white as surf, his face colorless; even his lips were white. "I'm thirsty. I need a glass of water."

Alex found a glass over a large, paint-covered sink. He let the tap run until it was clear of rust, filled the glass, and brought it over to the old man whose hands shook, holding it to his lips.

Alex stared down into salt blue eyes that seemed bigger than any eyes he had ever seen before. They were desperate eyes that reminded him of Iris's as he had seen them in his dreams: so desperate that they drank in everything around them.

"I thought you'd left me here to die," the old man said, catching his breath.

Alex hesitated. "Why would I do that?"

"I don't know what goes on in your mind, Peter. But I thought I would die. Where did you go?"

"I was looking for somebody."

"You won't find her, Peter. You're going to neglect me and let me die if you don't stop it. She's left you, can't you understand that? She's left you."

"How do you mean, she's left me?"

"People change, Peter, people change."

"But I need to find her."

"You don't need to find her. If you find her, what good will it do?"

"It will mean everything," Alex said, "if I can talk to her. I just want to talk to her, now, that's all. I just want to tell her what she's meant to me."

"She knows, Peter, she knows, don't you worry, she knows. You must stop. You have your life to live and life is such a complicated thing. There are so many colors in it, Peter."

"But I won't stop; I won't stop until I find her," Alex said. "Don't worry. I'll never stop."

"What for? Why all the folly?"

"Because I am not a Michelman," Alex said. "I am a Barton."

"A who?"

"A Barton."

"You elude me. What do you mean a Barton?"

"Alex Barton," Alex said. "Alex Barton."

The old man dropped his glass of water and it smashed on the thin, worn carpet at Alex's feet. "It is *you. You . . .*" The white-haired man breathed fast, shallow breaths, his chest moving up and down quickly. "Step closer and give me your hand, please give me your hand."

"I'm anxious to find her. I'm dangerous. I don't want to hurt you, Mr. Volenti," Alex said. "But you must tell me where my wife is." He held his hands up as if he were going to strangle him.

But the man merely reached up, took one of Alex's hands and tried to bring it down to his chest. "Patience, patience, young man. I am old and I'm ready to die. You won't get anything out of me like this."

"Where is she?" Alex said, drawing away.

"I'll help you find her, but first you must listen to me . . . you'll understand, you'll understand if you listen to me carefully, listen to every word I have to tell you. I'll tell you a story, young man; I'll tell you a story that really happened, a true story that started long ago." He coughed, his eyes watered, drops slipped down the wrinkled skin at their corners, his face had become even paler. He cried quietly for a moment.

CHAPTER **5 9**

A MAN has been loving you
though you don't know him and he doesn't know you. He loves
you more than he loves himself, more than he loves God," the
old man said.

He began reaching for Alex's hand again, but Alex stayed
back. Finally the old man let his arms fall next to him on the
bed as he looked up at the peeling paint on the ceiling.

"I too had a rough time as a boy. I grew up so poor. Would
you believe it if I told you that I feel more at home in this messy
studio than I would in a real house? I was born in the back of
a wagon, a circus wagon." The old man coughed again. "Born
in the hay between Rome and Rimini in Italy.

"Circuses . . . Their blood runs so deep in my family that my
ancestors must have been born in the rings of the great Circus
Maximus. Strange things, are they not? Circuses are strange
things. Wherever I've gone throuhout my life I've heard their
footsteps behind me. Only later did I find out that circuses were
in my heart all along. But I'm still amazed by them, still taken
by surprise, still shocked by them.

"My mother died while giving birth to me, and later that same day my father fell seventy feet to his death in a ring outside of Rome. His catcher said he never came out of the tuck during the flip. I knew nothing of what other children know—I only knew the ring: hay and sawdust, canvas and sweat. I was fathered and mothered by acrobats, clowns, roustabouts, and publicists. My first memory was of looking up high into the arena to a flying act. I didn't think I wanted to join them. But one day I woke up and there I was eighty feet above sawdust, flying through the air toward the hands of a catcher—I was eight years old.

"Even then I didn't remember thinking that I was any different from other kids. Other kids went outside and played. I climbed the ladder and swung and swung and flew . . .

"When I was ten years old I joined the Finelli family as one of their flyers. By twelve I was a star in many countries, a prodigy acrobat. I was the biggest circus draw since Tom Thumb. The show got rich. They couldn't sell enough tickets to the crowds. We moved into bigger and bigger tents, and I was on the front page of every newspaper and magazine in Europe and the United States.

"The show was my family . . . had I left they would have lost their shirts. But I loved them so much I wouldn't have thought of it. They were my blood.

"By the time I turned sixteen, I wasn't such a freak—there are others at that age who become good at the trapeze—but I kept getting better at my act. I was doing the triple—the somersault of death as the Spanish call it—and I had already begun working on the quadruple. I may have been on my way to becoming the greatest trapeze artist of all time.

"But then something strange began to happen. Dreams began flooding into my life. At night I would wake up scared and shaking. They were the clearest dreams you can imagine. I'd see the world from high above—and everywhere on earth I'd see nothing but tents.

"I was dreaming of a world of circuses, the whole planet from the Sahara to the Himalayas to the Grand Canyon covered with circuses, a planet of tents and performers where everything born was born for the sake of an act . . .

"At first I wasn't in these dreams. They were just the opposite of my real life when sometimes I'd go into a magazine shop and see my picture on the cover of two or three magazines. In my dreams, you see, I was nowhere to be found. There were hoards of performers and animals, but I wasn't among them. I was the flying man high above, but I was invisible.

"And then these dreams changed. I did begin to show up in them. I'd be running down a dirt road somewhere in Africa, I think, running between the endless tents screaming—screaming about what? I didn't know. When I woke up I'd try to remember what it was all about, what I was afraid of, what I was saying. I'd try to write it down, but I could never remember. I'd wake up in my circus trailer in a terrible sweat. Usually my bloody screams roused the whole show. Other times I'd sleepwalk: once I woke up a mile away from the tents in a strange town. My feet were bleeding from running down the road.

"Of course every clown, every manager, every worker thought they knew what was wrong with me. Some thought I needed a girlfriend and set up dates for me. But I only laughed at this. I was good to the girls; I'd try not to hurt their feelings.

"Other people thought that my nightmares were from becoming famous so early in life. Some of the older people thought I needed a parent. I remember one person saying, 'He's had more than most people get in terms of kindness, but who is the boy's father?'

"Because of my terrible nightmares, I was often afraid of going to sleep. Soon I became so tired that I could no longer do the triple flip—I shouldn't have been in the air at all. I began to miss the hands of my catcher. One time while flipping, my feet slammed into my catcher's head. I fell and he fell on top of me into the net. After a short while, I wasn't even a draw for the show.

"One day a magician joined our circus for a short stint. His name was Joseph. He was able to make an elephant disappear in a ring surrounded 360 degrees by an audience. He was also a mind reader. I didn't care if his tricks could be explained rationally. I was frightened of him, more frightened than I've ever been of anyone. He made me feel like a little boy. He'd follow me with his big round eyes whenever I'd pass his dressing room. If I stayed to watch his act—which I stopped doing—he'd watch me from the arena, as if I were the only one in the audience.

"His eyes were mesmerizing. I felt as if he were drawing me into a tunnel of blackness leading to an evil, evil world . . . but I also felt something else . . . I felt like somebody was looking at me, truly looking at me. I felt he might be the answer to a certain problem that had been on my mind for a long time.

"At night my nightmares kept changing. I'd still be running between the tents in Africa or some Far Eastern country, but at some point I'd see him peeking from between the tent flaps, smiling, drawing me in with his eyes. Yes, I still woke up screaming, but now I had something to focus my fears on: Joseph's eyes.

"Finally, in my dream once, I stopped running, turned to him from the dirt road, and yelled: 'What do you want from me? What is it that you want?'

"And he said, 'Who is watching?'

" 'Watching what?' I said.

" 'Your shows.'

" 'My shows? What do you mean?'

"He pointed with his cane over the tents, which spread out as far as you could see, thousands, hundreds of thousands of circuses.

" 'They're mine?' I yelled, still standing away from him.

" 'Who's watching?'

"I began running from tent to tent. In each one there were

acts being performed, but there was nobody in the audience. In each ring there were stars of the circus, but not a single spectator. There was band music, there were glittering costumes, there were spotlights and everything that makes up a circus, but there were no spectators.

"I went back to the road where I'd seen Joseph. He was still there peering out of the dark flap of canvas. He lifted his hat to bow, and I saw broken feathers instead of hair. Once again I began to scream.

"The next day, I decided to ask the ringmaster to fire him. I planned to tell him that the man was making it too hard to perform and that I couldn't stay in the show with him. It was either me or him.

" 'He's gone,' the ringmaster said.

" 'What do you mean?'

" 'He left a week ago.'

" 'What?' I cried. 'But where did he go?'

" 'He performs only long enough to survive. He says that performing destroys the mind first and then the body.' "

"My nightmares went away soon afterward, but in my waking life I began to look for something. I didn't quite know what it was. I thought it might have been a father or mother. I thought the old people were right. But now I know better. I was looking for the perfect member of the audience—the perfect person to watch me.

"In every town, I asked the ringmaster to turn on the lights after my act so that I could see the audience clearly. Then I'd walk in a circle around the arena and stare out at them. In my heart, I wasn't sure that I could identify the person I was looking for merely by the face, but I secretly hoped he or she would come forward, that somebody would help me with my problem of being seen, my need to be looked at in a certain way.

"My search went on for what seemed forever—until I was

twenty-three. How many faces, how many crevices, how many strange country roads and little towns did I search for this person—and how empty the world seemed without the person. I was more lonely and scared than ever.

"Then I began to see things more clearly, less drunkenly, more coldly. The circus lost its magic for me. Finally, I gave up looking for the right spectator. No sooner did I do that than my flying act became as routine a job as working in a bank.

"Just as I was about to quit the circus for good, the owner of it died and bequeathed the whole show to me. I took over as manager and before I knew it I was even more firmly tied to it than before.

"Ten years later, by buying up other circuses, through a combination of good fortune and, I guess, a shrewd business sense—not as shrewd as Barnum, oh no, not quite like that, but shrewd, very shrewd—I got rich, so rich that I began to see my face on the covers of magazines again, and there were stories speculating as to whom I would choose for a wife. One day, at a party in France, I was introduced to an actress related to the great P. T. Barnum.

"Vera wasn't beautiful by any means. She always said what was on her mind. In fact, one of our first conversations turned into an argument.

" 'Circus performers are second-rate compared to actors and actresses—they risk only their physical lives. Risking one's emotions and ego is the deepest risk that one can take.' I remember her words well.

"I hate conversations like that. But what she had said didn't seem fair after what I'd been through. Somehow I started defending the very thing I didn't like—the circus.

" 'There is no danger but physical danger! Show your great-grandfather and his work at least that much respect!' I said. 'Theater is fun and games. That's why actors are so full of themselves.'

"I didn't see her for over a year, not until in Paris I saw a

play she was in . . . and then I went to every one of her shows
for a week.

"You see, she really was risking something new and important
during each performance.

"The next time I saw her she and a few other actors were
walking along the cobblestones of a Paris street. I knelt in front
of her and kissed the back of her hand. 'I'm so sorry,' I said.
'I've seen what you can do. You were in greater danger than I
ever was on the trapeze.'

"A year later we were married."

"After the Nazis' invasion of Poland, I sold my shows, one after
the next, and moved to America. On the way over here with
Vera, I heard that German spies had been planted in the Ringling
Brothers show to study for military purposes how they moved
their heavy equipment and troops of people. After getting off
the boat we went to the U.S. military and told them our names
and began telling them our secrets. Not only did they learn our
methods of moving men and equipment, but they also learned
performance techniques for soldiers.

"We in the circus believe in death the way a soldier must
believe in it. The knowledge that I passed on wasn't new to
circuses. It was knowledge, I'm sure, passed on through the ages
since the Egyptians' first circuses and the Roman arenas.

"Just after the war our first child was born in New York. We
called him Kismet after a tiger.

"The child, a young boy, brought us happiness for three years,
and I began to dream of a future, a future for my family. I used
to toss him up in the air, toss him high. He'd laugh so hard.
That little boy became my hopes, my dreams. The only thing
I looked forward to was playing with him, making him laugh,
and he laughed a lot, he really did." Volenti stopped. He was

staring at the ceiling. "He laughed a lot. He really laughed a lot." His voice trailed off and then he was silent, his eyes searching the ceiling for something. "And then something bad happened. One day during a Broadway play, the boy was taken from us. He was kidnapped."

He turned toward Alex. His eyebrows came down and he spoke with intensity.

"Vera and I were ready to pay as much ransom as they wanted, to give up everything we owned just to have the boy back, to become poor again even, but our prayers weren't answered. No ransom note ever turned up. We hired detectives to find him, plenty of them. But not a clue was left behind.

"I was sure that performers had stolen him—performers mad at the way I had used them in Europe.

"But this might not be true . . . I don't know who took our son. All I knew then was the world had played a gigantic cruel trick on us.

"During this time a question kept coming to mind: If there is a God, why this cruel, cruel trick? Did Vera and I really deserve such a thing? What's his reasoning?

"Then I began to feel a certain way about it all. Even if there is a God, his maxim must be this: Pretend that I don't exist. Live your life as if I do not exist! Live for life's sake, act for acting's sake, perform for the sake of the performance!

"That was part of the answer to the question I had asked Joseph in my dream. I must accept that there is no spectator, nobody who can really see me, even if there really is somebody who can. Soon after that Vera became pregnant.

"Once again I thought about circuses. I saw them as my ticket back into life. I didn't know why this was. Maybe everyone falls back on their childhood when they're in a mess. And what a mess I was in!

"At that time I got to know a young American Indian who had a mysterious understanding of circuses. He didn't like them. His ancestors, he told me, had been forced into a circus to survive long ago. They had been made to perform religious dances involving their sacred hoop in the ring for white people. The sad effects of this cruelty were passed down through generations to him. Circuses had been following him throughout his life the way they followed me."

Volenti took a deep breath. His voice changed. He spoke more quietly and personally to Alex.

"Not long ago, Alex, this friend was making his own valiant attempt to get away from circuses. But circuses are powerful, take it from me. I've since learned that he took his own life."

The old man watched Alex for a moment, then turned his head so that he was looking at the ceiling.

"But back then, after learning about my dreams, my Indian friend showed me a place where I could realize them, an island, an island of dreams, he called it, an island that had been owned by the army and had lain dormant for years. Friends in the army helped me acquire it.

"And after it was mine, my vision began to take shape. The island would be an island for performers, circuses without spectators, circuses for circuses, jugglers for jugglers, acrobats for acrobats, roustabouts for roustabouts, and armies for armies, doctors for doctors, workers for workers, people for people. A Circus of the Sea! What an idea—the island would become a kind of show, the blue show, performed for God? Or maybe for nothing. Soon it had a life of its own.

"You can imagine what a strange childhood it was for our children. They grew up in a beautiful château where Vera began practicing to become a contortionist. When my oldest daughter turned twelve, Vera sent her to a boarding school called St. Mary's.

"One time when she came back on vacation we noticed that she had changed. She was distant. Her heart and mind were somewhere else. Finally she said that she had fallen in love, deeply in love. My wife and I wouldn't have taken such a young girl's proclamation seriously if the change in her hadn't seemed so big.

" 'Who are you in love with?' I asked her.

" 'A boy,' she said.

" 'And how did you meet him?'

" 'I didn't meet him. He was visiting us from another school. He got stage fright.'

"The next time she was back on the island, I asked her if she was still in love.

" 'Yes,' she said. And later, when I asked if the boy she was in love with was in love with her, she said, 'He doesn't even know I exist.'

"When she was eighteen, she was still distant. Her heart was still somewhere else. I thought she had a touch of madness in her. She left the island for New York and I followed her.

"While I was following her in New York, I discovered we both had something in common: she was following somebody herself, the boy she had fallen in love with.

"She didn't go near him for three years. She only watched him, watched his every step.

"I was upset by what I saw, and whenever she returned for Christmas, I tried to ask her about her life. Then she found out that I knew about her obsession, and she left the island for good, vowing never to come back. It was as if she were protecting something inside of herself.

"I again followed her, but found out she had already started going out with the man. When she wants something, she'll let few things get in her way, believe me. They fell in love . . . truly . . . and soon they were married without a wedding—I think my daughter liked the idea of getting married like that after the way she was brought up . . . I got the keys to their apartment once when they left them in their mailbox." Volenti reached up and took Alex's hand.

"And I was there the winter that her husband was in a play,

and I knew the story about that. She got him to go on stage, for what reason I don't fully know, but she thought it important. Maybe by seeing him on stage again she would find out something about him or about herself, or maybe she wanted to help him with that moment, that most painful moment she had told her mother about when she was young.

"On stage the boy showed me everything. Not only did I see into him when he got stage fright and started mumbling something, but I saw into myself. The words that he mumbled were the same four words that I had heard long ago the moment I found out that my first son was taken from us in the theater. The words were spoken by actors in the play on the stage below our box. *'The child will follow.'* I still don't know if that line was actually in the play . . . I had no idea what it meant. The child will follow, but where? Where and what will he follow? Was there some meaning behind this horrible event that nearly destroyed my life? Or was it merely a coincidence that the line had been uttered? I kept hearing the line in my head for years.

"I went to the boy's old high school and there I found out about his past. I contacted the first family who had adopted him and found out who he really was."

He stopped and looked at Alex. His lips were wet with spittle. He stared into Alex's eyes.

"The agency where he was adopted had a strange story to tell about finding him. A fisherman found him clinging to some boards at sea. The brine-soaked boy was naked . . . he was two and a half years old at the time. He couldn't speak. They had dumped him overboard but hadn't killed him. He had clung to the hull of a broken rowboat . . .

"I didn't go up to him. I didn't let him know who he was. I remember staying in a hotel room in New York, one moment sweating from such a high fever that I thought I would die, the next wrapped in every blanket in the room, shaking with cold, my teeth chattering. All the time I was crying.

"I had found him. How happy I was. But the next minute I

knew that another trick was being played on me. He was married to his sister. He was in love with his sister. And not just in love with her. If he had only been in love with her that would have been another thing.

"I began to think of a way to make the marriage disappear. This marriage, this bond, meant something else, something crucial, so crucial that it was life-threatening to him.

"Then I had an intuition. It was what I had learned myself when I had lost him. Only one thing in this world, in this universe would succeed in separating him from her and would be his salvation at the same time. Somebody had to save you, Alex!"

Volenti's pale blue eyes were staring at Alex, and Alex was staring back into them. The eyes seemed to grow wider and wider. They became enormous. Far back in one of them Alex could see something dark: a tunnel, a tunnel that was beckoning him. Slowly, he moved toward it until he realized that he was walking, walking up a hill into the tunnel of the eyes.

For a second, he thought he was climbing through the tunnel inside the mountain.

Then he was flying, flying into an infinite space.

"Never trust a circus, never, never, never trust a circus!" the old man said and laughed. "They'll tell you one thing and they'll do another. They take pride in their dirty lies, they think lies are funny, lies add spice to life, they revel in lying, happily, ever so happily. Never believe a circus, Alex! Never believe a word a circus tells you! A circus is as obstinate and righteous as a wicked little school boy whom you'll never ever discipline. A circus is as hard as nails, a pigheaded mendicant, a pickpocket, a petty thief who will never change the course of his sordid and immoral ways. To rely on a circus for anything is unforgivable, a mistake, a terrible unforgivable mistake . . . Count on a circus, Alex, count on a circus . . ." Volenti's voice began shaking. He stopped speaking and caught his breath, then let it out, wheezing slowly. A dead silence fell.

CHAPTER 60

IN the silence Alex walked along the wall to a window with four panes. Through the panes, a few feet away, he could see the thick trunk of a tree, its branches casting layers of shadows over the fallen pine needles on the earth. At the base of the tree a striped chipmunk sat back on its haunches gnawing at a seed.

Alex began to speak. But he stuttered and stumbled over syllables until finally the only words that came out were: "You're a circus man . . . a *circus* man . . . that's what you said . . ."

And then he could hear Volenti's heavy breathing, the wheezing in his chest, and it was as if he were waiting for an answer to a question that he had been unable to ask.

"One day, Alex, a young flying man lost a friend, a woman so dear and so close to him that she meant more to him than his own life." Volenti drew in a long breath. "So sad was the young flying man that he left his ring and everything in the world that he knew to find her.

"First he headed east, flying into the rising sun as far as he could go, but he could not find her anywhere. So then he turned around and flew west toward the setting sun until he had reached the end of the west where his search again turned up nothing. He tried flying north into the cold but soon he realized she was not there either. Finally he started flying south and when he had flown as far south as he could go, he knew he could not turn back, he could never come home and he could never land without her, so he kept on going, flying higher and higher out into space.

"For many many years he looked for her. He flew through all the space of all the universes and galaxies, and he used up all time, as many millennia, as many light-years as there were. And after all this time he grew very old and frail, and he realized that he could not stay aloft much longer and he would have to land. He still missed her terribly and he knew in his heart that when he did land he would die. And so he began to come down.

"And as his feet touched the earth, he kept his eyes closed and when he opened them, he suddenly found himself in a very strange and a very beautiful place. He had returned to the ring from which he had begun. He had been flying for all these years in a circle. Looking around at the ring, he saw that the only difference was that its color had changed to blue."

Volenti took a breath, and then his voice changed; it lost its boldness. It became sad and melancholy.

"But that story, I'm afraid, Alex, that story is an illusion, a trap. Because no circle, no ring is perfect, nor is there a perfect act. Every ring has a fissure along its border, a minute crack, a flash of darkness. And if the flying man had flown for long enough, eventually he would have been sucked through that crack, he would never have reached his blue ring . . ."

"You're wrong," Alex said. "Wrong."

"What do you mean, wrong?" Volenti said.

"Wrong, just that, it's a theory, a theory that's all."

"But those are *Iris's* words, you understand, those aren't my words, those are *her* words."

"She said that to you?" Alex said. "Then you must have talked to her. Where did you talk to her?"

"I talked to her here."

"She was here, in this room? When?"

"Two hours ago, this morning. I saw her for the first time since her disappearance."

"Where did she go? Did she leave anything behind when she left here?"

"No, nothing."

"No proof that she's been here?"

"No. Take my word," Volenti said, finally. "What more can I give you right now?"

The chipmunk dropped the shell of its seed, cleaned its little paws, and scampered through the shadows on the pine needles and into a dark hole in the side of the tree.

"Don't you know where she went? You do know, don't you? You do know."

"I'm not sure."

"Tell me, please, tell me. Was she looking for me? Was she?"

Alex looked over at Volenti who nodded his head, slowly.

"What did you tell her?" Alex asked.

"I told her what I thought had really happened to you."

"And what was that?"

"That you had drowned, that you must have found a way to do yourself in. It was a mystery where you were after the first year." There was silence. Then a kind of inner coughing came from Volenti's throat, as if he were choking.

Alex turned and saw a glistening pool of tears had filled the man's eyes. The tears began to spill along the wrinkles in his face.

Alex went to his side. "Please, Mr. Volenti, if you know, if you have any—"

Volenti cried harder and harder. He could barely speak. "She's missed you." Sobs shook his chest and his throat. "She's missed

you . . . my God . . . like I've never seen a person . . . it was
making her . . . I thought she would make it, but . . ."

"But what—please, please—"

"She told me something before she left, she told me she
wanted to go to where she'd seen you last . . . that's where she
went . . . that's where . . . I know . . ."

Volenti was crying so hard that he could not speak at all. His
cheeks were wet and red. He no longer looked like an old man
but like a baby, a newborn baby.

CHAPTER 61

THREE hours later, he was at the Boston airport. He had to wait only fifteen minutes for a connecting flight to Verre, and he assumed he was catching up to her—the last flight had left only a half hour before, and it was the only one she could have caught.

He had to call a taxi once he landed in Verre because there were none waiting; maybe she had had trouble getting a taxi too.

He begged the driver to speed, and the driver did so, even on the dirt road. Throwing money down onto the seat, Alex jumped from the car and rushed across the field. He could hear the waves crashing. The surf was very high.

From the top of the dunes he saw a fisherman on the beach casting a line out from a long fishing pole. He was dressed in a dark, glistening yellow slicker with a hat with a very long bill and tall rubber waders. Alex ran down to him.

"Has somebody gone in?" he yelled over the roar of the surf. But the fisherman did not seem to hear.

"Gone in," Alex said. "Has somebody gone—"

The man lifted his hand and pointed beyond the breakers.

The light yellow back of a fish arced out of the water. Another fish arced, then another. A school of them were angling away from shore, out toward the setting sun.

"A person!" Alex yelled. "I'm looking for a person!"

The man was reeling in his line. But something struck his lure; the pole bent over violently. He leaned against its force, but was drawn down to the water, up to his waist in the white surf.

Alex turned to the beach. Above him, near the dunes he saw a pile of clothes. He ran to them: her sneakers, her socks, her jeans and underwear, and her faded red shirt. He turned back to the water. The fish he saw were making their way toward the gold line of the sun. He stripped and dove in and began to swim, stroking as hard as he could.

Out past the breakers he lost his wind and slowed down, pacing himself, lifting his mouth for air on every stroke.

As he swam he raised his head only a few times to look ahead of him. Each time the light on the water was different. The sun was lowering.

After a long while he felt cramps in the back of his legs. Slowly the cramps moved up to his hips, then to his stomach.

The sun went all the way down below the edge of the sea, and the water darkened and became still.

He kept going, doing the crawl, blowing air out underwater, sidestroking, even lying on his back and kicking. The stars came out faintly at first and then brighter, and he could see the tip of the moon rising above the horizon. He glanced over his shoulder to shore; lights were not visible.

He stopped and lay on his back for a moment. Then he went on, but soon realized that he'd sink if he pushed himself any farther. He stopped again and treaded water, looking carefully out at the darkness. An occasional glimmer of starlight came up from the calm surface.

He began breathing out deeply, pushing air from his lungs, more and more air. At last, he took in a deep breath, the deepest breath he had ever taken, and with it he yelled at the very top of his lungs, louder than he had ever yelled before.

"Iris!"

His voice echoed across the ocean.

He listened, and his eyes searched the dark sea carefully.

Then he saw it on the far horizon. It was rising off the water: the color, the blue color, fainter than the moon at dawn. It grew, blooming up into the sky, flooding the heavens and the earth together and shining back down on Alex.

He still waited. He waited for what he thought was an eternity having given his loudest cry, his last cry.

And then he heard it: a sound, a sound that turned into a voice that spoke a word.

"Alex!"

Circus World Museum, Baraboo, Wisconsin.